A LOYAL SPY

A LOYAL SPY

SIMON CONWAY

HODDER &
STOUGHTON

First published in Great Britain in 2010 by Hodder & Stoughton
An Hachette UK company

1

Copyright © Simon Conway 2010

A CIP catalogue record for this title is
available from the British Library

Hardback ISBN 978 0 340 83966 9
Trade Paperback ISBN 978 0 340 83967 6

Typeset in Plantin Light by Ellipsis Books Limited, Glasgow

Printed and bound in the UK by Clays Ltd, St Ives plc

Hodder & Stoughton policy is to use papers that are
natural, renewable and recyclable products and
made from wood grown in sustainable forests.
The logging and manufacturing processes are
expected to conform to the environmental
regulations of the country of origin.

Hodder and Stoughton
338 Euston Road
London NW1 3BH

www.hodder.co.uk

For Sarah

Thanks: Phil Robertson, Steve Russ, Juliet Bremner, Misha Glenny, Ahmed Siddiali, Samantha Bolton, Raza Shah Khan, Nick Sayers, David Corn, Rowan Somerville, Thomas Nash, Hedvig Boserup, Auden Witter, Chris Alexander, Wendell Steavenson, David Smith, Guy Willoughby, Dai Baker, Aslan Mintaev, Anne Clarke, Paddy Nicoll and Mark Urban.

'Lodestone Oil foresees a thousand mile long oil pipeline that will extend south through Afghanistan to an export terminal that will be constructed on the Pakistan coast. The estimated cost of the project is $2.5 billion.'

Hearing before the Committee
on International Relations,
United States House of
Representatives, 1996

'We are not talking about soapflakes or leisurewear here.'

Dick Cheney, Institute of
Petroleum autumn lunch, 1999

JONAH

The Graveyard of Empires

'The river of death has brimmed his banks,
And England's far, and Honour a name,
But the voice of a schoolboy rallies the ranks,
'Play up! Play up! And play the game!'
Henry Newbolt, *'Vitaï Lampada'*

I go chop your dollar

Jonah arrived in Freetown on a Saturday, the day of the weekly soccer match on the beach between amputees and polio victims from the nearby Médecins Sans Frontières camp. He met up with his contact in the reception of the Cockle Bay guest house, opposite the squalid shacks of salvaged timber and blue all-weather sheeting that constituted the camp. Dennis was wearing a Tupac Shakur T-shirt. So were most of the RUF fighters who had been hanging around in Freetown, the capital of Sierra Leone, since the 1999 peace accords. They loved Tupac. He'd been dead for nearly three years, shot up in a drive-by shooting in Las Vegas, after watching the Tyson–Seldon fight, and that was how they all wanted it to end, in a blaze of booze, dollars and gunfire. Like Tupac, they wanted their ashes rolled up and smoked with weed.

It was a convincing disguise. Dennis wasn't really an RUF fighter. He wasn't even from Sierra Leone. He was from Shepherd's Bush. He had Jamaican parents who'd come over to Britain on the *Empire Windrush* in 1948.

We're all at it, Jonah thought: Poles build your new extension, Lithuanians sand your reclaimed wood floors, Nigerians clean your office, Indian doctors treat you when you are sick, Filipino nurses change your NHS bedlinen, Ghanaians drive your minicabs, and if you can afford it Hungarian nannies or Czech au pairs look after your kids. And some of us – usually second generation and sufficiently acclimatised – work for a cash-strapped branch of British military intelligence known only as the Department and do your dirtiest spying for you. And, it goes without saying, it's a thankless task.

They walked over to watch the match. Jonah stood beside a limbless man who was smoking a cigarette perched between the wire twists of a coat hanger on the end of a stump.

It had been five years since President Kabbah had called on his citizens to join hands for the future of Sierra Leone. The RUF had responded by dumping sacks of amputated human hands on the steps of the presidential palace, embarking on a spree of amputations that left several thousand people without limbs.

'Aziz Nassour and two others flew into Liberia last Friday,' Dennis told him. 'They were met by Liberian police and escorted straight past immigration and customs.'

Aziz Nassour was a Lebanese diamond broker on the UN Security Council watch list, whose presence in neighbouring Liberia was in contravention of Security Council Resolution 1343, which sought to end the illicit trade in conflict diamonds.

'From the airfield they were driven straight to a known Hezbollah safe house owned by a Senegalese diamond trafficker named Ibrahim Bah.'

Ibrahim Bah was also on the UN watch list. And he had pedigree. Jonah assumed Bah was the reason that he'd been flown in. Bah had fought in Afghanistan with the mujahedin and in Lebanon with Hezbollah. He was also thought to have been involved in training Charles Taylor, Liberia's despotic president, and Foday Sankoh, the psychotic leader of the RUF, when they were in Libya in the eighties.

'The day after they arrived they met with an RUF general, known as General Mosquito, who is a middleman involved in smuggling diamonds out of Sierra Leone. They asked Mosquito to double production of diamonds from the mother lode for the next two months, and they are offering to pay over the odds for them.'

Somebody was looking to change large amounts of cash into easily transportable commodities and looking to do it quick.

'Where's this information coming from?' Jonah asked.

'Local informant.'

'Reliable?'

Dennis shrugged his skinny shoulders. It was one of the Department's mantras – the more you pay someone the more you can rely upon them to tell you what you want to hear. It was the same with torture. Neither was a reliable route to the truth.

'Who are the two men with Nassour?' Jonah asked.

'The informant didn't recognise any of the faces on the Hezbollah list.'

That summer most intelligence analysts imagined that Hezbollah, the Iranian-backed and Lebanese-based terrorist network, posed the greatest threat to western interests. 'Have the Americans been informed?' Jonah asked.

Dennis shrugged again. 'Couldn't tell you . . .'

'So where do I fit in?'

'We believe they've crossed into RUF-held territory to take a look at diamond production. We need you to go up there and try to identify them.'

'Alone?'

'We have a contact up there who will host you.'

'Who is he?'

'A diamond broker by the name of Farouz – he's a Lebanese Shiite from Barital in the Bekaa Valley. The family is up to its elbows in the counterfeiting business. The Metropolitan Police arrested his nephew in a London casino a couple of weeks back with a hundred thousand pounds of fake currency. Farouz has been offered a deal – cooperation with us will ensure that his nephew gets off on a technicality.'

'So he knows that I'm a British spy?'

Dennis shrugged. 'Believe me, he doesn't want to know.'

'What kind of back-up have I got?'

'There's an Increment team on stand-by in Ascension.'

The Increment was the executive arm of the General Support Branch – a group of specialists usually serving Special Forces, though in these days of recognised security organisations and private military companies you could never be sure – that provided the special operations capability for MI6. In Jonah's experience they had a tendency to measure their success in terms of quantity of ammunition expended, and he was as likely to die in the crossfire as survive any future rescue attempt. It wasn't exactly reassuring.

'I've filled out a mop for you,' said Dennis, meaning a UN Movement of Personnel (MOP) form. 'You're booked on a UN chopper tomorrow.'

'Don't tell me it's got a Ukrainian crew?'

'It's got a Ukrainian crew. But don't worry, the pilot never takes a drink before lunchtime.'

'What time is the flight?'

'Depends what time lunch finishes.'

'Thanks, Dennis. You're a bundle of laughs.'

There was a cheer as the amputees scored. Dennis shook his head sadly and said, 'The wheels have fallen off this place.'

The man beside him was scratching at Jonah's leg with his coat-hanger prosthetics. Jonah gave him a dollar. He had to tuck it directly into his pocket.

There was a battalion of Zambian peacekeepers stationed in Kenema, the capital of Sierra Leone's Eastern Province, and Jonah rode up there on a resupply flight in the back of an Mi-8 helicopter with a fresh platoon of soldiers. They say the Mi-8, formerly mass produced in the Soviet Union, has a Jesus screw. A single threaded bolt that attaches the rotor to the frame. If for some reason the bolt should become unscrewed and the rotor's blades unattached, then – in the absence of lift – you fall. Like a brick. In such circumstances all you can say, all you have time to say, is: 'Jesus . . .'

Jonah was asleep before the chopper took off.

He opened his eyes on a different world. An impenetrable forest-green canopy lay below, dotted with cloud shadows. The engine shuddered and his ears pulsed.

They passed over a circle of open space, a village clearing. In it he could see naked black children staring up, each one pegged to a shadow, and the chopper's shadow blurring on thatched roofs and then flickering over the forest again. He watched the Zambian soldiers bunched around the porthole windows, their ivory eyes staring down. The forest stretched to the horizon.

Jonah walked up Kenema's Hangha Road, shouldering through the melee of hawkers standing outside Lebanese stores selling racks of boom boxes, shortwave radios and Sony Walkmans, past the bullet-riddled police station, plastered with Red Cross posters of missing children, and a café playing Nigerian rap:

> You be the mugu, I be the master
> Oyinbo man I go chop your dollar
> I go take your money and disappear.

He stopped in front of a shop displaying a dilapidated wooden sign with a cut diamond painted on it. He took a deep breath and stepped inside.

The Lebanese had arrived in Sierra Leone over a hundred years earlier, and unlike the Europeans, who lacked the enthusiasm to penetrate the bush, they made straight for the interior. Before long they could be found on every street corner peddling mirrors, pots and pans, jewellery and cheap imported textiles. By the late 1950s they dominated the two most lucrative sectors of the economy: agriculture and diamond dealing; and by the late nineties they had it all sewn up, diamonds and gold, finance, construction and real estate. It was said that it was Lebanese money that Liberian president Charles Taylor had used to bankroll the RUF, when they seized control of the diamond fields.

Farouz was a large man sitting behind a small desk in a threadbare office at the back of the shop. There was a black velvet pad in the centre of the desk with a couple of magnifiers and a jeweller's loupe on it, and a folded camp bed in the corner of the room. Farouz had a black carpet of chest hair and a heavy gold chain. He sipped at a tiny cup of Lebanese coffee while he examined Jonah's letters of introduction from an Antwerp cutting house and periodically attempted, without much success, to light a fat Havana cigar. When he was finished reading he jabbed the cigar at Jonah.

'So you want me to teach you about diamonds? We used to see a lot of delinquent kids offloaded down here to cut their teeth. It's been happening for as long as anyone can remember. They'd fuck the local whores and beat their chauffeurs and when they were done they'd run back home to Beirut to take over the family business. You think you're here to play?'

I'm here to play because of your delinquent nephew's weakness for blackjack, Jonah was tempted to say, but he wouldn't. It was an elaborate charade. A dance conducted, Jonah assumed, for the benefit of eavesdroppers. 'Do I look like a delinquent?'

Farouz leant back in his chair, which squealed in protest. 'You look like you've been in a car crash.'

'I've been in several,' Jonah acknowledged. It was true: the scars were there to see. Front- and rear-end impacts, rolls, pile-ups, the whole shebang. It was a hazard of the job. And explosions too; in 1994 in Bosnia he'd driven over an anti-tank mine in a Land Rover and had been catapulted into the sky. That one had cost him an eye.

'What do you want?'

'I want to learn the trade,' Jonah told him, going through the motions.

'I'm sure you do,' said Farouz, leaning forward again and leafing through Jonah's papers with a sceptical look on his face. 'Your references are impeccable. Best I've ever seen.'

Jonah silently cursed General Support Branch, which consistently failed to heed its own dictum – *keep it ordinary*. Farouz jabbed the cigar at him again. 'What I don't know is whether you have the stomach for this business.'

'I've been around the block.'

Farouz snorted. 'You have some scars. That's nothing to boast about. Tell me, have you ever seen a diamond mine?'

'No.'

'You see a polished rock on a pretty young woman's finger, white, no inclusions – flawless. You have a naive belief in the idea

of the purity of marriage. But this is nothing. It's just a sentimental idea. Here in the jungle, diamond mining is a kind of
robbery with violence. You grab what you can get. To do it, you
need only brute force, which is nothing but an accident caused
by the weakness of others. It is not a pretty thing to see.'

'I'm not a pretty thing to see,' Jonah retorted.

And Farouz laughed – a belly-shaking rumble that caused
further protest from the springs in his chair. 'If you want to see
the mines you have to get up early.'

'I don't sleep much.' Which was also true: he'd been a raging
insomniac since his wife had left him two years before.

'Nobody sleeps here,' Farouz told him. 'There's too much money
to be made.'

'So when can I see the mines?' Jonah asked.

'Tomorrow. Why not . . .?'

An old friend back from the dead

July 2001

The following morning it was as if they were at the bottom of a deep oceanic trench, moving along a footpath through shafts of dusty sunlight that filtered through the forest canopy far above. The air in the forest was cool and dark, and the path ahead of them stretched out without visible end. They hurdled columns of venomous black ants, and stepped between the husks of mangoes discarded by diamond diggers on their way to the mines. Farouz proved to be nimbler than he looked.

Twice they passed through collections of mud huts with thatched roofs in clearings of hard-packed red dirt. Old people and children lounged sleepy eyed in front of their huts and stared impassively at them from porches and stools while chickens pecked at the earth around them.

'In the dry season I take a backpack filled with diamonds and ride a motorbike through the jungle trails to Guinea and from there to the capital, Conakry,' Farouz explained. 'That way the customer avoids paying licence fees and export tax. In Conakry, I go to a bank and deposit the parcel in a safe deposit box. Soon after, we meet somewhere, a hotel lobby or a café, then I take you to the bank and you get to inspect the goods. Once the sale is agreed, you transfer the money from your end and it is converted to cash at the bank. Next the diamonds are inspected by Guinean customs and they issue a certificate of authenticity confirming that they originated in Guinea. After that they are legitimate. You send a small plane down and pick them up and you have the diamonds in Antwerp by nightfall.'

'And in the wet season . . .?'

'We do it via Freetown. The overheads are higher because the customs officials are greedier, but it is just as straightforward.'

'Can you bring them out via Liberia instead of Guinea?'

Farouz glanced at Jonah suspiciously. 'It's costly but feasible. It requires more security, but the basic process is the same.'

One moment they were in the jungle and then the next they had stepped on to the banks of a giant hole, awesome and volcanic, that had been gouged in the jungle.

Men with guns swarmed on the banks and earthen ledges and around the pumps and wooden troughs that led to the water, and the pools were filled with gangs of skinny men stripped to their shorts and covered with mud and slime. They slung rocks and gravel around in circular shake-shakes, washing the red clay and silt away from the stones, watching for the grey and white ones among the quartz chips, their helot faces dripping with sweat.

Diamonds are born of heat and pressure. Millions of years ago, deposits of compressed carbon crystallised under extreme heat and pressure miles beneath the earth. Then subterranean volcanoes erupted, punching through the layers of earth, shooting the diamonds to the surface in geysers. Today you can find them sprinkled in the sand and gravel of Sierra Leone's alluvial plains.

Farouz greeted a gang leader who was standing beside a conical mound of drying gravel high above the pits. 'How'da body?' he called. Their handshake ended with a flourish, a snap of the fingers.

Jonah crouched at the edge of the pit. Beneath them a man in the water stopped and lifted his shake-shake and immediately the guards were on him, a foreman reaching in and plucking out the stone. He washed it in the water to remove the last of the clay and held it up between his thumb and forefinger.

'Boss,' he called.

Beside them the gang leader nodded and the stone was passed from hand to hand up the earthen ledges. It was placed in the palm of Farouz's hand. He held it up to the sun and squinted at it.

'Two carat,' he said.

Then he passed it to Jonah, who mimicked him – holding it up to his remaining eye for scrutiny. It looked like an impossibly large grain of salt. Jonah had read that once upon a time diamonds were said to reveal the guilt or innocence of accused criminals and adulterers by the colours they reflected. By rights, in Sierra Leone, Jonah thought, the diamonds should be blood red.

There was the sound of a throat being cleared close behind him and the cold O-ring of a muzzle was placed against the back of Jonah's neck. The sound of insects thickened around him.

'Put your hands up,' said a voice that was calm but authoritative, and suddenly familiar from a long-ago children's game. Silwood Park in the endless summer of 1976: a skinny boy pointing a stick at him. Jonah glanced at Farouz, who shrugged and mopped his brow. So much for a deal cut on behalf of his delinquent nephew.

The muzzle was removed. The man with the voice that had sent him spinning back through time stepped back, safely out of reach. 'Turn around.'

It couldn't be.

Jonah took a deep breath and obeyed.

There were three of them and he recognised them immediately. One of them he knew from grainy mugshots in 'most wanted' posters, Ahmed Khalfan Ghailani. Ghailani had bought the truck that carried the bomb that destroyed the US embassy in Dar es Salaam in 1998. The second was Aziz Nassour, the Lebanese diamond broker on the UN watch list, and the third, the one who was pointing a pistol at him – a black moulded-polymer sub-compact – was the custodian of a deep, dark secret. Jonah would say that Nor ed-Din had been his best student and his oldest and dearest friend, but the last time he had seen him he was lying face down in a pool of icy water in the Khyber Pass, and for many years Jonah had been under the impression that he had killed him there.

Nor held out his hand for the diamond and Jonah dropped it into his upturned palm. He wanted to say, 'Hey, Nor, welcome

back from the dead.' But Nor was a professional secret-keeper –
trained by the best – and it seemed from the expression on his
face that they had never met.

'What are you doing here?' asked Nor in Arabic.

'Buying diamonds,' Jonah replied, also in Arabic.

'The diamonds here are no longer available for sale.'

'Then I guess I'd better go back the way I came,' Jonah told
him, but he could see from the expression on their faces that this
was not an option. 'I don't want any trouble.'

'Nevertheless, trouble has come,' said Nor, and gestured to the
guards with a flick of his narrow, tapered fingers. 'Take him.'

They dragged Jonah down a jungle trail to a clearing with a
single breeze-block hut and threw him inside. For several hours
he listened to the steady footfall of the guards circling the hut
and occasionally the sound of Nigerian Alpha jet fighters buzzing
the jungle to the west.

Afternoon sun poured through the gaps in the thatch roof and
created pools of light on the dirt floor. Jonah squatted on his
haunches and watched as a fly writhed on its back in its death
throes. Soon afterwards an ant emerged from a crack in the
breeze-block wall. It darted this way and that with its antennae
writhing. It found the fly carcass, circled it, and then went back
to a second scout. They met antenna to antenna as if talking and
then the second scout returned to the crack. Almost immediately
a column of ants marched out and smothered the fly. They
dismembered it and carried the pieces back to the nest.

The next time he saw it happen, he waited for the second
scout to return to the crack and then reached down and removed
the fly. Sure enough, a column emerged but when they found
no fly they turned on the scout and tore it limb from limb. It
occurred to him that the impulse to kill the bearer of bad news
is hard-wired into all creatures.

He couldn't help wondering whether he had been dealt a similar
fate.

Pipe dreams

It was 27 September. On an elevated traffic island outside Kabul's presidential palace the corpse of former president Mohammed Najibullah was strung up by his neck. His clothes were drenched in blood and the pockets of his coat and his mouth were stuffed with afghanis, the country's almost worthless currency. Kabul had fallen to the Taliban and the motley collection of British soldiers and spooks known as the Afghan Guides were now officially surplus to requirements.

Jonah was called to a meeting with Fisher-King to be given the news in his carpeted rooms at 85 Vauxhall Cross, the headquarters of MI6. He left the Department and walked down Whitehall and along the Embankment, past Parliament and MI5, and crossed Vauxhall Bridge. Approaching the building with the sun rising behind it, you could see why it was known as the 'inca jukebox'. It was surprisingly brash for a building that housed a secret arm of the government.

Fisher-King met him by the lift in shirtsleeves and socks and guided him by the elbow past Immaculate Margo, his formidable secretary, and on into his inner sanctum with its privileged view of the Thames.

'Looking back on it, who'd have thought a band of bloodthirsty tribesmen would bring the Soviet Union to its knees,' he drawled in his effortlessly patrician voice. 'Darjeeling?'

'No thanks.'

'Have a seat.' He waved in the direction of a chesterfield.

Jonah sat carefully. The first time he had been called to Fisher-

King's office a chair had collapsed beneath him, and although he had suspected that the incident had been manufactured, it had nonetheless had the desired effect; ever since he had felt ill at ease in Fisher-King's presence.

Fisher-King crossed to his broad, uncluttered desk and paused for a moment with his hand resting on his high-backed chair. 'Afghanistan has been through a whirlwind of intrigue and deception in the years since the Soviets left, and during that time your friend Nor has offered us an unparalleled insight into Pakistani meddling.'

'And I think he still could,' Jonah said.

Fisher-King sat and leant back in his chair with his fingers clasped behind his head. 'We hung on in longer than most, Jonah. Long after the Americans had lost interest. You can't say fairer than that, can you?'

'No,' Jonah conceded.

'Now it's time to move on, to invest in new areas. The Pakistanis have put the Taliban in power in Kabul and on reflection we think that's a good thing. In fact it's good news across the region. We gave Saddam a bloody nose in '91 and now he's contained. In Tehran, President Rafsanjani has taken the mullahs in hand. He's a moderate, a thoroughly good chap. And Arafat's returned to the West Bank. You couldn't have predicted that. I think we'll look back in a few years time and say 1996 was the turning point for Middle East peace. You played a part in that and, of course, we're bloody grateful. We know what you've been through. Both of you.'

Fisher-King smiled broadly.

'That's it?' Jonah demanded.

'We can't be expected to shoulder your costs indefinitely,' Fisher-King protested. 'After all, you're not really one of us, Jonah.'

Fisher-King had always treated the collection of misfits at the Department at best as poor relations, at worst as rank amateurs. He was of the opinion that military intelligence was a contradiction in terms and Jonah was forced to admit that for the most part he agreed.

'How is Monteith?' Fisher-King asked. 'Is he still growing roses?'

Monteith was Jonah's boss, a fiery terrier of a man who ran the Department out of the gloomy basement beneath the Old War Office in Whitehall.

'I have serious doubts about the Taliban,' Jonah told him.

Fisher-King sighed. 'Of course you do, Jonah, and so do we, but it's a trade-off. It's always a trade-off, in this case between peace and security on the one hand and human rights on the other. Right now Afghanistan needs peace more than anything. The Taliban could play a central role in restoring centralised government in Afghanistan. The Americans agree. They are going to run a thousand miles of pipeline straight through the middle of it and pump a million barrels of oil a day. The oil companies are opening offices in Kandahar.'

'And the missing Stingers . . .?' Jonah asked. 'Shouldn't we be trying to get them back?'

The CIA had given away more than two thousand of the easy-to-use, shoulder-fired missiles during the war against the Soviets. The Stinger automated heat-seeking guidance system was uncannily accurate, and they had brought down scores of helicopters and transport aircraft, sowing fear among Soviet pilots and troops alike. Jonah had seen recent intelligence that suggested that six hundred Stingers were still at large.

Fisher-King dismissed the idea with a wave of the hand. 'The Americans are even as we speak negotiating with Mullah Omar to buy them back. They're offering a hundred thousand dollars for each one. There's nothing we can bring to that particular table. We don't have the resources. You'll tell Nor, won't you? It's best coming from you. He's your joe . . .'

'Tell him what exactly?'

'What I've just told you: job well done. Thanks very much.'

'And what do you expect him to do?'

'Same as he does now.' Fisher-King smiled winningly and sprang to his feet. 'I'm sure the Pakistanis will keep him busy.' He removed his double-breasted suit jacket from a rack and put it on, sweeping together the silk-lined flaps and buttoning it up.

'Got to go,' he said. 'Top Floor is waiting. You know your way out.'

Jonah found Monteith sitting on a plastic chair in front of the Afghan ops board in one of the largest of his basement rooms. As was his daily custom, he was wearing a hand-stitched tweed suit and polished brogues. It was difficult to tell whether the suit was forty years old or simply looked it.

'They want me to pack it up in boxes and stick it in an archive,' Monteith muttered angrily, staring intently at the board. 'Fisher-King says it should be in a museum. I was thinking of donating it to my old school.'

Monteith's Afghan ops board was a legend across the intelligence services. It was known as the Khyber Collage. It was a mishmash of satellite photos, mugshots, maps, waybills, freight certificates, Post-it notes, bills of lading, company accounts and bank records, transcripts of phone intercepts, letters and newspaper cuttings. Things were crossed out and new bits superimposed and glued on. It was maddeningly complex, like an alchemistic experiment. When Jonah had joined the Department it covered a single wall, now it was two. Only Monteith professed to see all the links. Only Monteith could claim to have been following the growth of the broad and diverse movement that was radical Islamic militancy, going back decades, to its roots in the jihad against the Soviets, when the Americans and the Saudis, without any thought for the consequences, funnelled money to a diverse range of Afghan fighters. Funds that went to tens of thousands of people, some operating as individuals, others as mujahedin groups – groups that had over time dissolved or gruesomely mutated.

At the centre of the board, there was a photograph cut from a newspaper of a donnish-looking man with a high forehead and bifocals perched on his nose. It was Monteith's arch-nemesis, Brigadier Javid Aslam Khan, known to the Department as 'The Hidden Hand'. Khan was head of the Afghan Bureau of the ISI, the Directorate for Inter-Services Intelligence, Pakistan's shadowy and all-powerful intelligence agency. Monteith maintained that it was Khan who was responsible for channelling Saudi and American funds to the most unsavoury and extremist elements of the mujahedin during the Soviet occupation. It was Khan who was directly responsible for the brutal civil war that followed the Soviet withdrawal when the mujahedin groups turned on each other and fought over the rubble. And it was Khan who created and nurtured the Taliban for a purpose that was yet to be fully revealed, but which kept Monteith awake at night.

Khan was also Nor's ISI handler. Nor was one of the roving sets of eyes and ears that Khan maintained in the shifting jihadi groups that he subsidised in Afghanistan. Nor fed information to Khan and Nor fed information to Monteith. He was the Department's best Afghan source, and Jonah suspected that there was nothing that Monteith hated more than the sense that Khan had finally prevailed.

'We stride boldly away from the twentieth century with too much confidence and too little reflection. We wrap ourselves in self-serving half-truths and comic-book tag-lines: the triumph of the West, the end of history.' He snorted. 'The unipolar American moment. It's ridiculously naive.'

'What do you want me to tell Nor?' Jonah asked.

Monteith glared at him. 'Tell him that he can expect no further assistance from us, either financial or legal. Tell him that if he shows his face here we will deny that we ever had anything to do with him.'

'How do you think he's going to react to that?'

'I don't expect him to react well. What do you think?'

'I think he's going to throw a fit.'

'Thank you for your insight. You'd better head off if you're going to catch your plane.'

On his way out, Jonah saw that some wag had written 'only connect' on the back of the door.

A week later, in the final days of the 'hundred-and-twenty-day wind', when the Afghan plains were lashed with dust storms and the sky was the colour of a bruise, Jonah slipped silently into Kandahar.

Tradecraft dictated that they meet in the privacy of the cemetery behind the Chawk Madad, among the tattered green martyrs' flags and upright shards of stone. Nor strode back and forth, his thoughts and words running into each other, gesticulating with his hands as tears rolled down his cheeks. Nor had always been emotionally extravagant: he swerved from one extreme to the other, from unblinking stillness to this staccato jumble of speech.

'You must be fucking joking,' Nor said. 'I'm not hearing this.'

Jonah had just told Nor that he must learn to live without him.

'They pulled the funding,' Jonah explained.

'So what am I supposed to do now?' demanded Nor. 'Stand by and watch while this country rolls back into the Dark Ages? Because that's what's going to happen, Jonah, they're going to wind the clock all the way back to zero. They're going to break the fucking springs.'

'They're delivering peace,' Jonah said, lamely.

Nor stopped and stared. His accusing silence, as always, was worse than his mania.

'Afghanistan has a chance that it hasn't had in a generation,' Jonah told him. 'The Americans are going to run a pipeline through it.'

Nor sat down and buried his head in his hands.

'I can't believe I'm hearing this,' he said.

And Jonah couldn't believe that he was saying it.

'What's happened to you?' asked Nor suddenly.

Jonah wondered whether to tell him: I have bought a dilapidated farmhouse on an island on the west coast of Scotland, somewhere as far away from Afghanistan as it is possible to get, and I'm going to repair it and live in it; I am to become the father of a baby girl and I have a marriage that I want to make right again, and that is all I care about.

'The Department is downsizing,' Jonah told him instead. 'The Afghan Guides have been consigned to history. I'm retiring.'

'What the fuck are you talking about? How can you retire? You're not even thirty years old.'

'I'm done.'

'I'll never forgive you for this.'

The mullah wants to parley

January 1999

It was in early 1999, just over two years after he was deemed to be surplus to requirements in the new Taliban era, that Nor got back in touch with the Department. The message that he conveyed was simple – *the mullah wants to parley*.

By that stage it was already clear to anyone who was a student of Afghan affairs that the Taliban, under the command of Mullah Omar, were not the pliable yokels that it had been assumed they were. In August 1998, the Clinton administration had launched a cruise missile attack on terrorist training camps near Khost in retaliation for the Nairobi and Dar es Salaam truck bombings, and the US oil giant Lodestone and its rival Unocal, the Taliban's only corporate friends, had suspended work and closed their Kandahar offices. In November 1998 the Manhattan Federal Court had issued an indictment chronicling 238 separate charges against Osama Bin Laden, from participating in the 1993 World Trade Centre bombing and funding Islamist groups in New Jersey to conspiring with Sudan, Iran and Iraq to attack US installations. And the following month, the UN Security Council had passed a motion of censure on the Taliban for its failure to conclude a ceasefire with the Northern Alliance, the slaughter of thousands of ethnic Hazaras in Mazari Sharif, profiting from the lucrative heroin trade and harbouring terrorists.

Jonah was living on the Hebridean island of Islay, with his wife Sarah and Esme, his baby daughter. He remembered the sense of relief when the call came and the sense of palpable excitement in the Department when he arrived. He also recognised, with the clarity of hindsight, the significance of Sarah's parting question, delivered across the kitchen table: 'Is that what you're going to do? You're going to keep leaving us?'

What could he say? He had come to his own conclusion. As miserable as it was, his job was what he was. It was his calling. He was nothing without it.

Monteith called them together before the Khyber Collage. He had clearly ignored the directive to dismantle and send it to a museum. It had grown larger in size in the last two years, spilling over to fill half of another wall of the briefing room with more newspaper clippings, photographs of fire-breathing imams, and frame grabs of jihadist websites and satellite channels. Strings of ribbon showed an intricate web of alliances among Sunni extremists worldwide, including Chechen rebel groups, Palestinian radicals, Kashmiri militants, the Abu Sayyaf in the Philippines and the Islamic Movement of Uzbekistan. It was Monteith's assertion that it had only been since 1996, when the Taliban swarmed into Kabul and Bin Laden returned to Afghanistan after half a decade in Sudan – at about the same time as the Afghan Guides were disbanded, Monteith liked to point out – that al-Qaeda had taken on its current incarnation as a worldwide revolutionary vanguard operating in more than sixty countries from a secure base in the Hindu Kush. A base provided by the Taliban and their Pakistani masters. Monteith called them an army of occupation, Pakistani proxies ruling a client state, and he hated them with a passion.

The Taliban sat at the centre of the Collage, fed by three distinct streams: the first, weapons and money from Saudi Arabia via the ISI; the second, a ready source of fanatical foot-soldiers from the Pakistani madrasas; and the third, revenue from the opium trade, with Helmand province as the centre of production. And in each case the hand of the ISI's chief of Afghan intelligence, Brigadier Javid Khan, Monteith's arch-nemesis, was detected and highlighted for all to see.

For the sceptics at the Foreign Office and within MI6 who

regarded Afghanistan as a backward hellhole and posed the question of why the Pakistanis or for that matter the Saudis should bother with it, Monteith liked to describe the Taliban regime as an ideological picket fence, a buffer zone built by the Pakistanis against the Soviets, and those who came after – the Russians and the Central Asians – to block their access to the Indian Ocean. As for the Saudis, he said that they would always need somewhere to dump their delinquent sons.

The team was five strong, including Monteith. He said that any more would be a crowd given the liaison difficulties at the other end, but Jonah suspected that they were the only ones who were not dead or had not refused to come out of retirement. They sat on white plastic chairs facing the collage: Jonah, Beech, Lennard and Alex.

Monteith liked to call them his waifs and strays. They were the British Afghans – the Afghan Guides. Between them they spoke Mandarin, Dari, Pashtun, Russian, Armenian and Arabic. They spanned fifteen years of war and civil war in Afghanistan. 'Chinese' Lennard, the oldest, the son of a Lancastrian construction engineer and a Chinese merchant's daughter from Singapore, had carried Blowpipe missiles manufactured by Short's in Belfast to Abdol Haq's mujahedin group Hezbe Islami, and showed him how to use them to knock out the Soviets' Sukhoi bombers. He was a graduate of St Martin's School of Art, and carried a wooden paintbox in his pack. He painted watercolours, capturing the Afghan fighters' grizzled, battle-scarred features, their jutting chins and enormous hands.

Andy Beech was the son of a Church of Scotland minister and an Armenian tapestry weaver. A graduate in theology, he'd taught Ahmad Shah Massoud's commanders in the Panjshir valley to use burst transmission radios provided by the CIA to coordinate attacks on the Soviet-trained Afghan army in the Salang Tunnel and at Bagram airbase.

Alex Ross was the youngest and brashest, an orphan wolf-child. The son of a Para sergeant who'd won a George Medal and drunk himself to death, and a German barmaid from Munster. He was Monteith's fixer – his ever-eager 'foster' son.

Then there was Jonah – Chewbacca behind his back. The polyglot son of a Palestinian scientist and a black English barrister; he'd been the Arabic-speaking interpreter who'd worked for Monteith when he reluctantly returned to regular soldiering and commanded a battle group in the first Gulf War. Monteith referred to Jonah as his bluntest instrument – an unstoppable force and an indestructible object.

The Guides knew each other's secrets, each other's skills and weaknesses. They'd shared shell scrapes, and brewed tea together in the midst of other people's firefights. They knew that you measure out captured land, outcrop by rocky outcrop, in brews of tea. They forgave Monteith everything for the way he protected and shielded them from outside interference.

Monteith hurried through the door, followed by one of his assistants clutching a folder. A few seconds later Fisher-King stepped in, silent as an interloper. He leant against the wall at the back of the room and offered no comment.

'Mullah Omar, the leader of the Taliban and Afghanistan's de facto head of state, is seeking advice on how to deal with Bin Laden,' Monteith explained, briskly. 'He recognises and acknowledges that the presence of the Saudi is detrimental to the reputation and international standing of his regime, but he says that he cannot expel him because he has been a guest of the Afghan nation since the days of the jihad. He'd like to meet with us.'

'What does he want?' Beech asked.

Monteith flared his nostrils and cleared his throat. He'd never liked being interrupted. 'We know the mullah is seeking assurance that if Bin Laden is given up his dependants will be cared for. We know the Saudis have offered shelter to his family. As for what else he wants, we'll have to hear what he has to say.'

'And what do the Americans think?' Beech asked.

'Let's just say the Americans do not recognise the Taliban need for a face-saving formula. There was no common language. All the Americans can say is "Give up Bin Laden!". The Taliban are saying, "Do something to help us give him up." The Americans have not engaged these people creatively. There have been missed opportunities.'

'What kind of opportunities?' Lennard asked.

'Opportunities to resolve the issue,' Monteith replied.

Lennard and Jonah exchanged puzzled glances.

'Let me get this straight, you think that we're going to have a sit-down meeting with Mullah Omar, make some promises you know we can't keep, and at the end of it he's going to hand over Bin Laden to us?' Beech asked.

'Perhaps,' Monteith snapped. 'Next question . . .'

'When do we leave?' Alex called out.

It was the kind of question that was more to Monteith's taste. He clapped his hands together and said, 'Next plane. Dress warm. It's going to be cold.'

Jonah glanced over his shoulder to see that Fisher-King had slipped unnoticed from the room.

The promise of Uncle Sam
and the promise of God

Monteith swept the distant ridge with his binoculars, standing among the broken glass and upturned chairs on the rooftop of the Kabul InterContinental.

'Towards the end, Hekmatyar had his rocket batteries there,' he said.

'They fell upon us like a plague,' Yakoob Beg agreed, pulling at his beard thoughtfully.

'And Dostum was there to the east,' Monteith said, pointing towards the ancient citadel that the Uzbek warlord Dostum had occupied in 1992.

'We were surrounded.'

The contrast between the two men was stark: Yakoob Beg was large and round in a white robe and turban. He was flat nosed, Chinese looking, with characteristic Hazara features inherited from thirteenth-century Mogul invaders – the so-called y-chromosome of Genghis Khan. Monteith, by contrast, was hunched and squat, with his weight concentrated in his shoulders. His legendary red hair was mostly grey now, but his Celtic ancestry was clear to see in the rash of freckles on his hands and face.

Jonah joined them at the blown-out window. Looking out at the ruins of Kabul and the barren ridge-lines that surrounded it, you could be forgiven for thinking that an act of God, perhaps an earthquake, had sent the city tumbling down a funnel, leaving nothing but a heap of rubble at the bottom. But it was a man-made cataclysm. A medieval war. He knew. He'd slipped in and out of the city a couple of times to carry messages from Monteith to Yakoob Beg in the mid-nineties, during the siege, when Kabul had been a battleground for competing warlords: Ahmad Shah Massoud, the Lion of the Panjshir; Dostum, the Uzbek butcher; Gulbuddin Hekmatyar, the Islamist fanatic. They'd slaughtered each other for the right to rape and steal. They'd flattened mud-brick block after mud-brick block. They'd seeded the rubble with thousands of mines and unexploded shells.

As they watched, a column of red Toyota Hi-Luxes, with armed men crouching in the beds of the trucks, drove up the hill and turned off on the road north to the Salang Pass in the direction of the Northern Alliance lines.

'The Taliban are preparing for a fresh offensive,' Yakoob Beg observed.

As a Hazara and a Shiite, Yakoob Beg was a member of an ethnic group that had been declared infidels by the Taliban – more than eight thousand Hazaras had been killed in Mazar only a few months previously. But Yakoob Beg was first and foremost a survivor. Like so many of his fellow residents of Kabul, he had developed a capacity to adapt his behaviour to accommodate whoever was in charge, while keeping a watchful eye out for whoever might come next. He maintained high-level contacts with the Northern Alliance, who were occupying front lines north of the city, and the Taliban, who currently controlled it. Presumably, he paid them both. He lived in Wazir Akbar Khan district, one of the city's most prestigious neighbourhoods, in a large compound that had remained miraculously untouched by the years of occupation and civil war. Most of the houses that surrounded his were now occupied by the elderly warriors from Kandahar who made up the bulk of the Taliban leadership, and their Arab allies. Jonah knew that Yakoob Beg had received a regular stipend from the Department throughout the late eighties and early nineties, when he had provided information and other services to the Afghan Guides, but as to his main source of income, that was well known. He was an opium trader.

'The Taliban delivered us from anarchy,' Yakoob Beg said. 'They were the only ones single minded and brutal enough to achieve it. The people of Kabul had lost all hope. The Taliban gave it back. So they were prepared to put up with a great deal in order to prevent the past from returning. Even fear.'

'The people are frightened?'

'The Taliban have become increasingly extreme in their methods. At first they were attractive, fascinating even, from a certain point of view, but in the end they were just like all those that came before.'

'What are the people saying?' Monteith asked.

'That the Arabs bring money every month and the Pakistanis bring guns and without their support the Taliban could not hold the city.'

'Do you believe that?' Monteith asked.

'Outsiders have always sought to determine events in Afghanistan,' Yakoob Beg replied. 'We have had many puppet-masters: the British, the Russians, now the Pakistanis . . .'

'And the Afghans have always sought outside assistance to gain local advantage,' Monteith retorted.

'It is our curse.'

'It is your game.'

Yakoob Beg smiled. 'And yours . . .'

'But if the Arabs were to withdraw their support?'

Yakoob Beg seemed to be laughing at him. 'Do you think that you can outbid the Arabs?'

They drove for hours across a vast snow-covered plain scored by eroded river beds, towards the shark's-teeth of a distant mountain range. Huge black vultures soared on the thermals overhead. Pylon lines, long since stripped of wire, ran along the roadside as reminders of a time when Afghanistan had ready supplies of electricity. There were three of them crammed in the back of a taxi: Jonah, Monteith and Alex. Beech and Lennard had remained as backstop in Kabul, maintaining communications with London from the roof of the InterContinental.

The approach to Kandahar was dominated by gibbets festooned with ribbons of cassette tape and pyramids of smashed television sets. The painted arch called the chicken post at the eastern gate was guarded by kohl-eyed Taliban wrapped in blankets. They poked their Kalashnikovs through the windows, smashed the taxi driver's Hindi cassettes and unspooled the tape to the wind. Jonah reflected that Nor's prediction, made in the cemetery in 1996, had been right – Afghanistan had slid into the Dark Ages.

Inside the city, the taxi edged between market stalls, sliding in the icy slush. Packs of starving orphans detached themselves from the mud and ran alongside the car until they were driven off by men with whips. There were no longer any women to be seen, and for some reason that was what bothered Jonah the most.

They parked beside a small nondescript door in a high-walled compound and armed Taliban surrounded the vehicle, forming an attentive perimeter. Two youngish chowkidars with white turbans and fuzzy beards came in close and opened the doors. Jonah eased himself carefully along the back seat and out into the street. One of the men took him by the arm and guided him to the wall. There were traces of lipstick on his lips and he was smiling in a way that Jonah found unnerving. The man pressed his groin against the back of Jonah's thigh and searched him. His hands moved under Jonah's armpits, across his ribs and stomach and between his legs, where they rested for a few seconds, cupping his balls.

'Turn around,' said a voice in broken English. The young man removed his hands and Jonah turned with his back to the wall to find himself staring down the barrels of several guns. Beside him Monteith and Alex shared nervous glances. An older man wearing a white turban studied them carefully.

'This way,' he said. They followed him through the door and into a dirt yard littered with car parts.

There was a man, unmistakably an American, sitting on the steps of a single-storey house with an MI6 resting on his lap. He had a shaved head, a goatee, shades, black chest-webbing, and his muscled arms were 'fully sleeved' – tattooed from shoulder to wrist. On his head there was a black baseball cap with a logo on it of a wolf's head in a rifle's cross hairs. The man was clearly a bodyguard, a private security contractor.

'Who the fuck are you?' he growled.

A second American emerged from the house and came towards them. He was wearing chinos and a navy blue windbreaker. His hair and moustache were silvery white and expensively groomed. CIA or State Department, Jonah guessed.

'I didn't see who it was at first,' the man said.

'How are you, Jim?' Monteith asked.

'I've had better days.'

'Who the fuck are they?' the bodyguard demanded again.

'You're a soldier. They're soldiers,' the man identified as Jim said to his colleague. 'I know these guys. They're Brits. And mostly harmless. Go get in the car.'

When the bodyguard had stepped out into the street, Jim paused briefly in the doorway to the compound, looking at Monteith and then at Jonah. 'Our assessment is that Bin Laden is neither weak nor stupid enough to leave Afghanistan and the Taliban are unlikely to ask him to leave, which means that there is no business to be done here. You're wasting your time.'

'What did you say to them?' Monteith asked.

'I told them we know that he's guilty. I told them to turn him over or face the consequences.'

'And what did they reply?'

'They say they're going to do something but they'll do exactly nothing. So when they're done with you, you should go home and tell whichever multinational is paying for your ticket to stay the fuck away from the Taliban.'

'Our ticket is paid for by the British government.'

Jim laughed. 'You crack me up.'

He stepped out onto the street. They listened to a vehicle engine start up on the other side of the wall.

'Who the hell was that?' Alex asked.

'James Patrick Kiernan. He used to be CIA Head of Station down in Islamabad,' Monteith told them.

'Friend of yours?' Alex asked.

'Not exactly,' Monteith admitted.

The man in the white turban, who had remained impassive

during the exchange with the Americans, indicated for them to enter the house. Monteith led the way. They were shown to a meeting room, where they were offered sugared almonds while they waited. Half an hour passed.

Eventually the man with the white turban reappeared and escorted them down a dimly lit corridor to an office with a bare, metal-topped desk. A row of elderly men with weathered faces and grey stringy beards, peg-legs and plastic arms occupied the chairs that lined the walls. Monteith called them 'junkyard demons' and said that they were impossible to kill, and you could see what he meant: with their outsize features and scar tissue, shrapnel-filled bodies and ill-fitting prosthetics, they looked like monsters in a cheap horror flick. These were the men who had hammered the Soviet Union into submission. They were unstoppable.

A door opened, a different door to the one they came in by, and a man in a black turban limped in.

'Welcome to my house, Englishmen, welcome,' the black-turbaned man said. His handshake was soft but he had a straight gaze that was grey-green and gave the impression of being visionary. 'My name is Wakil Jalil Khalili. We are honoured by your presence.'

He spoke in English and gestured to the three nearest empty chairs.

'Please take a seat.'

Watching Wakil sit was like watching an old bed frame collapse. He removed his prosthetic leg and rubbed the stump. 'The Mullah Mohammed Omar regrets that he cannot speak with you in person but he has asked me to offer you his greetings.'

'Thank you,' Monteith replied. 'Please convey our greetings to him also.'

'You have come a long way,' Wakil said, standing his leg on the floor by his chair. 'It is cold. This year it is very cold.' He leant forward across the desk and clapped his hands together lightly. 'You will take tea?'

A tea boy appeared with a tray filled with a variety of mismatched cups and saucers and a metal teapot, and served them all tea. The old men poured the tea into their saucers and slurped at it. After the tea boy had retreated and Monteith had made several compliments on the sweetness of the tea, he began.

'Several weeks ago an emissary of yours approached us to discuss a problem.'

'Yes?'

'The problem relates to the presence of Sheikh Osama Bin Laden in your country.'

'I see, yes, a serious matter.' Wakil's face showed no emotion.

'We appreciate this opportunity to discuss this difficult matter with you and we hope that we can be of assistance. We recognise that Osama Bin Laden has been a guest and an ally of your country since the time of the jihad against the Soviets. We acknowledge the long-standing Pashtun tradition of hospitality.'

Wakil made a brief humming sound and nodded his head in encouragement.

'At the same time, we are concerned that the presence of Osama Bin Laden is having a very negative effect on the reputation of Afghanistan.'

Wakil nodded, giving the appearance of understanding. 'Mullah Omar has also asked me to inform you that I am authorised to discuss certain matters on his behalf, including the matter of our guest, Sheikh Osama Bin Laden.'

'We know that the Americans have already made representations to you on this matter and that you are giving consideration to their request, but we also feel that there may be a role for us, perhaps in facilitating further dialogue or clarifying misunderstandings to prevent either side reaching the wrong conclusions.'

Monteith sat back in his chair in order to show that he had volunteered his assistance and that he was acting in good faith. He offered a friendly glance to everyone in the room.

After a lengthy pause, during which he impassively considered the surface of his desk, Wakil said, 'We are considering two different promises. One is the promise of God. The other is that of the Americans. The promise of God is that if you journey on His path you can reside anywhere on this earth and you will be protected. The promise of the Americans is that there is no place where you can hide that we cannot find you. Frankly speaking, we prefer to believe in the promise of God.'

'We do not wish to contradict the promise of God,' Monteith replied, after a suitable pause.

'The Americans lecture us about evolution and a thousand years of progress but all we see is a dark age of suffering and perdition.'

'My country is a small one,' Monteith said. 'We are no longer in the business of issuing ultimatums. Rather, we are interested in finding a common language in the hope that we may discover a way to solve this problem that recognises the sensitivities involved and that is agreeable to both sides. We are here to listen, sir.'

'I will tell you, we ourselves are victims of terrorism,' Wakil replied. 'We are harassed by Russia and we are struck by American cruise missiles, and sometimes devastated by car bombs and sabotage. Other countries interfere in our internal affairs and we are subjected to international sanctions. In regards to Osama Bin Laden, he was once championed as a mujahid fighting the Russians, but now he is called a terrorist. The issue is not terrorism, it is Islam. There is a struggle in progress between Islam and the Kuffar.'

The door behind Wakil opened, and a young man entered and whispered in Wakil's ear. With a start, Jonah recognised Nor. He was thinner and there were fresh lines etched at the corners of his eyes. When he had finished speaking he took a seat at Wakil's shoulder. Jonah had the feeling that he been listening to them. It occurred to him that they were in an anteroom and that the real business of the meeting was being discussed elsewhere.

Wakil's face was stony. 'I'm sorry to disappoint you, but I have been informed that Sheikh Osama left his residence near Khost some days ago without telling us where he was going.'

One of the men lining the sides of the room coughed and another dropped his feet from his chair and slipped on his sandals. Wakil strapped his prosthetic back on. The meeting was being brought hurriedly to a close.

'Do you have any idea where he might be headed?' Monteith asked, glancing at Jonah, a hint of disappointment in his voice.

Wakil shook his head. 'The sheikh surrendered his satellite telephone to us several weeks ago at our request. Contact with him has now been broken. I'm afraid our guest is missing. We cannot help you any further.'

He got up from behind his desk and limped out, as if commanded, through one of the inner doors. Seconds later, without a backward glance, Nor followed.

Again, just as they had done a couple of years earlier, they met in the cemetery behind the Chawk Madad. Nor came hurrying through the piles of dirty snow and the profusion of freshly erected martyrs' flags with his black turban obscuring his face.

'What's going on?' Jonah demanded, his breath forming ice crystals in front of his face. It was less than half an hour since Wakil had ended the meeting with them. 'This isn't going anywhere.'

'You're not listening,' Nor responded, curtly. 'Missing is their way of saying Bin Laden is not under their protection. It means he's on the move. They're giving him to you, Jonah.'

'What do you mean?'

'Do I need to spell it out to you? They're giving you permission.'

'Permission . . .?'

'Yes, to deal with him.'

'We don't do that,' Jonah said carefully, after a pause.

'Of course you don't. But you know people who do, for the right price. Bin Laden's currently at a place called Farm Hadda on the Kabul river. He's due to return to the al-Badr camp near Khost on Sunday and he's taking the Jalalabad road. You ambush him there. The Northern Alliance will take the blame. Problem solved.'

A Moleskine and a pencil

January 1999

The following night Jonah climbed the steps to the roof of the Kabul InterContinental and found Beech and Lennard there, sharing a flask of Scotch. They had set a couple of the chairs in front of the windows and they were sitting with their feet on the ledge, contemplating the dark outline of the city. Jonah picked up a chair, brushed broken glass off the seat and carried it over to join them.

Beech held out the flask and Jonah sipped the warm, peaty alcohol before handing it on to Lennard. He looked around. Monteith was hunched over on the far side of the roof, whispering into the satellite phone. He'd spent most of his time since their return from Kandahar on the phone.

'Who's he talking to?' Jonah asked.

'Fisher-King,' Beech replied.

Lennard grunted, 'That bastard.'

The flask went around again.

'I have a question,' Jonah said.

Beech looked at him. 'Go on.'

'Do you know a CIA guy named Jim Kiernan?'

'Sure,' Beech acknowledged. 'He used to be Head of Station in Islamabad. I think he's at the CIA Counter Terrorism Centre now.'

'He's Deputy Chief of Operations,' Lennard added. 'He oversees the Manson family.'

The Manson family was the nickname of the unit within the CIA's Counter Terrorism Centre that was charged with hunting

Bin Laden and his top lieutenants. It was said that within the CIA they had acquired a reputation for crazed alarmism about the rising al-Qaeda threat.

'We bumped into him in Kandahar,' Jonah told them, 'down in the mullah's compound. When Monteith caught sight of him, I swear his whole face fell. I've never seen him look so pained. What's between those two?'

Beech and Lennard shared a glance.

'Come on,' Jonah urged.

'It goes back to the siege of Kabul,' Beech explained, 'a difference of opinion on how to prosecute the war.'

'Which is a polite way of saying Monteith stabbed him with a pencil,' added Lennard, tapping the ash from his cigar against the heel of his boot.

'A pencil?'

Lennard shrugged. 'He was angry.'

'I need more information,' Jonah demanded.

'You'd better tell Chewy the tale,' Lennard said to Beech.

'OK,' Beech agreed, stroking his beard, assuming the character of the most senior of the Guides. 'Let's see, once upon a time, which is how these things begin, there was an evil empire that was nearing the end of its days, a fire-breathing dragon called President Najibullah sitting on a pile of loot, and two warriors, Kiernan and Monteith, one rich and one poor, with very different views of how to hasten the empire's collapse and kill the dragon. Monteith, the pluckier of our two warriors, argued that the CIA should stop the flow of weapons and money to the Pakistanis, our double-dealing, so-called allies in the war against the evil empire. He wanted to cut them out of the picture entirely and to deal directly with the mujahedin. He wanted targeted support for one commander, a genuine leader with Western sympathies who could slay the dragon, take control of the country and rebuild it.'

'Monteith was backing Abdol Haq, who ran Hezbe Islami, which was one of the mujahedin groups operating in the Kabul area,' Lennard explained. 'He had a plan for Haq's men to infiltrate the city and overthrow the Najibullah regime as soon as the Soviets skipped town.'

'It was a fairy tale,' Beech recounted. 'Instead the CIA, encouraged by Kiernan, who was CIA station chief in Islamabad and had the deepest pockets in town, stepped up the supply of weapons to the Pakistanis. We're talking about hundreds of millions of dollars' worth of military supplies, including Chinese and Egyptian 122mm artillery rockets. The Pakistanis passed them on to all and sundry with the largest share to Hekmatyar, their pet Islamopath. With the rockets they could hit the city from twenty-five kilometres away, which meant everybody and anybody could have a pop at the dragon without much risk to themselves. Pretty soon a couple of hundred rockets a week were crashing down in Kabul and ordinary people were dying in droves. Monteith was furious. So was his protégé, Abdol Haq. He accused the other mujahedin groups of behaving like terrorists and blamed the Americans and the Pakistanis for arming them. Monteith fired off a rant to London and the issue was raised by the MI6 liaison officer in Washington in a weekly meeting with his counterpart at the CIA. As you know, shit flows downhill, and pretty soon afterwards Kiernan went careening up the Great Trunk Route to our office in Peshawar to confront Monteith. At that time the Guides were located in a suite of rooms on the second floor of a dilapidated colonial-era building near the bazaar. It was freezing in the winter and boiling in the summer. Monteith had his own office, right by the stairs at the entrance, where he could see exactly who was coming and going. It wasn't much more than a broom cupboard. He had a desk and a chair. That's it. There were never any papers. He was convinced that the landlord was being paid by the ISI to spy on us, which he probably was, and so he never wrote anything down. He kept everything in his head. The only thing that he had on his desk was a row of pencils. He'd sit in that office and whenever he needed a job done he'd throw a pencil at whoever was walking past. If you got hit you did the job. We'd pile past that door at top speed but he'd always get you. He was a deadly shot. The story was that he'd been the army's javelin champion as a junior officer. The angrier he got, the more he'd sharpen the pencils. So on this particular day, Kiernan storms into the office and he and Monteith proceed to have a furious stand-up argument. Kiernan tells Monteith that the idea that there is one mujahedin leader who can bind the country together is the same old naive, messianic bullshit – in fact the Afghans have been selling it as an idea to the British since Queen Victoria's time and still the Brits are falling for it and there's no way that the Americans will. He tells him that Haq is no better than any of the other warlords. In fact, he says, they are all rapists and murderers – what of it?' Beech paused to take a swig at the flask. 'Now, for Monteith that was the final straw. He lost it. He grabbed the nearest thing, which in this case was a pencil, and flung it at Kiernan. It went right through his cheek. Imagine the scene: Monteith was standing there, totally mortified by what he'd done, and Kiernan had a pencil sticking out of his face. You can guess what followed. The CIA demanded Monteith's head on a platter and London threatened to return him to regular soldiering. There was no way Monteith was prepared to go back to square-bashing and so he had to write a letter of fulsome apology. And that's why the two don't exactly see eye to eye.'

'And it's why Monteith stopped throwing pencils,' Lennard added. He took the flask from Beech, had a swig and passed it to Jonah.

Monteith looked thoughtful. He'd walked across the roof to them with his hands deep in his pockets.

'They want their bloody pipeline,' he said. 'They think that with Bin Laden out of the picture the negotiations can open again.'

Yakoob Beg leant forward with his face reflecting the dull red embers of the brazier in the centre of the room. Monteith sat opposite him, shifting uncomfortably on his haunches. Jonah was squatting in the shadows in the corner of the room beside a small round-faced boy who was holding a plate of dried mulberries. They were in the *hujra,* or guest room, of Yakoob Beg's villa in the Kabul suburb of Wazir Akhbar Khan. Twenty-four hours had passed since their return from Kandahar and Monteith was growing increasingly restless.

'Tell me,' he said.

Yakoob Beg glanced down at the pages of the open Moleskine notebook in his lap. 'The facts as I understand them are these, my friend. Since he left Kandahar Bin Laden has been making enquiries about somewhere to house his family in comfort and safety. The old Soviet collective farm at Hadda has become available and we understand that he is inspecting it for suitability.'

It was said that if you could get hold of Yakoob Beg's Moleskine you would learn the identity of every commodity trader and protection racketeer from Marseilles to Mumbai – Turkish heroin syndicates, Bulgarian people smugglers, etc. It was also said that the Moleskine had been an impromptu gift from Monteith back in the eighties, and written on the inside front cover, next to *In case of loss please return to*, was Monteith's name and the address of a long-forgotten safe house in Bloomsbury.

'You are confirming that what Nor has told us is credible?' Monteith insisted.

'It's credible.'

'And you have identified a group prepared to undertake the task?'

Yakoob Beg pursed his fleshy lips. 'Of course, it can be arranged if you are prepared to pay the right amount. But it is short notice and there are fewer groups available for hire than there were before the Taliban. I cannot guarantee that those available are best suited to the task.'

'It is not a pleasant task,' Monteith told him. 'I don't expect pleasant people.'

'I have asked the Uzbeks to come,' Yakoob Beg said, 'at your request, but I cannot vouch for them. You must make your own judgement. You have an expression in Latin, *caveat emptor*, yes? It means buyer beware.'

The moon and the frost lent everything the silvery patina of an old photograph. They were standing in the shadows beside the outer wall of the compound. They had abandoned their room full of sleeping bags for fear of eavesdroppers. Monteith was speaking, his voice barely rising above a whisper. 'I've been told that capturing Bin Laden alive could deepen complications. According to the Americans, evidence that he ordered the Nairobi and Dar es Salaam bombings might be difficult to produce in court. None of the informants involved in the case have direct knowledge of his involvement. Trying him could prove embarrassing, particularly if it comes to light that the Clinton administration has concocted a secret policy with Pakistan and Saudi Arabia to tolerate the creation and rise to power of the Taliban.'

'So we do as Nor suggests,' Alex said.

'The Americans cannot sanction an assassination,' Monteith explained. 'They have a presidential executive order preventing it.'

'But they want their pipeline,' Beech said.

'They want their pipeline,' Monteith agreed.

'So they want us to do their dirty work for them?'

'Something like that,' Monteith replied.

Alex shrugged. 'Nor is right. If we kill Bin Laden the chief suspects will be Massoud's Northern Alliance.'

Beech glanced at Jonah, who couldn't help but feel that what was being discussed involved crossing an invisible line, beyond which the consequences were difficult to determine.

'Can we be certain of Nor?' Beech asked.

'He's never lied to me before,' Jonah replied, uneasily.

'We abandoned him,' Beech said. 'Can anybody tell me what he's been doing for the last two years?'

'Not really,' Jonah replied. Nor had been vague on the specifics of his activities when Jonah had questioned him. He claimed that he had remained in touch with Brigadier Khan, his handler in the ISI, that he had taught at one of the camps near Khost, but had offered no specific details.

'Can we double-check with the Pakistanis?' Beech asked.

'There's no time,' Alex said, 'and no indication that they would share the information with us.'

'Nor was the best bloody source we had here,' Monteith replied, making no effort to hide his irritation. 'He never let us down.'

'But we let him down,' Beech argued. 'And what about Yakoob Beg's Uzbeks? Do you really think that they are appropriate for this task?'

'Appropriate?' Monteith growled. 'They are entirely appropriate for the task.'

'They are available,' Alex added, 'and within our price range.'

'Do they know the identity of the target?' Lennard asked.

'There's no reason for them to know,' Alex said.

'Killing people in wartime or even in self-defence is one thing,' Beech said. 'Arming and training people fighting for their freedom is another. What is being discussed here is an assassination. Cold-blooded murder.'

'Are you taking the piss?' Alex retorted. 'This is Afghanistan.'

'We do this and we step outside the boundaries of what is legal,' Beech insisted. 'There's a reason the Americans have a law against it.'

'We stand in the eye of a storm,' Monteith said. It was obvious from the set of his shoulders and his upturned nose, the expression of the terrier-like quality that he was renowned for, that Monteith would brook no opposition. 'If we don't act now and stop Bin Laden, mark my words, we face the prospect of a resurgence of terrorist violence the like of which the world has never seen.'

As he was speaking, Jonah observed a man step out of the shadows close to the far wall. He came towards them along a path through the thorny outlines of denuded rose bushes. Others flitted through the shadows behind him. Moonlight glinted on rifle sights and loops of ammunition. The courtyard was deserted, and for a moment Jonah thought that they were about to be attacked. He reached for his pistol but Monteith put his hand on Jonah's to restrain him.

'I am a friend,' the man said. 'I am Khalil. I was crossing the courtyard to your rooms when I saw you.'

'You have good eyes,' Monteith replied, glancing towards the shapes hanging back in the rose bushes.

'I understand that you want to speak to me?' Khalil asked. He was wearing a *chitrali* cap and had a blanket around his shoulders, and it was difficult to make out much of his face, except that his smile gave the set of his jaws a starved and skeletal look.

'Are your men ready?' Monteith asked.

'They are,' Khalil replied. His smile broadened menacingly. 'We will meet you tomorrow night.'

Killing an Arab

They were perfectly camouflaged. One moment there was only the ghostly, stippled bark of the gum trees and then there was a gentle rustle of the leaves, a breath of wind, and it was as if the trees were moving of their own volition, the bark unravelling. You could hear the padding of tiny feet.

'Birnam Wood,' whispered Beech.

It was close to midnight. They were waiting at a bridge west of Jalalabad. They had been standing for an hour on the concrete apron at the eastern end of the bridge when Khalil's gang emerged from the eucalyptus plantation to greet them.

There was a collective intake of breath. 'Jesus, they're kids.'

They were a pack of fifty or so, dressed in motley: tennis shoes, army jackboots, chequered scarves, haj and *chitrali* caps, turbans and Kalashnikovs. They had dark fuzz instead of beards and their starved, lupine faces shimmered in the moonlight. They were skittish, jockeying for position at the front of the pack, and grinning. The oldest among them could not have been more than twelve.

'This is fucked,' Lennard muttered.

'It's the fucking Lost Boys!' Beech turned on Monteith. 'You're not serious?'

Lennard whistled. 'And blow me, it's Captain Hook . . .'

Khalil stepped out of the trees with a whip in his hand. He raised it and the boys nearest to him flinched. They scattered and then circled back again, pressing in behind him. He stepped forward, and tapped Monteith's chest with the whip.

'Yakoob Beg has confirmed that he is holding the money,' he said. 'So we are yours to command.'

'This is unacceptable,' Monteith told him.

'What is unacceptable?' Khalil asked.

'These are children. I will not fight with them.'

'Then you will not fight,' Khalil replied.

They stared at each other. Jonah swore softly under his breath. Monteith looked as if he was going to explode.

Beech left later that night. He divided his rations and ammunition between them while Monteith sat some way off on a boulder, seething.

'Technically of course this is desertion,' Lennard said, accepting a block of Kendal mint cake and a bottle of Tabasco.

'We don't exist,' Beech told him. 'I don't. You don't. This mission doesn't.'

They bear-hugged.

'You're letting the team down,' Alex told him, shaking his head. There had been shouting earlier. Monteith had produced a pistol and pointed it at Beech, who had simply turned his back on him. Monteith had stood there visibly shaking, before storming off.

Beech turned to Jonah. There was a pause. 'You're better than this,' he said, sadly.

They hugged, Jonah gripping him in the darkness.

At dawn they began the long walk to the ambush position. Down a steep valley, and up the facing mountainside, their feet sinking in scree and snow, clutching at rocks to pull themselves upwards, Jonah afflicted every step of the way by Beech's accusation. He stifled the voice, which was his own, telling him that anything, even this, was better than throwing it all in and going back to an empty life and a wife who no longer loved him. He concentrated on the sounds around him: the howling wind in the rocks, the shifting scree and the frightened chatter of the boys. Icy fog closed in on them. He wondered whether the route might be a figment of Khalil's imagination or even a trap. He kept going, numb fingers reaching for icy rocks, terrified that if he did not keep going he'd be lost in the void. The path widened again, the fog lifted, and they came on to a ridge that seemed to overlook the whole world. Deep gorges and jagged peaks stretched away on either side. The going was easier. The path along the top of the ridge was wide, and the boulders larger and more easily navigable. They passed an old fortress, adobe-walled and crumbling, topping the ridge.

In less than five hours they stood above the gorge of the Kabul River, with the thin strip of the road running through it. Khalil spoke for the first time, turning back to them. 'We will do it here, where the valley narrows.' He smiled. 'They say that the Pash-tuns killed many English here.'

'Let's get this done,' Monteith growled.

Another hour passed as they hiked down to within range of the road. Years of neglect, flooding and rockslides had almost destroyed it, breaking up the tarmac, leaving huge craters. Alex sat down on a rock and blew on his fingers, before reaching into his pack for an entrenching tool. He began digging a shell scrape, a shallow two-man trench. Khalil and Monteith went to deploy the cut-off teams. Jonah stood, staring at the road. It was the oldest Afghan trick: lure the invaders into the narrows of the Kabul river gorge and cut off their means of escape.

It was all up to Nor.

The boy crouched among the jumbled rocks and dirty clumps of snow with his weapon disguised in rags. There was a hammer and sickle badge pinned to his *chitrali* cap. He looked about eleven years old.

Jonah had been watching the boy since dawn. He was located with the main ambush team, sharing a shallow scrape with Alex on the crest of a ridge overlooking the gorge. The boy was shivering, his oval eyes darting this way and that. When he had first become aware of Jonah staring at him, the boy had glared back at him, an expression that was both defiant and fearful.

Afghanistan was full of orphans.

★

There were times, Jonah thought, in an ambush, for instance, when soldiers could experience a sense of being of one mind, like a shoal of fishes that swerves as one under the surface of the ocean, times when an older, lower brain rises to the fore.

'Three vehicles heading east,' whispered Lennard from one of the cut-off teams, in Jonah's earpiece.

It was one in the afternoon. Three mud-caked Shoguns with blackened windows and jerrycans lashed to the roof raced into the narrow, steep-sided ravine.

There was a collective intake of breath.

Jonah began to count: *one, two . . .*

He glanced to his left. Monteith was a few feet away, in a scrape with Khalil.

Three . . .

The mud beneath him smelt of the wind, of ozone.

Four . . .

For a brief moment he had no awareness of future or past, just the Uzbeks in the rocks around him and the lines of cable running to him along the hillside from the charges placed where the ravine tapered at either end.

Five.

'Now,' said Monteith, as the convoy drew level with him, his voice barely audible above the roar of the Kabul river.

Jonah pressed the button and spun the key on the Russian exploder.

Events unfolded in unison: the charges exploded, rocks tumbled into the ravine in billowing clouds of dust and the road collapsed; the lead vehicle slewed sideways and rolled, tumbling into the gorge below; and the Uzbeks opened up as one with everything they had – assault rifles, machine guns, rocket-propelled grenades. The air crackled and swirled. Brass cases cascaded down the slope. The fuel tanks on both vehicles exploded.

It was over in seconds but it went on for several deafening minutes. In the next scrape Monteith gesticulated furiously at Khalil. Jonah could imagine his anger and frustration at the ill-disciplined expenditure of ammunition. Soon the bodies would be unidentifiable. It was potentially disastrous. They needed proof, photographs of the dead Arab, if the mission was to be successful.

Abruptly Khalil stood and his gang rose as one to join him. And as they did so, they let out a triumphant wailing sound, *wulla-wulla-wulla,* from the back of their throats. The hillside seethed with sudden movement. The Uzbeks swarmed down the slope, whooping and yelling, sliding in the scree. At the bottom, they surrounded the vehicles and dragged the passengers out.

'Go take a look,' yelled Monteith.

Jonah scrambled down the slope with Alex at his shoulder and plunged into the crowd, trying to get to where the bodies were being fought over. He was instantly disoriented. Acrid black smoke was pouring from the vehicles. The boys were pushing and shoving. Leering faces surged at him out of the smoke. Hands pulled at his clothing and his rifle. He pushed back, slamming his elbows into the nearest faces. He stamped on legs and feet. He barrelled forward. He caught a glimpse of a body. The blood and charred skin and rags of clothing made it difficult to identify. Then he got a clear sight of a familiar hammer and sickle badge and the boy wearing it, with arms bloody to the elbows; in one of his hands he held a machete and in the other a dismembered head. Despite the bruised and bloody features, Jonah recognised the face immediately.

It was Jim Kiernan, the former CIA station chief from Islamabad.

They'd killed an American.

I'll never forgive you for this. Nor's words from two years before, disregarded at the time, brought sharply back into focus; and immediately following them, the absolute certainty that the Americans would never forgive them for this. Jonah turned and fought his way back through the crowd, desperate to find some space in which to breathe. Breaking free, he dropped to his hands and knees and retched, and retched.

'Boss, you'd better get down here,' Alex called, from beside him.

'Did we get him?' Monteith shouted.

'You really need to see this.'

Jonah rolled over on to his back. Alex was standing with his rifle hanging loosely from its sling. 'This is so fucked,' he said, and slumped to the ground.

Monteith hurried down the slope. 'What is it?' he demanded.

'Go and look for yourself,' Jonah said, bitterly.

Monteith shouldered his way into the crowd and returned a few minutes later, ashen faced. He strode back and forth, kicking up dust.

'What are we going to do?' Jonah asked.

'We're fucked,' Alex said.

'No we're not,' Monteith snarled. 'There's nothing to tie us to this.'

Jonah looked up at him. 'What do you mean?'

'You know exactly what I mean.'

Vultures wheeled above the smoke. The ambush site was scorched and streaked with ash, and a bonfire burned in a crater. The boys squatted singly and in small groups, staring passively at the flames. The wreckage of the vehicles had been pushed off the road and into the gorge. The bodies were blackened sticks on the fire. Soon there would be nothing to recover.

'What do we do about Nor?' Jonah asked.

'You finish him,' Monteith said. 'Find him and kill him.'

'OK,' Jonah said. He stood up.

Alex glanced up at him. 'You want me to come?'

Jonah shook his head.

'You think you'll find him?' Alex asked.

'I'll find him.'

'We'll be waiting for you in Peshawar,' said Monteith.

It took him less than a week. It was easier than he had imagined. There was nothing surreptitious about it. He checked into the Spinghar Hotel in Jalalabad and simply waited. Three days later an Afghan carrying a Kalashnikov approached him across the hotel's neatly clipped lawn and invited him casually to drive out of town.

The highway east of Jalalabad was littered with boulders and the man steered carefully around them. They overtook gaudily decorated trucks and lines of trudging camels, their breath condensing in the bitter cold. Soon it began to rain. There were no wipers and the man reached through the window with a rag to wipe the misting windscreen. An hour later, he stopped the car beside a slope of shale.

'Go that way,' he said, pointing to a rough track that led up a ravine.

Jonah set off on foot up the mountain, hunched, with his collar turned up against the wind and sleet, and only his anger to propel him forward. After a further hour he had climbed above the cloud layer and the moon shone down on the road ahead. He walked past a frozen waterfall.

Without warning, a man stepped out from behind a rock up ahead. It was Nor. He appeared to be unarmed.

They faced each other by moonlight. Nor saw Jonah's face, metallic in the moonlight, with an expression wild enough to raise a warning in him, but instead of fleeing he set his face hard against his former friend and said insolently, 'What's your problem, Jonah? You betrayed me. I betrayed you. What can be fairer that that?'

Maddened, Jonah smashed his forehead into Nor's face. Nor's nose split like a ripe fruit and he fell to the ground. All Jonah's tolerance, his forbearance in the face of years of careless insults – beginning with Nor's jibes about Jonah's never-to-be-fulfilled desire to be white, his houseboy manners, his emotional inadequacy, the sneering asides about his wife, all of it culminating in the betrayal in the Kabul River Gorge – was turned outward in pent-up fury. He was going to kill him. He struck Nor with wild, lashing blows. '*Die!*' he yelled. He dragged him down the slope to an ice-covered pool. He flung him on to it and the surface splintered and cracked. He waded into the icy water and began to pummel Nor with his fists. Nor's face was covered in mud and blood. Jonah went on pummelling him until Nor's misshapen head slid under, leaving only a trail of bubbles breaking the surface.

Then he trudged back down the mountain filled with a murderer's remorse and flagged down the first car that passed. It was an ancient white Lada, driving back down from Kabul to Peshawar. Jonah pushed a wad of dollars into the Pashtun driver's hands and curled up on the back seat, shivering.

Hours later, safely back in Green's Hotel in Peshawar, with his hands shaking uncontrollably, he poured himself a whisky and gulped it down; then another and another and another.

The next morning Jonah met with the other Guides in the courtyard of Green's Hotel and told them that Nor was dead. All loose ends were tied. There was no reason for anyone to know about their involvement in the death of the CIA agent Jim Kiernan. Crisis averted. Monteith and the Department in the clear. And that was what Jonah believed until the muzzle of a gun was placed against the back of his neck beside the open pit of a diamond mine in Sierra Leone and he turned to find himself face to face with his oldest friend and bitterest foe.

Amputation is for ever

July 2001

They came for Jonah in the night, in the darkest hour, when the insects produced a roaring wall of sound. There were four of them, RUF fighters in raggedy T-shirts and flip-flops. They stormed into the hut on a wave of cane hooch and Jonah rose to meet them, swinging his fists like jackhammers. He knocked two of them flat before a rifle butt crashed into the side of his head. He felt a tremendous shock. The next moment his knees failed and he was falling, his head smacking the ground with a thump. The dirt floor in front of him receded to a great distance. He blacked out.

When he came round, he found that he had been dragged out of the hut and into the forest. There were men standing over him, poking him in his chest and abdomen with the barrels of their guns. Behind them the stars glittered and the sound of the insects pulsed in waves. A voice that seemed familiar, but which he struggled to recognise, said, 'Now it's your turn.'

His turn for what?

A man wearing a Tupac T-shirt slung his AK over his shoulder, straddled Jonah and bound his hands with a cable tie, tightening it so that the plastic sliced into the flesh of his wrists. The pain brought him an insight – he was in Africa. But why? He hardly ever went to Africa. He didn't speak any of the languages. The man slapped him across the face a couple of times.

The familiar voice said, 'Bring him.'

He was lifted to his feet and pushed and pulled along a narrow path through the forest. He stumbled in the darkness and fell several times. Each time the men kicked him and pummelled him with their rifle stocks before lifting him to his feet and pushing and pulling him along.

At some point he decided that he must be dreaming. He wasn't in the jungle at all. In fact, it turned out that he was being carried off the rugby pitch with a concussion. There were boys either side of him gripping him by his arms and legs and his shirt and shorts. It took a whole line-up to lift him. They were sloshing through the mud towards the touchline. The sky was a cloudless, cobalt blue. He was pleased to see that Nor was there, running alongside him, shouting words of encouragement through his gumshield. Nor was the most recent addition to the first fifteen, the new scrum half, lithe and fast. Jonah was the number eight, the anchor of the scrum.

Back in the dream, the path opened out into a large sandy clearing lit by the stars. At the centre of the clearing was a massive tree stump with a broad, flat surface. Its shadow reached across the clearing like a fist. They dragged him to the stump and kicked his feet out from behind him, so that he fell to his knees like a supplicant before an altar. They lifted his hands and placed them on its scarred surface.

Nor squatted before him, with the sweat on his face glistening in the starlight, and placed his hands over Jonah's.

'Fight and slay the pagans wherever ye find them,' Nor said, quietly at first, then angrily, then shouting, 'Lie in wait for them and seize them!'

It was difficult to understand him with the gumshield in his mouth. And he was talking in Arabic. In those days, the sword verses were Nor's favourite bit of the Koran, possibly the only bit he knew. He'd growl them at the opposing scrum. He was nicknamed the Saracen.

'A limb for a limb,' a voice said, in his dream. He felt its searing breath on his face.

'Who's limb?' Jonah wondered.

'In revenge there is life.'

'What are you talking about?'

'The bogeyman's here.'

Jonah's eyes were drawn to the treeline. A man stepped out of the shadows at the forest's edge. He was naked and smeared with ash. He had a bandana tied around his shaven skull and a machete in his hand.

'He's come to take your hands . . .'

Jonah began to struggle, but the men had him pinned down, their arms hooked through his elbows. His hands were numb, all the blood drained out. The bogeyman approached.

Nor lifted his hands off Jonah's and the men tightened their grip on his forearms. His fingers poked out like sticks. The bogeyman raised his machete, swinging it in a great arc. The starlight glinted blue on the nicked blade.

Nor's eyes shone.

He hit the fast-reverse button: it was moments before the concussion. The scrum was holding. Jonah was dug in and low against the ground, with a string of pain from his heels to his thighs. The ball was in the thicket of feet in front of him. Looking back through his legs, he saw Nor just behind him, impossibly low, as if he were on starter's blocks, waiting for the ball.

Nor's eye shone. *Go on, Chewy . . .*

Jonah heaved.

Yes . . .

Jonah imagined the wet crunch of the blade on flesh and bone and his severed hands flopping on to the grass. He saw himself as the limbless beggar from the football match, pleading with his coat-hanger claws.

Go on . . .

He bared his teeth and gave up his thoughts. He swung to the right and bit off an ear. The man screamed.

The blade came slicing down and Jonah surged upwards and to the side and the screaming man on his right tumbled forward on to the stump and into the path of the falling machete. His skull split like a melon. Jonah's forehead connected with the jaw of the man on his left. Teeth flew. Then he was on his feet, swaying and snorting like an enraged bear. He spat the lump of gristle in his mouth on to the ground. Things leapt in and out of focus. He looked from right to left: Nor was squatting, very still, on the balls of his feet; one man was hunched over the stump; another was spreadeagled on his back; a third man, the one in the Tupac T-shirt, was stumbling in the direction of the treeline and the bogeyman was on his knees crawling after him. The killing was not done. With his bound hands Jonah tugged the machete out of the man's head. He took five steps, sloshing through the mud. He counted them, one after the other. Focus came and went. The bogeyman rolled into a ball, like a frightened millipede. Jonah thought *you're dead*. He brought up the blade and swung it down and brought it up and swung it down.

'*Stop!*' A shout.

He staggered backwards, staring wildly.

There was a loud *crack* and he wondered for a moment whether he'd been shot. Missed. Nor would not miss again. He closed his eyes, giving himself to the coming bullet. Nothing. He opened his eyes. Nor was standing with the stock of the Kalashnikov fitted to his shoulder, his eyes narrow as slits and his tongue thrust deep into his cheek; his finger tightening on the trigger for a second time. *Crack*. He shot the remaining fighter just a couple of steps short of the treeline. Then he turned to Jonah, pointing the rifle at him.

'I'll shoot you dead.'

Jonah exhaled, staggering back and forth. His head was thumping like a hammer. He sank to his knees. 'I don't have it in me to take you on.'

Nor acknowledged Jonah's response with a quick nod of the head and walked among the wounded, dispatching them, one at a time, with the barrel pressed to each forehead before gently squeezing the trigger.

Then he turned to Jonah, pointing the rifle at him again. 'Tell Monteith to beware the sky.'

A moment's pause. *The sky?* 'Why?'

'A whirlwind is coming, Jonah,' Nor said softly. 'When it has passed nothing will ever be the same.' Then he ejected the cartridge, cleared the breech and threw the rifle to the ground. 'You'd better run for your life.'

Jonah staggered into the jungle. Soon afterwards he heard the hammering of automatic-weapons fire.

A storm came. He couldn't see more than a couple of steps ahead. In the darkness, there was no boundary between land and sky. Rain poured down from the canopy and rushed along the forest floor. He was stumbling along a path that had become a torrent of water. There were crashing sounds all around that he was convinced were trees falling. He kept moving forward. Leaves and vines whipped him. Thorns ripped at his face and clothes. The ground gave way and abruptly he was tumbling in a mudslide. He slammed into a tree. He folded around it. He was numb and cold; only the cuts on his face felt real.

A family of charcoal burners found him in the wake of the storm. He was unconscious and still clinging to the tree, his fingers gripping the bark. They had to prise them off, one by one, before cutting off the plastic cuffs. He was too large to carry, so they made a sled from fertiliser bags and dragged him through the forest to their camp.

When he woke up he was on the sandy floor of a tent, lying wrapped in blankets. There was a fire burning beside him. The logs were crackling, sparks falling on the ground.

One of the charcoal burners was leaning over him. 'Who are you?'

He almost laughed. It was such a great excuse to be an amnesiac, to be reborn. Unfortunately, he remembered everything.

'The cat's out of the bag,' he said.

'You have a fever,' the man said.

And a splitting headache.

With Nor dead there had been some hope of keeping the assassination of Kiernan a secret and avoiding a vengeful American response; with Nor alive there was no such hope. They would always live with the fear that Nor would talk. And he would talk,

Jonah was sure of that. The only possible reason Nor hadn't done it in the last two years was because he was keeping it up his sleeve, ready to produce it with a flourish for maximum, catastrophic effect.

Some day Nor would talk.

The fallen towers

September 2001

The message was written in the layer of white ash on the hood of an abandoned car on Broadway: PUNISH. It wasn't clear whether the person who had used a finger to scrawl the message was referring to what had happened or to some future act of retribution. Standing on the pavement beside the car, Jonah watched another convoy of Humvees, dump trucks, bulldozers and backhoes trundle south through the parted sawhorse barriers.

'*A whirlwind is coming,*' Nor had told him, two months before in Sierra Leone. '*When it has passed nothing will ever be the same . . .*' He'd been right. You could tell by the look on people's faces that something terrible had happened. And that many Americans were thinking that this was the worst thing that had ever happened – the world had turned on its head in a day.

'We've spent five years trying to get people to listen. But nobody took us seriously. They were oblivious. It was too exotic a threat. Too primitive . . .'

Jonah glanced across at Mikulski, who was staring at the pillar of ash spiralling upwards, hundreds of feet over Manhattan and the Hudson. It was the first time that Mikulski had spoken since Jonah had met him at the barricade on the corner of Varrick and Houston. Mikulski had produced his Treasury Department ID and soldiers dressed in flak jackets and gas masks had waved them through. They had walked together down the empty, ash-covered pavements into the Financial District.

Mikulski looked as if he had hardly slept for several days. He had a steely expression on his face that suggested deep-rooted anger.

'I said to people: you don't understand. Random slaughter is a way of life out there, from Algeria to Afghanistan. Bombs, earthquakes, mass starvation – whole regions of the world strewn with failing states. They just didn't get it. People thought that we were immune, that somehow our ideals and beliefs would shield us.'

Mikulski was right, Jonah thought; in the world that he knew this sort of thing happened every day. Hatred, not love, was all around. Eventually, inevitably, it had found its way to America.

'Where were you?' Jonah asked.

'When the first plane hit? I was walking down West Broadway. I heard the roar of the engines. I looked up and it struck the North Tower.' He glanced across at Jonah. 'I was still standing there with my mouth open when the second plane hit.'

Mikulski's office had been in the US Customs House in World Trade Centre 6, the eight-storey building that was destroyed when the North Tower collapsed on it. They had been due to meet there on the afternoon of the 11th. Mikulski was on loan to the US Treasury from the FBI's Foreign Intelligence office. His particular speciality was tracking terrorist financial links.

Mikulski returned the question. 'Where were you?'

'On a plane,' Jonah replied, 'on my way here.'

It was already clear that 9/11 was the fixed point around which they would orientate themselves for the foreseeable future. In the immediate aftermath of the attack, Jonah's 747 had been diverted to an air force base at Gander in Newfoundland. It had joined thirty other passenger jets that were parked on a runway built for cold-war-era nuclear bombers in expectation of a very different kind of Armageddon. The small, dilapidated town adjacent to the runway had struggled to accommodate several thousand unexpected guests, and by the time Jonah and his fellow passengers had disembarked from their plane, the only remaining place to sleep was the benches of a Pentecostal church. He had spent five nights in the church.

'What will happen now?' Jonah asked.

Mikulski unfolded his newspaper and held it up for Jonah to

see. On the cover was a picture of President George W. Bush and below it the headline: *Justice will be done.*

'We'll go after them, wherever they are. We'll hunt them down.'

Revenge was the word on everyone's lips. In the early hours of one morning in Gander, Jonah had found himself sitting on a pew in the church next to a straight-backed, grey-faced woman with a Bible on her lap. He hadn't meant to intrude on her prayers but it was the only pew without someone stretched out on it, and she had offered him a weary smile. He had spoken to her out of politeness and in return she had confided in him. She spoke softly, without betraying any emotion: her daughter had been 'taken' in the attacks. She had been 'judged'. The daughter had worked at Cantor Fitzgerald on the 104th floor of the North Tower, just above the point of impact. Jonah had been stunned by the woman's composure.

'We have sinned against Almighty God, at the highest level of our government,' the woman explained. 'We've stuck our finger in His eye. The Supreme Court has insulted Him over and over. They've taken His Bible away from the schools. They've forbidden little children to pray.'

Jonah tried to ease himself out of the pew, but there was an unstoppable momentum to her softly spoken words.

'The battle of America has begun,' she told him. 'In the cities of these people, which the Lord thy God doth give thee for an inheritance, thou shalt save alive nothing that breatheth. Retribution will be terrible to behold.'

Not everybody in America had considered they were immune or out of reach, Jonah reflected. Plenty of people had been expecting it. They were the ones counting down the hours to the rapture. It was easy to understand how religious fundamentalists would latch on to the destruction of the towers as a foreshadow of the coming Armageddon. And both sides were at it: the symbolism was both biblical and Koranic. In the Bible, the people who built the tower of Babel were punished for their presumption; in the Koran, the people who failed to heed God's messengers were destroyed in the punishment stories. As far as Jonah was concerned,

Islamism and Christian fundamentalism were no different from each other – their adherents were both scrambling rabidly for the next piece of carnage.

'This way,' Mikulski said, producing a torch from his battered leather coat. They entered the Century 21 department store and picked their way through the rubble and smashed goods to the emergency stairwell. They climbed to the fifth floor and entered the offices of a law firm. Walking over to the windows, which were blown out, they stepped out on to the ledge.

'There,' Mikulski said.

They were looking right into the heart of it, an enormous pile of smouldering wreckage. Parts of it were on fire. In the glare of the spotlights, they stood and watched firemen digging in the rubble and twisted metal. Just looking at it sucked all the hope out of you.

'You have your answer, don't you?' Mikulski said. 'You know now why they were converting cash into easily transportable assets, because they know that we are going to come for them like a whirlwind and they know that if they can't carry it they'll lose it. Diamonds are among the easiest, and by far the most valuable by weight, of commodities to move. They don't set off metal detectors. They don't have any scent. You take a diamond that's been cut and polished and there's no human being on earth who can tell with certainty where that stone came from.'

'We think they purchased about twenty million dollars' worth.'

'They want to be able to fund future attacks,' Mikulski told him. 'This abomination isn't enough for them; it's not big enough or grotesque enough. Not by a long way. It's only the opening salvo.'

Within the counter-terrorism community, Mikulski had a reputation for being a maverick but also for plain speaking and honesty. He was the son of Polish immigrants, a former Baltimore homicide cop turned FBI agent. When Jonah had first contacted him after his return from Sierra Leone he had hoped that Mikulski would be able to offer some advice on how to track the sale of the diamonds, in the hope that it might lead to Nor, but that wasn't his only motivation for asking for a meeting. Jonah had been ready to tell all. In the weeks following his return from Sierra Leone, he had convinced himself that it was better to confess and hope for clemency than leave it to Nor to reveal all in some spectacular stunt. He had not consulted Monteith before arranging the meeting. He was in no doubt that Monteith would regard what he was contemplating doing as treason. But he had reasoned that he was under a greater obligation to tell the truth than to simply protect the Department.

By the time he had boarded the plane for New York, Jonah had made his mind up. He was going to confess. But events had intervened. Terrorists had crashed planes into the World Trade Centre and the Pentagon. Standing beside Mikulski in the window of the legal firm, and staring down at the fiery inferno that was all that was left of the towers, he knew that there would be no confession. The world had irreversibly changed. He was as tied to the lie as the rest of the Guides.

MIRANDA

Hijra: Flight

'I take refuge with the Lord of the Daybreak from the evil of what He has created, from the evil of darkness when it gathers, from the evil of the women who blow on knots, from the evil of an envier when he envies.'

Koran, Sura 113

The woman who blew on knots

2 September 2005

Some time before dawn she found herself at the door to the farm-house, sure in the knowledge that there would be no further sleep that night. She stood for a while, naked in the doorway, staring out across the water at the mainland. The air was cold and thick with the smell of brine, and soon the first mist would roll off the water. The chill burned her cheeks, breasts and thighs. She thought, as she had so often done before, that her life was a mystery that had unravelled in directions unforeseen.

The dog slid between her legs and sprinted off after distant rabbits. She didn't feel tired. She felt lost. She had no cable, no lifeline, to show her the way. She turned from the doorway and retreated to the kitchen. From the freezer box in the fridge she removed a bottle of lemon vodka, the last of the batch. She poured herself a measure in an empty jam jar from the draining board and downed it in one gulp. It burned.

She felt a rush of sudden anger. There were times when it felt as if a band of steel were tightening against her skull.

Even in his absence Barnhill was full of Jonah's presence. She often started, her head turning as fast as whiplash to catch him, but she was always too slow. He was never there. It was just his ghost haunting her, an invisible companion to the dog that followed everywhere at her heels.

She glanced at the postcard tacked to the fridge door; Jonah's only message since he had left the island. The picture was a photograph of the Bala Hissar fortress in Peshawar. She turned it over.

The stamps were from Pakistan, postmarked Peshawar. She had contemplated buying a ticket for Pakistan and setting out in pursuit of him – after all, she knew Peshawar well – but something had made her stay put. She distrusted the postcard's provenance. There was a simple written message, *I have things to take care of,* and the address written in a scrawl beside it. The subtext eluded her. She clung to the thought that there might be some further communication from him, some sort of explanation.

Then there was her job, if it could be called that. From the beginning of April she had been employed by Scottish Natural Heritage to monitor the habitat of rare orchids on the island's machair, the sand-dune pasture on the windward side of the isle of Jura that was classified as a special conservation area. In the last two months she had logged frog, Hebridean, northern March and early purple orchids, as well as sea bindweed, yellow rattle and red clover among the carpet flowers. She had even spotted Irish ladies' tresses, a native orchid of Greenland, its seed probably deposited by migrating Greenland white-fronted geese in their droppings. Then there were the birds: corncrake, twite, dunlin, redshank and ringed plover. After Jonah had left she simply continued with her daily routine of hiking, note-taking and observations. If nothing else, it had provided a ready excuse for her restless meandering.

Beyond that, it was a struggle to remember how she had spent the time. There were piles of books, fragments of diary notes and observations, clues here and there, but nothing concrete, and certainly nothing to distinguish one day from another. They'd run together like goulash.

She was almost forty.

She didn't even own a car.

She left the kitchen and walked down the hallway, her fingertips sliding along the wall. There was a black Karrimor rucksack hanging on a peg on the wall, its straps fastidiously folded and taped. Her crash-bag, Jonah had called it. The night before he had left, he'd packed it and insisted that she keep it ready for instant departure.

'You need to be ready at a moment's notice,' he'd told her.

'Why?' she'd asked, amused by the gravity of his expression. She'd put such things behind her. That was why they had come to Barnhill, to put their wildness behind them. She'd imagined it was simply force of habit in him.

'Trust me,' Jonah had said. It was only much later, days after he'd gone, that it occurred to her that these were the very the same words that she'd used to him in Baghdad in March 2003 in the last days before the war, when falling for him felt like utter madness, when everything that she did, every word she said, every man she fucked or betrayed, everything she revealed and the many things that she kept concealed, all of it was about getting back her stolen child.

She drifted from room to room in a sleepy daze with the dog following. There was a thin layer of peat dust from the fires in the kitchen and the drawing room that covered everything. It needed dusting. She needed to find a morning routine again.

She opened the door to Jonah's study and stared at the empty desk and the wall beside it, which had a profusion of jottings, press cuttings, photographs and maps pinned to it. The collage, he called it – the research matter for his memoir. She sat in the swivel chair and leant back to study the wall. She had taken to randomly reading the press cuttings, the items of interest to Jonah that were highlighted in fluorescent yellow marker. This time, she read a cutting from the *Daily Mail* – '*Aviation International Services do not now and have never conducted so-called rendition flights*'. Beneath it there was an article from the *Washington Post* with the headline: '*Al Qaeda Cash Tied to Diamond Trade*'. Beside that, with an arrow linking the two, there was a 2004 print-out from Wikinews: '*The bodies of eleven disembowelled people have been found in a mass grave in the Sulaymaniyah region of Kurdistan, according to the United States military in Iraq. The bodies have not yet been identified. Reports quote an estimate that the bodies may be more than a year old.*'

Then there were the faces. She recognised some of them – the obvious ones, including Bin Laden and his deputy, Ayman al-Zawahiri, US vice-president Dick Cheney and the Abu Ghraib guard Lynndie England. There was a Polaroid photograph of Monteith, head of the shadowy unit of the Ministry of Defence known only as the Department, and until 2003 Jonah's boss. Then there were other faces, faces remembered from her own past, the evidence of an unexpected and at times troubling intersection between her life and Jonah's. There was a Pakistani brigadier, whose face she remembered glimpsing in a tunnel in the Tora Bora mountain range of Afghanistan. There was even a photograph of her husband Bakr, the father of her son. He was sitting in a restaurant in Kuwait City in 1990, looking sleek and well fed a few months before the Iraqi invasion.

Others she did not recognise, including one of a man at the centre of the collage, a head shot taken for an Interpol Red Notice. Nor ed-Din, it said in large text above the photo. Beneath it, under the heading 'Aliases', were half a dozen names.

He was smiling.

A wry, self-mocking smile that made a parody of the mugshot. He was good looking too, beautiful even, with large, oval eyes with dark, almost feminine eyelashes, a straight nose, defined cheekbones and full lips. There was something about him that reminded her of her husband as a young man, when she had first met him in the North-West Frontier, and had felt intoxicated by his beauty and his elusiveness. His eyes seemed to follow her around the room.

It wasn't the only photograph of Nor. There were several. One of him in the midst of a crowd at a demonstration protesting about the plight of Muslims in Bosnia; another of him in ranks of uniformed officer cadets, with the caption *Somme Company, Royal Military Academy, Sandhurst*; and finally, a Polaroid of two young boys in swimming trunks with the sea and what looked like a Crusader castle in the background. In the margin of the photograph *Jonah + Nor, Lebanon* had been written in purple felt-tip pen.

Childhood friend, soldier, activist, criminal . . .

She wondered about Nor ed-Din's place in Jonah's confessional memoir. There had been plenty of opportunities to read Jonah's work-in-progress but she had deliberately not taken them. It wasn't through lack of interest; more that she was unwilling to be drawn into a situation where she felt obliged to reciprocate. She had concluded long ago that there was a limit to what she was prepared to share. She had not told Jonah that she recognised the Pakistani brigadier. There were certain things that she kept back.

She went upstairs. In the bedroom she picked up her dressing gown from the floor and hung it on the back of the door, a half-hearted attempt at tidying. She hesitated at the foot of the bed. Feeling disconsolate she remained standing there, staring at Jonah's side. She remembered sleepless nights listening to his breathing and his night-time mutters. He slept face down, spreadeagled, arms and legs outstretched, often poking out of the covers, his pillows discarded on the floor. For several weeks after he had left, she slept with one of his pillows sandwiched between her thighs.

Perhaps she should have been more open with him.

She missed their lovemaking. She missed his hands, the walnuts of bone and sinew at the knuckles, the flat and broad pads of his fingertips tracing conversations over her skin, and the way he brought her to climax.

She slipped into the unmade bed, her fingers reaching between her legs. She came with her eyes closed and her mouth open, out of time for a few seconds. The little death. Oblivious. Nowhere.

She missed the way he flexed his fingers when he was talking to himself, conducting his interior monologues. He was lousy at disguising his dreaming. His eyes took on a faraway look. For someone so transparent it was amazing to her that he should be able to keep so much hidden.

She missed his shambling gait and his scarred skull, the bear-like qualities that he ruefully acknowledged. She missed his suspicion of closed doors; his need for an immediate exit close to hand. She missed his irrepressible daughter Esme, the bear cub, who swept through the house like a typhoon – a wild-haired mess of cuts and grazes and half-finished sentences.

She missed his curious stare.

She felt a constricting sensation in her chest. There were times when she dismissed Jonah as a child, one who imagined a dream and its fulfilment as one. She had come to despise the impulsiveness in him.

She dressed in sweatpants and a sleeveless top and went back down the stairs to the kitchen. She stared again at the postcard Blu-tacked to the fridge. Beyond it the vodka ticked like a clock.

She turned away and drifted again from room to room. Passing a window, she saw that two roe deer had appeared out of the mist and were crossing the track: a female and a fawn heading towards the far corner of the garden. She could see from the fawn's kidney-shaped rump patch that it was a male – a mother and son. Sometimes it felt as if even nature was mocking her.

At dawn she rolled out her yoga mat on the grass and for an hour or so the cadence of her breathing marked the boundaries of her world.

She saluted the pale orb of the sun, her body moving to the rhythm of her breath, rising on the in-breath and falling on the out-breath. Up dog. Down dog. At the end of each cycle she leapt to the front of her mat and in doing so became a virtually unconscious being, in a pure present, free of the past or any anxiety about the future. She held warrior pose, sinking deep in the lunge with her arms outstretched. She turned her hands this way and that, to deflect the pain. She held the pose for longer than she had ever done before, feeling the strings of muscle running down her arms as taut as cables.

She finished with a headstand, and held it for several minutes before easing down, and pausing in corpse pose to let the tension run like water out of her neck and spine. She rolled over on to her back, closed her eyes and felt herself sinking, sinking.

For a while she slept.

Eventually she woke, rolled over on to her right side and got slowly to her feet. She squatted and rolled up her mat. There was no anger in her, only sadness. She padded back into the kitchen and drank from the tap. Then fed wood into the Aga, put the kettle on the hob and switched on the radio to listen to the *Today* programme, another of his morning rituals. He'd flip the switch and lean against the sink with his arms outstretched like an athlete limbering up and wait for the hourly bulletin. Always he expected some new terror, and they rolled in like waves: Beslan, Madrid, Istanbul, Marrakesh and London.

She listened for a while: reports from New Orleans of the descent into anarchy in the aftermath of Hurricane Katrina and at a benefit concert the rapper Kanye West saying, 'George Bush doesn't care about black people'; in Iraq a surge in car bombings, bomb explosions and shootings as the country sank inexorably into sectarian civil war and the historian Francis Fukayama saying, 'We do not know what outcome we will face in Iraq. We do know that four years after 9/11, our whole foreign policy seems destined to rise or fall on the outcome of a war only marginally related to the source of what befell us on that day'; and a report from the Stratford Street mosque in Beeston in Leeds on the origins of the 7 July London bombers, a commentator saying, 'It is easy for such movements as Hizb-ut-Tahrir to get into the minds of young-sters who are to an extent empty vessels. The information is easily accepted because of its seeming coherence and, more importantly, because many of those they seek to indoctrinate have nothing to offer in return. This is not discovery through the exchange of ideas. This is writing on to a blank page.'

In her twenties Miranda had been married to a man who intro-duced her to the intimate workings of guns and bombs. He had scooped her up like flotsam in the courtyard at Green's Hotel in Peshawar in Pakistan's North-West Frontier and taken her away to the Lion's Den, the al-Ansar Camp in the Tora Bora mountain range. She remembered sitting on a wooden bench in a segregated classroom of pious female students who were as careless with their own lives as they were with others'. She'd watched him in front of the blackboard, scratching his chalk diagrams from right to left, his lessons randomly punctuated by the sudden rattle of tins and the sprint for the shelters as the Russian Sukhois roared overhead. She knew how easy it was to make tricycloacetone peroxide from the combination of hydrogen peroxide, acetone and sulphuric acid, ingredients readily available in paint thinner, antiseptic and drain cleaner. The key was in the percentages and maintaining a stable temperature.

She knew that the AK47 assault rifle has only eight moving parts. It can be stripped in under a minute and cleaned quickly in almost any climactic conditions. She could close her eyes and recite the order: release magazine catch, remove magazine, cock rifle, release the catch on the right side of rear sight, push piston assembly cover forward and detach from piston assembly and bolt.

She had glided between worlds of opulence and worlds of desolation. She had become pregnant in a cave in the Lion's Den and given birth to a boy nine months later in an air-conditioned palace in Saudi Arabia. She had called him Omar, firstborn. She had drifted between cities: Riyadh, Beirut, Kuwait City, Baghdad . . .

In 1991 the Iraqis had snatched her from occupied Kuwait and incarcerated her in the prison at Abu Ghraib. On a Thursday they had come into her cell and removed her son. It had taken her ten years of searching to find his grave.

Her father had been a fighter. His father had been a fighter. The Isaaq clan were fighters. When she was five, her father, who had fought the Ethiopians in the Ogaden and turned against his former mentor, the dictator Siad Barre, would clench a fist that was mottled pink with scars and hold it out.

'Are you tough, little bird?' he would ask.

'I'm tough,' she would say.

'Then hit my fist.'

She swung, crushing the knuckles of her tiny hand.

'Is that as hard as you can hit? Do it again, harder this time.'

She swung again.

'Are you tough?'

'I'm tough.'

'Hit me again.'

She struck again, sobbing, the tears rolling down her cheeks.

'Come on. You're tougher than that. Hit me.'

An uncle once said that she was tougher than her father – the same uncle that felt her up when she was fifteen. The second time that he tried it she'd been ready for him. It was Eid. They were upstairs at her parent's house. When her uncle pressed himself against her she slipped a draughtsman's blade from her sleeve and sliced through the fabric of his trousers, causing him to widen his eyes comically. She had told him that if he ever attempted to touch her again she would cut off his penis.

After a shower she stared at herself in the full-length mirror. Five foot ten in bare feet, she stood with one hand on the taut plain of her stomach and the other on her forehead, pushing back the unruly strands of her hair. She had strong cheekbones and knowing eyes. She could be thirty.

She bared her teeth. She said, 'You used to frighten people.'

She wondered when something would happen.

Inspectors call

She was hiking down off the moor when she spotted the car coming around a bend in the hard-core track, some five or six miles distant. It was pelting with rain and a scouring wind was coming in from the north-east. She stopped in the shadow of a basalt outcrop and called the dog to her side. It came alert and raised its snout to the air.

'Stay,' she murmured.

She studied the approaching car through her binoculars. It was a Peugeot 206, white with red stripes, and marked Metropolitan Police. It was a long way from London in a 206. Be careful what you wish for, she thought. She briefly considered making a break for the mainland but quickly discounted the idea. There was chaos in Baghdad, New Orleans, London, a thousand other places . . . what possible reason could there be for her to leave the island? She resumed walking and the dog stayed close by her side.

The car was still some way off when she entered the cottage, rolled down her waterproofs and stepped out of her wellingtons. She fed the dog with a handful of dried food in its bowl, caught her reflection in the mirror on the wall and tucked a lock of hair behind an ear.

She put the kettle on the Aga and waited for the knock on the door. Wait, she told herself. Wait a beat.

There were three of them: two in uniform at the fore and, behind them, a third in a knee-length leather coat and mud-spattered jeans. The policemen stood sheltering from the rain in the porch, with their shoulders hunched and water dripping off the peaks of their caps. The third stood out in the yard, his unshaven face locked in a ferocious grimace.

'This is Barnhill, is it, ma'am?' asked the taller policeman, with a moustache.

'Yes,' she said. 'What can I do for you?'

'Mrs Miranda Abd al'Aswr, is that correct?' asked the shorter one, taking his time to pronounce her name correctly. He removed his peaked cap and tucked it under his arm. His hair was plastered against his scalp. She almost felt sorry for them but their expressions were devoid of good humour.

'Yes, I'm Miranda.'

'I hope we're not disturbing you?'

'What do you want?' she asked. *What was there to disturb?*

'We're making enquiries about a Mr Jonah Said,' said the shorter one.

'What is it?' She heard her voice becoming strident. Inside she quaked.

'We understand that you are an acquaintance of Mr Said, a close friend?'

'What's happened to him?'

An insolent silence followed. They seem to be deliberating whether to answer.

Eventually, the taller man replied. 'He's missing.'

'Unless he's here?' added the shorter one.

'He's not here,' she told them. 'He left a couple of weeks ago.'

The kettle began to whistle on the hob. The taller one looked over her shoulder into the kitchen. 'Can we come in?'

She turned her back on them, went over to the Aga and removed the kettle. When she turned back they were standing in the kitchen, dripping on the floorboards. The taller one removed his cap. She couldn't see the third.

'I need to see some identification,' she said.

Begrudgingly they showed her their passes. They looked real enough. So did the uniforms. The taller one with the moustache was an inspector and the shorter one a sergeant. Their names were Coyle and Mulvey.

'Tea?' she asked.

'Please,' said the taller one, the inspector named Coyle. 'Both white. No sugar for me.'

'I'll have two,' Mulvey told her, and after a pause he said, 'Please.'

The third man slipped through the door and stood by the entrance to the hall, in a rapidly expanding puddle of water.

'And your friend . . .?'

Sergeant Mulvey stared at her for a moment without comprehension.

The man dug around in the pocket of his leather coat and retrieved a crumpled business card, which he offered to her. It said *Mark Mikulski, Federal Bureau of Investigation.*

'I'm only here to, uh, observe . . .' he said, in a North American accent.

'Do you want tea?' she asked.

He shook his head, dislodging further droplets of rain. Then he looked around and, spotting a chair by the wall, he sat down in it. Inspector Coyle frowned, as if sitting amounted to a breach of protocol. There was clearly tension between these neatly turned out policemen and their unshaven companion.

She made three teas and was careful to discard the tea bags in the compost bin. Coyle stepped aside to let her get the milk carton from the fridge. She sniffed at it before pouring.

'There isn't any sugar,' she explained.

'Just as it comes, then,' said Mulvey.

Turning to hand them their mugs, she saw that the dog was sitting in front of the American Mikulski and having his ears scratched.

'Mr Said is a difficult man to track down,' said Coyle. 'He isn't very popular with his ex-wife. He is no longer employed by the army.'

'Who reported him missing?' she asked, leaning back on the Aga rail.

They didn't reply.

She sipped at her tea.

'Is this from him?' asked Coyle, pointing to the postcard tacked to the fridge. 'May I?'

She nodded in assent and he peeled the postcard off the door.

'Is this his handwriting?'

'Yes.'

'*I have things to take care of*,' he read out loud. 'What do you suppose that means?'

'I don't know.'

'People often go missing from Peshawar. I mean, Peshawar is a staging post, for people heading for the tribal areas and Afghanistan, isn't that so?'

'You believe Jonah's in Afghanistan?'

'Not any more,' said Coyle.

'Have you been to Afghanistan, Ms Abd al'Aswr?' Mulvey asked.

'I have.'

'May I ask what you were doing there?'

'I was driving a truck.'

Coyle looked around him, at the dog, now curled up on the sofa, the breakfast things and two-day-old newspapers still on the table, the empty bottle of vodka and her socks slung over the back of a chair.

'You're on your own, then?' he asked, in a tone that suggested that she lived in a state of disarray.

'Since he left,' she acknowledged.

'You don't have a telephone,' observed Mulvey.

'The line doesn't reach this far.'

'And you have a part-time job with Scottish Natural Heritage?'

'Yes. I monitor the orchids.'

'Orchids?'

'There is a species of rare orchid on the moor. I keep watch over them.'

'To deter thieves?'

'Partly.'

'When did Mr Said travel abroad?' Coyle asked.

'I don't know. Have you checked with the airlines?'

They glanced at each other.

'Did you discuss his departure?' Coyle demanded.

'No,' she said.

'You just woke up one morning and he was gone?' asked Coyle
sceptically.

'No. I came back off the moor one afternoon and he was gone.'

'Did he leave a note?'

'No.'

'And has he made contact since?'

'No.'

'Except for the postcard,' said Coyle, standing very close to
her.

'Except for the postcard,' she agreed. She held out her hand
for it and reluctantly he gave it to her.

'What was he doing in Peshawar?' asked Mulvey, from the far
side of the room, as he sifted through the papers on the table.
'Mr Said, I mean.'

'I have no idea. You won't find anything interesting there.'

Mulvey picked up a book and rifled through the pages. 'You
speak Arabic?'

'Yes.'

Their eyes were on her. She sipped at her tea.

'Abd al'Aswr is an interesting name.'

'It was my husband's name. He was from Saudi Arabia.'

'Where is he now?'

'He's dead.'

Coyle and Mulvey looked at each other.

'Mr Said has some Middle Eastern ancestry,' Coyle told her.

'Not all Arabs are terrorists,' she said defiantly.

'Goodness, no,' said Coyle. 'We wouldn't for a second enter-
tain that thought. Would we, Mulvey?'

'Not for a second.'

Coyle removed a passport-size photo from his wallet and held
it up, pinched between his thumb and forefinger for her to see.

'Do you recognise this man?'

The photo was the same as the mugshot pinned to the wall at the centre of the collage in Jonah's study, the man with the wry, self-mocking smile.

'His name is Nor ed-Din,' Coyle explained. 'He's a British citizen of Jordanian extraction. Do you recognise him?'

'No,' she lied.

'Do you have access to the Internet?'

'No.'

'This gentleman recently appeared in a video. I think you would call it a sort of confession. In it he makes certain threats against the security of this country. Serious threats. I repeat, do you know Nor ed-Din?'

'I've never seen him before.'

Coyle regarded her sceptically. 'We believe that your friend Jonah was a colleague of his. The Department, have you heard of that?'

'No.'

'What about Richard Winthrop?' Mikulski asked, leaning forward in his chair.

Coyle looked up sharply and Miranda had the feeling that Mikulski had deviated from a prepared set of questions.

'No,' she replied.

There was a pause.

'Did Mr Said take much with him, when he left?' asked Mulvey.

'A change of clothes, that's about it.'

'A mobile phone?'

'I'm not sure that he had one. They aren't much use up here. There's no signal.'

'Did he possess a passport in another name?'

'I don't know.'

'Did he talk to you about what line of work he was in?'

'We never discussed it.'

'You don't seem to have discussed very much.'

'We had a predominantly physical relationship,' she said. 'We fucked a lot.'

Mulvey wagged a finger at her. 'Now you're teasing us.'

'I don't think I can help you any further,' she said.

'You've been very kind, ma'am, and we've overstayed our welcome,' Coyle replied. He handed her a card. *Inspector Coyle. Counter-Terrorism Command.* 'Give us a call, if you remember anything that might help. And if Mr Said rings or writes, or turns up as suddenly as he disappeared, or you remember anything or hear something from a third party which could be of assistance in locating him or Mr Nor ed-Din, then please let us know.'

'I will.'

'Of course you will,' said Mulvey.

'It's an interesting house,' said Coyle.

'A bit remote for my taste,' added Mulvey.

Mikulski rolled his eyes and got up from the chair.

The policemen put their mugs on the table before they left. Neither of them had touched the tea. She stood by the sink and watched through the window as the police car rattled back down the track with the American's head visible in the rear window, staring back at the house.

As soon as the car had turned the corner she hurried down the hall to Jonah's study.

In addition to the photographs of Nor ed-Din she found three references to Richard Winthrop on Jonah's board. The first was a clipping from the *Baltimore Sun*, dated May 2003, a block of text highlighted with a yellow fluorescent marker:

> Like dirty money, tainted reputations can be laundered, as the
> Bush Administration fervently hopes in the case of Richard
> Winthrop. Now at the White House National Security
> Council, Winthrop has been chosen to go to Iraq to serve as
> deputy to Coalition Provisional Authority Chief L. Paul
> Bremer. As part of President Reagan's policy of supporting
> anti-communist forces in the 1980s, hundreds of millions of
> dollars in United States aid was funneled to the Salvadorean

Army, and a team of 55 Special Forces advisors, led for several years by Richard Winthrop, trained front-line battalions that were accused of significant human rights abuses.

The second reference was from the *New York Times*, dated 28 June 2004, the headline '*Bremer Leaves after Iraqi Sovereignty Transfer*', and beneath it a photograph showing CPA chief Bremer striding towards a waiting plane in his trademark tan suit and Timberland boots. At his side, his head circled with a black marker pen, was a taller and equally determined-looking man in a suit. Beneath the photograph the caption read: '*L. Paul Bremer and his deputy Richard Winthrop IV stage an exit in one plane for the press and then fly out on another*'.

The third reference was in a cutting from the *Wall Street Journal* dated February 2005, an announcement by the security company Greysteel USA that it had hired a new vice-chairman:

'Richard Winthrop brings with him thirty years of experience in combating terrorism around the globe and absolute devotion to freedom and democracy and the United States of America,' said Greysteel owner, Thaddeus Clay. 'We are honoured to have him return to our great team.'

With leadership drawn from the Executive Branch of the United States Government, Greysteel has the practical experience and the network to mitigate any security issue.

She sat back in the chair.

On the one hand there was Nor, with an obvious childhood link to Jonah and other parallels: both soldiers, possibly both members of the Department, both missing, both wanted by the police and the FBI. On the other hand an American, a Republican ideologue with a past connection to Salvadorean death squads, one-time deputy to the proconsul of Iraq, and now vice-chairman of one of the largest security companies in the world.

Where was the link?

Who's been sleeping in my bed?

4–5 September 2005

Miranda got off the bus at the bottom of Bowmore's Main Street and walked towards the round whitewashed Presbyterian church at the top of the hill. It was a beautiful clear day on Islay without a cloud in the sky. The dog followed at her heels. At the Co-op she crossed the road and headed diagonally across the square past the usual huddle of teenagers standing around the telephone box and walked towards the school.

She knew that she could not approach Esme at home. The level of antagonism between Jonah and his ex-wife Sarah and her new husband Douglas was such that she would not be allowed to speak to Jonah's daughter if she showed up at their front door. She also understood the reason for it.

In mid-1999, soon after Sarah announced that the marriage was over and that she had found someone else, Douglas was kidnapped and held in captivity for several days in a remote corner of Sutherland in northern Scotland. Jonah had not approved the kidnapping, he had not been involved in the planning or the execution of it, but he had been lured up to Sutherland in great secrecy on an unrelated pretext.

Jonah had described to her the ferocious mixture of emotions that followed on seeing Douglas lying face down on a bed of straw, naked but for a pair of underpants; the mixture of horror at what had been done in his name and a visceral anger at the man who had made a cuckold of him. There was no way that Douglas could have identified him – it was dark, he'd been wearing a balaclava. But Douglas had known that it was him, squatting in the cattle shed beside him, of course he had. Who else could it be?

The subsequent police investigation had failed to uncover any evidence to tie Jonah to the crime. He had an alibi and no desire to confess. But he remained a suspect. It was Jonah's colleague Alex Ross who had recruited the team and undertaken the kidnapping. He had done so on behalf of Jonah's employers in the intelligence services, who devised it as a means to blackmail him. All it would take was for one of the kidnappers to come forward and, in return for immunity, place Jonah in the cattle shed. He'd be discredited and imprisoned. Neutralised.

'Why would they do that to you?' she had asked.

'Because I know things,' he told her, 'a secret that must never be told.'

'What kind of secret?'

'It's better if you don't know.'

She wondered whether it was because of the secret that must never be told that he had disappeared and the police had come calling at her door.

It was break time and the playground was full of children. Miranda stood by the fence and almost instantly spotted Esme. She was unmissable. She was playing hopscotch in a headlong rush, tripping from square to square, her wild and unruly hair streaming behind her. As she darted to the back of the queue, Miranda raised her arm and waved. The dog panted excitedly. Esme peeled away and ran over to the fence.

'Hi, Esme.'

'Hi, Miranda. Hi, dog.'

Miranda squatted down so they were face to face through the chain links, with their noses almost touching. Esme reached through and scratched under the dog's chin and behind his ears.

'Are you going to tell me?'

A sly smile crossed Esme's face and she shook her head vigorously.

'How about a clue?'

It was a game that they'd been playing since her arrival in
Scotland. Give the dog a name . . .

'Dog,' Esme replied, after consideration.

'It's not very specific as names go,' Miranda said.

'Dog,' Esme repeated.

Miranda smiled. She wanted to reach through the links and
hug the little girl. 'Dog, then.'

'Has he caught many rabbits?' Esme asked.

'Plenty.'

'He's as fast as the wind.'

'Esme.'

'Yes?'

'I wondered if you'd heard anything from your dad,' Miranda
said. 'Has he called you or written to you?'

Esme looked at her feet.

'I just want to know that he is OK. That's all.'

She wouldn't meet Miranda's eye.

'It's OK, Esme. It's me.'

'You mustn't tell anyone,' Esme said, after a pause.

'I won't. I promise.'

'Wait.'

Esme turned on her heels and ran across to the far side of the
playground. The dog stuck his snout through the fence, eager to
follow. Esme stopped next to an older girl and they had a short
discussion. The older girl glanced at Miranda. Something was
exchanged and Esme sprinted back over to the fence. In her hand
she held two dog-eared postcards that had been folded in half.

'You mustn't tell,' she said.

'It's all right,' Miranda told her.

Esme passed the cards through the fence. On one was a photograph of Wadi Rum. She turned it over. It was addressed to E
and signed 'Bear'. It said: *I miss you, sweetpea*. The stamps were
from Jordan, postmarked Amman. The other was of the Bala
Hissar, identical to the one sent to her from Peshawar. It said:
I'm thinking about you. She was beginning to put together a sense
of his movements. He had been in Peshawar, Pakistan, and then

Afghanistan, and then just a few days ago Amman in Jordan.

'He sends them to Elisabeth, that's the big girl over there,' Esme explained, 'she brings them to school and reads them to me.' She shifted from foot to foot and then she glanced around. 'I've got to go,' she said.

'It's nice to see you,' Miranda said.

'Say hi to Dad,' she said, and for a moment her face was transformed by a glowing gap-toothed smile. Then she sprinted away.

'I will,' Miranda said to herself, 'I will.'

She walked back to the bus stop with the dog following.

She had to wait an hour at Port Askaig for the ferry back to Jura, and she sat at a picnic table outside the hotel and nursed a vodka and tonic. She stared across the sound. Unusually the surface of the water was as still as a mirror. She flicked through the local newspaper but the words blurred and she could not hold the sense of them. Why hadn't Jonah sent her a postcard from Amman at the same time as he had sent the one to Esme with the message *I miss you sweetpea*?

Did he miss her too? All he'd written to her was: *I have things to take care of.* She felt angry. Had she wasted two years of her life, wandering the island, while he wrote his stupid memoir? Why had he stopped writing to her? And what was he doing in Amman? Just as Inspector Coyle had described Peshawar as a staging post for Afghanistan, she knew that Amman was a staging post for Iraq. Was that where he was?

It had been in Iraq during the 2003 invasion that Jonah had invited her to come back to the UK with him. He'd told her that he loved her, and in the heady, supercharged atmosphere of those first few days of the war – so-called *shock and awe* – it had seemed possible that it was true. She herself had felt a strong desire for it to be true. After all, there was nothing left for her in the Gulf. She had learned that her son was dead. She had a British passport. There was nothing to stop her. Why not go with him?

The ferry set off across the sound towards her. It had been August 2003 when they had arrived in Scotland and taken up residence at Barnhill on Jura. And there they had lived for two years, ostensibly because Jonah's daughter lived with her mother on Islay, the adjacent island, but in fact in a sort of self-imposed exile. She hadn't set foot on the mainland for two years. Jonah had been over to visit his parents but never for more than three or four days. Then one afternoon, he had returned from Craighouse, Jura's only village, and she understood immediately from the brooding expression on his face that something was up. He had said to her, 'I have to go away for a few days. It may be nothing.'

She had felt then that she deserved more of an explanation. He'd told her that he was going to the island of Barra in the Outer Hebrides to speak to a former colleague named Andy Beech.

'I won't be gone long,' he'd said, distractedly, 'I'll come straight back.'

She rode the short distance to Jura standing at the ferry's ramp, and a tourist couple gave her a ride as far as the hotel in Craighouse. She had another vodka and tonic in the empty public bar. By the time she left it was school closing time, and as she was crossing the street to the bus stop she saw Moira Campbell and her four boys. Moira lived in a stone cottage at the river crossing at Lealt, about seven kilometres south of Barnhill.

'Need a lift?' Moira called.

'Please.'

The kids squeezed in the back of the Land Rover with the dogs and Miranda rode in the front beside Moira. Moira's husband Graeme was the gamekeeper for the estate, and he was one of the very few people that she had encountered in her wanderings on the moor in the previous months.

'Graeme's been meaning to stop by and talk to you,' Moira said.

Miranda glanced across at her. Moira's face was plain, honest and open. She wondered how it was that they had never become friends, but even as she floated the question she knew the answer. She hadn't made the effort. For too long she'd kept entirely to herself. Someone had once told her that she had the independence of a cat. Afghanistan, Iraq and all the other places had hardened her to the point of numbness. There was a kind of aloofness that did not earn her many friends, particularly among other women. Besides, she had a bad habit of fucking their husbands.

'He found a dinghy yesterday,' Moira told her, 'in one of the caves up beyond Glengarrisdale. He says there are strangers on the moor.'

Miranda felt suddenly light headed, struggling to understand what Moira was saying to her, the vodka doing its work.

They left the county road at Ardlussa, and followed the track through the strip of ancient woodland that hugged the coast all the way to the island's northern tip. They emerged on to the moor at Lealt. First she saw the outline of the motionless wind turbine and then the house and finally Graeme by one of the outbuildings with an axe in his hands and a pile of newly split logs by his feet. The kids burst out of the car and dashed for the climbing frame.

Graeme walked over to her and shook her hand. His grip was bone-crushing, his hand several times larger than hers. Graeme was a retired Royal Marine, a softly spoken giant with a shaved head and a long walrus moustache that made a pirate of him. The islands seemed to be full of retired soldiers.

'How are you?' he asked.

'Fine,' she replied, automatically. *Fine*. It was what she always said.

'Did Moira tell you about the boat?'

'Yes.'

'They've made an effort to conceal themselves. The boat is under a camouflage net and the sand at the mouth of the cave has been swept. There are two of them, I think.'

'What do you think they are here for?' she forced herself to ask.

'Eggs from the eagles probably. I guess there's a chance they're here for your orchids.' His eyes narrowed. 'You want to stay here tonight?'

'No, I'll keep going,' she said firmly.

'I'll give you a lift,' he offered.

'I'd rather walk. I need to clear my head.'

'Have you heard from Jonah?' he asked.

'No,' she replied.

They stood in silence for a few moments, and she would not meet his gaze. The dog rubbed itself against the back of her knee. She had no capacity for conversation about Jonah.

'Be careful,' he said, eventually. 'If you find them don't get yourself into a confrontation.'

'I won't,' she said.

She waved to Moira and the kids and set off north on the track across the moor.

An hour and a half later she walked over the brow of the hill and saw the house again. The lights were off and the yard was empty. Approaching, she willed herself to study the footprints in the mud of the courtyard. She spotted Coyle and Mulvey's next to the ruts left by their car. Her own Caterpillars. There were others, though, and they looked new.

She took five steps into the kitchen and stopped. She stood still and listened. She breathed in slowly with both her mouth and her nose and caught a whiff of sweat on the warm, still air and stale cigarette smoke. Someone had come and the lack of wind had betrayed them.

She hung her bag on a hook in the passageway and stepped carefully down the passage towards the study. Halfway along, she caught it again: the same faint whiff of cigarette smoke. Not smoked here, that would be an elementary mistake, but carried into the house on someone's clothes.

She entered Jonah's study and stood for a moment, refamiliarising herself with the room. She ran her finger across the undisturbed dust on the writing desk. She sat in the swivel chair and wondered what they could have found apart from what they were supposed to find. Her passport and emergency money were hidden, away from the house. Everything else was on the flash disk that Jonah wore at all times around his neck, even in bed. He'd taken his laptop with him when he left. She pulled open a drawer. It contained pens and pencils, a box of drawing pins – nothing out of the ordinary. Nothing seemed to be missing.

She swivelled in the chair, glancing at the walls.

Something was different.

Shit.

She wouldn't have noticed it, the collage was such a jumble, but she'd spent so much time since Jonah left just sitting here staring at the collage, reading highlighted text and wondering at the connections, that she had developed a strong sense of what was where on the wall.

The postcard had been pinned directly on top of a map of Kandahar City. It showed a pier with a crane and a yellow hydraulic ram between two huge metal clamshells that rose out of the water, their striated surfaces shining like gold in the late afternoon light. In the background were the distinctive tent poles of the Millennium Dome. She pulled it off the wall and turned it over. On the other side was printed *Thames Barrier, London*. It had not been there before.

She put it on the desk and returned to studying the collage. The postcard was not the only addition. There was a diagram of a ship: line drawings of it from above and from the starboard side and between the drawings a scale with an overall length of 440 feet. She was a freighter, by the looks of it, with five holds and hatches, and three masts and derricks. Using a pen, someone had drawn two score marks through the third hold just forward of the deckhouse. Beside the drawings, also in pen, someone had written a latitude and a longitude.

51 28 00 N

00 47 01 E

She ripped it off the wall and threw it on the desk with the postcard.

Below the ship's diagram there was a colour print-out of a website page pinned over the top of the photo of Monteith. She tore it down as well. The page contained a table, a graph and a map. It was produced by the National Tidal and Sea Level Facility & Tide Gauge Network and had the title: *High and low water times and heights for SHEERNESS*. The map showed the location of tidal gauges in the UK, including the one at Sheerness in the Thames Estuary. The graph showed the predicted variance in tidal heights for September, ranging from zero to six metres, and the table gave the high and low water times in GMT for each day in the month ahead. A date ten days hence with a predicted high water level of six metres at 11.00 p.m. had been ringed with a fluorescent marker. The date was 12 September.

She sat back in the chair and stared again at the collage. There was something else. Nothing more appeared to have been added. Things had been taken away. They'd removed all reference to the American Richard Winthrop. They must have come, whoever they were, ripped down the newspaper clippings of Winthrop and then pinned the postcard, the diagram and the page to the cork board.

Why do it? Except to remove incriminating evidence and plant incriminating evidence? She couldn't think of any other explanation.

Angrily, she went upstairs. Smoke again. She hadn't smoked a cigarette for over a year and she had come to detest the habit. In the bedroom more stale smoke. Perhaps there were other things here that had been planted.

She sat on the bed and quickly reviewed events. She had crossed to Islay and in her absence they had come and tampered with the collage, removed evidence, added evidence; which probably meant that they were ready to swoop. So she presumed they were watching the house, even now. Two close observers in a concealed hide. There could be others. Someone might have followed her all the way to Bowmore. With a sinking feeling she realised that someone might have observed her talking to Esme. Her mind rifled through the passengers on the ferry, looking for anyone out of the ordinary, but it was the time of year for tourists. There could have been an observer with a half-decent set of binoculars, indistinguishable from the scores of birdwatchers that descended on the island, anywhere along the sound. Once she was off the island they had free rein.

Outside, the sun was sinking towards the moor. Now she was back and it was time for action. It was time to run.

She took her rucksack, her 'crash-bag', down off the peg in the passageway, unpacked it on the kitchen table and inspected the contents: a sleeping bag, a bivvy bag and a North Face pile jacket, all in compression sacks; three pairs of black cotton underwear and three rolled pairs of socks in a waterproof bag, because he'd said there was nothing worse than being short of underwear when you are on the run; wash kit and sewing kit for running repairs; a packet of wet wipes for luxury; mess tin/dog bowl; a black beanie hat, a boot cleaning kit and her pair of Caterpillar boots.

She turned the bag inside out and ran her fingers along the seams, looking for anything out of the ordinary. A locator. Nothing. She repacked the bag.

She rolled up her yoga mat. Then she shovelled several hand-fuls of dog food into a plastic bag and tied a knot in it. It went in the rucksack, on top of her Caterpillar boots. As an after-thought she pulled the postcard off the fridge and returned to Jonah's study to pick up the papers that she had torn off the wall. They went in the crash-bag's lid.

She slung the rucksack across her back and tightened the shoulder straps, then stepped into her wellingtons and pulled her waterproof trousers back up her legs to her waist.

Ready.

'Come,' she said.

The dog sprang off the sofa.

She eased herself back down the passageway to the drawing room and slipped out of the window into the lengthening shadows of the hollow on the house's eastward side. Keeping the house between her and the mass of the hill beyond, she sprinted the hundred metres to the treeline, counting each breath as she went.

Then she was in the tangle of alder, rhododendrons and stunted oak trees. She kept heading east until she reached the cliff edge and then followed the line of cliffs northwards towards Kinu-adrachd.

After a kilometre or so she dropped down into a narrow ravine between fractured stone walls that was filled with leaves and followed it down to a tiny natural harbour that was hemmed in by foliage. Jonah kept a dinghy, its outboard removed, under a tarpaulin in the rhododendrons. She stopped for a moment and listened to the gentle lapping of the waves. Nothing appeared to have been tampered with.

She headed back up the ravine to the woods. She dug with her hands in the soft earth near an oak tree. Buried there, contained within a metal locker and immersed in grease, was the outboard. Beside the locker was a jerrycan of fuel and beneath it a sealed plastic envelope. She zipped the envelope into the lid of her bag and carried the outboard down to the dinghy. Then she went back for the jerrycan.

She dragged the dinghy down to the shoreline and set about fixing the outboard. As she worked, she expected them to appear through the trees at any moment. She struggled to keep her mind clear and her actions orderly.

The outboard started first time. The dog sat beside her in the boat, its snout raised to the air. Together, they headed east across the placid water.

They spent a fitful night in a small wood beside a river, some-where on the Craignish peninsula. Miranda woke every hour or so – the wood was full of noises, rustlings, the dapple of the moon and the melancholy hoots of owls – and felt the dog shift in response in its nest at the bottom of her sleeping bag. She realised that, lying on her back in an unknown wood, nobody knew where she was and she hardly knew where she was herself. She didn't feel fear. Not as such. It was a long time since she had felt afraid. Though she could remember circumstances similar to these in which she had felt real fear, the kind of fear that would not let her sleep: nights spent wrapped in a blanket beside a temperamental Zil truck in the Hindu Kush, anticipating another day of playing cat and mouse with the Sukhois and Hinds of the Afghan air force.

She lay there, watching the sky lighten, and she thought of her life. Things had always happened to her. Events swirled around her like gusts of sand in a desert storm. Sometimes she stood in the eye. Then, inevitably, there was another gust of wind, a buckle of thunder in the air, and she was carried onward. There was no point trying to fight it.

Abruptly the dog scrambled up through the bag and raced off into the dawn. When she had recovered she retrieved Jonah's postcard from the crash-bag, which had been her pillow. She stared at it: the photograph of the Bala Hissar fortress in Peshawar in Pakistan. Bala Hissar meant high fort in Farsi. She vividly remembered the slow swirl of bicycles, donkey carts, trucks, auto-rickshaws and cars around the hulking fortress. It was possible to say that her own journey had begun in Peshawar one spring, when riotous thickets of sweetpeas climbed the walls like weeds. That another man, not Jonah, had taken her by the hand and first led her into the storm.

An accidental collision

'I've been watching you,' the stranger said, in perfect English. She was sitting in the courtyard at Green's Hotel in Peshawar. She had been there for several days while her boyfriend 'Digger' limped around the market in an unravelling plaster cast, searching for cut-price parts for the truck. She was eighteen.

The stranger was wearing a white shalwar kameez – the white of redemption – and later, when he removed it, she saw that his body was criss-crossed with scars. And he had beautiful eyes that, even then, seemed to contain several gazes. They'd glide across her and then away like a lighthouse beam, leaving her wanting more.

'And I've been watching you too,' she said. It was March 1988, and the Soviet army was about to begin its withdrawal from Afghanistan.

He laughed at her boldness and reached out to take her right hand, turned it in his so that the web of skin between her thumb and forefinger was uppermost. His thumb rubbed the blue letter inked there.

'R for right?'

'Yes,' she said, defiantly. 'Digger' had broken his leg two days before they were due to leave England and had spent the trip in a plaster cast. She'd driven the truck and its load of disposable gas stoves all the way from Dover, with L for left written on one hand and R for right on the other. She told him that she'd never made a wrong turn.

'We'll call this an accidental collision,' he said. 'My name is Bakr. I come from the Lion's Den.'

She had decided to sleep with him then. Later, beneath him in his bedroom, while her discarded boyfriend searched the corridors for her, an unexpected shudder passed through her body like a bolt of lightning. And afterwards, outstretched on the sheet, softly panting, she whispered, 'Will you take me to the Lion's Den?'

The first leg of their journey was a seven-hour bus trip up to the Tochi Valley in the tribal areas bordering Afghanistan. Bakr had secured her a place as a volunteer at a hospital in an Afghan refugee camp. It wasn't the Lion's Den. It was a stop on the way.

The camp was a squalid collection of low, dun-coloured buildings gathered around a square of baked earth. First, she was introduced to the camp administrator, who treated Bakr with a degree of deference which suggested that he was an important figure. The administrator served them tea and asked her questions about her family and origins. She told how her father had fought the Soviet-backed military regime in Somalia. He appeared satisfied with her responses.

They were given their own hut, with a white plastic chair and a mattress resting on a pallet.

'There's a catch,' he said.

'Which is?'

'We have to get married.'

Why not? she thought. He showed her how. She spoke the words: *I have wedded you myself.* She stated the agreed term of two years and her dowry, a basil plant in an old paint can. He said: *I accept.*

They made love on the mattress and again he brought her effortlessly to climax.

He was gone the next day.

There were very few antibiotics or medicines. She spent her mornings improvising dressings for the wounded and mopping the floors. In the afternoon she worked in the office. Occasionally the Red Crescent sent supplies, and she'd scrupulously check the delivery note against the invoice.

It wasn't really a hospital, at least not as she understood the term after an exile's childhood in London. It was a first-aid post. It was built of rough breeze blocks with a tin roof. There were two connected rooms and each one held two rows of fifteen beds. Most of the wounded were in their thirties, though there were a few who were older – haggard, toothless old fighters who to her untutored eye could have been seventy or forty. There were no women.

Across the camp, women were almost invisible. She'd see them in their burqas, flitting between huts like ghosts. The men ignored her. She wore a headscarf, but even the wounded turned their faces from her. Only the children befriended her. She'd sit on a stone outside her hut, with the basil plant beside her, and the young girls would sit at her feet and teach her the Pashtun words for things.

Bakr brought her a gramophone that he claimed to have recovered from the ruins of a house that had been occupied by a Soviet general in the Wazir Akbar Khan district of Kabul, along with some 45s. The general's taste was distinctly capitalist, bourgeois even. They wound the gramophone up like a clock and danced to 'Strangers in the Night' and danced to it again. It made them think they were in another place, another time.

He was gone the next morning.

Everybody had a gun, even the wounded, who kept their Kalashnikovs hanging from the bedstead or lying beside them. On several occasions, she watched as boxes of AKs were unloaded from trucks, and stored in a concrete bunker at the edge of the camp.

As the summer temperature rose, the number of men passing through the camp increased. They were mainly Pakistanis, but there were others, Arabs from Egypt, Algeria and Saudi Arabia. They were on their way over the border to train in Afghanistan. She envied them. They were on their way to Bakr.

The Arabs set up a makeshift firing range beyond the camp perimeter and spent the day shooting at improvised targets. When she wasn't working, she'd go and sit on the ridge above the range, on a flat stone veined with marble. She'd watch them squatting and lying, with the stock of their weapons against their shoulders.

It was the camp administrator who told her to expect him. Bakr arrived the next day. He was filthy. His body was bruised and his feet were raw. He stank of cordite. She shooed away the children, dragged the door shut and pushed him down on the bed.

'Teach me to fire a gun,' she demanded, straddling him, pulling him up inside her.

In the night, Bakr got up and opened the door and cold air flooded the hut. In the moonlight his body was perfect, dark as a polished nut. He leant over slightly to light a cigarette, cupping his hand to protect the flame, and his palms and face were illuminated by the lighter. She slipped out of bed to join him and they shared the cigarette, standing naked side by side.

She never tired of looking at him, at his perfection, and it did not seem possible that she ever would.

'All right,' he said.

He took her hand and led her back to the bed. He kissed her, his full lips on hers. She could taste the tobacco in his mouth and the Russian vodka they had drunk earlier out of coffee jars. He was aroused again. She folded her legs around his waist, lifting herself towards him.

Bakr went down on one knee behind her, with the muscle of his thigh against the back of her leg and his right arm hooked around her midriff.

'Load the weapon,' he said, softly in her ear.

She tapped the magazine against the stock as she had been shown to ensure the rounds were sitting correctly on the spring and slotted it into the rifle. She pulled the cocking handle, feeding the first bullet into the firing chamber.

He reached across to the fire selector with his left hand and clicked it down two notches for semi-automatic fire. She breathed out slowly and settled slightly, her buttocks pressing against him, feeling the extent of his arousal.

He gripped her forearm. She inhaled and pressed the weapon against her cheek. She closed her left eye and aligned the front and back sights. The target was a hundred metres away, a tin of powdered milk on a rock.

'It kicks to the left, always aim a little to the right of the target.'

The dusk light shimmered. She felt light headed, as if she were about to fall. He was the only thing that was holding her up, cradling her between his thighs and his biceps, the pennant of his cock against her buttocks. She breathed out.

'Pull the trigger gently, it will go back farther than you expect,' he said.

She inhaled . . . exhaled . . .

She pulled the trigger.

She turned, breathless from sprinting, surprised that she had beaten him to the rocks. Bakr waved. She saw that he was holding her headscarf and understood that he had stopped to pick it up. She looked around and located the tin can lying on its side. She picked it up and stuck her finger in the hole.

'Look,' she shouted.

'You're a natural,' he said, handing her the scarf.

They lay side by side on a broad rock.

'I'm bored here,' she said. 'I want to learn how to be a fighter.'

He laughed.

'I'm serious!'

She punched him in the ribs, harder than she'd meant to. He doubled up, winded. 'I've never been so sure of anything in my life,' she said, leaning over him, pulling at his tunic. He fluttered a hand at her while he caught his breath. 'You said you'd take me to the Lion's Den.'

'I did,' he gasped.

'So take me.'

He stretched out and looked up at her, panting.

'I can match any man,' she said.

He shook his head in what seemed to her to be wonderment. 'I believe you could.'

'Take me,' she insisted.

He propped himself on one elbow and looked at her. 'You know that when they want to praise a woman here they say she is quiet and shy and obedient.'

'I'm not looking for praise. I want to do something, something meaningful.'

'Some say that there are only two places for an Afghan woman, in her husband's house, and in the graveyard.'

'I'm not an Afghan woman. And you're not an Afghan man.'

He pulled a face. 'That's true.'

'So take me.'

He became serious. 'There are some women at al-Ma'asada, Arab women who are being trained for the jihad. They are . . .' He paused. '. . . set apart. It is said that they have left one place but not yet reached the other.'

He did not tell her that the other place was death.

The Lion's Den

'There is a road. It runs through the mountains from Pakistan to Afghanistan and from the caves to the front line, wherever it might be. Sometimes there are landslides and we lose the road. Sometimes it is destroyed by the Russians. Sometimes it will be there but you will not see it at first. But there will always be a road, because the road keeps our struggle alive. We are fighting against a country that thinks it is strong but it is weak. Our road is stronger than their bombs. And if you cannot find the road, then you make a new one.'

She sat at the back of the classroom, with her face covered and her head bowed like a penitent. The Algerian instructor did not acknowledge her presence. He scowled as he limped back and forth in front of the blackboard. 'When you are scared or when you are cold or hungry, tell yourself that you are not important. What is important is what you carry. Enough rifles for five hundred men. Who cares about your lives? Your truck is everything.'

It was said that he had been injured in the battle for Jaji, where only a few dozen Arab fighters led by Sheikh Osama Bin Laden had fought off the Soviets. The same Bin Laden who had provided the bulldozers that built the caves and the road.

She attended classes from dawn until dusk: driver training, vehicle maintenance, convoy drills, weapons handling and religious instruction. She was hungry and dirty. Her fingernails were cracked and her feet were blistered. The only interruptions to the lessons were the call to prayer and the incessant air-raid warnings.

At night, she slept on a blanket laid across a wooden pallet in a small cave that was segregated from the men. Each morning, she washed in a bucket, wet a washcloth and, holding it above her head, squeezed the freezing water on to herself. She hurried down the tunnels with her head bowed, clutching her textbook: *Military Studies in the Jihad against the Tyrants.*

She would not meet anyone's eye. She stayed away from the darkest tunnels.

There were three other female students. One was Algerian, the other two Egyptian. Four women in a cave complex full of angry young men. Their husbands were jihadis who had died in the fighting in Khost, leaving them without protection or resources. Unable to return to their home countries for fear of arrest and imprisonment, and unwelcome in a camp whose populace regarded them as a rebuke and an embarrassment, they were treated as pariahs.

They did not expect to survive.

She had no idea where Bakr might be. She felt his absence like a stabbing pain. She could not reconcile him – the extravagance of his physical passion or the tenderness of his speech – with the columns of angry, repressed young men in the tunnels. She wondered whether he had abandoned her.

A student asked, 'What is it like when the Russians bomb?'

'It's like the wind, as if the wind came from hell,' the instructor replied, his eyes shining like polished stones. 'Or like the sun as if it came down to earth.'

'The Russians are the enemy of the earth,' the cleric declared.

'*I wish I could raid and be slain, and then raid and be slain, and then raid and be slain,*' they chanted in unison. There were moments of exaltation, when the recitations and the chanting combined to create a tumult of passion in her chest. '*Many a small band has, by God's grace, vanquished a mighty army.*'

Their enemies were numerous and powerful: heretics, pagans, crusaders – but their belief and their willingness to sacrifice their own lives to establish God's rule on earth made them all but invincible.

'Our duty will not end with victory in Afghanistan,' the cleric told them. 'Jihad will remain an individual obligation until all other lands that were Muslim are returned to us so that Islam will reign again: Palestine, Bokhara, Lebanon, Chad, Eritrea, Somalia, Philippines, Burma, Yemen, Tashkent and Andalusia.'

Jalalabad. A mighty battle was coming. The rumour spread through the tunnels like wildfire. Finally they were taking the battle directly to the enemy. For the first time she saw Pakistani advisers in the tunnels – it was said that they were demanding a tangible victory that would fatally undermine Najibullah's puppet regime. The city of Jalalabad at the head of the Great Trunk Road was the target. Weapons and cash poured in from across the border. The young men hurried with renewed vigour down the tunnels.

At night she sat on her palette and cleaned her gun. Once, she saw Sheikh Bin Laden in the tunnels with his pack of Egyptian bodyguards. He was impossibly tall and slender, somehow too fragile for the task. But you only had to look into the Egyptians' eyes to see the fury that would carry them and anyone along-side them to careless death. She folded herself against the wall as they passed and was trembling for minutes afterwards.

Bakr came and she realised that what she wanted from him was shamefully little. A night of warmth and the consolation of his body. The oblivion of sex. The raw simplicity of it. He led her to a cave that showed signs of being hastily vacated by others. People always made way for him. He was like a prince who could part the tides, not like the sheikh, who was constantly besieged by followers, but special nonetheless. He undressed her, taking his time with each button. Naked, they wrapped themselves in sheepskins. With his penis inside her she felt almost complete. And suddenly hungry for more, for permanence – she raised her pelvis to him, to retain every last drop of his sperm. He whispered the words of a poet in her ear: '*You are more precious than my days, more beautiful than my dreams.*'

She would give him something even more precious than herself.

She was sure of it. Before he left he told her that the battle would begin with an assault by ten thousand warriors.

They drove their loads of guns, blankets and gas stoves to meet the southbound trucks at the exchange point on a high plateau and swapped the loads for wounded men and broken equipment to be taken to the caves. They drove at night with only the moon to light their way, twenty-five trucks in single file. During the day they slept, or at least tried to, among the rocks in the deepest valleys, with camouflage tarpaulins covering the trucks. Just before dawn, when the convoy stopped, the four women would cook food together and share a cigarette, before wrapping themselves in blankets and huddling together out of the wind.

As the weeks passed the number of wounded increased, and news carried by them was all bad. The assault had started well enough with the capture of the village of Samarkhel and the Jalal-abad airfield but it had soon foundered on well-defended Afghan army positions around the city. The wounded described the withering fire from bunkers and trenches, and the screams of the dying caught in the minefields and low wire entanglements. The Afghan air force flew a hundred sorties a day over the city. Antonov transport planes, modified to carry bombs, flew at high altitude out of range of the Stinger missiles. They dropped their payloads of cluster munitions on the battlefield, saturating the hillsides with flying shrapnel. And Scud missiles, fired by Soviet troops deployed around Kabul, rained down.

There were so many wounded that it was impossible to conceal them all at night. The risk of the convoy being found by the Afghan air force increased with each passing day.

Several times, they were forced to halt and wait for several days while the wounded died in droves and gangs of men with AKs strapped to their backs broke rocks and shovelled snow to open the road. That was when she felt most exposed, when her hands most often reached for the reassurance of her own AK.

She would not have long to wait to be tested.

★

A giant strode through the mountains towards them. It was dusk and she was sitting in the truck's cab, staring fearfully at the sky, when the Russian Sukhois found them. It was beyond anything she could have imagined.

They had been stuck in a bottleneck for eighteen hours, jammed like sardines in a tin. The road was closed by a rockslide at the end of a long and narrow ravine. Her truck was near the back of the convoy, her view of the road ahead blocked by a dog-leg in the ravine. The other women were in the trucks behind her. There was nothing for them to do but pray.

After the first detonation, the ground buckled like molten plastic and a tide of pulverised stone came rolling down the ravine, turned the corner and engulfed the truck. The windshield turned white and shattered. She was thrown across the cabin, bounced off the passenger door and rolled into a ball in the footwell. A blast of heat forced her to cover her face with her hands. Beside her the plastic seat cover bubbled and melted. She could feel her eyebrows singed off and struggled for breath as the heat sucked the air out of the cab. The second detonation blew her out of the cab. She hit the ground and rolled into a ball.

The ground was bouncing up and down. Further detonations followed, with sheets of flame. Flying stone chips grazed her forearms and her shoulders. She crawled behind a boulder and dug into the dirt with her hands.

She felt the warmth of his hands, holding hers, drawing her up out of the cold and darkness. She opened her eyes. Bakr was sitting there, beside the hospital bed with her hands in his.

'Is . . . is . . .?' She couldn't find the words.

He knew what she was asking. He smiled. 'The baby is fine.'

She gasped, her jaw falling slackly open, giving her breath and her thanks to the air.

'I'm taking you home,' he said.

She closed her eyes again. As she drifted back into unconsciousness, she found herself wondering where that home might be.

The woman in the dunes

What had she expected? Not the air-conditioned chill of Saudi palaces and shopping malls, the chauffeur-driven limousines and the all-enveloping tentacles of the family conglomerate. Not Bakr's purposeless drifting or his incessant womanising. Not the admission that in Afghanistan he was at times a reluctant spy for the Saudi intelligence services, sending back reports on the kingdom's most famous prodigal, Osama Bin Laden. She had not known what to expect. How could she have done? She had married a pauper, who had nothing to offer her but a few words of poetry and a basil plant in a can of paint. How could she have expected that he would turn out to be a wastrel, the dissolute younger son of an incredibly wealthy family?

'Come to Saudi Arabia,' Bakr had said, in a casual manner, at the hospital in Peshawar. Why not, she thought, she was sick of Afghanistan. It was no place to have a child.

'I'd follow you to the ends of the earth,' she told him.

Shortly after the birth of her son Omar in Saudi Arabia, Miranda was told that her womb would have to be surgically removed because the placenta had grown into and through the wall of her uterus. She was in her early twenties. It didn't seem fair.

She loathed Saudi Arabia. It *was* the ends of the earth. What am I doing in this appalling country that does not deserve its riches, she thought, where I'm not even allowed to drive, when it's the only skill that I possess?

When Bakr was offered a position revamping a failing import/export business in Kuwait City she encouraged him to take it – anything to get out of Saudi. The business was an offshoot of one of the holding companies run by the family conglomerate. It specialised in importing luxury Western goods into Iraq. It was being run by one of Bakr's uncles, Ebrahim, who had founded it back in the seventies but was old and diabetic now, and more interested in the small nomad museum that he owned in Kuwait City than forging relationships with Iraqi traders.

Who could have expected that Bakr would take to the work with such zeal? Or that there was nothing he would not do to close a deal . . .

Miranda wrenched the car door's handle, stumbled away from the Mercedes and stood bent with her hands on her knees, nauseous, barely staying upright, her gaze lifted towards the distant horizon. She wanted somebody to come out of the shimmering desert air and save her. Far away she saw the ripple of a mirage: a burning death in Afghanistan, like that of her Egyptian friend, whose charred corpse was pried from a burned-out Zil; or a parade of lovers, Bakr passing her, like a gift tied with ribbons, from one man to another; having to fuck her way out of a nightmare in which she was sinking as if into quicksand.

She wanted to yell in Bakr's face, *When did I stop being precious to you?*

She held her head between her knees and waited of the mirage to fade.

It was Bakr's uncle Ebrahim whose comment had caused her to storm out of the building and drive out into the desert until she couldn't drive any more. He'd said, 'Are you concerned that Bakr may take another wife?'

She didn't know why it had upset her so much. It wasn't as if Bakr's womanising was what bothered her most. There was something hopeless and unresolved about his behaviour, which was what had made him so attractive to her, and was probably what appealed to the women who fell for him.

She straightened up and rubbed the small of her back with her hands. Three months had passed since the hysterectomy and she could count on one hand the number of times that she'd had a civil conversation with Bakr in that time. Any attempt at discussion made him furious. Of course he'll take another wife, she wanted to scream – this man that I married that is as elusive as a wisp of smoke. Gulf men wanted sons. Now that she was not capable of delivering another it was inevitable.

She turned and walked back to the car.

Omar's huge eyes followed her as she reached into the footwell and recovered the small, floppy-eared rabbit that had fallen there. She tucked it in under one of the straps of the child car seat and nuzzled Omar's tummy with her nose. He reached for her face with his tiny fingers.

'I love you,' she whispered. He smiled.

She got back in the car, turned it around and drove back into Kuwait City. She found Ebrahim standing on the steps of the nomad museum with a repentant expression on his face.

'I'm sorry,' he said, 'I'm just a foolish old man.'

It wasn't Bakr's womanising that bothered her; what bothered her was being offered by her husband to his business partners for their sexual gratification.

Miranda and Bakr divided their time between Kuwait City, where the import/export business was based, and Baghdad, where the bulk of the business was done.

Baghdad terrified her. She loved it at first, though. There was something febrile about it back then, in 1990, before the first Gulf War, like a pulse of blood that made your skin tingle. On the Al-Arasat Road, she could drink and dance all night. It was a new beginning: for her, for Bakr and for Iraq. The eight-year war with Iran was over and Saddam had won an overwhelming victory in the presidential election. He had announced new economic policies, companies were privatised and hundreds of licences were issued to people to start up construction and other companies. Bakr was flying goods in by the planeload from Kuwait

City and delivering them into the hands of this new breed of Iraqi traders, who were intimately linked to Saddam Hussein's regime.

They became rich. They had everything: cars, fashionable clothes, a beautiful apartment, a nanny for Omar. But it was not enough. It was never enough. There was always another deal, and with each deal Bakr edged closer to Saddam Hussein's immediate family. The family were the real prize. That was where the riches were. Cut a deal with a family member – the exclusive provision of Christian Dior suits and Dimple whisky to Saddam's son Uday, for instance – and you were made. But the Hussein family always extracted a harsh toll for making you rich. And as the deals grew larger in scale, the incentives that must be offered to secure the deals had to increase similarly in significance. Until there was only one thing left to offer.

'I'm not your whore,' she screamed at him.

'Then what use are you?' he sneered.

In Kuwait City, she spent her days at the nomad museum, where she had befriended Bakr's uncle, Ebrahim. The old man had been more than happy to hand over the day-to-day running of the company, and he was enchanted by Bakr's young wife and baby son. For Miranda, the low lighting and air conditioning of the basement museum provided a welcome respite from the heat, a welcome respite from Bakr.

Ebrahim was a small man, round at the edges; he was always whistling and humming, singing to himself as a he fussed around the exhibits in their glass cases. The museum displayed a large variety of Arab artefacts ranging from ceramics to costumes and textiles. A collection of manuscripts charted the development of calligraphy. Cabinets displayed ornate weapons, silver jewellery and boxes inlaid with mother-of-pearl. Omar crawled along the polished floors.

Her favourite item was a painting by the Orientalist David Roberts, *Lady Jane Digby el-Mezrab*, a portrait of a Western woman in Bedouin costume, with Roman columns behind her.

One afternoon, Ebrahim told her the story of the beautiful and headstrong English woman who scandalised nineteenth-century Europe with a succession of husbands and lovers and eventually married an Arab sheikh of the Sba'a tribe of Syria. His eyes twinkled mischievously as he spoke.

'From her father she inherited a taste for that which did not belong to her. He was a pirate, an English privateer who made his money by seizing a Spanish treasure ship. From her mother she inherited great beauty and desirability. Her lovers included the very best of the nobility of Europe – earls, barons, and counts, Ludwig I of Bavaria and the Greek king. There was even an Albanian brigand, who kept her in a cave and made her queen of his rabble army. At the age of forty-six, she travelled to the Middle East; there she fell in love with Sheikh Medjuel el-Mezrab of the Sba'a tribe. They were married and remained so until her death twenty-eight years later. She adopted Arab dress and learned Arabic in addition to the other eight languages in which she was fluent. Half of each year was spent in the nomadic style, living in goat-hair tents in the desert, while the rest was spent in the palatial villa she built in Damascus.'

Were you happy, Lady Jane? she wondered.

'We're getting on like a house on fire,' Ebrahim said from the bottom of the steps.

Bakr was standing at the top of the steps, holding the heavy wooden doors wide open so that a blast of heat from the street swept through the vestibule. She felt dizzy and she could hardly breathe. She hadn't seen him for more than a week. Not since he had punched her outside the National Restaurant in Baghdad. It was July 1990 and he was furious about something. 'What are you doing here?' he demanded. There was a tightening around his eyes that suggested a perpetual hangover.

'Your wife is helping me with the displays,' Ebrahim added, in fearful defiance. 'She has a good eye.'

Ebrahim winced at his choice of words. Her right eye was still purple and black.

Bakr sneered. 'You stupid old man. Do you think that any of this is going to matter in a few weeks' time?' His gaze glided across her and Omar and then away, leaving her feeling that they had been spared.

Bakr turned and left. The doors slammed closed again. Ebrahim raised his almost blind eyes to the ceiling and whispered words of thanks to his maker. She eased herself down into the nearest chair and held out her arms for Omar to climb into her lap.

'What does he mean?' she asked.

'I don't know.'

The Iraqi army invaded on 2 August. Bakr disappeared into Iraq a week later. She remained in Kuwait City with Omar and helped Ebrahim to box up and hide the museum's artefacts from marauding Iraqi soldiers.

Monday, 15 January 1991. It was sunny but surprisingly cold. Heavy rain fell at intervals through the morning, drenching the hapless conscripts in their trenches.

Miranda had just finished breakfast when Iraqi Republican Guard soldiers surrounded the house. She was given no time to pack her things. She was driven north into Iraq.

The Allied airstrikes began two days later.

She remembered lying awake, night after night, in the fluorescent glare, listening to the sounds of the cell blocks, the footsteps of the night guards, the clatter of their keys and the slow breathing of Omar by her side.

It was her second month in Abu Ghraib. She lived among women who had murdered their husbands or smothered their children. There were junkies and thieves, and dissidents and whores. They lived and breathed by permission of Saddam Hussein, and his emissaries, their jailers.

Fifteenth March 1991. They came into the cell and took her son. Nobody who hadn't experienced it could possibly imagine what it was like to have your child taken away from you. She relived it in spasms, sudden flashes of memory and nightmares.

It was a Thursday. The first she knew they were coming for someone was when one of the prisoners began shouting at the far end of the corridor. She turned away from the tiny barred window, from the thorn bush that offered a glimpse of freedom, and walked to the door. She pressed her cheek to the wire-core glass of the viewing pane and watched as the jailers advanced down the corridor. She remembered glancing back at Omar, who was playing on the floor, pushing a small block of wood with bottle-tops for wheels, back and forth on the cell floor. He looked up at her smiled. She turned back to the pane of glass and found herself staring into the eyes of one of the jailers.

The bolt rattled in the lock. She spun around, gathered Omar up in her arms and backed towards the wall. Two of them stepped into the room, a man and a woman. Others waited in the corridor outside. The man was carrying an electric cattle prod. He was short and stocky, his underarms ringed with sweat, his bald head glistening by the light of the room's single bulb.

'Put the child on the bed and step into the corner,' he said.

She shrank farther against the wall. 'What do you want?'

The woman held out her arms to take the boy. 'I'm sorry,' she whispered.

'No!'

She tightened her grip on Omar. The man held the cattle prod so that it was just inches from her face. 'Give up the child or I will shock you both.'

'Please, in the name of Allah,' she pleaded, understanding that she had been completely forsaken.

'Give up the child.'

The woman stepped forward and pried her fingers loose from Omar's clothes. Omar shrieked in the woman's arms and Miranda felt his desperation like a punch to the stomach.

'He is mine,' she screamed. 'He is mine.'

JONAH

The Sort of the Dark Side

'We also have to work, through, sort of the dark side, if you will. We've got to spend time in the shadows in the intelligence world.'

Dick Cheney, *Meet the Press*, 2001

We're all New Yorkers now

December 2001

Monteith was worrying the cuffs of his Barbour jacket when a sudden shaft of wintry light cut through the dappled branches of the plane trees and caught him in its corrosive radiance. He stopped, dazzled, and shut his eyes. Beside him, Jonah turned his back on the sun and stared, struck by the unnatural dimensions of Monteith's shadow on the pathway. Like an ogre from a storybook, something to scare children with. Jonah had heard him called *Yoda* behind his back by the callow young assistants who fetched and carried for him. More than ever Jonah wanted to tell him to go to hell. The cloud cover shifted and the moment passed. They moved on.

It was 28 December 2001 and they were in St James's Park, ten minutes' walk from the warren of windowless cubicles beneath the Old War Office building that constituted Monteith's office and, with the exception of a few terse footnotes here and there in intelligence reports, the only ostensible evidence of the Department's existence. Usually, Monteith liked to keep his operatives dispersed or at arm's length. He often claimed that being a wild card was his strength, but since Jonah's return from Sierra Leone he had kept him close by his side.

Jonah had his fists hidden inside the sleeves of his sweater, his fingertips securing the frayed ends. It was bloody cold. Monteith was delivering him on foot to an informal grilling at the hands of the head of the Operations Sub Group (OSG), a super-secret offshoot of the US National Security Council's Special Situation Group (SSG).

'A good double's not pretending, Jonah,' Monteith insisted. He seemed unusually defensive. 'He's playing both ways. When he is with us he is with us. When he's with them he is with them. The trick is to get the best end of the arrangement. You can't cast an agent like Nor adrift and expect him not to go native.'

'Is that what you want me to say?' Jonah asked.

'Of course I don't want you to say that. In fact I'd be bloody careful if I were you. There's a high degree of paranoia involved. If you're not with them you're against them.'

'So what do you want me to say?'

But Monteith was just getting into his stride. 'They've got it into their heads that there is no law but the discretion of the United States. They're bypassing the regular operations of intelligence, military and law-enforcement agencies and stovepiping raw intelligence to the very top. The politicians are picking and choosing without any realistic evaluation. They're conjuring threats out of thin air. They're going to invade Iraq.'

Jonah wondered briefly whether he had heard him correctly – had he said Iraq? Jonah was not aware of any imminent threat from Iraq. To his mind, Iraq was a can of worms with the lid best left on.

'We'll help them too,' Monteith protested. He seemed genuinely outraged. 'You'll see. Down at the Vauxhall Cross they've obligingly coughed up a report on one of Saddam's little helpers shopping for uranium yellow cake in Niger. That's what your man's doing here. Come to pick it up by hand – it'll be on Cheney's desk by tomorrow morning. Mark my words. We are entering a period of consequences.'

Behind Horse Guards the London Eye slowly rotated. That morning Al Jazeera had released new videotape footage of Bin Laden in his Afghan cave, claiming that 'the awakening has started'. It seemed to Jonah that there were more important things to worry about than Iraq.

Monteith stopped and tipped a nod towards the tall American who was standing at the centre of the bridge and staring intently at the surface of the lake. 'It's impressive, the level of influence they have. They call themselves the Cabal. They've convinced themselves that they're on the side of the angels and everybody else is a fool.'

'I'm used to being considered a fool,' Jonah told him with some satisfaction. After all, it was Monteith who had taught him that the greatest compliment you could pay to a secret agent was to take him for a fool.

'Like I said, I'd be careful if I were you,' Monteith replied sternly.

'I'll be charming.'

'That would be a first,' Monteith said, and then, 'You'll have to come clean. Word has come down from on high. We're all New Yorkers now.'

'What is that supposed to mean?'

'It means that they've seen the files on Nor up until the fall of Kabul in '96 when we cut him adrift. They know nothing about him getting back in touch with the invitation from the mullah and they know nothing about his involvement in the death of Kiernan. And they won't learn a thing by poking about in the cupboards because it's all been shredded. It means that you are to answer his questions truthfully and to the best of your ability, and it means that if necessary you're to lie through your teeth. And when you're done you are to come scurrying back to me with a verbatim report. And Jonah . . .'

'Sir?'

'Remember where your allegiance lies.' Monteith nodded in the direction of the Palace, turned on his heel and strode away.

Jonah was taken aback. It was unlike Monteith to invoke allegiance. Jonah wondered what it meant. Jonah didn't much believe in the monarchy, or for that matter the nation-state. As a general rule, he held to Dr Johnson's view that patriotism is the last resort of scoundrels. He had come to the conclusion that intelligence was an attribute of individuals and that groups – clans, tribes, nations – were intelligent in inverse proportion to their size and influence: the bigger the stupider, the stronger the dumber. In fact, if he had to label himself, he thought the term disbeliever fitted him best. He disbelieved in New Labour, in the Taliban, in Defense Planning Guidance and the Operations Sub Group.

Richard Winthrop IV's hair was parted on a knife edge and his shoes were polished like conkers; Jonah guessed by his own hand. He was wearing a blue button-down shirt and his suit was grey, some sort of subtle check that Jonah did not recognise. His nose was as sharp as a compass and he had a fat signet ring on – he was Yale Skull and Bones, and after that Georgetown Law School and the American Enterprise Institute – according to Monteith, his family dated back to the Massachusetts Bay Company, to the founding myth of America; a perfect sanctuary – *New Jerusalem* – built on virgin land. He burned with brash intensity. His grip was earnest. It was what Jonah had come to expect of the new breed in power in Washington.

'Walk?' Winthrop suggested.

'Fine by me,' Jonah replied.

They passed the swamp cypresses, heading in the direction of the Palace.

'When I first meet people I like to share with them a saying from the Pirke Avot, the Hebrew book of ethics,' Winthrop said. 'It goes like this: *It is not for you to complete the work, but neither are you free to withdraw from it.*'

His pale, almost colourless eyes focused on Jonah. 'Are you a believer?' he asked.

And Jonah thought that, although he was a disbeliever, he didn't much believe in that either. 'I was raised a Roman Catholic,' he responded reflectively, wondering whether that counted in some way. But he knew it didn't. The behaviour of the priests responsible for his school education had ruled out taking it seriously.

'We are vassals in a shared endeavour, Jonah,' Winthrop told him. 'We face an enemy that targets and kills innocent civilians. They lie in the shadows, they don't sign treaties. They don't owe allegiance to any country. They don't fight according to the Geneva Conventions. They do not cherish life. Every day they are manufacturing small amounts of nuclear materials.'

Jonah frowned and wondered whether he had heard right – *nuclear materials?*

'Tell me, are we supposed to wait passively, like the Kurds did in Halabja, for Saddam to rain chemical weapons down on us?' Winthrop demanded. Jonah remembered vividly the footage of the bodies of women and children lying in the streets of Halabja, taken by an Iranian TV crew a few hours after the Iraqi air force used gas on the inhabitants. It formed a part of the reasoning behind his abhorrence for the murderous activities of Saddam's regime. But then again he could reel off a list of loathsome states, and it was quite a leap from gassing your own people to a chemical assault on the most powerful nation on earth, especially on the back of a decade of sanctions, but Winthrop was clearly at ease with the leap. 'Are we supposed to wait for more planes to plunge out of clear blue skies?' he demanded. 'Or should we act decisively now, utilising our military advantage, and like a boa constrictor squeeze out the terrorists and the regimes that support them? You want to know why we were attacked. I'll tell you why: because we were weak. We didn't see how we had failed and how our enemies had seen us fail. We didn't see the pattern. How we failed to rescue the embassy hostages in Iran, how we lost Marines in Lebanon and Rangers in Mogadishu, the 1991 ceasefire against Iraq, Lockerbie, the 1993 attacks on the World Trade Centre, the 1998 attacks in Dar Es Salaam and Nairobi. We face a unique convergence of tyranny, terrorism and technology, and in response to it there can be no room for half-measures. We cannot repeat the mistake of 1991 in not going far enough. We cannot rely on consensus. We cannot allow our actions to be dictated by weaker partners.'

For Jonah, who had participated in the rout of the Iraqi army in 1991 and witnessed first-hand the carnage of the Mutla Ridge, the first Gulf War could not have ended a day sooner.

Winthrop was in his stride, punctuating his remarks with short jabs of his forefinger. 'Since 1991, Saddam has worked to rebuild his chemical and biological weapons stock, his missile delivery capacity and his nuclear programme. He is building centrifuges.

He has mobile bio-weapons labs and unmanned drone delivery systems. He has given aid, comfort and sanctuary to terrorists, including al-Qaeda members.'

'You have evidence of this?' Jonah asked, sceptically.

'We have solid reporting of senior-level contacts between Iraq and al-Qaeda going back a decade,' Winthrop snapped. 'We know that Mani al-Tikrit, the director of Iraqi intelligence, met with Bin Laden at his farm in Sudan in July 1996.'

A silence followed while Jonah stared at a huddle of miserable-looking ducks and reflected on the fact that there was no way that Bin Laden could have been in Sudan in July '96 and there was no way he was prepared to share that information with Winthrop. Bin Laden was in Afghanistan that summer, and Nor was shadowing him.

'We have reports that place Mohammed Atta, the lead 9/11 hijacker, and Iraqi intelligence agents in Prague in April 2001,' Winthrop told him.

Monteith was right, Jonah thought: they really were going to invade Iraq.

'You take a strong man like Saddam out of the equation and you've got to be prepared for the consequences,' Jonah told him. 'There's a real risk of civil war between the Sunnis and Shiites and Kurds.'

'We know what we're doing,' Winthrop told him.

I doubt that very much, Jonah thought. He stamped his feet. It really was bloody cold. He wished that Winthrop would come to the point. 'What is it you want from me?' he asked.

'You're an interesting case, Jonah. I've been reading your file.'

'Don't believe half of what you read.'

'It says that you're arrogant and opinionated.'

'Obviously some of it's true,' Jonah conceded.

'In my book that makes you a bad work colleague.'

'I've been told that.'

'But it also says that you show an aptitude for working under pressure and on your own. It seems to suggest that you are one of those solitary people who make a virtue of not needing company.'

'Perhaps.'

'And you're an American citizen.'

'Yes,' Jonah acknowledged.

'And for three years from 1993 to 1996 you ran a double agent inside the ISI, the Pakistani intelligence service?'

'That's right.'

'And then you terminated the relationship?'

'Yes. The funding was withdrawn.'

'Am I right to say that Nor was in conflict with your department at the end?'

'He was always in conflict with the Department,' Jonah replied. 'It was in his nature.'

Winthrop shook his head in irritation. 'But specifically by the end?'

Jonah sighed. 'He thought that we had abandoned the people of Afghanistan. He thought that we had abandoned him.'

'And what did you think?'

'Mostly, I agreed with him.'

'He was your friend,' Winthrop observed.

'Yes, he was my friend, but he was also the only person we had inside the ISI and the best live source we had on Afghanistan. We knew the ISI were operating outside the control of their own government and that they were up to their elbows in Afghanistan, and he was the living proof of it. He knew every warlord, every drug baron, every tribal chief, every loose-cannon jihadi and every mullah on the make. To me, it didn't make any sense for us to abandon him.'

Winthrop's eyes narrowed, angrily. 'And at any stage did you for one moment think to yourself that we should have been informed that you had a so-called asset inside the ISI?'

'I ran him as an agent, I didn't control who had access to the information that he generated. For that you need to speak to my superiors.'

'We have, Jonah, and we have expressed our anger and disappointment in the clearest terms. You ran a covert operation with a clearly unstable agent in an allied intelligence service and when you were done with him you cut him dead and in doing so shepherded him straight into the hands of the enemy. In doing so, you compromised not only your own security but that of all of us.'

In the silence that followed this outburst, Jonah's apprehensions gave way to something like rejoicing. The Americans didn't know about Kiernan.

Qala-i-Jangi

December 2001

They circled back on the south side of the lake, past an empty playground and a boarded-up ice-cream stand.

'Tell me again how you recruited him,' Winthrop said.

Jonah replied cautiously, aware that he should be on his guard against the suggestion that he had conspired with Nor since the very beginning.

'When I first met him he was all over the place.'

'That was at school?'

'Yes, at school. He was a couple of years younger than me. My father and his father were academics in the biology division at the same university. I guess he looked up to me – there weren't many pupils from ethnic minorities. It wasn't exactly overt racism, but there was a lot of hostility. I tried to protect him.'

'Protect him how exactly?'

'Help him curb his temper. Stop him rising to the bait. It worked for a short time and he was a model student, but then I left and he punched a magistrate's son. Then he got caught drinking. Then he got caught smoking cannabis. Eventually the school expelled him. His father washed his hands of him. Some relatives came up with some money and sent him back to Jordan. The next I heard from him he'd travelled to Pakistan and from there crossed into Afghanistan. He wrote to tell me that he had joined the mujahedin.'

'He was a Muslim?'

'And a Baathist, and a Sufist, and an anarchist and an atheist.

I don't think he really believed in anything. Like I said, he was all over the place.'

'And when did you next see him?'

'At Sandhurst. Out of the blue he'd joined the British Army.'

'Why?'

'Why did he join the army?'

'Yes.'

'I suppose he did it because I had.'

'He looked up to you?'

'Yes, I suppose. He idealised me.'

'And by that stage you were in military intelligence?'

'Yes.'

'And you recruited him?'

'Yes.'

'It didn't bother you that he was your friend?'

'No. I couldn't see him lasting in the regular army. I couldn't believe he'd got in. He stuck out like a sore thumb.'

'More than you?'

Winthrop had a point. 'I didn't see why he should have to put up with what I did. I thought what we were offering him would suit him better.'

'And what were you offering him?'

'The Department manufactured an incident for him and had him slung out of the army on a trumped-up drugs-smuggling charge in 1993. We inserted him in the Islamist group Hizb-ut-Tahrir, who were active in East London at the time, and it was at that point that the ISI first noticed him. From there he embarked for Bosnia with a relief convoy. In Split on the Bosnian border he met up with a Pakistani veteran of the war against the Soviets, who we knew to be an agent of the ISI. At the time the ISI were monitoring the so called "Afghan Arabs", who were active in the tribal areas. Nor fitted the profile: he was Jordanian and Sunni, disaffected with First World military skills; a golden boy gone wrong. The ISI recruited him on spec and sent him off to Afghanistan for training with the extremist group Harkat-ul-Mujahideen, the HUM. He became the backbone of the Afghan

Guides. He was our man on the inside, feeding us information about the composition of extremist groups in Afghanistan and the extent of Pakistani meddling there.'

'Why do you think he took the assignment?'

Countless reasons, Jonah wanted to reply: because he was a maverick; because he fit the army like an ill-fitting suit; because he was without anchor; because he was bored; because he was too intelligent; because I asked him to do it. 'I think it was the challenge. He relished the excitement.'

'And then you cut him dead?'

'It wasn't my decision.'

'Did you feel let down?' Winthrop asked.

'Yes, I suppose I did.'

'And you left the service at about the same time?'

'Yes.'

'Why?'

'They closed down the Afghan Guides and downsized the Department and my wife gave birth to our daughter. I took it as an opportunity to try a different life.'

There was a pause. 'But that life didn't agree with you?'

'It didn't work out. My marriage broke up.'

'You were married in 1990 and your wife left you for another man in 1999.'

'That's correct.'

Another pause. It was inconceivable that Winthrop did not know about the kidnapping but he chose not to mention it. It hung there unspoken between them.

'And then you came back to the Department?'

'Yes. Monteith offered me my old job back.'

'And at no stage did you attempt to recontact Nor?'

'At no stage,' Jonah replied. He was right; it was Nor who had contacted them.

Winthrop stopped and contemplated the pelicans on their rock at the centre of the steaming lake.

'We've got him,' he said.

For a split second Jonah didn't understand and went on staring at the pelicans as they shifted from foot to foot and folded and unfolded their wings, then he spun on his heels and found himself face to face with Winthrop.

'Where?' Jonah demanded.

'Afghanistan. In the military intelligence compound at Kandahar airport.'

'Where did you find him?'

'He was captured by Northern Alliance forces at the fall of Kunduz in November. From there he was transported to Qala-i-Jangi. He may or may not have been involved in the subsequent disturbances. He was pulled out of the cellars by US Special Forces a month later.'

The massacre at Qala-i-Jangi had been widely reported in the Western media, largely because it involved the first American death in combat in Afghanistan. After the surrender of the Kunduz garrison, General Dostum's Northern Alliance forces had loaded four hundred prisoners on to trucks and transported them to his citadel at Qala-i-Jangi. With night falling, Dostum's men failed to body-search the prisoners and during the night eight killed themselves with concealed hand grenades. The following morning, a fight broke out when one of the prisoners made a lunge at Mike Spann, one of the two CIA interrogators assigned to the Uzbeks. Spann shot several prisoners before being beaten to death. The prisoners then broke into one of the fort's armouries and seized mortars and grenade launchers. The fighting continued for four days, growing in ferocity as Dostum's men, supported by US Special Forces and SAS soldiers, pounded the citadel before moving in and pouring burning oil into the cellars. The last eighty starving survivors had not emerged until the middle of December.

'Is he talking?' Jonah asked.

'He hasn't said a word.' Winthrop ran a hand through his hair. 'You think you can coax him back into the fold?'

'Are you making me an offer?'

Winthrop snorted. 'This isn't a fucking courtship, Jonah. Just because you've been forsaken by your country doesn't mean that we're going to leap at the chance.'

'I have citizenship,' Jonah protested.

'We have room for but one flag, Jonah, the American flag. There can be no divided allegiance here. Any man who says he is an American but something else also isn't an American at all.'

'So what do you want from me?' Jonah asked.

'We want you to go to Kandahar and get him to talk.'

Monteith was standing, straight backed, ever the soldier, on the edge of Horse Guards. Seeing Jonah emerge from the park, he fell in beside him. 'Well?'

'They've got Nor.'

'Christ,' said Monteith, unconvincingly, Jonah thought. He reflected on Winthrop's jibe – *just because you've been forsaken by your country*.

'Is he talking?' Monteith asked.

Jonah shook his head. According to Winthrop, Nor hadn't said a word since he had been hauled out of the cellars of Qala-i-Jangi.

Monteith breathed a sigh of relief. 'Thank God for that.'

'I'm leaving for Kandahar tomorrow night.'

Monteith nodded eagerly. 'It's best if you speak to Nor first. Find out what he wants.'

'It's only a matter of time,' Jonah told him. 'And then we're all in trouble.'

Plaques and tangles

December 2001

It was Monteith who was responsible for the departmental mantra that *the best lies are sandwiched between truths.* You have to believe it yourself, Monteith would say. And mostly he did.

He was Jonah Said, spawn of a Palestinian biologist and a black barrister of Guyanan descent. He had been born in the USA, while his father was studying for a PhD and his mother was volunteering at a civil rights centre. But he was raised and educated in England, in suburban obscurity, and as far back as he could remember the things he had aligned himself with were designed to outrage his parents' liberal sensitivity. He ran wild at school, failed his O-levels, was a pothead from fourteen to seventeen and deemed responsible for a flurry of hastily terminated teenage pregnancies. He pulled himself together briefly enough to sit his A-levels at a community college, and against all expectations secured a university place in Edinburgh to study Arabic. On obtaining an undistinguished degree, he spent a couple of years back in the USA, mostly in New York, where he lived a nocturnal life, tending bar and sampling the range of available drugs, settling on crack as his narcotic of choice. He lost touch with his parents. His abiding memory of that time was of travelling down a tunnel, a shaft of light crackling at the edges – night after night – from the stack of liquors to the customer to the till. He joined the British Army in 1989, catching a plane back to the UK and walking into a London recruiting centre. It was a characteristically impulsive gesture that possibly was prompted by the death of a friend in New York as the result of a heroin overdose (an occurrence that he failed to mention in his interview for the Regular Commissions Board). Against all expectation he was awarded a commission. It was conceivable that the army was under some pressure to recruit from ethnic minorities, and after all, his parents were by that stage pillars of the establishment, his father an eminent professor and his mother a Queen's Counsel, soon to be elevated to the House of Lords. In quick succession he attended the Royal Military Academy at Sandhurst and the Platoon Commanders Battle Course in Warminster. His army career was at best undistinguished. He served as an interpreter in the first Gulf War, a platoon commander in West Belfast, a liaison officer in Bosnia, and most recently as an instructor at Catterick Army Garrison in Yorkshire.

Other facts were hidden. That he was polyglot; that he obtained a master's degree in Dari and Pashtun at London's School of Oriental and African Studies under an assumed name. That he had earned but was deprived of the right to wear both the Commando dagger and the Parachute wings. That he had completed selection at Hereford. That he was on permanent attachment to a super-secret arm of the UK Defence Intelligence Agency colloquially known as the Department, which had been cut adrift of the Ministry of Defence and was nominally answerable to the Secret Service, MI6, but utterly deniable in the event of compromise. That it was his home. And his garden was the failed, failing or rogue state. He slipped in and out of ransacked cities, jungle hideaways and mountain caves.

What was also clear was that all those years ago, when he rode a train out of the suburbs, he had no intention of ever going back.

It was always strange to be back. It was 29 December, the day after his meeting with Winthrop. He was due to fly to Afghanistan that night. He had decided to visit his father first.

He parked the car under an old yew tree and sat for a while listening to the slow swish of the wipers on the windscreen, staring fondly over the steering wheel at the large and rambling red-brick Victorian building with its wooden clock tower and glass conservatories.

He remembered a wildcat childhood spent clambering across its roofs and racing through its hothouses, hiding in long-neglected cupboards, pulling open drawers of pinned butterflies and beetles and peering at specimen jars filled with coiled, unsettling shapes floating in formaldehyde.

Built in the 1870s, and set in twenty-four acres of Berkshire parkland dotted with fishponds, Silwood Park was the home of Imperial College's research station and had been the location of his father's office for as long as Jonah could recall. It was also at Silwood, at the start of an unusually hot summer, when the whole of England reeled in the heat, that Rashid ed-Din, a young Jordanian biologist with a doctorate from the American University in Beirut, had arrived at the faculty and moved into an office across the hall from Jonah's father. He had brought with him a veiled wife and three children, including a quicksilver son named Nor.

Jonah had first spotted the boy from a lookout post in an unruly thicket of rhododendrons on the outer edge of the ornamental gardens. He had almost completed his first cycle of daily perimeter checks and was wondering how the day would unfold. It must have been mid-morning, and already the sun was baking hot. He lay among the leaf litter and stared across a drought-racked lawn at the boy, who was sitting by one of the fishponds, with his feet immersed in the water. Nor was wearing only a pair of shorts, and the first thing that Jonah had registered was that his skin tone was not so very different from his own. In such circumstances boldness was required. He had crawled out of his hide, climbed to his feet and approached slowly, careful to remain out of the boy's line of sight. He remembered that the ground was hot beneath the soles of his feet.

He had been almost within touching distance, when Nor had casually glanced over his shoulder at him. 'I thought it rained here?'

'Not this summer,' Jonah had replied, mid-step.

'Do you always sneak up on people?'

'Not always.'

'Where are you from?'

Jonah had shrugged uneasily. 'Here.'

'You don't look like you're from here.'

'Neither do you.'

'I'm not,' Nor had said, indignantly.

Every year on 5 November, the anniversary of the Gunpowder Plot – the failed assassination attempt against King James I by a group of English Catholics in 1605 – a straw-stuffed guy in the likeness of one of the academics was burned on a bonfire down by the largest pond. Jonah remembered the excitement that had filled him the year that his father was chosen. It seemed strange now: after all, his father was a Palestinian Catholic.

He had driven the twenty-five miles from London to Silwood Park ostensibly at his mother's request, though the request had been made some weeks before. He was in a rented car. He didn't own his own car, or much of anything else for that matter. He'd been divorced for over two years. That brief chapter – *house, car, dog* – was now over. He got out of the car and stood in the drizzle. His shoulders ached from driving down through the mist and he stretched, working the blood into his muscles. He had not seen his father for six months, not since before Sierra Leone and 9/11. His mother had briefed him on what to expect. Even so, it was still a surprise to see the collection of BBC Bristol vans and caravans parked on the gravel forecourt and on the lawns.

He followed electrical cables up the steps and into the building. Inside it was almost unbearably hot and he caught a whiff of something earthy with a hint of decay in the still air. He didn't recognise it. He slipped off his jacket and eased his way down the passage towards the great hall.

Viewed from the entrance to the hall the raiding colony seemed to be a single living thing, the feeder columns writhing from side to side on the lengths of dockyard rope that coiled through the rooms. He stepped between the rails laid for a track dolly and followed one of the suspended ropes down a corridor towards his father's office.

In a side room he glimpsed one of his father's PhD students emptying out a bucket of leaves and petals on to an old billiard table. She was wearing a white paper suit and a shower cap. He saw that the table legs were standing in plastic buckets filled with water. She waved as he passed. His father had always had a devoted student following.

He went down the steps into the atrium and stood among the African palms, staring upwards at the ropes converging to form a single trunk that ran the length of the hothouses. Up in the foliage a camera panned on the end of a gib-arm. Across the room, a cameraman sat in front of a flickering monitor. Jonah walked over and stood at his shoulder for a while. On the screen an apparently endless column of worker ants carried leaf fragments in one direction and a line of unburdened workers advanced purposefully in the other. Wedge-headed soldiers with massive jaws flanked the gangways, separating the opposing columns and maintaining the direction of travel. It was difficult to comprehend the scale of the enterprise.

'There is no mind,' Joseph Said called out as he hurried across the atrium towards him. He stopped just short of him and looked Jonah up and down, as if he were a stranger. There was a bright yellow butterfly on the shoulder of his threadbare tweed jacket. 'It's shaped but leaderless.'

He was thinner. He seemed to get thinner each time Jonah saw him, thinner and taller, as if he were being stretched. He was an old man, with dark spots on his hands and neck, but his eyes were still striking. They sparkled with amusement. For a moment Jonah wondered whether he recognised him.

'It's the largest colony of leafcutters outside the Amazonian rainforest,' his father told him. 'They range sixty metres on the longest rope. They've taken over the whole building.'

'It's impressive,' Jonah said, after a pause.

His father held him at arm's length and winked. 'They let me get away with anything now.'

They kissed three times on the cheeks, the Palestinian way. His mother's comment to Jonah, over a teacake in the tea room at the House of Lords, had been: 'He's completely out of control. You have to speak to him.'

Jonah wondered what it was that he was expected to say. It was usually Jonah's sister who acted as intermediary between his mother and father, who edited and softened, protecting them from each other's more fervent outbursts. He settled on the mundane. 'How do you keep them from escaping?'

His father grinned. 'Vaseline on the steel hawsers that hold the rope. The students keep them greased. We've only had a few minor breakouts.'

The cameraman beside him stifled a chuckle. 'Relatively minor, then. They are pretty vigorous.'

Jonah wanted to say, *I love you, old man.* But they did not do large talk. Instead his father took Jonah by the arm. 'It's the closest thing to farming in nature. Workers go out foraging for leaves, which they cut up with their jaws and carry back to the nest. The leaves are used as compost to cultivate garden colonies of fungi. Enzymes from the fungi digest the cellulose cell walls of the leaves and make them suitable for eating. The garden is vital for the ants' survival; without the continuous farming and feeding of the fungal colonies, the ant colony will die. Come, let me show you the nest.'

They walked down a corridor that had seemed endless to Jonah as a child, ducking to avoid the teeming trunk.

Standing at the entrance to the lecture theatre, with the river of ants just above his head, Jonah was reminded of a scene from the film *Close Encounters of the Third Kind.* The nest resembled a mountain: a pile of leaf litter and humus, rising several metres from a huge glass tank that took up most of the stage.

'How many of them are there?' Jonah asked.

'It's hard to say, eight million or so. As many as live in London.'

'What are you hoping to learn?' Jonah asked.

His father's fingers tightened around his bicep. 'On the face of it, we're trying to study their reproductive cycle.'

'But in fact?'

His father pointed across the aisle to the nearest row of seats. 'Sit down.'

They sat side by side and contemplated the teeming mound.

'It's a city,' explained Joseph Said. 'A mega-city. It's no less artificial or volatile than any other city. London. New York. Bombay. Here in captivity, with its population prevented from escape, it resembles a city under siege. I've christened it Gaza City.'

'Is this a protest?' Jonah asked gently.

'Not really.'

'But you're making a point?'

His father smiled ruefully and patted Jonah on the knee. 'The truth is I find their mindlessness comforting.'

It was too painful, and Jonah turned away to stare at the far wall. It wasn't fair.

'We lifted this nest from a remote corner of Venezuela, where stunning flat-topped mountains called *tepuis* rise out of the forest. It's an ecologically pristine environment. And it's doomed. Their flat tops mean that the animals have nowhere colder to climb to if the temperature rises. Darwin's dice have rolled badly for the planet, I think.'

He paused.

'Come to my office,' he said abruptly, and got to his feet. 'Let's sit and have a coffee. You can do your mother's bidding.'

Jonah followed him back down the corridor to his office with its view of the grounds. He looked around, searching for familiar items. He spotted the narghile pipe on the top of a bookcase and on the wall the framed deeds to the family home in Bethlehem, where his father had been born and which Jonah had never seen. The house was now occupied by an Israeli family that his father had been conducting good-humoured correspondence with for several decades. His father pulled a bag of coffee out of a drawer and ducked out into the corridor to fill his dented aluminium coffee pot with water. A familiar ritual.

'Where have you been?' he called out.

Jonah waited for him to return.

'I was in Sierra Leone,' Jonah told him, 'and after that New York. I'm flying to Afghanistan tonight.'

'Wherever there is trouble, that's where you are,' said his father, lighting the gas-ring stove he kept on a table beside his desk. He set the pot on the stove. 'When are you going to tell your mother what you do?'

'I'm not in any hurry,' Jonah replied.

'You should tell her what you do,' his father said. 'Soon I'm going to forget. Somebody in the family should know.'

This was how they communicated, in this particularly English way, by means of hint and pause, in which what was happening to his father was described by what was not said rather than what was. Funny, really, when you thought about it, given that neither of them was really English.

'Mum says that the faculty is threatening to have you evicted.'

'Really?'

His father didn't seem much concerned. 'She's worried,' Jonah said.

'They can't evict me. The nest's too big to move and besides we have a TV crew now. I'm a celebrity. I'm invulnerable, for now at least.'

The coffee boiled and he filled two cups.

'Here,' he said. 'Drink that.'

The coffee was thick, black and gritty, which is how he had always drunk it. They stared at each other over the rims of their cups. It was time to do his mother's bidding.

'How are you?' Jonah asked.

His father pulled a face. 'It's happening gradually: a misplaced word here and there. Memories slip away. I forget people's faces. I get my students to wear name tags. I've got one for you in a drawer somewhere. Under your name it says *son* – you'll know when it's time to start wearing it. We'll be able to get to know each other all over again every time.'

'Mum says you've stopped coming home.'

'Someone needs to keep an eye on the nest. I have a camp bed here. It's not uncomfortable.'

'Mum wants you to come home.'

'Your mother has an aversion to events that are out of her control.'

'She's worried about you.'

'Lots of people are worried about me. They like to tell me how worried they are. I'd really appreciate it if you didn't join them.'

'I promised I'd try, Dad.'

'Well done. You tried. Now, drink your coffee.' He took a packet of cigarettes out of the drawer. 'Smoke?'

'No thanks.'

'I've taken it up,' his father said. 'After all, why not?'

It had been six months since his father had been diagnosed as having Alzheimer's, six months in which to contemplate the inevitability of his physical and mental decline. There was nothing good to say about Alzheimer's.

'Are you still staying in that place on Black Prince Road?' his father asked.

'Yes,' Jonah replied.

'Have you got yourself a girlfriend?'

'No.'

'You can't always live in the past,' his father told him gently. 'It's just memories. You've got to look to the future. That's what I'm doing.'

'I'll try, Dad.'

Jonah looked at his watch. It was time that he left. He had to drive back up to London and pack for the flight to Afghanistan. He set his coffee cup down on its saucer.

'Shall I walk you out?' his father asked.

'I'd like that.'

His father accompanied Jonah down the corridor and through the glasshouses, to the great hall and beyond it the main entrance. It was a long walk. Jonah reflected that they hadn't always made each other's lives easy. He was an irritating and difficult son. His father could be short-tempered. But that was all gone now, there was no more competition. Alzheimer's had rubbed it away, leaving them with just this moment. They paused on the steps and embraced clumsily. It had stopped raining, and the lawns sparkled with droplets of water.

'I'm glad that we had time to get to know each other,' his father told him.

It was only later, when he was on his own, that he realised that his father had said goodbye. He was lying on his back, with his backpack as a pillow, staring at the ceiling of a hangar at RAF Brize Norton, when it came to him. It had been almost matter-of-fact, as if the issue had already been decided and he had been aware of it as an outcome for some time – a sad and precious parting.

For hours, while he waited for the plane, he turned the thought over in his mind.

In the cages with Silent Bob

December 2001–January 2002

Jonah corkscrewed into Kandahar by night with a cargo of freshly captured prisoners, the plane's descent near vertical to deter Stinger missile attack. They hit the ground with a bone-jarring thud, and bounced down the rutted runway towards the darkened terminal building, while the cargo ramp descended and airmen in insect-like goggles and flak jackets pulled the manacled and hooded prisoners to their feet. Jonah tightened the straps on his backpack and tapped the magazine on his rifle to check that it was secure.

The plane spun on its axis at the end of the runway and military policemen swarmed out of the icy darkness with red-lensed torches. An airman yelled, '*Move!*', and the ragged line of prisoners stumbled down the ramp, their breath escaping in clouds through the burlap sacks over their heads. Everyone was screaming – MPs, prisoners, airmen – the stream of commands and obscenities inaudible as the spinning plane's engines roared in preparation for take-off.

Jonah followed the line of prisoners across the tarmac and through a sheet-metal door, into a barbed-wire enclosure lit up with stadium lights and overlooked by watchtowers manned by armed MPs. The prisoners were hurled into sandbag pin-downs where MPs in surgical gloves cut away their rags with scissors. A huge MP flashed his torch in Jonah's face and demanded that he identify himself.

'Jonah. OGA attached,' Jonah shouted back at him, supplying the words that he had been given. OGA – *Other Government Agency* – CIA nomenclature.

'You are now in a combat zone,' the MP yelled. 'You will keep the magazine in your rifle at all times. You will never leave your rifle more than an arm's length from you. You will engage any target that threatens you. Is that clear?'

'Yes.'

'This way.' The MP led him down an abattoir-like tent tunnel past a line of naked prisoners and a doctor who was screening them, his gloved hands moving across their skin and probing their mouths. They hurried through a cloud of lice powder and past piles of rubber-soled shoes, blankets and brightly coloured jumpsuits. At the end of the tent a couple of FBI agents with cameras and flashguns were waiting expectantly for the first of the processed prisoners. The MP led Jonah past them, out of the tent and past a row of smoking oil barrels giving off the sweet, sickly scent of burning human excrement. They went through another sheet-metal door into a mud-walled compound with eight large tents, each one surrounded by concertina wire. They skirted the row of tents, stepping between the stumps of apple trees, and exited through another door.

The MP walked over to the first of a huddle of olive-drab tents, tapped on the pole and stuck his head inside the flap.

'Got the OGA for Silent Bob here, sir.'

'Send him in,' someone called.

The MP stepped back and held the flap open for Jonah. 'In you go, sir.'

Inside, a group of army interrogators and analysts, bundled up in flannel shirts and winter parkas, sat in camp chairs tapping away at laptops or lying sprawled on cot beds. One of them, wearing a sergeant's stripes, looked up from a sheaf of papers and said, 'You're OGA Jonah?'

'That's me.'

'You're late.'

Jonah recognised the type: hard working and fiercely proud, trying to hold together his team in the bleakest conditions. And every day getting walked all over by outside agencies – it was no wonder he resented the intrusion.

'I'm here now,' Jonah told him in a neutral tone.

'Tired?'

'Not particularly,' Jonah replied, though in truth he was exhausted by a trip that had brought him from Rhein-Mein US Air Force base in Germany via Incirlik in Turkey and a former Soviet air force base in Uzbekistan to Bagram airbase on the outskirts of Kabul, where they had picked up the consignment of prisoners, and now, finally, Kandahar. He was determined not to show it. 'I'd like to see the prisoner immediately.'

'Let's do it, then. Nakamura, take him to the Joint Interrogation Facility, and you there, Heaney, go and fetch Silent Bob from the cages.'

A young Japanese American with a crew cut looked up from his laptop and gave a quick nod, while behind him a tall and skinny white man rolled off his cot with a groan and stuck his bare feet in a pair of boots.

'This way, sir,' said the soldier named Nakamura, pulling a woollen cap down over his ears. He led Jonah from the tent past a ramshackle collection of bomb-damaged buildings towards a large metal gate at the entrance to a walled compound. The gate was topped with barbed wire and was marked with a spray-painted sign that said NO ENTRY. There were guard towers manned by MPs with machine guns and the area beyond the gate was lit up with stadium lighting.

An MP opened the gate and waved them in.

'Welcome to the Rock,' Nakamura said.

Inside, they walked down a passage between the outer tin wall and an inner mud wall that was fifteen feet high and decorated with a mural with the silhouettes of the Twin Towers superimposed on an image of the Pentagon. Underneath were the words WE WILL NEVER FORGET.

Nakamura led him past murals of the New York Police Department and Fire Department shields, and through a beaten metal door into a high-walled compound with a set of six round tents in two rows surrounded by barbed wire. Each tent had a piece of cardboard above its entrance with a number from 1 to 6 written on it. At the end of the compound, between the rows of tents, there was a fire burning in a halved oil barrel. A huddle of inter-rogators and MPs were standing around it, feeding cardboard into the fire. They looked up as Jonah approached.

'You're the guy here to see Silent Bob?' asked one of the inter-rogators.

'You think he's going to talk to you?' added another.

'Maybe,' Jonah replied.

'You better watch him real close,' said one of the MPs, 'he bites. He just about took one of Lopez's ears off.'

'Here he comes,' said another.

The door at the far end of the compound clattered open and a prisoner in a blue jumpsuit, handcuffs and leg irons was hauled through it and forced to race with baby steps by an MP on each arm. His head was covered in a sandbag and steam rose out of the pointy ends like devil's horns. Nakamura pointed to the nearest tent and the MPs took the prisoner inside.

'You want me in there with you?' Nakamura asked.

'No, I'm fine, thanks,' Jonah replied. He felt excitement rising in him like a wave and rubbed his face in an involuntary spasm.

The MPs emerged. 'Do your best,' one of them said.

Jonah ducked through the flap. There was a propane tank in the corner with a coil that spurted flame and a huge MP standing to one side with a wooden baton. The prisoner was sitting on a camp chair, still wearing his hood. Opposite him was a second chair. Jonah sat in it. The first thing that he noticed was the smell – a sharp, animal reek – rising off the prisoner, and then his still-ness. The hands lightly cupped in his lap, his knuckles covered in scabs. He struggled to remember, *was Nor ever this still?*

'Shall I remove the hood, sir?' the MP asked.

Jonah nodded.

The MP stepped forward and with a flourish pulled off the sandbag.

Jonah stifled a gasp. He barely recognised him. Nor's face was a death mask, a skull-like landscape of ridges and flint-like points with the skin stretched taut across them. His neck was impossibly thin and his shaven head was covered in faded, yellowing bruises. His lips were cracked and purple from the cold, and strings of frozen snot hung from his nostrils. Looking at him, with his head hanging and his hands and feet in chains, Jonah was filled with shame at seeing his friend so degraded.

'Can you take off the cuffs?' he asked.

'No, sir,' the MP told him firmly.

Nor lifted his head and accused Jonah with his hard and cavernous eyes.

'I came as quickly as I could,' Jonah said, and in doing so acknowledged that there was never going to be an end to his sense of responsibility. From the schoolyard to the parade square, from the Home Counties to the North-West Frontier, Jonah had been his keeper and his mentor. 'You have to talk to me,' he told Nor, 'if you want to get out of here.'

Nor closed his eyes and tipped his head back, exposing the tiny purple veins in his eyelids, displaying a sort of weary fatalism.

'If you don't talk to me they'll send you to Guantanamo. Once you're there you won't get out.'

Nor opened his eyes, lowered his head and spoke in a voice that was barely a whisper: 'As for the unbelievers, their works are like a mirage in the desert. The thirsty traveller thinks it is water, but when he comes near he finds that it is nothing.'

Jonah recognised it as coming from the Koran's twenty-fourth sura, al-Nur, the Light. 'I'm here to offer you a deal.'

Nor raised his head again and studied Jonah. 'Of course you are,' he said. 'You're an errand boy.'

'Yeah, and you're Mr Kurtz. Fuck you.'

Jonah woke to the crackle of machine-gun fire in the darkness. Men were tumbling out of the camp beds around him and reaching for their boots, rifles and combat gear. After a couple of minutes of frantic fumbling someone shouted 'Let's move' and suddenly they were running – a scattering of adrenalin-filled shadows – towards the terminal building.

They took cover with a group of marines beside a burned-out

snack bar in the baggage reclaim area and listened for an hour or so to the sound of incoming machine-gun fire on the perimeter and the pop and crash of outgoing mortar fire. Rumours swirled like dust – the enemy were in the wire; there were suicide bombers at the gate.

Gradually the fire grew more sporadic and eventually Jonah relaxed. He engaged the safety catch of his rifle.

Beside him Nakamura said, 'I heard you got Silent Bob to speak?'

'Yes,' Jonah replied.

'In English?'

'Yes.'

Nakamura was incredulous. 'You know him?'

'We were at school together,' Jonah admitted. Though what he meant was that they were the best of friends: they collected spiders in jam jars in surburbia and fed them with insects; they sprinted from arrow-slit to arrow-slit in Crusader castles in Lebanon; they built traps and hides; and they perfected their battlefield death throes. Nor was best at dramatically dying – no surprises there!

'Nobody tells us anything,' Nakamura complained. 'How we're supposed to get any usable intelligence out of these people is beyond me.' He took off his helmet and lit a cigarette. He stared at the burning tip. 'My mother says these will kill me. That's funny in this place.'

Jonah nodded sympathetically.

'Would you say Bob's high value?' Nakamura asked.

'Yes,' Jonah responded. 'His real name is Nor.'

'That means light, right?'

'Yes, Nor means light.'

From what Jonah could gather from listening to the interrogators most of the prisoners in the cages were judged to be of dubious or little intelligence value: they were simply 'swept up', foot soldiers who had been lifted in combat operations and, for want of anything else to do with them, had been fed through the chain to Kandahar, a way-stage on the route that would eventually lead them to the recently opened camp at Guantanamo Bay in Cuba. It seemed that with every step his confidence in the War on Terror was further eroded.

'I don't want to speak out of turn,' Nakamura said, 'but I've talked to several guys I know in Special Forces who were camped on the outskirts of Kunduz with Dostum's fighters, in the days before the town fell. They said that right up until the end the Pakistanis were flying planes out of the city on an air corridor authorised by our own military command. We had intelligence that when we first laid siege to Kunduz, there were eight thousand or so Taliban and Arab fighters holed up in there. But by the time the city fell there were less than three thousand left. Everybody important got away. Our allies flew our enemies away. It's got to make you wonder. If your friend is genuinely high value and he was left behind, then he was left behind for a reason.'

'Or he chose to stay behind,' Jonah said, thoughtfully.

As they were walking back, they passed a soldier sitting in a deckchair outside his tent. He was wearing headphones and singing along to a song:

'*But we've wander'd monie a weary fit, sin auld lang syne . . .*'

'Happy New Year,' Nakamura told him.

The man gave him a thumbs-up. It was 2002.

Jonah rose just before dawn and stepped out of the tent, standing for a while beneath the purple sky, watching the sun on the horizon, its light casting the distant mountains in jagged silhouette. The barren and dusty earth stretched in every direction, and it seemed as if there was nothing alive in it. It was a landscape that had consumed armies – the Russians and the British – and it was difficult not to imagine that a similar fate awaited this most recent intervention.

His thoughts kept going back to his conversation with Nakamura the night before. A profound sense of unease had descended upon him, and the germ of an idea had begun to form in his mind. He ducked back into the tent and went over to Nakamura's cot. He knelt beside it and shook him awake.

'Has he been X-rayed?' Jonah asked.

Nakamura shuddered and blinked. 'No.'

'Is there an X-ray machine in the med centre?'

'I think so.'

'Get him over there. Let's take a look.'

It was darker than the surrounding organs, an opaque mass about the size of an egg lodged in the bowel. They were standing in a tent in the med centre. An army doctor was holding the X-ray sheet up to a light panel on the tent wall.

'What is it?' Nakamura asked.

Jonah ignored the question. 'Do you have a safe?' he asked.

'Yes.'

'Can you get it out of him?' Jonah asked.

The doctor nodded. 'Sure. We can give him an enema and monitor his bowel movements. It will take a few hours. It will be messy and unpleasant. But we'll get it out of him.'

'Do it.'

This time he brought cigarettes. The MP removed the sandbag from Nor's head and Jonah offered him one. His face was paler and the hollows of his eyes were if anything deeper and more cavernous. He shrugged in acceptance and Jonah put the cigarette filter directly into his mouth.

'Why didn't you fly out of Kunduz on the airlift when you had the chance?' Jonah asked.

For a few brief moments they were face to face as Nor leant forward to accept a light – only inches apart over the lighter flame – and it occurred to Jonah that if Nor genuinely harboured murderous desire then now was the time to attack. Behind them the MP cleared his throat and tapped the end of his baton against his thigh. Nor sat back in his seat and inhaled. He closed his eyes and exhaled a thin stream of smoke.

'You can fly out of here tonight, if you cooperate,' Jonah told him.

Nor opened his eyes, lifted his cuffed hands and removed the cigarette from between his lips.

'Do they know about Kiernan?' he asked, glancing at the MP.

'I ask the questions.'

Nor took another drag and paused before exhaling. 'Tit for tat. You answer my questions and I'll answer yours.'

It was no way to conduct an interrogation, but when dealing with your oldest friend and oldest joe there was no such thing as established procedure. 'Of course they don't know,' Jonah hissed.

'You must be shitting yourself.'

'Why were you left behind in Kunduz?' Jonah demanded, angrily.

'Why aren't you at home with your family, Jonah?'

Jonah stood up. 'We just pulled a Kinder Egg full of diamonds out of you, enough to finance a major terrorist operation. These people are going to go to work on you. They're champing at the bit. You haven't seen anything yet.'

He turned to leave the tent.

'Don't go,' Nor said to Jonah's back.

Jonah sighed and turned back. 'You need to talk to me.'

'The Pakistanis knew about the diamonds,' Nor explained. 'If I'd tried moving them out on the Kunduz airlift the ISI would have seized them as soon as I touched down in Peshawar. It seemed better to take my chances with the Northern Alliance. What happened to your marriage?'

'It didn't last.'

'You look like shit,' Nor told him.

There was a pause. 'You don't look so hot yourself,' Jonah said.

Nor laughed bitterly, and within seconds was doubled up by a racking cough.

'We need to get you out of here,' Jonah said, sorrowfully.

'Spare me your pity,' Nor hissed. 'Give me another cigarette.'

Jonah put another in his mouth and lit it for him. Nor inhaled hungrily and broke into a further fit of coughing.

'What do the Americans want me to do?' he rasped, eventually.

'They want you to agree to work for them.'

He didn't appear surprised. 'This place is full of spies. I can't just walk out of here.'

'They've manufactured an alibi. They're going to render you to a third nation. From there they'll arrange for you to escape.'

'So where am I going?'

'Moroccan-occupied Western Sahara. The Dark Prison in Layoune.'

Nor ground the butt of his cigarette into the cold sand with his heel.

'Nice,' he said.

'What are you up to?' Jonah asked.

Nor shook his head and smiled wryly. 'I'm your loyal soldier, Jonah, as always.'

It was textbook: *the liar's lean* – Nor's entire frame tilted towards the exit. The pleasure a liar shows when his lie is believed.

The MPs came for them in the night, rattling their batons on the sides of the cages, provoking howls of protest. They opened three cells and dragged the occupants – Nor and two others for cover – out on to the sand. They were strapped to rough-ground gurneys, each one with an all-terrain wheel, and their hands, feet and mouths were wrapped with duct tape. A hood was placed over each head. They were rolled out on to the runway to wait for the next plane.

Jonah delivered the diamonds to Winthrop in a nondescript business park in McLean, Virginia. It was after midnight. He'd flown into Andrews air force base on a troop transport flight from Incirlik. He was met on the tarmac by a large and unfriendly Persian-American with a flattened boxer's nose. He introduced himself as Pakravan.

'You're the bagman, right?'

'I'm the man with the bag,' Jonah confirmed.

Pakravan lead him to a beaten-up 4Runner and drove him off the base, around the outer loop of the Beltway and into Fairfax County.

The office resembled a dentist's waiting room, though without the out-of-date magazines. There was overhead strip lighting, a laminate desk with a swivel chair, a row of fabric-covered guest chairs and a rectangular window with off-white vertical blinds. At the desk, there was a man wearing a long, black *rekel* coat and the beard and uncut sideburns of a Hasid. In front of him on the desk was a velvet pad, a pair of tweezers and a jeweller's loupe. Winthrop was leaning against a bare wall on the far side of the room. No introductions were offered. Jonah emptied a specimen bottle containing the diamonds on to the pad and the man started inspecting them one at a time, while Jonah, Winthrop and Pakravan waited in silence.

The man put down his loupe. 'They are the real thing. Very good quality: brilliant cut, white, internally flawless with no visible inclusions. The smallest one is probably no less than two carats.'

Winthrop sprang off the wall with a grin on his face. He slapped Jonah on the back with one hand and gripped his upper arm with the other. 'You did well.'

'I'd like to go home now,' Jonah told him.

Winthrop retained his grip on Jonah's upper arm. 'Of course, take a few days back in London, but we're not done with you yet.'

'What does that mean?'

'We want you to go down to the Sahara and pick up Nor. Steer him to safety. By which I mean shepherd him for a day or two until it's time to hand him over to our people. He's just out of prison. We think he'd benefit from a familiar face. A school friend.'

Fire destruction horizon

January 2002

Jonah met Alex Ross, his former colleague from the Afghan Guides, at the top of the Monument, Wren's two-hundred-foot-tall Doric column erected to commemorate the Great Fire of London. Alex was nothing if not melodramatic. His bodyguards patted Jonah down before the turnstile at the foot of the spiral staircase. Jonah used to think that Alex's employees, with their short-barrelled names – Taff, Ginger, Smudge – were an affectation, a piece of razzmatazz to impress the clients who bought into the glossy brochures put out by his security company, filled with panic rooms and quick response units. But ever since Alex organised the kidnapping of his ex-wife's lover, Jonah had come to see the wisdom in it. These days, Jonah found Alex's presence a provocation; he'd beat him to a pulp given half the chance.

Jonah had got off the red-eye flight from Washington that morning, switched on his phone at baggage claim and received the instruction to meet at the Monument.

'Fuck it,' Jonah muttered. He wasn't going to trudge up the staircase like some old, wheezing knacker – he'd rather arrive warmed up for a fight, bellowing and dripping. He sprinted to the top and burst out of the stairwell on to the viewing platform.

He needn't have bothered. Alex was oblivious. He had settled upon a new, apocalyptic and very lucrative calling. He removed his sunglasses and gestured expansively for Jonah's benefit. 'The fire raged for five whole days, Jonah. The heat was so intense the roof of St Paul's collapsed and the streets ran with molten lead.

Thirteen thousand houses destroyed. Afterwards the stones of the buildings were calcinated and brilliant white. Can you imagine it, the city as a skeleton, white as bone and surrounded by ash as far as the eye could see?'

Panting, Jonah scanned the horizon, searching for signs of conflagration, of the city white as bone. The view to the north was of the financial heart of the City, the Lloyds Building with its steel guts on the outside, the NatWest tower and the unfinished Gherkin; and, to the south, the river, its bridges and tour boats; and after it the mass of the southern boroughs, its housing estates and gas holders.

'September 1666,' Alex explained. 'The diarist Samuel Pepys described it as a bow of flame about a mile in width. They stopped it short of the Tower by using gunpowder to demolish rows of houses.'

Beneath them traffic climbed the pavements as police cars edged forward, their sirens dopplering, pulsing in the air.

'The city has always been under threat. Did you know it burned to the ground fifteen times between AD 764 and 1227?'

Dutifully, Jonah fed him his cue. 'No, I don't think I knew that,' he gasped.

'The last time was on the twenty-ninth of December 1940 when the incendiaries fell like rain. Almost a third of the city was reduced to rubble and ash. Sixteen of Wren's churches were destroyed. Only St Paul's survived. You want statistics? In the first two months of the Blitz the Germans dropped thirty thousand bombs on the capital. Six hundred bombers came in waves on the first night. Six thousand civilians died in the first thirty days. Twice as many people as died in the Twin Towers.'

'And your point is, Alex?' Jonah asked.

'My point is that the city is not invulnerable. It never has been. Destruction on a massive scale is not some remote fantasy dreamed up by doomsayers. It's a credible risk. We live with it every day. And we know our enemy now. We know the deep wells of resentment and hatred out there. We know the ranks of young men willing to immolate themselves on the promise of paradise. And we know our own weaknesses, the nodes and pinch points where people are funnelled together: Liverpool Street, King's Cross, Paddington. The tube stations, nightclubs, shopping centres and cinemas. Our vulnerable termini. We may have only minutes to live. I don't know about you but it makes me feel inflamed. I get a hard-on just thinking about it.'

'Do folks pay for this performance?' Jonah asked.

Alex grinned wolfishly and ran a hand through his unruly blond hair. 'Of course. I bring all my City clients up here.'

'And with the sermon they get what?'

'Prime-quality risk analysis and an invoice to make your jaw drop. It's the future, Jonah. Even as we speak, the day-to-day burden of defending society against the threat of conflict is being transferred to the private sector. You know that I married?'

'No, Alex. I don't think you told me that.'

'I'd have invited you to the wedding, but you'd have stood out. It would have made you feel uneasy. None of the old people were there. Not one of the Guides. I hardly knew my best man.'

'Congratulations,' Jonah told him, unsure of whether to believe him.

'I have serious commitments now: a business, real estate, a Thames view, a child on the way. My wife has expensive tastes.'

'I guess it's lucky for you that 9/11 revived the security business.'

'You make your own luck, Jonah. You know that. When I left the Department, I spotted an opening and I'm making the most of it. I have an opportunity to build a future for my family. That's the most important thing to me. I'm not risking that for some Department fuck-up.' There was a pause. The preamble was over and they had arrived at the meat of the conversation: 'Do you think that anyone in authority here is going to lift a finger to defend us if it comes out that we murdered a CIA agent in an unsanctioned operation? Christ, I wouldn't even be saying it out loud if we weren't up here.'

Alex had committed sacrilege. It was the Department's one unbending rule: *never ever mention Kiernan's death out loud.*

'They'll throw us to the fucking wolves,' Alex growled. 'I'm not having it. I'm not going to prison for anyone.'

'It's not a situation that any of us likes,' Jonah told him.

'But you're the one who's in a position to do something about it.'

'What does that mean?'

'Don't play stupid with me. Do you think he'll talk?'

Jonah shrugged – it was not an easy question to answer. There was no science in the running of agents, any more than there was an understanding of the intricacies of childhood friendships, and Alex knew that as well as Jonah did.

'You understand Nor better than anyone,' Alex insisted.

'As you may recall, we abandoned him in Kandahar back in '96. He thinks we betrayed him.'

'Was he ever ours?' Alex responded.

'I used to think so. Now I'm not so sure.'

'You're not sure about much, are you?'

'Less and less by the day,' Jonah retorted.

'Let's concentrate on what we do know,' Alex said. 'The Americans, who seem to have difficulty distinguishing their friends from their foes in the War on Terror, allowed the Pakistanis to fly every terrorist of value out of Kunduz before the Northern Alliance could capture them. I'm talking about Chechens, Uzbeks, Afghans and Arabs – Pakistani military personnel, ISI, Taliban and al-Qaeda fighters. Why didn't the Pakistanis take Nor? He's a fucking Sith Lord, Jonah. Why did they leave him behind?'

'He says because the Pakistanis knew about the diamonds.'

'Do you believe that?'

Jonah shrugged. 'He says he was a mule for al-Qaeda. One of several that broke out of Kunduz carrying the diamonds. They were supposed to scatter and meet in northern Iraq, near the Iranian border, at a camp run by an al-Qaeda-linked Kurdish group.'

'These days all roads lead to Iraq,' Alex said.

'And that's exactly what the Americans want to hear,' Jonah said. 'They're intent on creating a link between Osama Bin Laden and Saddam Hussein. They'll use it as a pretext to invade.'

Alex's eyes narrowed. 'Where are the diamonds now?'

'The Americans have them.'

'Have they valued them?'

'A million dollars, apparently.'

Alex whistled. 'You know that's twice what it cost al-Qaeda to finance 9/11? The total estimated cost to the US of the 9/11 attacks, including direct costs as a result of systems sabotage and indirect costs as a result of security, insurance and policy changes, was five hundred billion dollars. That's a million to one return. Do you really think he's just a mule?'

'I don't see that there is anything I can do about it.'

'The Americans want you to handle him. They recognise that you're the best man to do it and that gives you an opportunity to get to him before there are damaging revelations.'

'What do you mean by *get* to him?'

'You want me to spell it out for you?'

'Yes, I think I do.'

'I mean kill him.'

There was a pause.

'You want me to kill Nor?'

'Yes. That's exactly what I mean. Go down there to the Sahara and kill him. We can't afford messy revelations.'

'Who do you mean by we?'

'Obviously, Monteith can't tell you himself. There has to be denial.'

Jonah watched a gull lift and wheel in a spiral of air. He reflected that Monteith had always preferred to conduct his dirty work at arm's length. He heard himself speak from some middle distance. 'Of course.'

'Don't be fucking childish. You know how this works.'

'I've known Nor since I was a child.'

Alex looked closely at Jonah. 'People are asking why Nor didn't kill you in Sierra Leone when he had the chance.'

Jonah returned his gaze. 'Which people?'

Alex's eyes narrowed. 'Maybe you're too close.'

Jonah frowned. People hurried past on the pavement below. 'Of course, I'm too close.'

Abruptly, Alex changed tack. He grinned and slapped Jonah on the shoulder. 'Come on. Let's go over to Bangla town and grab a curry.'

Black locusts

February 2002

The Moroccans called them black locusts, the thousands of illegal immigrants that gathered on the North African coast in the hope of reaching Europe by scaling the fences surrounding the tiny Spanish enclave of Melilla.

Scores had died on the fences, shot by border guards, and hundreds more had been captured. For several weeks the Moroccans had been cramming them into the back of trucks and driving them a thousand miles south across the desert to the 'Berm', the 2,400-kilometre-long earthwork fortification that divided the disputed territory of Western Sahara. At the Berm they were stripped of their belongings and ejected through the minefields into open desert.

The route was proven, the venality of the guards well established. It was simply a question of waiting. Nor would come. And when he did Jonah would face an impossible choice: kill his oldest friend or risk exposure of himself and his colleagues in the Department as the murderers of the CIA agent James Kiernan.

The plane's wheels extended with a dull thud that jerked him awake. Jonah was always awake for landing. He rubbed his face and, looking around, found the woman in the next seat staring at him. She was wearing a ribbed, white shawl that covered her hair and her hands were smeared with henna. He wondered whether he had called out in his sleep. Glancing out of the window, he saw only darkness, and then suddenly the lights of the city beneath him.

They landed and the engines screamed as they decelerated on the tarmac.

He went down the metal gangway and walked across the tarmac in the searing cold of the desert night. He had landed at the airport on the outskirts of the closed military city of Tindhouf, in the far south-west of Algeria. His name was Jonah and he was a British passport holder. He was a journalist, of sorts. He wrote half-hearted cant for a socialist Internet site. He had lost his eye to a welding spark as a child.

His contact was waiting in the terminal beyond, standing a head taller than the Saharawis around her, clutching a tatty Gladstone bag beneath her arm. She was wearing a T-shirt and flip-flops despite the cold and there were goose bumps on her tanned forearms. She had dirty blonde hair, unnerving blue eyes and almost no upper lip. She was wearing lipstick but it did not follow the contours of her mouth; for a moment, Jonah experienced a bizarre urge to reach out and wipe it away.

Her name was Justine. She was a former Sky News reporter, now reduced to acting as a freelance stringer for anyone unlikely enough to show interest in the plight of the dispossessed population of Western Sahara. The route that had led her to this remote outpost, as described in her file, was a painful one – a spectacular fall from grace, precipitated by mobile phone footage of her shouting at a rape victim in a field hospital in Sudan: '*Nobody gives a shit if there was only one of them. It's nothing. You have to say it was a gang rape. Look at the camera. Do it again, but four or five of them this time, you understand?*' The footage was posted by an outraged MSF doctor on YouTube and within days it had been downloaded by a million people worldwide. The self-righteous fury that followed had caused the network to ditch her and made her a virtual pariah.

'My God, look at you,' she said, and he could tell immediately from the shrewdness of her stare that she was unlikely to be satisfied until she understood the nature of his mission. She tucked her arm in his. 'Come on, there's a car outside.'

She led him to the far side of the car park, to a battered white Land Cruiser with a small group of men squatting beside it, drinking tea around a fire. As they approached a man in a faded army jacket and a black turban got up. He climbed in the car, turned the key in the ignition and it rattled into life.

'We had a pack of Spanish journalists fly in a couple of days back,' Justine explained, once he had squeezed on to the bench seat beside her. 'They have already crossed into the liberated zone. I presume that's where you want to go?'

'Yes,' he said.

'We'll overnight tonight in the one of the camps and set off tomorrow at first light.'

'Fine,' he said.

They skirted the city on a bypass lit up with sodium lamps that gave it a hallucinogenic orange glare. There were no other cars. There was no one to be seen. They circled a roundabout and turned off into the desert. There were no more street lamps and the only illumination came from their headlights on the road ahead. After a few miles they approached an Algerian military checkpoint. The driver slowed the car and flicked on the overhead lamp. A soldier emerged from his hut. Justine gave him a friendly grin and the soldier waved them through.

'Welcome to the Saharawi Arab Democratic Republic,' Justine said.

They turned off the road and bounced along a rutted track between low hills, and then they were on the camp's unpaved streets. The low, crude brick huts and rectangular tents were arranged in loose blocks.

'There are a hundred and something thousand Saharawi refugees spread across five camps,' Justine explained, staring at him. 'They have been here for thirty years, a whole generation stranded out here in the middle of nowhere, forgotten about by the international community while the Moroccans occupy their homes and plunder their phosphates and fishing banks. But I guess you knew that?'

They turned into an alley. He attempted to count off the shacks as they bounced past but it was no good. He had no idea where he was. The driver stopped and cut the engine and lights.

'They've maintained a ceasefire for fourteen years,' she said as they got out of the car. 'They've resisted the temptation to draw attention to themselves with spectacular acts of violence. These are the best-run refugee camps in the world.'

The driver led them to a large tent. He ducked under the guy ropes and through the flap at the entrance and Jonah and Justine followed. A short, round woman in a shawl got up to greet them. Justine put an arm around the woman's shoulder.

'This is Fatima,' she said. 'She is my auntie.'

Jonah shook hands with the woman. The driver closed the flap behind them. The large, windowless tent was bare except for a low table, a charcoal burner, a pile of blankets and a few cushions spread across the carpet. They sat and Fatima resumed making tea. Two teenage girls wearing thick woollen mittens entered the tent and sat opposite them, watching but saying nothing.

Jonah asked for details about the migrants.

'They've found ninety-five so far. Most of them have spent two or three days wandering in the desert before being picked up. They've been given shelter in a schoolhouse in Birlehlu, one of the settlements in the liberated zone. It's about six hours' drive west of here.'

'What nationality are the ones they've found?'

'West African mostly, Guineans, Ghanaians, Nigerians, Gambians . . . you name it. They've found a couple of Bangladeshis, also.'

'Any Arabs?'

'No Arabs,' she said, holding his gaze, no expression on her face.

He was passed a small glass filled with sweet black tea. He drank it and handed back the glass.

A man pushed aside the tent flap. He was tall, thin and bespectacled with a neat goatee beard. Jonah got up to shake his hand but the man motioned for him to remain seated.

'This is Ahmed,' Justine said. 'He is an official from Polisario.'

Polisario was the Saharawi independence movement, they controlled the refugee camps and the 'liberated zone', the stretch of mostly empty desert to the east of the Moroccan 'Berm'.

'You are welcome,' Ahmed said, solemnly, when he had sat down. He spoke very good English without a discernible accent. Jonah got the feeling that although he was polite, he did not welcome Jonah's presence. A second round of tea was served. Jonah checked his watch. It was after two.

'Are you tired?' Ahmed asked.

'I'm OK,' he replied.

'Why have you come?' Ahmed asked, in Arabic.

'I'm looking for someone,' Jonah replied, also in Arabic.

'You'll find no jihadis here,' Ahmed said, 'if that's what you've come for. There are no fundamentalists or suicide bombers.'

'I'm looking for a friend, that's all.'

'Our people on the other side of the Berm tell us that there has been a prison break in Layoune, from the Dark Prison. That is unprecedented. The identity of the escaped prisoners is unknown.'

'I just need to find my friend,' Jonah told him, 'and then we will leave. I don't mean to cause any difficulty.'

Ahmed said to Jonah in English, 'I have something to discuss with Justine. Please excuse us.'

They disappeared out of the tent.

Jonah sat back against a cushion and accepted a third glass of tea. After he had drunk it he checked his watch again. He closed his eyes. He became aware of someone standing at his shoulder. He opened his eyes again. Justine smiled sympathetically.

'You speak Arabic,' she observed.

Fatima and the girls had left the tent. The driver was asleep beneath a pile of blankets.

'You're not a spy, are you?' Justine asked.

'No.'

'OK.' She laughed. 'I'm not concerned.'

'No need to be.'

'My father was a spy,' she said.

'OK.'

'I don't know whether he was any good at it. He didn't like it much when the cold war ended. He said the Soviets were worthy adversaries. I think he'd have been happy if the Soviet Union never collapsed. What about you? What about your father?'

'My father is a biologist,' he told her.

'The birds and the bees,' she said, lightly. 'I expect that you were better prepared for the opposite sex than I was.'

'I doubt it.'

Eating, sleeping, fucking . . . that was what his father had described to him at an early age as the basic animal, and human, needs. Jonah wasn't sure that it had made him any better prepared for life and its inevitable disappointments.

'My father is a Palestinian,' he said, out of nowhere. He thought of adding: he is losing his mind.

Her eyes were watchful, ever alert. 'Then you know what it's like to be without a home.'

He felt torn. To agree would be dishonest: he had citizenship, there had always been a family home for him to go to, his parents, for all their difficulties, were still together; if he was homeless it was a result of his own bad choices, a bad marriage, an all-consuming job; but at the same time he had no wish to interfere in a fantasy of fraternity that might be all that Justine had to cling to.

'They've decided to help you,' she said.

'I see,' he said uncertainly.

'You can go where you like.' She smiled mischievously, and added, 'And I'm coming with you.'

'OK,' he said, after a pause.

'You'd better get some more sleep.'

They lay down beside each other, beneath piles of blankets. He woke up once and found her staring at him, her face just a few inches from his.

He was awake just before dawn and he pulled on his boots and went outside to stand in the bitter cold, watching the sky turn from deepest purple to palest blue streaked with pink.

It was eerily quiet.

'It's beautiful,' Justine said. He didn't hear her come up behind him. He turned to look at her. She had tied up her hair and she looked vulnerable in the dawn light. Beautiful, even. He felt his earlier antipathy to her melt away.

'They're wary of you,' she said. 'They're not sure whose side you're on. They don't want to incur the anger of the Americans. If it wasn't for me speaking up for you they wouldn't have let you enter the liberated zone.'

'Thank you,' he said.

'You're not a journalist, are you?'

He didn't reply.

'I still believe in my country,' she said, 'despite everything.'

'Like I said, I'm looking for a friend.'

'Do you have many friends?' she asked playfully, leaning into his shoulder.

'Not many,' he said ruefully.

They drove across a stark and barren landscape. Jonah sat on the bench seat with Justine squeezed in between him and the driver, with their thighs and elbows touching. He used a GPS to track their course as they left Algeria, cut across the northern tip of Mauritania and entered the 'liberated zone'.

Jonah discovered that the driver's name was Zalik and that he had originally been a road construction worker employed by a Spanish company, but that he had joined Polisario after the Spanish abandoned the colony and the Moroccans invaded.

After six hours they reached Birlehlu. There wasn't much there but a corral of junked trucks, a cluster of sheet-metal huts constructed from flattened oil barrels, a few shipping containers and, some distance off, an abandoned colonial-era schoolhouse that housed the rescued migrants. They arrived in the early afternoon when the sun was so bright you had to squint to see through the windscreen.

Jonah wandered from room to room through the schoolhouse with Justine following. In one a line of African men in ill-fitting, blue boiler suits queued up to be inspected by a Spanish medical team. In another, two Bangladeshis wrapped in silver-foil blankets were staring disconsolately at the floor. They had paid a people trafficker in Dhaka several thousand dollars each to smuggle them to Europe. They had been wandering in the desert for four days before a Polisario patrol found them.

'I thought I must die,' one of them said to Justine, in halting English.

There was no sign of Nor. Jonah stepped out into the courtyard, into the burning sunlight, and shaded his eyes with his hand. Sweat ran down his back at once.

'Where's he from, this friend of yours?' Justine asked.

'He's from Jordan,' Jonah replied, reluctantly.

'We need to go north if we are going to find him,' she said, 'towards the Berm.'

A pile of sardine tins stamped MAROC lying discarded in a dry river bed marked their passing. Zalik squatted down beside the tins and turned them over in his hands. 'They came this way,' he said, and then pointed to a nearby fold in the ground. 'There are mines there.'

They got back in the Land Cruiser and drove a few kilometres farther along the wadi, following tyre tracks in the soft sand.

At a waterhole in a place named Budib they encountered a nomad family with a herd of camels. A woman in black robes and her pigeon-chested son sat on a bank of sand, watching their camels gathered above a cluster-bomb canister that was being used as a water trough. Tennis-ball-shaped explosive sub-munitions were scattered across the floor and sides of the wadi.

Zalik spoke to the woman and her son for a while and Jonah stood listening. They had not seen any migrants for twenty-four hours. Jonah worried that the escape route might have closed.

'How long have you known this friend of yours?' Justine asked.

'We were at school together. His father knew mine.'

'What are you going to do when you find him?'

'Let's find him first,' he said.

'We are close to the Berm now,' Zalik said.

They parked the Land Cruiser at the base of a slope that was littered with hard black volcanic rock and set off up it on foot. They walked across a baking plateau. Zalik pointed to an escarpment that was about a kilometre away. It was the Berm. It was unmistakably man-made, a stark black line following the summit of the escarpment. Individual bunker positions and communications arrays were visible at intervals along the Berm. At the foot of the escarpment piles of stones at intervals marked the perimeter of the minefields.

They walked down a narrow gorge, and approached a line of sand dunes. Zalik showed them to a hollow that was dotted with thorn bushes.

'Wait here,' he said. He set off across the dunes.

The moonlight was blue and palpably cold. He sat in darkness, on the crest of the dune, waiting for the dawn. Zalik had vanished and Justine was huddled beside him in her sleeping bag. He glanced regularly at her, every few minutes, but his main focus was on the distant Berm, and the direction that Nor was expected to come from, if he came. Most likely it would not be this night. He listened to the sound of the wind rustling in the thorn bushes in the wadi below.

His life was such that he was often awake when others slept. He hadn't planned it that way. He hadn't envisaged it but that was how it had turned out.

Catching moles

September 1992–September 1993

He remembered his surprise on receiving the letter from Nor in which he told him that he had joined the British Army. He remembered thinking incredulously: what are you playing at? He remembered the subsequent drive up from the intelligence school at Chicksands to the military academy at Sandhurst. He had arrived after dark and found Nor lined up on show parade, the nightly punishment ritual in which those guilty of a transgression of discipline were forced to parade in their best uniform Blues in front of the college steps for inspection by a typically fearsome company sergeant major – Nor was on his fourteenth consecutive night of show parade. Jonah had hung back in the shadows at the edge of the square to watch.

'Show pockets clean,' the sergeant major had yelled, and the line of young officer cadets turned out their pockets and stood holding them between their forefingers and thumbs. The sergeant major had marched up the line with his pay stick tucked under his arm. He had clattered to a halt opposite Nor and bent almost double to inspect his pockets. After a few moments, he had straightened up, inhaled a lungful of breath and begun to yell.

'Sand! Sand!!! You've got sand in the seams of your pockets, Mr Din! I don't know where the fuck you think you are, you miserable little Ali Baba, but you're not in the fucking desert now! You're not buggering camels and gobbling sheep's eyes! You're not flying around on a fucking carpet! You're not wearing a tea towel on your head! Look around you. Can you see a shimmering oasis fringed with gently swaying palm trees? Can you?

A camel-hide tent filled with dancing virgins and burnished silver platters of Turkish Delight? Look at me, Mr Din, do I look like I jumped out of a lamp to grant you a fucking wish? I most certainly did not! You're at the Royal Military Academy Sandhurst, Mr Din. You're in Her Majesty's army, wearing Her Majesty's uniform. You are, without doubt, the most woeful example of a cadet that I have ever had the misfortune to attempt to turn into an officer, and if you don't want to spend a thousand and one nights on show parade you had better get your miserable house in order. Show again!'

And so Nor was sentenced to another night on show parade, and so it went on and on. The sergeant major had stalked off the parade square, leaving one of the colour sergeants to fall out the cadets.

Afterwards, Nor had walked back towards the accommodation blocks with his eyes downcast. Jonah had fallen into step beside him. Nor had looked up but did not appear surprised.

'This is your fault,' he had told Jonah. 'You have to get me out of here.'

It was close to midnight by the time he had turned off the dual carriageway, following the signs for the air force base. It was the spring of 1993, less than a week after Nor had been thrown out of the School of Infantry at Warminster, and dishonourably discharged from the army – less than a week since he had been set on a path that would eventually lead him to the North-West Frontier.

The entrance to the married quarters was a mile or so beyond the floodlit perimeter fence that surrounded the runway. He had almost missed it. People often did. There was a narrow lane with a dead-end sign, leading to an estate of red-brick 1950s housing tucked inconspicuously in a fold in the ground. He had driven between rows of identical houses on avenues named after distant battlefields, and turned into a cul-de-sac reserved for senior officers' families.

Monteith's cottage was located down a hard-core track that

ran alongside one of the houses and then branched off into a
stand of old oaks and overgrown rhododendrons. To get there
Jonah had to open a gate and drive noisily across a cattle grid.
It was typical of Monteith: of the military, but not in it.

It was said that the first true test of any fresh recruit to the
Afghan Guides was to find Monteith's cottage. There was even
a rumour that a kindly army padre had taken it upon himself
to gently inform luckless recruits that he found wandering the
mown lawns of the married quarters that their services were
no longer required and that they should return to unit. The
cottage was an old gatehouse protecting a long-neglected track
from the days before the air force base when the lands had
been part of a family estate. It was brick and wood, with a flint
tiled roof, mullioned windows and a carved oak doorway that
was bleached with age. It sat amidst dense vegetation surrounded
by a dogwood hedge that was clotted with clematis and honeysuckle.

Turning a corner in the track, he had been surprised to see
Flora's dented VW Beetle parked beside the hedge. As far as
he had been aware, Monteith and his daughter Flora were not
on speaking terms. Jonah hadn't seen her for more than six
months. He'd felt a sinking feeling. He'd said to himself, why
is everything so bloody complicated? He knew what his wife's
response, under different circumstances, might be: *Life* is *complicated.* But his wife hadn't been around to offer her particular
brand of wisdom and it wasn't a problem that he could go to
her with.

Jonah had pressed the bell. The door opened and they stood there
for a moment in the darkness. Then she'd reached up with her
hands resting on his chest and lightly brushed her lips against
his cheek. It was all he could do not to pick her up.

'Come this way,' she'd said, and stepped deftly out of reach.

He'd followed her down the hall, watching the sway of her hips
beneath her robe. In the kitchen, she had leant forward over the
porcelain sink, to stare out of the window facing the back garden.

He'd stood beside her for a moment and waited while his eyes grew accustomed to the darkness.

'He's been out there since the sun went down,' she had whispered. 'He hasn't moved an inch.'

Nor was squatting, balancing on the balls of his feet, in the centre of the lawn. His head was bowed and his hands were resting lightly on the grass. Jonah had felt his heart sink – Nor was losing it. It had taken him longer to locate Monteith. He was sitting with his back to a tree on the edge of the lawn.

'The whole county is infested,' Flora had said. 'You'd think there was plague.'

Jonah had struggled to make sense of the scene for a moment and then he recognised the irregular mounds that littered the lawn – *molehills*. He'd almost laughed out loud.

'He caught one last night,' she'd said. 'Just reached down and plucked it out of the hole. Amazing. Dad never taught me to catch moles.'

'Nor me,' Jonah had replied. 'In fact, the only advice that he gave me was to find a shadow and stand in it.'

'You're standing in a shadow now,' she'd said, without looking at him.

He'd shrugged in response. 'It's getting to be a habit.'

She had turned, and the little light there was shone on her face and her upturned nose and he'd wanted to reach out and kiss her.

'Stop it,' she'd whispered.

'I'm sorry.'

'What do you think you're playing at?'

'I don't know. I just, just . . .'

'Not that. *Him. Nor.* I thought you weren't supposed to get sentimental with your agents. Treat them like dirt and when you've finished with them throw them to the wolves – isn't that what your mentor, my precious father, says?'

'Nor's made for the work,' Jonah had protested.

'You've known him since you were a child,' Flora had said. 'He looks up to you. You should listen to him talking about you.

I've had to the last couple of days. He's practically in love with you. Are you ready to ditch him in some forgotten hellhole when it all goes wrong?'

'It won't come to that. We look after our people.'

'Who are you talking about? Who's this *we*? The Department? My father? Do you think he feels any loyalty to Nor? You know him better than that.'

Jonah had sighed. 'I need to talk to them.'

'You can go out there and join them. I'll leave you to it. Catch some moles. I'm going to bed.'

'Wait . . .' he said.

She had paused in the doorway to the hall, with her head down. 'What are you going to do, Jonah? Tell me that you love me, after all? You're married, remember.'

'Flora.'

She had seemed to shrink in the darkness as if it would provide camouflage.

'Flora.'

She had moaned softly. He had put his hand on her shoulder. She had shrugged it off and pulled away from him.

'And maybe there isn't a shred of loyalty in you either,' she'd hissed.

It was the summer of 1993 and a truck flying the black-and-white flag of the Hizb-ut-Tahrir led a crowd of about a thousand students down Brick Lane and along Whitechapel High Street past the East London mosque. Shopkeepers and local council tenants had spilled out on to the street to watch. Stewards in day-glo vests led the chanting: 'Jihad for Bosnia! Jihad for Palestine! Islam is the solution!'

A police van brought up the rear. The crowd was young and predominantly Bangladeshi. The boys wore baggy jeans and the women were veiled but shouted with a gusto equal to the men's.

Monteith had followed at a discreet distance with Jonah walking by his side. 'They don't look much like jihadis,' Jonah had observed.

'Hizb are the flame under the kettle,' Monteith had replied.

'It'll take time but eventually they'll reach boiling point.'

'Are they being watched?'

'You mean by someone other than us? MI5, for instance?' Monteith had snorted derisively. 'I told you when you joined that you would find it a lonely business working for me.'

Jonah remembered that on his first day as one of the Guides, Beech had told him that it was Monteith's curse to be an unfashionable prophet. A Cassandra. Monteith was widely derided across the intelligence community for conjuring threats out of thin air.

'Hizb are currently banned from preaching in the local mosques. But that's not going to stop them. The Hizb is organic. They don't need offices, mosques or schools. They have a cell structure and they spread like a cancer, by mutating and replicating. Each cell, or *halaqah*, has about five members. They meet once a week and are commanded by a *mushrif*, or teacher. They go out and recruit and break off to form new cells.'

At the front of the march, a young man had climbed the tailgate of the truck and was shouting into a megaphone: 'Brothers, we are bringing jihad to the streets of the capital of the *kuffar*, the unbelievers.'

The crowd cheered.

'A year ago nobody was using the word jihad. Hizb brought it here.'

'What do they want?'

'The Hizb? Destroy the West and its puppet regimes in the Muslim lands. A global Muslim nation. More immediately they are looking for volunteers to be trained overseas and sent back here to form the nucleus of a future uprising. Talk of the devil, look there. Your two o'clock. There he is.'

An older man with a limp was passing a dry cleaner's shop window, shadowing the crowd.

'His name is Farid. He's Pakistani,' Monteith had explained, 'a Pashtun from Quetta. He lost the leg to a Soviet mine in Afghanistan in 1984. He's over here recruiting for the training camps. He's also Pakistani intelligence, ISI through and through.'

As if on cue, Nor had climbed on to the truck and snatched

the megaphone. He had recently been thrown out of the army on a trumped-up charge of possessing drugs – but in reality, he was Monteith's latest recruit in the war on extremism, fresh from several months' training at the intelligence school at Chicksands. He'd shouted: 'Crusader, invader! Saladin is coming back!' A cheer went up from the crowd and Nor had rewarded them with his most ebullient grin. He'd started a new chant, 'USA! USA! You will pay!'

The older man had been watching Nor intently.

'Do you think Nor's ready?'

'He's ready,' Monteith said. 'Now it's up to the Pakistanis.'

Jonah kissed Flora beneath a riot of honeysuckle in Monteith's garden at the end of that summer. They had kissed with a ferocity born of two years of frustration and longing.

Monteith was having a party to celebrate Nor's successful penetration of the Hizb-ut-Tahrir. They were all there: Nor, Beech, Lennard, Alex and their wives, partners and children. Flora had rigged fairy lights in the garden. Even Monteith had been in a jovial mood.

It was after dark and they had found each other on one of the pathways through the lush foliage that almost swallowed the house, and Flora had taken him by the hand and led him farther into the shadows. They had been silhouettes in the darkness, reaching for each other, her hands on his shoulder and then cupping his face.

Afterwards, she had slipped out of his arms and gone back to join the party. He followed more slowly. He remembered his wife looking up at him as he approached with a question in her eyes. But he was a professional deceiver. A spinner of lies. Absent-mindedly he'd run his fingers through her hair.

A couple of weeks later Nor had left for Bosnia with an aid convoy. He'd been in Split, waiting for permission to cross the border, when he was approached by a Pakistani ISI agent and encouraged to travel to Pakistan. At the beginning of summer he had arrived at the HUM offices in Lahore and after a few days in the city had been sent up to Miram Shah, the dusty town close to Afghanistan that was used as a staging post for recruits heading to the training camps around Khost.

And so Nor's career as a double agent in the pay of both the Pakistani ISI and the British intelligence services began.

A loyal spy

Justine woke, her large eyes blinking uncertainly. She wriggled in the bag and fought to get an arm clear. She ran her fingers through her hair, shaking the sand out.

'Have you been awake all night?' she asked.

He shrugged. 'I've been thinking.'

'About your friend?'

He did not answer.

'You must be freezing,' she said.

It was true, he was cold.

'Come here,' she said, and partially unzipped the sleeping bag. She worked her body close to his. He put an arm around her shoulders and she rested her head against his chest, her hair against his chin.

The dawn was coming. With his binoculars he scanned the horizon. There was no sign of Zalik or of Nor. He sensed through his arm the shiver of her body. He felt a chasm inside himself and a corresponding emptiness in her.

'It's bloody cold,' she mumbled.

He surprised himself by brushing aside a strand of her hair and kissing the nape of her neck. She looked up at him and he cupped her face in his hands and her eyes did not close. They kissed ardently.

She pulled down the zipper farther. He slipped in, pushing his boots against the bag's stitching, and heaved his weight against her. She reached behind him and pulled up as much of the zip as she could. He kissed her again. He ran his hands under her blouse. Her nipples were as hard as stones against the rough palms of his hands. She pushed down her jeans and he slid his hands downward and pressed his fingers between the cleft in her legs, parting the folds of flesh, hooking a finger inside her. She shifted against him and moaned softly. He kissed her neck, her nipples and the lobes of her ears. He unbuttoned himself. She kicked out of a trouser leg, raised one thigh and, reaching down, steered him inside her. He gasped. They were two patches of heat in the expanse of night. He plunged into her and he felt the zipper tear against the small of his back.

They were filled with wildness and abandon. She came quickly, with her eyes wide open. He took longer, and when he finally came, rearing above her, it felt as if some part of him had torn inside.

Afterwards, they drank from his bottle of duty-free. Then he crawled out of the bag and did up his buttons, refeeding his belt through the loops. They did not speak again. He assumed that she was embarrassed or even frightened. He had been told once that the expression on his face when he was coming was terrifying.

He lifted the binoculars and scanned the horizon.

Zalik returned soon after, appearing soundlessly from behind a nearby acacia tree. He squatted on the sand beside them. Jonah wondered whether he'd been watching them. Justine wouldn't look at him.

'Two men crossed the Berm last night,' Zalik said. 'They passed east of here. One of them is injured.'

'Are you sure there were two?' Jonah asked.

Zalik did not reply.

After a pause, Jonah asked, 'Can you take us to them?'

Zalik stood up and, without answering, started walking back towards the car. Justine hurriedly bundled up the sleeping bag and stuffed it into her bag. They followed.

He was sitting slumped in the shadows of a cave. One of his legs was bent under him so that he appeared to be kneeling. The other was outstretched but ended just below the knee in a bloody stump. They had followed the trail of blood up the rocky slope from the wadi floor. For a moment, standing at the mouth of the cave, Jonah felt a momentary sense of relief that events had been taken out of his hands, but it was soon followed by shame and a plunging sense of desolation. This was not the way for it to end.

Beside him, Zalik flicked on the torch. The cave was decorated with ancient pigment: hundreds of handprints pressed into the walls and roof by long-forgotten hunters. He wondered whether it represented some kind of warning. Kneeling beside the dead man, Jonah touched his face. His skin was still warm. His eyes were open. It was not Nor. Jonah breathed deeply from his abdomen and, despite everything, gave brief thanks. He glanced up at Zalik, who was standing, watching him. 'The other one?' he asked.

Zalik shrugged.

They headed back down through the piles of rock to where Justine was waiting. Turning a corner in the narrow wadi bottom, they found her dancing barefoot on the sand, her hips swaying to some interior rhythm, with a bottle of vodka in one hand and a cigarette in the other; Nor was sitting cross-legged on the boulder beside her with his head covered by a black turban. They were smiling. Seeing them together, with their smiles connecting, Jonah felt a sudden stab of what could only be described as jealousy.

'He says that you're the devil and that you tried to take away his God, Jonah,' Justine announced. She pirouetted, and shook her bottom at him as she offered the bottle to Nor, who declined graciously. 'He also says that he was your best student. He says that you taught him everything he knows.'

All Jonah could think of was that the old Nor would have accepted the bottle, the old Nor had a passion for vodka. The old Nor didn't have a God to appease.

'You took your time, Sensei,' Nor teased.

'Who's your friend in the cave?' Jonah asked, stonily.

Nor's mouth narrowed to a pout. He didn't want the mood broken. 'A fellow traveller. One less fortunate.'

'Who was he?' Jonah demanded furiously.

'A Saudi. He was rendered out of Kandahar on the same flight as I was. Does that satisfy you?' With that Nor sprang down off the rock. He was still pale and far too thin but his face was flushed with excitement. They shook hands and then, to Jonah's surprise, Nor embraced him. In all the time they had known each other Nor had never once embraced him. Afterwards, they stood with Nor's hands grasping Jonah's upper arms. 'You should be happy. You were going to have to kill him anyway, to maintain my cover.' Then he leant forward and whispered in Jonah's ear, 'Unless of course it was me you were planning to kill?'

'I'm here to make sure you're OK,' Jonah replied, stiffly. Not for the first time he wondered how it was that Nor saw through him so easily.

'I'm OK,' Nor told him, serious for a moment. 'Now where are we going?'

'South,' Jonah told him. 'People are waiting for you.'

Nor reached out and took Justine by the hand. 'So show me to my next mission,' he said, and he tightened his grip on Justine's hand as he grinned at Jonah. 'It's the beginning of a great adventure.'

They camped on the plain, beside a jumble of volcanic boulders close to the Mauritanian border. While Zalik made tea, and Justine carried a bucket of water into the thorn bushes to wash, Jonah and Nor climbed the rocks. They sat side by side on the summit and watched as the red orb of the sun sunk below the western horizon. Jonah glanced sidelong at Nor, who had his eyes closed and his chin raised and appeared to be speaking under his breath. He wondered whether Nor was praying. He did not know what to make of this new, serious-minded Nor. He couldn't help but remember Sierra Leone, the moonlight on the nicked edge of a raised machete, his arms outstretched and Nor squatting over him, his words venomously spoken: *fight and slay the pagans wherever ye find them*. He did not know whether the piety disguised a murderous fanaticism. Carefully, Jonah slid his Gerber blade out of its sheath and rested it against his thigh, so that it was hidden from view, with his hand resting on the moulded plastic grip.

Eventually Nor opened his eyes, and finding Jonah staring at him, smiled gently.

'How are you?' Jonah asked.

'I wouldn't recommend the Dark Prison, even for a long weekend.'

'They couldn't just release you,' Jonah explained patiently – agent to joe – reflecting on how easy it would be to slip back into the old roles. 'It was necessary to maintain your cover.'

Nor rolled his eyes and lit a cigarette. 'You never could tell when I was teasing you. Have you really stopped smoking?'

'Yes.' It was always Jonah's role to be the ham-fisted one. Nor had an unerring capacity to make him feel like the bluntest of instruments.

'I'm impressed. How's Monteith?'

'Worried about what you might tell the Americans,' Jonah replied, tightening his grip on the knife. His mouth was dry and he felt a plunging sensation in the pit of his stomach.

'I bet he is. And I expect he's not the only one. How's Alex?'

'Alex has made a new life for himself in risk consultancy and he's feeling very protective of it.'

'Protective enough to have me silenced?'

There was a pause. Jonah chose his words carefully. 'What do you think?'

Nor hung his head and nodded as if to acknowledge the direction in which they were heading. 'And the others? What about Lennard?'

'He's in a monastery in Burma. He has a new and unpronounceable name. I don't suppose he cares.'

'And Beech?'

'Beech is a policeman on a small Hebridean island off the west coast of Scotland. He married Flora a couple of years ago.'

Nor looked up sharply. 'Beech married Flora Monteith?

'Yes.'

'You should have married Flora.'

Jonah shrugged. 'It didn't work out that way. She's pregnant, I think.'

'I'm sorry.'

'I'm not,' he lied.

Jonah had gone in search of Flora right after his marriage broke up. Of course he had. It was the summer of '99 and she was living in a flat near the tube station in Ladbroke Grove. He'd buzzed the entryphone of her flat at 2 a.m. after spending several sleepless hours pounding the streets rehearsing what he wanted to say. 'What are you doing here?' she'd asked, standing in the doorway, once he'd made his way up the stairs.

'You know why I'm here,' he'd said.

'Stop right there,' she'd told him, and then after a pause, in a soft voice, she'd dropped her bombshell. 'I'm getting married.'

He remembered being stunned. It had seemed so unfair. He'd married the wrong person and now he'd meant to put it right. How it always should have been. How could he be thwarted now? It was finally possible. Where was the justice in that?

'I didn't know,' he'd said.

'You will soon. You're the best man. I'm marrying Beech.'

And he hadn't known what to say.

'He's here if you want to speak to him,' she'd told him.

He'd staggered back down the stairs.

A couple of months later, he had stood beside Beech at the altar, in a morning suit that was bursting at the seams, with the ring tightly clenched in his oversized hands. And when the time had come for the priest to ask whether there were any objectors present, he had not said a word. What right did he have? He'd screwed up one marriage already. He had wanted to punch his hand through a wall.

Jonah and Nor sat side by side on the rock and the desert stretched away in all directions.

'And you?' Nor asked, staring at his feet. 'Do you care?'

'You were my joe and you betrayed me,' Jonah said, the fury there in the knot of his shoulders and in the grip of his hand on the knife.

'Did I?'

'You lied to me. As a result, we executed a CIA agent. For Christ's sake, the guy had a wife and two kids.'

'Are you going to kill me, then?' Nor asked.

There was a pause.

'I haven't decided,' Jonah replied, carefully.

Nor stubbed out his cigarette. 'I don't know whether you remember this, but you once offered me a definition of friendship, of true friendship. It was at Chicksands, at the intelligence school, when you were turning me into a spy. You told me that a true friend is someone who you could rely on to help you bury a body with no questions asked.'

'I remember.'

'Well. Kiernan had to die.'

'Why did he have to die?'

Nor looked across at him. 'He was poking his nose in where it wasn't welcome.'

'What does that mean?'

'It's best if you don't know.'

'Best?'

'Safer for you.'

'You're going to have to do better than that,' Jonah told him.

'Besides, you should be glad it's turned out so well. Killing Kiernan was an easy way to prove that my oath, my *bayyat*, meant something. It gave me instant credibility. It infiltrated me inside the upper echelons of al-Qaeda.'

Jonah was incredulous. 'What the hell are you talking about?'

'Nobody has got as close to Bin Laden as I have.'

'I can't believe I'm hearing this. You must be fucking crazy. We sacked you in '96.'

'And all this time I've been working for you, inching myself closer every day.'

'Why should I believe that?' Jonah asked softly.

'Because you want to,' Nor replied, 'because I'm your oldest friend and because I make you feel guilty.'

'I don't know who you are any more.'

'Come off it, Jonah. You never had a clue who I was or what I believed and you never bothered to find out. You were too busy playing the elder brother and protector and then, of course, your best role, the one you were meant for, agent and handler.'

'You were a willing volunteer.'

'Sure I was. I fell for it. All that patriotic duty shit. Playing the secret agent. I fell for it hook, line and sinker. You made me a traitor to my own race.'

'And what are you now?'

'I'm just the same as I always was. A loyal spy.'

'But who's loyal spy? Tell me why Kiernan had to die.'

Nor shook his head, and smiled wryly. 'You're not going to kill me, are you?'

'I couldn't,' replied Jonah. It was true. The anger had abated. He had decided that whatever happened would happen. He'd take the consequences. He thought: *You remind me too much of myself to kill you.* But of course there was a time, in Afghanistan back in 1999, when he thought he had.

The moon had risen but the sun had not yet fully set. They seemed to have fallen between times – an interstice, a truce. Below them Justine emerged from a thorn-bush-filled wadi wearing a sarong. Her hair hung in wet ringlets on her shoulders. She headed back to the fire that Zalik had built beside the Land Cruiser. Jonah would have liked to go back down to her but he guessed that the intimacy of the night before was unlikely to be repeated.

'Do you see much of your daughter?' Nor asked, matter-of-factly.

'When I can,' he replied. Despite his ex-wife's antagonism towards him she had continued to allow him to spend time with Esme when he was given leave. He supposed that he should be thankful for that.

'What are you going to tell Monteith?'

'The truth, that when it came down to it, we're too alike, you and I. I don't have it in me to kill you.'

'Will that satisfy him?'

'I doubt it. But there's not much he can do about it. After tomorrow you'll be an American asset, beyond his reach.'

'I won't tell them about Kiernan,' Nor said. 'Why should I? I don't want to end up back in the Dark Prison, any more than you do. Tell Monteith that your secret is safe with me.'

At first it appeared to be a trick of the dissolving horizon. They had been driving for what seemed like hours across the remnants of a vast and ancient lake, their tyres leaving tracks in the salt crust behind them. On Jonah's GPS the Land Cruiser's progress drew a line across an empty screen.

Then it crystallised out of the haze: a burnished Land Rover, bright as molten glass, driving towards them. Zalik stopped the engine and squinted over the steering wheel at the approaching vehicle as they freewheeled to a halt.

The Land Rover stopped alongside them.

A man got out. It was Pakravan, the Persian-American with the boxer's flattened nose. He was wearing the beard and shaven upper lip of a true believer. He walked over to the Land Cruiser and leant in the window, resting on his beefy forearms.

'Welcome to Eschatos,' he said.

A reverse rendition

February–June 2002

They knew in London that he'd failed to kill Nor as instructed long before he landed at Heathrow. There was a text message from Alex waiting for him when he switched on his phone at baggage reclaim, a command – *Footbridge at Vauxhall Bus Station. Now.*

It was time to face the consequences. He took the underground, travelling on the Piccadilly Line to Green Park and then on the Victoria line south to Vauxhall. He emerged from the underground and spotted the metal footbridge that spanned the roundabout. Alex was standing at the centre of it, leaning on the railings.

'Smile,' Alex greeted him, mirthlessly. 'You're on *Candid Camera.*' He nodded in the direction of the MI6 building. 'You've got to hand it to Terry Farrell. I mean, the man was not just an architect, he was a comic genius. Who would have thought of hiding our most secretive government offices inside a massive Inca pyramid on the banks of the most famous river in England? They were a bloodthirsty lot, the ancient Incas. And Terry Farrell was Maggie Thatcher's favourite architect. Can you believe that they've written me a cheque and asked me to evaluate the threat? I was like, are you serious? Between you and me, I'd have done it for Smarties.' He lit a cigarette. 'Of course, the IRA had a pop. They fired an RPG from Vauxhall Park. There, just the other side of the railway line. It didn't do any damage to speak of. Bollocks, really . . .' Something caught his eye and he pointed down the line of railway arches. 'Look down towards Albert

Embankment, our side of the road, beyond the gay spa and the Portuguese deli. What do you see?'

The bonnet of a police Range Rover was just visible poking out from under one of the arches.

'The Director of Special Forces arrives in an unmarked forest-green Land Rover every Thursday morning with an armed police escort who wait outside for him. He leaves a couple of hours later. I've had a rotation of my people, collecting make, model and registration numbers of vehicles going in and out. We're building a map. You're probably wondering why we haven't been spotted. I'll tell you why. There's a large transient population around here. Winos and junkies. So despite all the surveillance cameras – and as you've no doubt already clocked, there are plenty of them – it's still difficult to keep track of individuals over an extended period.'

'That's fascinating,' Jonah droned, attempting to convey his wish for Alex to get to the point.

'It's not funny, mate. Well, it is, actually. There are a couple of grocer's shops not five minutes from here in Oval that will sell you Tamil Tiger training videos under the counter. I've been watching them. The assault on Jaffna is particularly instructive: swarms of suicide bombers – men, women and children – all of them sprinting like fuck straight at enemy lines. They completely overwhelmed the Sri Lankan army and took the peninsula. You know the Tigers invented the suicide bomber?'

'Is that how you'd do it?' Jonah asked, caving in, as he usually did.

'They're certainly vulnerable,' Alex said, thoughtfully. 'Crisps and soda pops would be their downfall. Twice a week, regular as clockwork, you've got loaded vans delivering pallets of soft drinks and confectionery for the vending machines. You hijack one of those, pack it with explosives and drive it in. You kidnap the driver's family, threaten his wife and kids with electric drills, sure enough he'll get the gate opened. You wouldn't need to get as far as the underground car park, the chicane at the entrance would do. Detonate it and then swarm the place with jihadis with shaped charges. You make your own access. You could send a bulldozer in after the truck to mount the ramps and get access to the foundations in the car park, that's if you wanted to bring the whole building down. But basically you're looking for the server. Knock that out and England's flying blind. All the secrets up in smoke. Of course, to spread the confusion, you could set off secondary devices at the police station two doors down opposite the Esso garage, Fire Brigade HQ up by Lambeth Bridge and behind us at Cobalt Square.'

'You know, you have every teenage boy's fantasy job?'

Alex grinned expansively. 'Of course I do.' The grin disappeared just as suddenly. 'Which is why I take personal fucking affront when I learn that somebody, who clearly hasn't been listening, fails to perform a simple task as instructed and as a result puts all of this in jeopardy. What happened?'

There wasn't much point in a lengthy explanation. 'I couldn't do it.'

'That doesn't cut much ice with Fisher-King.'

'Is that who you are answering to now?' Jonah asked.

'Fisher-King is who we are all answerable to: you, me, Monteith.'

'What do you want?' Jonah demanded.

'Hear me and believe what I say. I have been given unequivocal direction. If Nor fucks up, this country will no longer be safe for you. Witnesses will come forward and be offered immunity from prosecution in return for testimony that you conspired to kidnap your wife's lover. Do you understand?'

Jonah thought of his one-bedroom flat in London and his bolt-hole in Edinburgh that the Department might or might not know about – the meagre threads of his life. Ever since the Department had conspired to organise the kidnap of his wife's lover and frame him for it, he had been aware that, one day, he might be forced to leave the country or face the prospect of disgrace and a lengthy prison sentence.

'I understand,' he said.

'Come on,' Alex said. 'Fisher-King wants to speak to you.' He strode off along the footbridge.

★

They fell into step with Fisher-King, heading north on Albert Embankment towards Lambeth Bridge.

'He doesn't want you in the building,' Alex had explained as they hurried to catch up with him. 'He'll brief you on the way to his weekly meet with Five.'

Fisher-King glanced at Jonah briefly and returned his attention to the pavement ahead. He wore a pinstriped suit, knee-length cashmere coat, silk scarf, gleaming handmade shoes. As ever he looked immaculate.

'You have jeopardised us all.'

Jonah waited. This wasn't going to be a dressing-down; that wasn't the way Fisher-King operated. That was what Alex was for.

'Winthrop has asked for you again,' Fisher-King informed him. 'Nor's your joe. Winthrop wants you to run him again.'

'Why?'

'I think his idea is to put Nor back inside al-Qaeda.'

'That's insane,' Jonah protested. 'How could we ever rely on anything that Nor told us? How would we know he was on our side?'

'Winthrop has Vice President Cheney's ear. That has allowed him to bypass the usual channels. He's a force unto himself.'

'You can't agree to this,' Jonah told him.

'I don't believe that you have left us with much choice.' Fisher-King came to a sudden halt and turned on Jonah. 'You need to control this. You need to control Nor.' He looked at his watch. 'I'm late.'

He strode away.

Jonah glanced back, down the length of the nave towards the church doors, and saw Monteith approaching with his head bowed. Droplets of rain covered the shoulders of his Barbour jacket and the brim of the hat that he clutched to his chest.

Monteith sat in a pew beside him. He looked up at the main altar and nodded in respectful acknowledgement. His gaze returned to Jonah, and he looked directly into his eyes.

'Nor is being held at a camp in the Nevada desert, under the auspices of a CIA programme named Anabasis,' Monteith said. 'It's a covert operation to equip and deploy Iraqi defectors, mostly former Iraqi army, to destabilise Saddam's regime. That's the cover. I think that Eschatos is Winthrop's creation, a programme hidden within a programme, to shield it from congressional oversight. And that's about all I know.'

'Winthrop wants me in Nevada?'

'Yes.'

'And you want me to go?'

'It doesn't matter what I want. Fisher-King is calling the shots. I've been given my orders. So have you. When the Americans say jump, you jump. They'll let you know when they need you.'

'And until then?'

'Lie low. Stay out of trouble.'

It was still dark when Jonah arrived at Prestwick Airport, about forty miles west of Glasgow. Several months had passed since his return from the Sahara, months of kicking his heels at Dreghorn Barracks in Edinburgh, but then, finally, in June 2002, the summons came and he was on his way to Nevada.

His transport across the Atlantic was a Gulfstream V on the return leg of a rendition. As it fuelled, in a remote corner near the freight terminals, he stood on the grass beside the tarmac, rubbing the back of his neck in the rain. There was no one else to be seen. The only marking on the Gulfstream was the company name on the tail – AVIATION INTERNATIONAL SERVICES.

When fuelling was complete he was invited on board. Jonah sat in a window seat, buckled up and stared out at the parking apron.

Presently, the Gulfstream trundled out on to the runway. Rain swept the window pane beside him, the drops driven diagonally by the wind. Inside the plane it smelled of disinfectant and some of the stains on the upholstery may have been blood and shit. There were boxes of adult nappies stacked at the back of the plane. Staring around him, Jonah felt something like a moral objection. But he knew that in the post-9/11 world objections like these had been overridden. It seemed that anything was permitted in the name of homeland security.

The plane's crew were deeply suntanned and almost indistinguishable. They smiled constantly and they had an eye-glazed gonzo look.

'This is a very strange war,' he told the loadmaster, who offered him orange juice in a paper cup.

'Yes, it's weird,' the man acknowledged, 'we can't even talk about it.'

Nothing could be talked about. Jonah was on his way to Eschatos, which was hidden inside Anabasis. On his way to his oldest friend, who was also his bitterest enemy.

Greeks, diamondbacks, scorpions

The Anabasis camp was located on a derelict air force base at an Energy Department nuclear test site in the Nevada desert. Jonah was met at McCarran Airport in Las Vegas by Pakravan, who drove him in air-conditioned silence, sixty miles across a baking salt pan, to the camp.

'We don't usually welcome outsiders here,' Pakravan told him, after half an hour or so.

'I'm not here to get in your way,' Jonah told him.

'Some people criticise us as warmongers,' Pakravan said pointedly. 'That's always the way with those who want to create freedom and a better life.'

As they approached the outskirts of the camp, they drove past a squad of men on an assault course. Black stick-like figures in the shimmering heat haze. Pakravan told him that they were Iraqis and that they called themselves Scorpions 77 Alpha, after a former Special Forces unit disbanded by Saddam Hussein. 'As soon as we get the green light, they're going in behind enemy lines.'

They drove across the base, past abandoned hangars and tarpaper shacks, to its farthest reaches. Pakravan parked beside a stack of sea containers. He got out of the car and pointed across the desert in the direction of a pile of boulders, at a blazing point of light.

'He's over there,' Pakravan told him. He got back in the car and drove off.

At first, Jonah thought it was a huge mirror, solar panels perhaps, but as he approached he saw that it was a classic

Airstream – a silver-skinned, bullet-shaped trailer. There was a cardboard sign with BACK TO BAGHDAD written above the door and a young Arab sitting, smoking a cigarette, on the steps. He had dark eyes and hair, the lush curls framing his face, and an adolescent's slim hips. Nor's taste, Jonah thought.

'Is Nor inside?' he asked.

The young man shook his head. Beside the trailer there was a washing line with a length of what looked like snakeskin pegged to it. The skin was marked with a diamond pattern and it was as long as Jonah was tall.

'Where is he?' Jonah asked.

The young man pointed to a nearby trail. Jonah held his hand up to shield his eyes from the sun and squinted in the direction that the young man was pointing. The trail crossed an empty salt pan, shining white under the sun. It seemed to be heading in the direction of a distant mesa.

It took him half an hour to cross the salt pan. From there he made his way up a volcanic slope and followed the crest of a ridge north-west. The back of his shirt was soaked in sweat. Twice he saw drags – the S-shaped tracks left by snakes in the sand. And once a hairball, the remains of a rodent. At the end of the ridge was a rockslide, a jumble of rocks and shadowy spaces, with the trail leading down. Snake country. Nor was sitting among the rocks, about halfway down, with a garden pump sprayer, an axe and a six-foot length of cane by his side. He looked up as Jonah topped the rockslide.

Jonah paused for a moment and then, when Nor inclined his head in invitation, eased himself down through the rocks towards him.

Nor passed him the pump sprayer; from the smell it was full of petrol. 'You took your time,' he whispered. He lifted the cane. There was a fish hook attached to the end of it. He nodded towards the hole beside him. 'Give it a good dose.'

With the tank in his left hand and the sprayer in his right and several loops of hose in between, Jonah leant forward and inserted the nozzle in the hole. He pumped the tank several times. The hole filled with the smell of petrol.

'Out the way,' Nor hissed. Jonah scrambled backwards.

Swiftly, Nor poked the cane in the hole. A flick of the wrist, and then the rattlesnake was out of its den, taut as a spring on the end of the hook. Nor brought it crashing down on a rock, scooped up the axe and decapitated it.

They sat back and watched as the body writhed and the mouth opened and closed on the severed head. '*There are in Medina "Jinns" who have accepted Islam, so when you see any one of them, pronounce a warning to it for three days, and if they appear before you after that, then kill it for that is a devil*,' Nor said, quoting from the Hadiths. 'It's a western diamondback. Good eating. Better than MREs – Meals Rejected by Ethiopians – which are about the only other food available here. Have you met the neighbours?'

'You mean the Iraqis?' Jonah asked.

'Sure. Are they still clambering all over their play park?'

'You've been making friends,' Jonah observed, wryly.

'Why should I make friends?'

'It could save your life.'

'Please don't insult my intelligence.'

The snake was finally still and Nor looped it around his neck. He picked up the cane and the axe, leaving Jonah to follow with the pump sprayer. They hiked back along the ridge and down the slope on to the salt pan.

'What do you know about Xenophon?' asked Nor.

Jonah shrugged. 'It's all Greek to me.'

'Ha ha. You're funny, but not as funny as these chimps trying to pass off a disaster as a victory. Anabasis! I studied Greek, remember. At that school that we went to, which for some inexplicable reason you seemed to love.'

'I hated it too.'

'Don't give me that. You loved it. You're a fucking slave to institutions. Altar boy, soldier, spy – you'll always belong to some club or other.'

'And you'll always be getting thrown out of them,' Jonah
retorted.

Nor grinned. 'Very good.'

'You were giving me a lesson in Greek,' Jonah told him.

'Sure. I was giving you the benefit of my insight and wisdom.
I'll tell you about Anabasis. *Anabasis* is a book written by
Xenophon. It tells the story of the invasion of Persia in 400 BC
by a force of ten thousand Greek mercenaries led by Cyrus the
Younger. The Greeks won the first battle, at a place called Cunaxa.
So far so good. But what no one here seems to have taken on
board is that Cyrus died on the battlefield. The expedition
collapsed. The Greeks had to fight all the way back to the Black
Sea. They were swallowed by the sand.'

'So they score low in ancient Greek. What about Eschatos?'

'That's just scary end-of-the-world shit. Wait until you meet
Pastor Bob. These guys have rebuilding Solomon's temple on
their agenda.'

'What do they want you to do?'

'Me? Deep penetration job.'

'In Iraq?'

'Of course in Iraq. We're all going to Iraq: armies, agents, sabo-
teurs – *the whole shebang*. Saddam is history.' He put on an accent,
in mockery of Pakravan, and said: 'The president has said so,
and he's a man of his word.'

Nor cooked the snake on a propane gas stove, under the camouflage net strung alongside the Airstream. First he skinned it and
then stripped out the intestine. He sliced it into roundels, which
he flash-fried in a skillet with a splash of tequila and some chilli
flakes. He was drinking again, helping himself to the tequila as
he cooked.

'I've given up on Islam for a while,' he told Jonah. 'I couldn't
keep up with the fury.'

Jonah sat on a breeze block with a beer in his hand. He could
see the lights of the Iraqi camp on the far side of the base.

'Why do they want you to go to Iraq?'

'They want access to the diamonds and their shadowy controller.'

'The diamonds are in Iraq?'

'If we were separated, our instructions as carriers were to make our way to the Ansar al-Islam enclave in Kurdistan.'

Jonah considered this information. Ansar al-Islam was a Wahhabi Sunni group, from the Kurdish-controlled northern provinces of Iraq near the Iranian border, an area that was beyond Saddam's reach. He'd read intelligence reports which suggested that Ansar al-Islam had offered safe haven to al-Qaeda in the wake of the 11 September attacks. It seemed believable that al-Qaeda might move the diamonds there.

'And what are your orders?'

'You know. The usual shit: listen and observe, identify conspirators.'

'Who will you report to?'

'You.'

'Me?'

'And you'll report to your American friend Winthrop,' Nor replied. 'Now there's a man of vision and daring. So help me God, if I have to listen to any more of his shit . . .'

'And if I report to Winthrop that you're a lying sack of shit who is in all likelihood working for al-Qaeda?'

'Nice turn of phrase,' Nor replied, 'but I wouldn't advise it. I mean, you wouldn't want me to feel obliged to tell him about Kiernan, would you? How do you think that would go down in London?'

Just before they ate, the young Arab who had been waiting on the steps of the Airstream earlier reappeared with a bag of coffee. His name was Mohammed and he was a Sunni, from Fallujah. His father had been a brigadier in the Iraqi army but had defected to the West and settled in Detroit.

They ate the snake off paper plates. It tasted remarkably like chicken, as Nor had said it would. Then they drank coffee.

'Winthrop is coming tomorrow with an entourage,' Nor told

Jonah, 'his fussy Jews and his overweight pastor. You should go and greet him.'

'You know I was never an altar boy,' Jonah told him.

'Are you sure? I was counting on your experience to assist me tomorrow.'

'What are you talking about?'

'You'll see.'

Eschatos

June 2002–February 2003

Winthrop arrived by helicopter in the mid-afternoon heat, wearing pressed chinos, tasselled loafers and a button-down blue Oxford shirt. He ran out from under the rotor's downwash into the fierce Nevadan sunlight with a crowd-pleaser's easy smile, and insisted on shaking the hand of every one of the fifty or so Iraqis lined up on parade to meet him.

At Winthrop's heels were two Pentagon policy warriors: Jabotinsky and Scholem – nicknamed by Nor *the Murids*, the Arabic word for disciple. They emerged squinting from the helicopter as if unused to sunlight. After the Murids, a balding, red-faced man in a linen suit eased himself out of the helicopter. He was bearded and the hair of his whiskers and moustache outlined the pinkness and fleshiness of his lips. Jonah guessed that he was Winthrop's pastor.

As soon as Winthrop was done pressing flesh, Pakravan led them across the parade square and into a nearby hangar.

'There are nearly two hundred sovereign states in the world,' Winthrop told them. They were assembled on a half-dozen plastic chairs. Winthrop had loosened his tie and rolled up his sleeves. He strutted across the hangar like a politician on a stage. 'Most are unstable, veering between democracy and tyranny. Many are riddled with corruption and dominated by organised crime. Whole regions of the world – much of Africa, southern Asia, Russia, the Balkans and the Caucasus, and parts of South America – are strewn with corroded or failed states. Obliviously, we imagined that we were immune to the fallout from such chaos. We were not and we are not. We had our eyes closed. We didn't see it coming. We got hit by a truck.'

'Amen,' growled Pastor Bob, who'd scorned a chair and was standing with his thumbs hooked in the belt loops of his crumpled linen trousers.

'Gentlemen, we can no longer turn a blind eye to what is going on in distant lands,' Winthrop continued. 'We have entered a new era in history, a time of consequences. And it has fallen upon us, a chosen few, to bear the ark of the liberties of the world. An obligation rests upon us, not to go back on those that sacrificed their lives in the Twin Towers and in the Pentagon, but to see this thing through, to see it through to the end and make good on their sacrifice. Nothing less than the liberation and salvation of the world depends on it.'

Jonah was watching Nor out of the corner of his eye. He seemed to be studying the giant display that spread across several free-standing partitions, and served as Winthrop's backdrop. It was known as the spiderweb, and it was the hyperactive nephew of Monteith's collage. Nor had told him that Jabotinsky and Scholem had brought it down from DC, panel by panel, over several weeks, after they'd been stripped of their Pentagon security clearance. The rumour was that the CIA and the FBI had mounted a concerted operation to have them thrown out of the Pentagon and they'd been forced to proceed covertly here in Nevada. Which didn't mean to say that they weren't listened to back in the Pentagon; Scholem liked to say how Deputy Defense Secretary Wolfowitz had once spent forty-five minutes in front of the display. It was a mass of linkages and associations, spaghetti lines in marker pen and cotton thread. It depicted the 9/11 attacks as a multi-headed conspiracy carried out by al-Qaeda but assisted by Hezbollah, financed by the Saudis and sponsored by Saddam. It cast the Salman Pak training facility south of Baghdad as the nexus of an international family of terrorist organisations, including Abu Nidal, Hamas, Ansar al-Islam and Jund al-Sham. The spaghetti lines from Abu Nidal led to Lebanon and from there to al-Qaeda in Afghanistan. It showed an expressway from Tora Bora in Afghanistan to the Ansar al-Islam enclave in northern Iraq. It was, in Jonah's view, a dangerous exercise in wishful thinking. Abu Nidal was defunct. Ansar al-Islam was bitterly opposed to Saddam's Baathist regime. And the idea that Hezbollah Shiites were in league with Saudi Sunnis was utterly nonsensical.

'The Eschatos programme was established specifically in the face of new and apocalyptic threats,' Winthrop explained. 'Our mandate is to identify and infiltrate enemy structures, and to act pre-emptively to interdict them. We're a red team unit, a black ops team. Our first job is to know our enemy, to understand his means and his methods.'

He gestured to Jabotinsky, who took up the baton. He sprang out of his seat and strode back and forth in front of the spider-web brandishing an electronic pointer in his hand, like a college professor in front of a blackboard. 'Between 1996 and 2001 al-Qaeda acted like a venture capitalist firm, sponsoring projects submitted by a variety of groups or individuals from Morocco to Malaysia. However, in the weeks following 9/11 over a hundred million dollars of assets in operational accounts linked to al-Qaeda members and in clandestine feeder accounts of associated char-ities and companies were seized. We believed erroneously that we had interrupted their capacity to continue funding large-scale projects. However, our enemy has proved more resourceful than we expected . . .'

Winthrop held up a hand, stopping him mid-flow, and said, 'Tell us about the diamonds, Nor.'

Jabotinsky returned to his seat. After a pause, Nor rose to his feet and approached the spiderweb. He stood before it and faced the audience.

'In early 2001 I was approached in Jalalabad by a senior offi-cial in al-Qaeda, one of the Egyptians close to Ayman al-Zawahiri, Bin Laden's chief lieutenant. I was asked to travel to Tora Bora, where I met with al-Zawahiri.'

Nor tapped a photograph of Zawahiri on the wall, a grainy black-and-white enlargement that showed a man in white glasses and a turban, with a broad, meaty face and fleshy lips. Nor lingered for a moment with his finger on the photograph and then continued, and Jonah wondered whether he was the only one to note the mocking echo of Winthrop's sermon about the chosen few in his softly spoken words: 'Zawahiri told me that when the *umma*, the worldwide community of Muslims, goes astray, God sends an individual or small group of people to rescue it from perdition and restore it to the path of truth. I was invited to join an elite band prepared to sacrifice their lives in order to bring victory to those ambitions and principles as described by Sheikh Osama Bin Laden. I was told that a mighty blow was about to be struck against the Crusaders and that I would be a crucial element in ensuring the survival of al-Qaeda when the Americans and their client states responded. Zawahiri told me that he was expecting an American invasion, and that, like the Soviets before them, the Americans would be swallowed up by Afghanistan and it would bring their empire to its knees.'

'Go on,' Winthrop urged, impatiently.

'I was offered and accepted a job providing close protection for the transport of twenty million dollars in cash from the United Arab Emirates to Sierra Leone, where the money would be traded for rough diamonds, about two months' output of the Kenema lode,' Nor explained. 'The twenty million dollars was given into my possession at the Dubai Islamic Bank and I travelled with it to Liberia. I was escorted from the bank in Dubai by an al-Qaeda operative named Ahmed Khalfan Ghailani. I was always escorted. I was never left alone with the money. In Liberia we met up with a Lebanese diamond broker called Aziz Nassour and we travelled together to Kenema in Sierra Leone, where we handed the money over in exchange for the diamonds. The stones were carried back out through Liberia and transported by private jet to Bombay for polishing and cutting. My task was complete on arrival in Bombay. I was paid and I returned to Afghanistan.'

'And then?' demanded Winthrop.

'I was approached again. I was invited to join a select group of international couriers who were tasked with carrying the diamonds. I was told that there were twenty couriers, each one with a Western passport and a capacity to move freely across continents. I was not introduced to any of my fellow couriers, nor was I given any further clues as to their identity. However, I was told that we were going to be dispersed across Afghanistan in twelve different locations, but with instructions to flee overseas in the event of an invasion and regroup in the Ansar al-Islam enclave in northern Iraq. After my briefing and taking receipt of the diamonds, I was sent to Kunduz in the north of Afghanistan, where I joined a number of other Arabs and Pakistani ISI intelligence advisers. It was at that stage that it became clear to me that the ISI were aware of the existence of the diamonds and likely to seize them if given the opportunity. For that reason I chose not to escape on the air corridor set up during the siege. I was subsequently captured by Dostum's Uzbeks. You know the rest of the story.'

'Describe to us the purpose of the stones,' Winthrop said.

'I was told that they are intended to finance one-off, out-of-the-blue spectacular events.'

'So called *black swans*,' Scholem called out, from the front row.

'World-changing events,' Winthrop added. He nodded to Scholem, who took over from Nor in front of the spiderweb. Scholem was small, with an impish quality that suggested an excess of zeal. 'As before, groups and individuals are invited to submit proposals to al-Qaeda for terrorist attacks. When a project has been approved by a panel headed by al-Qaeda's Director of External Operations and a budget decided, a courier is mobilised,' he explained. 'The courier carries an agreed quantity of diamonds to London. In London the diamonds are sold at the sight market at De Beers. Cut and polished stones are untraceable, so there is nothing to alert De Beers to their source as conflict diamonds or their role in financing terrorist attacks. The cash generated from the sale is dispersed to the selected group or individual through the informal Hawala banking system, without financial or governmental scrutiny or accountability.'

'There are known to be a number of British-based Hawala

traders located in London, Birmingham, Halifax, Cardiff, et cetera, with ties to international extremist groups,' Jabotinsky told them. 'The way it works is this: the courier deposits the agreed funds with the trader and the trader then makes a call to a counterpart overseas, who is in touch with the selected terrorist group, and the counterpart makes a withdrawal, passing the funds to the terrorists. The system is a network that operates on the basis of trust and word of mouth. Codes and cell phones are changed constantly. It's almost impossible to monitor.'

'As expected, the September eleventh attacks provoked an American invasion and the couriers were spread to the four winds,' Winthrop said. 'We believe that they are now regrouping in northern Iraq and that al-Qaeda has already reasserted control over a substantial quantity of the diamonds. I don't need to tell you how dangerous that is. The September eleventh attacks are estimated to have cost al-Qaeda less than half a million dollars. Between them the couriers are carrying the funds for a further forty attacks on a similar scale. Let me repeat that: forty 9/11 attacks. We should all be very frightened.'

'What are you going to do about it?' Pakravan called out.

'We're going to infiltrate the courier network and unmask the operations that they fund. We're going to identify each and every courier and we're going to follow the lines of communication all the way up to the al-Qaeda leadership and down to the terrorist groups on the ground. We're going to seize the funds and eliminate the terrorists. To do that, we have to get in close. We have to identify the couriers. We have to have eyes and ears inside the Ansar al-Islam enclave. That's where Nor comes in. We're going to fill him back up with al-Qaeda diamonds and send him in to blow the operation wide open.'

And suddenly all eyes were on Nor, who stood before them with the spiderweb as his backdrop. He ducked his head and smiled shyly. *You should get an Oscar*, Jonah thought, *this is your greatest performance.*

There was more to come. A desert conversion.

*

Nor knelt in the dusk beneath a flaming pink sky. Pastor Bob drew himself up in magisterial fashion with the Bible in one hand and the other resting on the crown of Nor's head.

'Dear God, I believe in you and need you in my life,' repeated Nor, with his eyes firmly shut. 'Have mercy on me as a sinner. Lord Jesus, as best I know how, I want to follow you. Cleanse me of my sins and come into my life as my saviour and Lord.'

'Amen,' shouted Pastor Bob. 'Jesus has come to live within your heart. Your sins are forgotten . . . you are saved . . . you have received eternal life . . . you are now the Child of God . . . the Holy Spirit abides within you . . . You have become a new person. Your life begins here.' He beamed at Winthrop, who was grinning like an overgrown boy. 'God has chosen to move within Nor's heart . . .'

Later Pakravan's team of instructors arranged a barbecue and Winthrop insisted on manning the grill. He basted huge slabs of steak in honey and lemon juice while Pakravan poured cranberry juice for the Iraqis. In Winthrop's presence, Nor was transformed into a conspiracy theorist, an advocate of the school of thought that had the 9/11 hijacker Mohammed Atta visiting the Iraqi intelligence cell office in Prague in April 2001.

'Of course it's credible,' Nor exclaimed, 'moving the Sheikh's money was getting more and more difficult.' He had also taken to calling Bin Laden the Sheikh in company. 'But Saddam had readily available and freshly laundered funds. It was a marriage of convenience. Saddam and the Sheikh might be opposite ends of the spectrum – a secular Baathist and a fanatical Islamist – but there was something in it for both sides: state sponsorship with its considerable resources on one side and the global reach of a worldwide jihadi network on the other.'

Clearly this kind of talk was a big hit with Winthrop, who waved his tongs to punctuate a point. 'There's no way the attack could have been carried out solely by a ragtag bunch of terrorists plotting in Afghanistan. It needed a state sponsor. That's what needs to be seen, but it is what the CIA in its incompetence is unable to see. You can't expect evidence to verify the connection because both parties to the pact have hidden the ties so well. That's what I keep telling people: when operational security is good, absence of evidence is not evidence of absence. In fact, it's the opposite – the less evidence there is the greater the likelihood that something is going on.'

'Absolutely,' Nor told him, his wide eyes shining. Only Jonah could see the mocking laughter that lurked behind the lopsided grin.

'The end times are coming, Jonah,' Winthrop told him, by the dying light of the embers of the barbecue, 'and I for one am looking forward to seeing them come. But for that to happen Jerusalem and the Holy Land have to belong to the Jews again. That's what it says in the Bible – isn't that right, Pastor Bob?'

'The end is coming,' Pastor Bob agreed, 'that's why things are such a mess.'

'There's just no way for it to happen without bloodshed,' Winthrop continued, 'without a certain amount of destruction. Muslims will have to die. I regret that. I don't have anything against Muslims other than that they are wrong on a fundamental level. Some of my best friends are Muslims. Pakravan prays to Mecca every day. I don't hate him. These Iraqis here in the desert are working hard every day because they want their freedoms. I respect them. The American people are prepared to sacrifice Christian blood for Iraqi freedom. It's just what is written, is all.'

Winthrop left with Pastor Bob and the Murids at first light. As the helicopter took off and sheared away, Jonah turned to Nor. 'Was Atta really in Prague?' he asked.

'Yeah, yeah,' Nor laughed contemptuously, 'and Elvis was there too.'

'And the diamond couriers? Do they even exist?'

Nor grinned. 'You'll see.'

Jonah shook his head. 'You're playing a dangerous game.'

'I'm doing what spies do the world over,' Nor replied, 'I'm elaborating and embellishing.'

'You're lying.'

'Come on! It's all lies. All of it! Every speck. These guys aren't interested in the truth. Despite all their talk of venture capitalism, they can't bear the idea that al-Qaeda is an independent force with its own finances. It doesn't fit their world view. They just want an unbeatable excuse to do the wrong thing. They want an excuse to invade Iraq.'

'And you mean to give it to them?'

Nor shrugged. 'I don't see that I have much choice.'

Nor was put back into play in September 2002 and he was monitored every step of the way. To get him close to where he started, Winthrop called on the help of certain Colombian acquaintances. Nor was flown by light plane from a jungle airstrip in Brazil to the African narco-state Guinea Bissau, landing at a former Soviet air base near a village called Kuffar, on a route most recently utilised for the transport of cocaine.

From Guinea Bissau, Nor crossed into Guinea Conakry and from there to Mali, where he established contact with a representative of al-Qaeda in the Maghreb. They knew about his escape from the Dark Prison. He was already a legend across the western desert. He joined the 'terrorist underground', and was transported overland by a combination of truck, bus and train to Khartoum in Sudan. From Khartoum he flew to Istanbul and from there to Diyarbakir near the Iraqi border. He changed taxis in Silopi and crossed into Kurdish-controlled Iraq. It was the beginning of 2003. He was carrying a gutful of diamonds and a GPS tracker.

Winthrop and Jonah took a less prosaic route. Together with the Murids they crossed into Iraq in January, travelling in a convoy of Toyota Super Saloons with a detail of Skorpion bodyguards from the Anabasis programme. They followed the tracker's route to Sulaymaniyah, where Winthrop met with Kurdish leaders to discuss the imminent invasion. He was upbeat. Saddam's regime was approaching its endgame and the tracker showed Nor crossing into the Ansar al-Islam enclave.

The world was about to begin a new chapter.

Then it all began to unravel. The tracker was on the move again, heading east out of the enclave towards Iran. On 6 February 2003, US Secretary of State Colin Powell addressed a plenary session of the United Nations Security Council. As well as insisting that Saddam was in possession of biological weapons and was working to obtain key components to produce nuclear weapons, Powell used the existence of the Ansar al-Islam enclave to draw a direct connection between intelligence agents of Saddam's regime and al-Qaeda operatives offered safe haven after the fall of Afghanistan. The following day the tracker crossed the border to the Iranian town of Marivan.

Winthrop moved the convoy to the Iranian border. They camped on the line separating Kurdish peshmerga on one side and the Iranian Republican Guard on the other. After a couple of uncomfortable nights sleeping in the cars, the Iranians sent a runner across the line with a message: 'Are you Winthrop?'

The following morning the tracker switched direction and came towards them. An Iranian customs official carried it across the border and handed it to Winthrop in a brown envelope together with a handwritten letter that said: *So long and thanks for the stones.*

Jonah expected Winthrop to explode. But he didn't. He just walked back to the Toyota, climbed inside and announced that they were going back to Turkey immediately. And Jonah could have sworn that for the briefest moment he saw the ghost of a smile on Winthrop's face.

Pariah

February–March 2003

Jonah and Alex were in the Tower restaurant on the roof of the National Museum of Scotland in Edinburgh on the night in February 2003 that the historic section of the old town known as the Cowgate caught fire. They were drinking champagne – Veuve Cliquot, the widow – which Alex had demanded. The old town was in flames behind his head.

'You were warned that this would happen.' Alex lifted his sunglasses and rubbed his eyes. He surveyed the abandoned tables and empty bar, the wash of spinning blue light against the far wall. He did a sudden double-take and spun around in his chair.

'What the fuck is going on out there?' he demanded, loudly.

Spectators glanced back from the glass wall.

'The Cowgate's on fire,' Jonah explained.

Alex seemed insulted. 'Does *anything* mundane ever happen to you?'

'What is that supposed to mean?'

'Is this what you wanted?'

'Fuck off,' Jonah told him. 'You are the one who is blackmailing me.'

Their waiter returned. He said, 'Is everything OK?'

'No, Kevin,' Alex replied. 'Things are not fucking OK. We need another bottle, two bottles, in fact.'

The waiter retreated.

Jonah had been back from northern Iraq for a week, staying in transit accommodation in Redford Barracks on the southern outskirts of the city. He was aware that he was being kept in isolation, at arm's length.

'I don't like this any more than you do,' said Alex. 'You were given a clear choice. Eliminate Nor or face the consequences. Instead, you stood by and allowed him to make a mockery of the Americans. They are absolutely furious. They are accusing you of being in league with Nor to steal the diamonds. For Christ's sake, they think you're a double agent! An al-Qaeda plant! They're demanding your head on a platter.'

'And you mean to give it to them?'

Alex exhaled loudly and pushed back his chair.

'Actually, no.'

'No?'

'Monteith has other plans for you. He has a job, an opportunity for you to redeem yourself if you survive. He's waiting for you in London.'

Jonah considered this unexpected development.

'What I don't understand is why you didn't just disappear when Nor did?'

'Maybe because I'm not in league with him,' Jonah retorted. 'Maybe it's because I'm not a traitor.'

Alex regarded him sceptically. 'You'd better go and catch the shuttle.'

'I need a proper drink first,' Jonah told him.

The following morning Jonah was sitting in a private briefing in Monteith's gloomy basement office. His head was thumping like a steel drum. He'd flown down on the first flight with his forehead pressed to the back of the seat in front. He was full to the brim with self-loathing.

'Her name is Miranda Abd al'Aswr,' Monteith told him, sliding the photograph across the Formica tabletop. 'She's a British national. Her father was a Somali dissident, living in exile here in London, and her mother a nurse from Surinam. Her background is as exotic as yours, though in her case the mix of races seems to have produced beauty rather than brawn. The parents died while she was still at school. A car crash. She was kicked out of school, she drifted for a while, then she dropped out of sight. We don't have anything on her until she turned up in Kuwait in the late eighties with a Saudi husband, Bakr Abd al'Aswr, a businessman who ran the Kuwaiti branch of a family conglomerate called Azzam Holdings. The family came out of the Hadhramaut, the same Yemeni province as Bin Laden. We have reliable reports that place Bakr in Afghanistan with Bin Laden in the mid-eighties, before relocating to Kuwait. He disappeared a few days after the Iraqi invasion in 1989. She stayed. She runs a museum of Arab and Islamic artefacts in the Hawalli district of Kuwait City. Clear so far?'

Jonah squinted at the photo. It was difficult to make anything out through the dark panes of his sunglasses. He couldn't take them off without revealing that he'd lost his glass eye while vomiting in the back of a cab the night before. He settled on a grunt that he hoped Monteith would interpret as an affirmative.

'We have intelligence that suggests that Bakr al'Aswr was involved in the procurement of weapons of mass destruction for Uday Hussein, Saddam's son. We understand that the invasion of Kuwait may have disrupted a plot to smuggle a cargo of something unsavoury out of the former Soviet Union. In the confusion of the invasion the cargo went missing. We understand that a sweep of loose containers conducted by an overzealous UN logistician may have thrown up the cargo again. It is close to being found and the plot has now been reactivated. According to our source, who is close to them, Miranda is in negotiations with a hybrid gang made up of cyber-criminals and former intelligence operatives who are searching for the cargo. The gang operates out of a travelling bazaar called the "sheep market" that moves around within the demilitarised zone between Iraq and Kuwait. We believe that they are close to finalising a deal to sell it to elements close to Saddam.'

Jonah frowned, struggling to understand. 'And what do you want me to do?'

'You know the drill. Penetrate. Listen. Observe. Maintain your cover.'

'And my cover is?'

'You're being rotated in as a British military observer attached to the United Nations Iraq Kuwait Observer Mission. That gives you free access to the demilitarised zone and the opportunity to make contact with Miranda and the hybrid gang. You'll go under your own name. If they do any digging they'll find a disaffected army officer under investigation for kidnapping. You have the perfect cover. You're in disgrace.'

'And if they find the cargo?'

'Stop them.'

A pause.

'And if I refuse to go?'

'Do not pass Go, do not collect two hundred pounds; in all likelihood a dishonourable discharge and off to prison for kidnapping.'

'And if I go?'

'We do you a deal. Witness retracts her statement and the police go back to chasing ordinary decent criminals.'

'And the Americans?'

'You pull this mission off and we'll give you a new identity and a bolthole. It'll blow over.'

'I don't have much choice, do I?'

'No, you don't.'

'Then I guess I'll go.'

'Good. You'll like the zone. It's your kind of place. It's drowning in the excrement of the devil.

'It's my kind of place,' Jonah agreed.

'And another thing . . .'

'Yes?'

'The Russians are paying an interest.'

Jonah groaned. 'Great.'

'I'd stay away from them if I were you.'

He staggered out of the office and down the corridor past the thumping boilers and into the men's room where he threw up in the nearest stall.

★

Beams of light shone out of nothingness and were fractured by a whirl of black cloth. Death was approaching, pulling at the hood of a robe. Jonah cowered in the corner. Then there was a torch in his face and his eye was filled with dazzling prisms.

He heard a woman's voice speaking in English. 'It's a clear violation of his rights and of your mandate. You can't hold him like this.'

A second voice, a man with a Russian accent, replied, 'The matter is he's a suspect.'

'Christ, Nikitin. There's such a thing as due process. Even here.'

The man identified as Nikitin protested, 'He stole a UN vehicle.'

'He's a UN observer. He's entitled to drive UN vehicles.'

'You say that.'

'He's UN. I'm telling you. He's just been posted in.'

'And the dead Norwegian?'

'Turn the body over to the embassy.'

'The incident is being investigated by the police.'

'The Iraqi police? The *Mook*? Don't make me laugh.'

A hand took Jonah's upper arm, and the woman said, 'On your feet.'

Within seconds they were out of the container and into a grotto of camouflage netting, and after it a blaze of light and then cool shadow, and the sensation of entering a medieval town. Rising above them was a warren of routes and dwellings, a jumble of wooden and steel stairways, exposed balconies, passageways and alleyways. Everywhere there were washing lines and TV and radio aerials.

Jonah was following a tall, dark-haired woman in a black robe as she strode across the stage created by the pool of downlight from a skylight far above. Russian soldiers struggled to keep up with them. Jonah could hear distant noises – an argument, chickens, pop music – and smell cooking, garbage, sweat and urine.

In the less than twenty-four hours since Jonah had touched down in Kuwait City, Odd Nordland, the UN logistician, had had his throat cut in a toilet stall in the Desert Palm bar on the

Iraqi side of Umm Qasr, and Jonah, who had fled the scene in Odd's car, had been tracked down and beaten up by Russian soldiers. After a bloody interrogation they'd thrown him in a shipping container.

He called out, 'Where am I?'

'Not Kansas,' the woman replied briskly.

'And you're not Judy Garland,' he retorted. *You're Miranda Abd al'Aswr.*

She spun around to face him, with her hands on her hips and her elbows out at angles, and anything else that he might have said became an irrelevance, because he was thinking that Miranda was by some distance the most beautiful woman that he had ever seen. Monteith's photo didn't do her justice. To his eye she was five-ten with a mane of hair as black as molasses. Her teeth were bright white, her grin a slash of light in the encircling gloom. He felt a heady rush of excitement.

'We're in the Russian compound in Umm Qasr port,' she said. 'There's about six or seven hundred Russian "peacekeepers" in here without a fan between them. They have no showers, no hot meals, and no place to take a shit. It tends to make them irritable. So, if it's OK with you, I'd like to leave.'

He wanted to reach out with one hand and touch her, to place his fingers against the slender curve of her neck. He saw the blood rise in her cheeks. She threw up her arms in exasperation, turned on her bare heels and strode away.

'Sure, let's go,' Jonah said. He hurried after her.

They emerged from the building into daylight. They were walking across a large courtyard formed by a wall of double-stacked freight containers. There was a battered Nissan Patrol parked on the far side of the yard. Jonah noticed that Miranda's ankles and the skin of her bare brown feet were covered in floral hennaod patterns.

'My name's Jonah,' he called out.

'I know,' she said.

There was a sudden commotion off to their flank and Miranda cursed. A Russian officer had appeared and he was shouting and gesticulating at the guards on the gate. Abruptly a hand gripped Jonah's shoulder and a group of soldiers placed themselves between him and the woman.

'*Ribbet*,' he called out. He was being dragged back to the container, his heels raising clouds of bone-dust.

'I'll get you out,' she shouted.

'*Ribbet!*'

'Why do you keeping saying that?'

'If you'd kissed me I'd have turned into a prince,' he shouted.

He met her again a few days later, at the British embassy. She was standing alone by the bar with a large gin and tonic in her hand. Just looking at her made him contemplate a lifelong relationship.

'Somebody kissed you,' she said.

'No, nothing so dramatic; I recovered my glass eye.'

'It suits you. You look good now the bruises have gone down. You have a kind of asymmetrical beauty.'

'Thank you,' he said. 'What are you doing here?'

'That's easy: I'm a Brit.'

'That's not really what I meant.'

She smiled wryly. 'I needed a drink and there isn't anywhere else to get a drink in this town. Don't you have bad nights?'

'Plenty.'

'You chew your nails,' she observed. 'You look the worse for wear.'

Jonah looked down and considered the seamed scar tissue and calloused ridges, the autobiography of his hands.

She said, 'I thought you'd be dead by now.'

He looked up from his hands. 'Why?'

'You seem to have a habit of being in the wrong place.'

He laughed. 'Story of my life.'

'How did you lose your eye?'

'I got blown up by a tank mine. In Gornji Vakuf.'

'I was in Zenica for a while,' she said, distantly. 'It was a tough time.'

'What were you doing there?'

'Looking for someone.'

'Someone?'

She frowned. 'I heard a rumour that my husband had been fighting with the Muj against the Serbs and I went looking for him.'

'Did you find him?'

She looked at him. 'No. And I didn't find him in Peshawar, or Kandahar or Grozny, either.'

'I guess you must have wanted to find him.'

'Are you mad?' she retorted. 'I wanted to know he was dead. Shit. That way I might get my son back.'

She lit a cigarette. Her eyes closed as she drew the smoke into her lungs – she radiated anger like heat from a fuel rod. 'They'd been gone for years by then but there were always rumours. When you live with uncertainty like that it can drive you crazy.'

She turned away from him and stared out across the city and beyond it to the desert, its vast blackness. It was later that night and they were standing on the roof of the nomad museum in Hawalli. Somewhere out in the darkness, there were three hundred thousand combat-ready Coalition troops, waiting for the order to move.

'There's a storm coming,' she said.

'You can tell?'

She looked back at him. 'I saw the weather forecast, that's all.'

He felt as though he were falling. He reached out with his fingers until they came into contact with her hair. He gathered it in a thick bunch in his hand and leant forward, drawing her lips to his. They kissed.

She told him that she wanted her son back and that she would do anything – *anything* – to get him back. It was easy to believe. He wanted to help her. He wanted nothing more than to fall in love.

MIRANDA

Tagiya: Dissimulation

a term used for the practice of some dissidents who concealed their true allegiance behind the outward veneer of conformity.

You don't look like a local

6 September 2005

At dawn Miranda went down to the river and washed her face
and hands. She filled her water bottle and rolled out her yoga
mat. She saluted the sun and gave herself for half an hour to the
rhythm of her breath.

When she was done she rolled up her mat and stuffed her
sleeping bag into the rucksack. She changed her underwear and
socks. She ran a brush through her hair.

It was time to stop dwelling in the past. Her son was dead,
buried in the graveyard of a Christian convent on the north side
of Baghdad. Her husband Bakr was dead, killed in a shoot-out
in a Shiite slum in 2003. She had spent two years guarding orchids
on a remote Scottish island, living in a kind of limbo. Now Jonah
had disappeared, the police were looking for him and it was up
to her to find him.

She strode down off the hill into the village of Ardfern with the
dog at her heels and crossed the square to the public toilets. In
one of the stalls she unzipped the lid of her crash-bag and removed
the plastic envelope that she had dug up the evening before.
Inside it in an ankle wallet there was a thousand pounds and a
thousand dollars in cash. Jonah was thorough; she had to give
him that. She switched her wellies for the Caterpillars and attached
the wallet around her left ankle with the Velcro fastening. She
packed her waterproofs in the crash-bag and put the beanie hat
on her head. She opened the stall door and the dog was sitting
there, waiting with his tongue hanging out. Five minutes later

she was striding down a road hemmed in by weathered stone walls.

She had decided to follow Jonah's trail. She didn't know of any alternative. She was going to Barra to find Jonah's friend and former colleague Andy Beech.

She continued down the road but faster, battling the urge to run.

She was standing at the side of the deserted, faintly steaming road, a solitary figure with a dog. She felt exposed in unsecured circumstances. The car whistled past with its stereo thumping, braked suddenly and backed up to where she was standing. It was a sleek, lozenge-shaped sports car in shiny aluminium. The music stopped and the window purred down.

'Does it bite?' he asked, just audible over the motor.

'Only when provoked,' she replied.

'Going north?'

She visibly hesitated. He shrugged and was already looking into his wing mirror when she surprised herself by opening the door. The dog slid in and hopped into the back. She got in after it.

'Thanks,' she said, squeezing her rucksack into the space between her feet.

'My pleasure,' he said. 'Where are you going?'

'North,' she said, looking at the road ahead.

A few seconds idled by. She pulled the seat belt across her chest. He glanced at her. His eyes were very blue, almost colourless. 'Just north?' he asked.

'Where are you going?' she responded.

'I haven't decided yet,' he said. 'Fort William to start with. I can drop you anywhere on the way.'

'Fine,' she said.

He accelerated rapidly away from the kerb and they drove for a while in silence. The car's interior was leather and chrome, with the intimacy of a cockpit. Now it was filled with paw prints and the damp, mossy smell of the dog. It leant forward between them with its eyes on the road. The minutes flashed by.

'I used to have a dog,' he said.

She glanced at him, surreptitiously studying him. He had sharp cheekbones and blond unruly hair that curled above the collar. She noted the curve of his brawny shoulders and the swell of his chest under his open-necked white linen shirt, and the Breitling watch on his wrist.

'Somebody stole her,' he explained. 'The dog, I mean.'

He was wearing a pair of leather driving gloves, which struck her as strangely anachronistic.

'Does he have a name?' he asked, meaning the dog.

She shook her head.

'He should have a name,' he chided her, gently.

They purred along the coast road, with open moorland on one side and the steely, reflective surface of a loch on the other.

'Were you waiting long?' he asked.

'I'm sorry?'

'When I picked you up,' he explained, 'had you been waiting long?'

'No.'

They turned a corner and the windscreen was awash with dazzling white light. He flipped down the sunshade with an impatient flick of his fingers and the sunlight flashed on the stainless-steel bezel of his watch.

'You don't look like a local,' he said.

'I'm just passing through.'

'Heading anywhere in particular?'

'Just travelling,' she said.

'My father was Scottish,' he said, apropos of nothing.

She had her own Scottish blood, on her mother's side; a great-great-grandfather who owned a plantation in Surinam, and bequeathed it to the young slave that he married on his deathbed. Like the Lebanese, the Scots seemed to get everywhere.

'It's so beautiful, you wonder why anyone would leave.'

Because they are no longer safe, she thought.

'It's a landscape to lose yourself in,' he said, and sighed. 'I had a messy split with a long-term girlfriend. I needed some space, some thinking time. You know. I've been driving, staying in local pubs, and walking. You can walk for hours without coming across another person.' His glanced up from the road and regarded her with intensity. 'Are you in a relationship?'

The question floored her. 'He's gone,' she said.

'Gone?'

She bit her lower lip and stared out of the window. It was more information than she had meant to share.

'Is he coming back?' he asked.

She shook her head. 'I don't know.'

'I'm sorry,' he said.

Then they were in the shadows, bracketed by dense forestry blocks – dark rows of Sitka spruce that rose hundreds of metres on either side of them. The dog leant with the curves. It was like being in a tunnel: suddenly dark and intimate, enough to make you paranoid.

'You think you know someone,' he said, with his eyes on the road. 'You live with them; you share your dreams and your secrets. And then just as suddenly they're gone and you're left wondering whether you knew them at all.' He paused and grimaced. 'I'm sorry. It must hurt.'

'Must it?' she wondered.

'We're running away,' he said, blithely.

She repeated the mantra. 'I'm just travelling.'

'I didn't know where she was at first,' he continued. 'I thought about following her, but I didn't. I don't know whether that was the right decision. Would you find him, if you could?'

'Maybe,' she murmured.

'Did he leave any clues?'

'No.'

She felt panic rising. When Oban came into view, she felt para- lysed. This was her stop. Her plan had been to take the direct ferry to Barra, but if she got out now she'd leave a trail a child could follow.

'Look,' he said, with a calculating smile on his face. It occurred to her that it was the smile of a man convinced of exactly what was going to happen next. 'I don't mind taking you wherever it is you want to go. I mean, I don't have much else to do.'

'Inverness,' she told him. 'That's where I'm going.'

'OK,' he said slowly, the smile faltering.

'Perhaps you could drop me in Fort William?'

'Sure,' he said.

They did not talk for a while. Outside Oban he opened out the throttle and the landscape streaked by. They crossed the bridge at Connell and drove north alongside the banks of a loch. What seemed like intimacy between them had turned into unease.

He switched on the radio. There was more news from hurricane ravaged New Orleans. A reporter was broadcasting from the Louisiana Superdome: 'We saw dead bodies. People are dying at the centre and there is no one to get them. We saw a grandmother in a wheelchair pushed up to the wall and covered with a sheet. Right next to her was another dead body wrapped in a white sheet. Right in front of us a man went into a seizure on the ground. No one here has medical training. There is nowhere to evacuate these people to. People have been sitting there without food and water and waiting. They are asking, "When are the buses coming? When are they coming to help us?"'

He turned off the radio.

'You scratch under the surface and there's anarchy,' he said. 'It doesn't matter where you are. It would be the same here, a flood like that. People would die in droves.'

They stopped at a service station on the outskirts of Spean Bridge for fuel. He paused with his key in the ignition, the engine vibrating beneath her soles.

'I don't mind taking you to Inverness,' he told her.

'Thank you,' she said.

While he was filling the tank she headed for the toilets. She was halfway across the concrete apron before she realised that she had left her bag in the car. She went back for it.

'I'm not going to do a runner,' he said in an amused tone.

'I need some stuff,' she said, lamely.

In the toilets, she released a jet of dark yellow piss into the pan. She was dehydrated and light headed, strangely otherworldly. She knew she must run. She finished and wiped herself. Next she unlatched and shoved the small frosted-glass window open to reveal a view of a row of bins and the pine woods on the hill-side beyond. She opened the window to its full extent, climbed on to the toilet seat and turned to pick up the dog. It went through the window first and then the rucksack and finally she squeezed out after it. She dropped to the ground on all fours.

She walked quickly past the bins and into the pine woods with the dog following. She quickly spotted a path and ran along it until she reached a Forestry Commission track. She could hear him shouting in the woods behind her. She followed the track for fifty metres or so and then struck out into the woods, with the morning sun behind her. Eventually she reached a tarmac road. A holidaying couple gave her a lift to Mallaig, where she caught the ferry to the Isle of Skye. Further lifts carried her northwards, the single-track roads unrolling like ribbons over the blind summits and plunging slopes of the island.

She spent her second night on the run in a grove of alders beside a river on the Trotternish Peninsula. She dreamt that night of the sea, of waves breaking on a desert shore and a voice calling her name. At first she thought it might be Jonah, but it was Nor, squatting on the sand some distance off with his hand reaching out to her. He was wearing the same mocking smile as on the Interpol poster; he was saying, 'Come and find me . . .'

In the morning she took the ferry to Barra.

Nor's confession

Miranda walked up the lane hunched against the spindrift rolling off the dunes. The house was dark granite with white-painted shutters, and the stone walls snaked across the waterlogged fields from it in a riot of brambles. Scuds of cloud raced across the sun and pools of water shimmered like mirrors. A toad leapt out of the brambles into the road and the dog followed it with his snout as it crossed to the opposite verge. Above the rock peak of a nearby hill a pair of choughs wheeled and cawed. She caught the smell of peat smoke on the offshore wind.

Approaching the house, she skirted the deepest mud in the yard, noted the Land Rover hard against the steading wall and stepped up to the door. She knocked and waited. Knocked again.

A window was heaved open on the upper storey and Miranda stepped back from the door to get a better view. A woman stuck her head out of the window, her long auburn hair blown across her face.

'It's Miranda,' she called up, 'I need to speak to you.'

The woman swept her hair away from her face.

'Miranda,' she repeated. 'I've come from Barnhill.'

'Barnhill?'

'On Jura. I'm Jonah's friend.'

'Wait,' replied the woman from the window.

Miranda waited. What else was she going to do? Where else was there to go? This was the only lead she had.

A minute or two later the door opened. The woman's eyes

were strikingly blue but she'd been crying and there were dark smudges under them. A small boy with large and reproachful eyes clung to her right leg. Small boys were the worst – they gave Miranda a plummeting feeling. She struggled to maintain her composure.

'You're Flora Beech?' Miranda asked. Jonah had told her that Andy Beech was married to Monteith's estranged daughter Flora.

'I am.'

'I need to speak to you.'

Flora Beech chewed on her fraying lower lip and stared suspiciously from the hallway.

'Please,' Miranda urged.

After a pause, Flora stepped back and the child shuffled after her, clinging to her leg.

'Come in.'

Miranda followed Flora and her son down a narrow and darkened corridor that was lined with a montage of framed photographs and into the kitchen. Flora stood for a few moments in a sleepy daze and then tucked a lock of hair behind her ear and wiped her nose. 'Tea?'

Miranda nodded. 'Please.'

Flora filled the kettle from the tap and set it on the Rayburn.

Miranda squatted down and smiled at the boy. 'What's your name?'

The boy shrank behind his mother's leg.

'His name's Calum,' Flora told her. 'What are you doing here?'

'I'm looking for Jonah.'

Her face twisted. She turned on Miranda angrily. 'He's not here any more.'

'Do you know where he is?'

'No.'

'Could I speak to your husband?'

'He's gone,' she said bitterly, and pressed a fist against her forehead.

'Do you know where he is?'

'No.'

Miranda considered this information gloomily. 'How long has he been missing?'

'He's not missing, he's just gone. He walked out.'

Miranda struggled to understand. 'Did he leave a note?'

Flora looked furious. 'No.'

Miranda tried to keep her voice as calm as possible. 'Have you told the police?'

'He is the police, and like I said, he's not missing. He left.'

The kettle began to whistle and Flora turned back to the Rayburn. She flung two tea bags into a teapot.

'Can I use your bathroom?' Miranda asked.

'Down the hall on the left,' Flora said without turning.

It took a moment for the dizziness to subside. Miranda sat with her head in her hands. Jonah was missing. His friend and colleague Beech appeared to have walked out on his wife and son. The policemen Mulvey and Coyle – if they were police – had suggested that there was a threat against the UK from a former colleague of Jonah's, Nor ed-Din. Persons unseen, possibly also the police, had broken into her house and planted evidence – if it was evidence – that seemed to give a date and rough location to the threat.

She had no idea what to do next – who to tell or what to tell them. That was the trouble: she didn't know what anything was about. Flora, who she knew little about beyond the fact that she was Monteith's daughter and Beech's wife, wasn't exactly being friendly.

On her way out of the bathroom she felt for the switch and lit up the hallway. A collage of framed family photos ran the length of the wall. There were generations of Beech ministers and their wives and children in colour and black and white: Calum clutching a collection of outsize shopping bags; Flora with flowers in her hair ducking through an arch of raised swords on their wedding day; and at the end of the hall a lurching revelation that caused Miranda to put her hand on her chest and feel her heart thumping.

She remembered Jonah's words, spoken to her the evening before he left: 'Beech and I worked together in Afghanistan.'

It was a group photo of five lean and bearded men on the knife-edge of a mountain ridge with an apparently endless succession of crumpled, dun-coloured ridges marching into the distance behind them. They were in mufti: patched and thread-bare shalwar kameez and chest webbing, with black turban cloth wrapped around their necks, and they were so caked in dust that they seemed camouflaged. Each one carried a rifle, a Kalashnikov, and they stared into the camera with defiant expressions.

Monteith, the short, barrel-shaped man with ginger hair who had interviewed her in London on her return from Iraq – Flora's father – was standing at the centre of the picture with the others flanking him. Jonah was standing on his left beside Beech and had his arm around the shoulders of a fourth man she did not recognise. And finally, lounging insouciantly on a slab of rock with his feet dangling, was the man who had picked her up in his sports car on the road north of Gallanach, and driven her as far as Spean Bridge.

'It was taken in Afghanistan. Jonah and Beech and my father were part of a Special Forces unit called the Afghan Guides,' Flora told her from the kitchen doorway. She held out a mug of tea, which Miranda gratefully accepted. Flora seemed to have calmed down a little. 'Beech said that if anything ever happened to him I should destroy the photo.'

'Why?' Miranda asked.

'Officially the Guides didn't exist.'

Miranda pointed at the man who had given her a lift. 'Who's he?'

Flora considered the photo. 'Alex Ross.'

'Is he still with the Department?'

'No. Well. Not overtly. It's complicated. Alex works for a private security firm that undertakes the kind of work that governments need done but don't like to be associated with.'

'He gave me a lift yesterday.'

Flora pursed her lips and said, 'He was probably the one that I liked the least.'

'I'm sorry if I've brought them here.'

Flora shrugged. 'Beech said you were trouble.'

Miranda smarted at the comment but let it go. After all, it was mostly true. She was trouble. It followed her everywhere she went. She felt chastened.

While Flora was bathing Calum and putting him to bed, Miranda drifted from room to room. Eventually, she found herself in the study, standing behind the broad expanse of a desk with a desktop computer on it, staring at the books – mostly well-thumbed paperbacks with cracked spines – crammed upright and on their sides on shelves that reached to the ceiling. The fireplace stacked with peat. A fistful of pens jammed in a mug. A litter of paper clips. A small wooden icon with flecks of gold leaf. She found herself reflecting on this need so evident in both Jonah and Beech to have somewhere away from the turmoil of the world. Jonah had spoken wistfully to her of his envy for Beech, who had chosen to walk away from a life of espionage in favour of the relative quiet of a policeman's life on a small Hebridean island. Looking around, she saw it as the mirror of the island hideaway that Jonah had chosen for himself twice now, first in his marriage and more recently with her at Barnhill, and which on both occasions he seemed to have been unable to sustain.

She looked up to find Flora standing in the doorway in a pair of jeans and a T-shirt. She was holding a plate with two pieces of buttered toast. 'Dinner?'

Miranda took a piece and Flora had the other. Flora paused between mouthfuls and said, 'I'm sorry about what I said earlier. About you being trouble. I had no right.'

'It's OK,' Miranda replied.

'Why did you come here?' Flora asked, after a pause.

'I'm looking for Jonah.'

'He did come here, right after he . . .' Flora tailed off awkwardly.

'. . . left me?' Miranda finished for her.

'It wasn't about you.'

'Then what was it about?' Miranda asked.

There was a pause.

'It wasn't about you,' Flora repeated, softly.

'The police came to Barnhill, looking for Jonah,' Miranda told her.

'Did they say why they were looking for him?' Flora asked.

'No.'

Flora nodded as if this was not unexpected. 'Anything else?'

'They showed me a photo of a British-born Jordanian called Nor ed-Din.'

'I'm sure they did,' Flora told her.

'What do you know?' Miranda demanded.

Flora stared at her for a second. Then she sighed. 'You might as well hear it from him.'

She went over to the computer and Miranda followed.

'Sit down,' Flora said, indicating the chair before the monitor. 'It's connected. The video link is on the first bookmarked site.'

Miranda sat and gripped the mouse. The monitor lit up. She clicked on the web browser and pulled down Bookmarks. The first was a page and download link grabbed from YouTube. Someone, presumably Beech or Flora, had originally typed *Nor ed-Din* into the search facility. Top of the list was a freeze-frame of Nor's face staring out of the tube and beside it the title:

A spy's confession

The Koran commands you to speak the truth, even if it be against your own selves (more)

Miranda glanced up at Flora, who was standing at her shoulder. 'Go on,' Flora said.

Miranda clicked on the screen and the clip played. Nor spoke slowly and carefully in English, as if he was reading from a prepared statement. He addressed the camera and began with a phrase that Miranda recognised as originating from the Egyptian Islamist movement, the Muslim Brotherhood, '*al-Islam huwa al-hull*' – Islam is the solution. He stated that given the continuing occupation of Islamic lands by the Crusader forces of America and Britain, he had no alternative but to go public with the details of the assassination of the CIA agent James Kiernan at the hands of rogue elements within the British intelligence services, and his hand in it. He briefly described his career as a British under-cover agent embedded in the Pakistani Intelligence Service, the ISI, and that organisation's extensive links to Islamist elements – including al-Qaeda – operating within Afghanistan and the tribal areas of Pakistan. He described how he was cruelly abandoned by the British for more than two years following the capture of Kabul by the Taliban and how in that time he found God's true path and nurtured within himself a murderous desire to seek vengeance upon the *kuffar*, the unbelievers, who had led him so far from the path of righteousness. He described the ease with which he tricked the British into killing Kiernan. He described the subsequent cover-up. He named the rogue intelligence unit known as the Department, and its controller, the war criminal Monteith. He committed himself to further acts of violence upon the agents of the Crusader nations, specifically revenge against the hateful British. He ended by saying, 'Soon I will come to your country and I will launch an attack that will amaze the whole world. A tide of destruction. I swear to God, the greatest tide that ever was remembered in England . . .'

The link froze.

'It was posted about a week before Jonah came here,' Flora told her.

Miranda ran her hands through her hair. 'Shit.'

'Beech said it was taken down off YouTube a couple of days after being uploaded, but not before it had been grabbed and circulated on a bunch of jihadi websites.'

'Will people believe it?' Miranda asked.

Flora shrugged. 'It's true.'

'They really killed a CIA agent?'

'According to Beech, yes, they did.'

'That's the secret,' Miranda said. 'That's the secret that he said must never be told.'

'It's no longer a secret,' Flora told her. 'I don't know about you but I could do with a drink.'

They returned to the kitchen. Flora retrieved a full bottle of Talisker from the back of a cupboard and two large glass tumblers from a shelf and set them on the table. 'Sit,' she said. She uncorked the bottle and poured two large measures. She slid one across the tabletop to Miranda and picked up the other. 'Drink that,' she said.

The whisky performed a slow burn down Miranda's throat. They sat in silence for a while. Miranda watched as Flora's nails worried the chipped surface of the table.

'Nor was one of my father's waifs and strays. A double agent, I suppose. Just as he said in the video, he was planted by my father inside Pakistani intelligence, the ISI, to keep an eye on what the Pakistanis were up to in Afghanistan during the civil war in the mid-nineties. Jonah was the one that recruited him. They were at school together, but different years. Jonah was a couple of years older, I think, but they were two Arab kids in a mostly white boarding school. It created a bond between them. Nor looked up to Jonah, hero-worshipped him. He followed him into the army. He didn't last long. They kicked him out on a drugs charge, I think. I wouldn't be surprised if it was a trumped-up charge to provide him with cover. My father sent him off to Afghanistan. For a while he fed them information, and then at some stage they dumped him. I don't think anyone felt good about it but that's what happened. Understandably, Nor felt betrayed. I don't know how bad things were for him on his own in Afghanistan without anyone to turn to, but I'm guessing pretty awful.'

'And now he's making threats?'

'Beech said that if it ever came out that elements in British intelligence had been complicit in the death of a senior CIA agent and covered it up, then the Department would be finished and everybody who had ever served in it would be thrown to the wolves.'

'You think that's what's happening?' Miranda asked.

'Isn't that what it looks like to you?'

'I guess it does,' Miranda conceded.

'We came here for a quiet life,' Flora said bitterly, 'to get away from the past.'

'Have you spoken to your father since Beech disappeared?'

'I phoned the Department's emergency number. And I phoned the cottage in Norfolk. Both lines are out of service. As far as I know the Department has been closed down and my father has disappeared.'

'Do you have any other means of contacting him?' Miranda asked.

Flora shook her head. 'If he has a mobile phone I don't have the number.' She reached for the bottle and filled her glass again. 'What are you going to do?'

'Is Nor really coming here?'

'Listening to him on that video, I think he's coming. I think he's angry enough to go through with his threat.'

Miranda stared into the bottom of her glass. 'I have to find Jonah.'

Miranda was standing in the doorway to Calum's bedroom. She'd followed Flora up the stairs. Calum was lying on his back with a tiny fist clenched in front of his face. Flora was kneeling in front of him, beside the bed, gathering the blankets to cover him again.

Flora looked back at her. Her eyes narrowed. 'Jonah said that you lost your son?'

Miranda turned away. There was no light in the corridor. She walked along it as if it were a tightrope, step by step, trying not to fall. She sat on the carpet at the top of the stairs and wiped her eyes with the back of her hand. She had found it so difficult to accept that he was gone. For years after he was snatched, she imagined that he was alive somewhere and playing with his toys. Some nights she would tell anyone who was prepared to listen, 'Omar's coming home tomorrow.' Often she dreamt that she saw him in a crowded playground and ran up to him and screamed,

Where have you been? And he wouldn't answer and she'd wake up in a cold sweat.

Once she dreamt that Omar was living in the desert with a beautiful dark-haired woman who had convinced him that she was his true mother. Miranda woke up from the dream and drove into the desert until dawn.

A murder of crows

'It's all I've ever known,' Flora told her. 'For years I had a camp bed in one of my father's offices. I'm sure it was completely forbidden, but what could he do? If he got called out in the night, he'd bundle me up in a blanket in the back of the car and drive me up to London. I spent entire weekends in those basements, cutting out newspaper clippings for his bloody collage; either that or in Norfolk, getting dragged along behind him while he strode up and down the beach. It was so bloody sad. My mother never gave him any notice. She just left one night. I got a note, an apology of sorts. She boarded a ferry from Dover and that was the last we heard of her. It was obvious that she'd learned from him and made careful preparations. At first, I thought he might go looking for her. But he was too proud. He just strode up and down the beach staring at the North Sea. I remember I used to imagine it was him daring the tide to come in, so he could wrestle with it. That's my abiding memory of my father from childhood: a little man with a lot of fight in him who was destined to lose. Beech always said they'd crucify my father if they knew even half of what he'd done.'

Miranda swore. 'The tide,' she gasped. 'That's it.' She gripped Flora by the shoulder. 'It's something to do with the tide in the Thames Estuary, ten days from now.'

It was after eleven and they were sitting on the floor of Flora's studio, surrounded by shelves of unfired pots, with their backs to the radiator and the kiln on the wall facing them. The whisky bottle sat on the floor between them.

'In the end I was the one who tracked my mother down,' Flora continued. 'She was living in Lisbon. Her new husband was a building contractor with his own business. I was twenty by then, at university. She told me that there wasn't any other way to do it. If she'd taken me with her my father would have followed her to the ends of the earth. She said she was sorry. We didn't have much else to say after that.'

'We have to watch the video again.' Miranda got up and held out her hand for Flora to grasp.

They splashed through the muddy courtyard back to the house.

'I swear to God,' Nor said, speaking out of the tube, 'the greatest tide that ever was remembered in England.'

Miranda was brandishing the items that she'd pulled down off the cork board in Jonah's study: the postcard, the ship's diagram, the print-out of the Sheerness tide tables. 'That's it! That's it! Don't you see? The tide! A six-metre high tide at eleven p.m. on September twelfth.'

'It's a bloody strange way of saying it. Wait.' Flora leaned over her, minimised the clip and called down Google from the browser menu. She typed in *the greatest tide that ever was remembered in England* and hit search.

'Look. It's Samuel Pepys, December seventh 1663. The full quote is *There was last night the greatest tide that ever was remembered in England to have been in this river, all Whitehall having been drowned.*'

'They're going to flood the city,' Miranda said.

Flora nodded. 'It looks that way.'

Miranda remembered what Alex Ross had said to her in his car about the events unfolding in New Orleans: *It would be the same here, a flood like that. People would die in droves.* She remembered her dream of the night before, an immense wall of water toppling towards her.

She felt a shiver down her spine. 'Jesus!'

'Give me those coordinates.'

Miranda handed her the ship's diagram with the latitude and longitude written on it. Flora clicked on the Google Earth icon on the desktop. It was preset to a satellite image of the earth with the UK at its centre. They plummeted and then raced eastwards from London along the Thames, with Flora keeping an eye on the racing ticker tape of coordinates on the bottom left of the screen.

'There.'

A bright blue expanse. The sea. Flora zoomed out again and used the ruler. A point about a mile and a half north-east of Sheerness, where the Thames Estuary met the North Sea.

'There's nothing there.'

'But maybe there will be on September twelfth,' Flora said. 'A ship perhaps?'

'We need to tell someone,' Miranda said.

'Who?'

They stared at each other.

'There's no one to tell,' Miranda said. She reached for the bottle.

Miranda was describing her ten-year search for her dead son. When looking for her son meant hunting for Bakr. A decade of cities that blurred into each other – Peshawar, Kandahar, Kabul, Grozny, Zenica – the refugee camps full of malnourished children, the hotels packed with journalists and the checkpoints manned by drunken militiamen. Thousands of dollars in envelopes of cash passed to policemen and pimps, guerrillas and gunrunners, all of it wasted on rumours of Bakr that never amounted to anything.

It was in Baghdad in March 2003, with missiles raining down upon the city, that she finally found her husband Bakr, and he agreed to take her to the grave of her son, in the cemetery of a Christian convent on the north side of the city.

'I wasted ten years of my life looking for him. But he was dead all that time. Why didn't I know, why didn't I feel it here, in my chest?' She pounded her ribcage. 'What kind of mother am I?'

They were on the sofa in Beech's study. Flora was holding her, her arm wrapped tightly around Miranda's shoulders.

'You wanted him to be alive. Any mother would. Do you think

I'd give up if Calum went missing? You did what any of us would have done.'

Miranda wailed.

They were in the middle of a field. Flora was squatting, pissing. Miranda was staggering but staring skywards. She couldn't remember the last time she had been this drunk.

'Take a line from the edge of the frying pan and from the centre of the upturned *w* and where the two lines meet,' she said and pointed, 'that's the North Star.'

Flora lurched towards Miranda. She grabbed her by the arms. 'Jonah's mother,' she says. 'You've got to find Jonah's mother. She's the one!'

'What are you talking about?'

'That's what Beech said. If anything ever happened to them, they should go to Jonah's mother. Jonah wasn't having any of it, but Beech said that's what they should do.'

'Why?'

'She's in the House of Lords. For Christ's sake, she's chair of the Parliamentary Intelligence and Security Committee.'

Miranda whistled.

'I cut a picture out of a magazine. It was a bear. A polar bear . . . sitting on its bum on the ice . . . looking sorry for itself . . . like it didn't belong. I gave it to him. I said you're like this bear. Look at it, I said. You're a fucking grumpy bear.' Flora was talking about Jonah. She'd been talking about him for some time, her gestures becoming more animated and the volume of her voice rising as they emptied the bottle.

Miranda was remembering the morning after she had first slept with him, surveying the contents of Jonah's wallet on the floorboards of the museum in Kuwait City. The usual selection of cards and two folded pieces of paper that caught her attention – a child's wax-crayon drawing and a picture cut from a magazine of a polar bear slumped on an ice floe. She remembered him looming above her like a baited bear, at a rowdy party at the British embassy the night before, telling her that more than anything he wanted to *roar like a fucking warlock*. She'd felt the spark of desire leap from eye to eye. She remembered that she wanted him then, wanted to capture the raw heat of him and have him burn through the icy mass of her heart. For a while she thought that he had, but something had gone wrong.

'He was so cut up by the divorce. It was infuriating . . . he didn't love her . . . she didn't love him. They should have split up years before,' Flora told her, indignantly. Miranda was hardly listening, shaking her head from side to side. They were on the floor in the kitchen. 'If they had back then I might have said yes when he asked . . . but I wasn't going to throw everything away on the rebound . . . on damaged goods. He was so bloody shocked that I got together with Andy.'

Miranda was trying to work out why it had gone wrong. Maybe there wasn't enough heat in him, or she was just too bloody cold.

'I tried to make it work.' Flora was crying, the tears running down her cheeks. 'I really tried. But it was hopeless. I couldn't get him out of my head. He was there. Every day. And I was screaming . . . how could you? What are you doing? What about Calum? But none of it mattered. I was falling. Then he said it. He was here . . . just speaking . . . here in this room. He said he felt the same.'

Or perhaps she wasn't the right woman. And then finally, in a moment of drunken clarity, Miranda understood the antagonism, the look on Flora's face that she now recognised – *I got there first*. She felt a rush of sudden anger. At that moment she hated Jonah with a ferocity that made her head reel.

'Is that what happened here?' she demanded. 'Did he tell you that he loved you? Is that why your husband left?'

'Oh God!' Flora stared at her, a startled expression on her face. 'I'm sorry. I really shouldn't have told you that.' She curled up on her side. 'Shit!'

Miranda grabbed the bottle, in need of its final mouthful.

★

The dog's whining woke her. He was on the bed beside her with his snout raised to the window. 'What is it, dog?'

She groaned, reached for her watch and squinted painfully at the screen by moonlight. It was four in the morning: the vulnerable hour. Her head was thumping. Flora was curled beside her in a tangle of sheets. A moment's groggy reflection and she remembered putting her to bed and then lying down beside her. She eased herself into a sitting position and then wished she hadn't moved so rapidly. The contents of her head shifted painfully. Her bladder was uncomfortably full. She rolled her feet off the bed and lurched towards the window, careful to remain in shadow. She stood, silently watching. The moon cast a sparkling glow on the yard.

She almost missed him. In the shadows by the Land Rover was the silhouette of a man, standing like a sentry. She shrunk back. The dog slid across the back of her knees. She glanced across at her bag, at her clothes strewn across the floor, and had to resist the urge to stuff the bag and flee. There had been so many times in the past when she had done just that. Breathe, she told herself. This was no time for panic. *Breathe.*

Minutes passed, cirrus cloud slid eastwards. A wave of nausea rolled through her.

The man stepped out of the shadows briefly and the moonlight made a wraith of him. He skirted the yard and was gone. Miranda remained standing, silently watching, as a wave of sudden anger took hold.

Not long after dawn she went from window to window upstairs. There was a gorse-clad hill to the north-west with a rock peak and a crumbling wall running up to it like a spoke, and it appeared to offer the best vantage point.

Just as earlier she had resisted the urge to flee, now she resisted the urge to make a beeline for the hill. She must control her anger. There was a system to searching. Dressed in black, in pile jacket and beanie hat, with her cash in her ankle wallet and the postcard and papers stuffed in the back pocket of her jeans, she went down the stairs with the dog at her heel.

She was halfway down the corridor on her way to the door when she stopped suddenly. There was an empty square on the wall, a picture hook but no picture. The photograph of the Afghan Guides had been removed.

She remembered Flora's words from the night before: *Officially the Guides didn't exist.*

Why remove the photo? After Nor's confession, the existence of the Afghan Guides was circulating on the Internet; it could be denied but not entirely erased. What Nor hadn't done was name the individual members of the unit. The photograph could be used to identify them – perhaps that was why it had been taken?

She let herself out of the house and began an anticlockwise spiral, working her way out from the house. She rolled over the walls. She stopped at any potential cover, squatted and inspected the ground. The pain in her head had settled to a steady throb.

Eventually she found what she was looking for: a mess of large, unmistakably male footprints behind a hunched, spindly blackthorn tree hard against the wall leading to the rock peak. Squatting, she stared at the house and found herself watching Flora moving back and forth in the bedroom window. The man had paused here and then advanced on the house. She looked back along the wall and saw beside it a line of footprints in the rough grass leading directly up the hill and disappearing into the gorse below the rock peak.

Nothing she had seen indicated more than one watcher. If he had been up all night then now was the time to sleep. Either that or he was watching her now and she was about to advance in full view across an interminable space. There was only one way to find out, and it seemed better to do it straight away before her courage failed.

She stayed low against the wall and sprinted for the peak, splashing across the field with the dog sprinting after her. She was at the gorse in no time. She rolled under the nearest bush into a shallow depression, a bowl of dry gorse needles with some sardine tins, biscuit wrappers and a water bottle. His bed. She curled into a ball, expecting blows, but none come. She glanced this way and that. The dog watched her from the lip of the depression.

He was gone. There was a trail of disturbed gorse needles leading back across the hill. She relaxed, lay back and breathed out. The dog licked her face and she pushed it away. She decided there was nothing for it but to continue.

She rolled on to her tummy and crawled forward, following the trail. After fifty metres or so the trail divided, one spur running up to the peak, the other appearing to lead towards the dunes and beyond them to the beach. She chose the route to the peak, and crawled along it. She hadn't gone far when she sniffed the first waft of decay, the nauseating sweetness that she associated with animal carcasses found on the machair. Then there were the flies, their hum as telling as the smell. They were as big as blue-bottles and they settled on her hands and face. She held a hand-kerchief over her mouth and nose and continued, dragging herself forward on one elbow.

The ground fell away and she dropped into a crevice, between walls of fractured rock. She moved forward, following the twists and turns of the rock, squeezing between the narrowest sections, leaving bands of lichen stains on her jacket. The flies were thicker now, hanging in a cloud in the still air of the crevice.

She turned a corner and found herself face to face with Beech. He was wedged upright so that he appeared to be standing. His body was pale, almost blue, and the choughs had been at his eyes, but there was no mistaking that it was him. He seemed to be frowning. She stumbled back and the flies surged in excitement and they were in her hair and eyes and ears. A moment later and she was scaling the rock, heading upwards out of the crevice and into the wind. She reached the top and found herself on a broad pan of rock overlooking the farm. She slumped to her knees and retched the contents of her stomach on to the rock.

She was in a state of spasm, her whole body shaking. She felt a sense of terrible risk: to her, to Flora and Calum.

She looked up and, as if on cue, a Peugeot 206 marked Metro-politan Police appeared at the junction and turned up the narrow lane to the farmhouse. It was Mulvey and Coyle. She watched its roof and blue lighting array running above the wall. Again, she must flee. If they'd just come off the ferry, she had maybe twenty minutes before the ferry left again. If she got a lift from a passing car she might make it in time to catch it.

She leapt across the gap, and descended the far side of the peak to the dunes. Soon she was stumbling along sand pathways. Her head was a blinding sheet of pain.

At some point the dog rejoined her.

The ferry rose and fell with the waves and she had to hold her glass tightly to stop it sliding across the table. It was her third vodka and tonic. It was only at the end of the second vodka that she'd stopped shaking. She could not get the image of the flies rising from Andy Beech's corpse out of her head. She finished her drink and decided to go outside for some air.

She went out on deck with the dog following and stood into the wind so that the spray struck her face. She stood that way for several minutes. She didn't know what to think or do. She was angry at Jonah for betraying her, but not as angry as she expected to be; she was resentful of Flora but appalled by what had happened to her husband. There was a voice that she had heard before, which was saying *Run . . .*

She was not incriminated by Nor's confession. There was no reason to feel loyalty to Jonah. Why shouldn't she just run?

As she turned to leave, something caught her attention. Another passenger, the only other passenger on the deck, was standing by the lifeboats. He had short cropped ginger hair and he was wearing a Barbour jacket. There was something frighteningly familiar about his stance. Now he was looking directly at her. Suddenly she was convinced that it was the man who had been standing in the shadows in the courtyard the night before.

Terrified, she hurried back into the bar and ordered another drink. For the rest of the journey she sat with her back to the bar, staring at the doorway.

JONAH
Pursuit

'the calculating people of the prudent isle were inclined to harbour the conceit, that for those very reasons he was the better qualified and set on edge, for a pursuit so full of rage and wildness as the bloody hunt of whales'

Herman Melville, *Moby-Dick*

An inside job

Jonah looked up, his hands hovering over the keyboard, as a shadow fell across his desk. A pony was pressing its lips and buck teeth against the windowpane. He reached up and tapped on the glass and the pony skittered away.

The ponies had been irregular companions to Jonah and Miranda since their arrival at Barnhill in the wake of the Iraq war. They appeared without warning and usually stayed for several weeks at a time, grazing the grass before moving on to other pastures. Jonah had also come across them now and then sheltering in the caves on the windward side of the island. He had developed a deep and inexplicable affection for them.

He was done with writing for the day. He shut down his laptop, unslotted the memory stick and secured it to the canvas sling around his neck. There were secrets on it that he would not let stray from his person. He'd found writing more difficult than he expected; too often it made him feel tired and helpless. He knew that eyewitness material was of necessity partial and incomplete, and in searching for the motivation of others he'd found that his natural inclination was towards understatement. There was meaning in pauses and glances and half-formed sentences, but he struggled to articulate it. He knew that he must overcome this if he was to unravel the threads of deception that had characterised his life. How do you explain that you have valued the loyalty of a childhood friend above the security of those nations that have offered you their protection and their citizenship?

He'd made no decision about what to do with the manuscript,

although periodically he printed it and posted a sealed copy to
his solicitors in Glasgow. There was really no question of publi-
cation, even as fiction – there were too many secrets. Rather, it
was protection. A bulwark against the Department's act of blackmail – the kidnapping of his ex-wife's lover – that had blighted
his relationship with his former wife; and which now dangled the
constant threat of imprisonment over his head.

He drifted through the house. It was lunchtime. Miranda was
still out on the moor with the dog but she would be back soon.
They often had sex when she came in. There was something about
the moor that made her hungry for it, that filled her with desire.
Then she would open a bottle of vodka and start drinking. If the
moor was where she fought with her demons then the house was
where she found release. The house was yoga and fucking and
vodka. And he had concluded, despite everything, that this was
what kept them there. It was why they had stayed so long.

The radio made him crazy and angry. There was chaos from
Afghanistan to the Mediterranean. The Middle East lurched from
one crisis to another. American promises of reform and democ-
ratisation had evaporated. In Iraq, a civil war between Sunni and
Shiite Arabs raged. Al-Qaeda was the main beneficiary. It had
evolved into a complex global network, with a decentralised structure of active and sleeper cells that had enabled it to spread across
the Arab world, Africa, Asia and Europe. They could not expect
to be unhurt at home.

He kept newspaper cuttings on the wall above his desk including
a montage of recent pornography from the prison at Abu Ghraib:
one of them was an effigy, an image of a hooded figure on a
cardboard box, with his hands held out in supplication and electric wires trailing from his fingers; another showed seven bodies
in a pile with their genitals exposed, a human coil like a massive
turd, with Specialist Charles Graner and Private Lynndie England
in the background giving a thumbs-up. He knew enough of Arabs,
of his own Arab half, to know that shame is a dirty thing. It must
be washed, and only bloody violence would wash it away. For

him, these images, with their strange mix of cold-blooded brutality and adolescent frivolity, marked the moment when the Iraq adventure was lost, when an indelible image of American depravity was imprinted on the entire Islamic world.

A firestorm was coming.

She had said the road to hell was paved with the ambition to make the world a better place. She told him that it was not his problem any more. Neither was it hers. They had turned their backs on it, she insisted. Now she protected rare plants. She walked through the house naked. There were days when they woke, fucked and tumbled back into sleep, to start afresh a couple of hours later with the sky leaking through the gaps in the curtains; and there were days when they woke, climbed out of bed and went their separate ways and did not speak again until dusk.

He was offered her file in London on his return from Iraq but he refused the offer. He didn't want to know anything unless she was the one who offered it to him. He knew that she had spent time in the madrasas in Pakistan, and Afghan caves; that she had spent the best part of a decade tracking her Islamist husband across the conflicts of the world; and he knew that she bore the torment of losing a child. But he had not pressed her for details. He wanted nothing unless it was freely given. Besides, he had his own secrets that, for her protection, he would rather not share.

He had reached thirty-eight. He'd been beaten up, knifed and shot at. He'd been married and divorced. He had outlived his father. He had learned something about facing adversity in life.

At the post office there was a postcard waiting for him of a stretch of deserted beach. It said – *We need to talk*. It was unsigned, postmarked the isle of Barra. He broke a five-pound note in the shop, and walked across to the phone box. He fed coins into the slot and dialled the number from memory. Beech picked it up on the fourth ring.

'It's Jonah. What is it?'

'I need to talk to you,' Beech said. 'I can't leave here.'

'It's OK, I'll come to you,' Jonah agreed, reluctantly.

He put the phone down and walked slowly back to the Land Rover, considering the implications of the card and the call with a creeping sense of dread. Beech was not given to melodrama. Something serious had happened. It had been naive to imagine that the world and its woes could be ignored for ever. He found Miranda stretching in the garden when he returned. She was incredibly strong and supple. She dedicated herself to things – exercise, drinking – with an intensity which at times he found disconcerting.

'I have to go away for a few days.'

She deserved more of an explanation. He didn't know what to say. There was a part of him that wondered if it was really Beech that he wanted to see. He wished that he could roll back time, to that night in Kuwait City, when just looking at her made him contemplate a lifelong relationship. He wished that he could rekindle that fire.

Instead he shrugged. 'It may be nothing.'

'And if it's something?' she asked, pausing with her arms out like blades. 'This time. The next time. Are you going to keep going?'

'What is it?' she asked, searching his face, her eyes wide and her pupils struggling to focus. They were kneeling on the carpet in front of the fire. It was almost midnight and she was most of the way into a bottle of vodka.

'We may not be safe here any more,' he said.

'You poor ragged bear,' she said, and cupped his face in her hands. 'You can't help yourself. They've sucked you in.'

'I won't be gone long,' he said. 'I'll come straight back.'

'I'll be waiting,' she murmured. He watched her eyes go sleepy.

'I'll not be here when you get back off the moor tomorrow,' he said. And then after a pause, 'You have to trust me.'

He took her by the hand and led her up the stairs to bed. He lay awake beside her, with the windows open, listening to the sound of breakers striking the shoreline. There was one final thing, perhaps too self-evident to need saying. She wanted to obliterate the outside world and he did not. He could not.

★

In the morning he took his crash-bag down off the peg where it hung beside hers, and methodically unpacked and repacked it in his study, checking it for cash, passport, phones, etc. He added his laptop. He strayed for a moment, contemplating the collage on the wall, and his hand reached reflexively for the memory stick at his neck. He might have need of his leverage.

He drove the Land Rover down to Feolin and took the ferry to Port Askaig. He drove across Islay, stopped briefly in Bowmore to touch fingers with Esme through the school fence, passed his ex-wife's Land Rover on the airport road, and made it in time to catch the morning ferry for the mainland from Port Ellen.

He spent a sleepless night in a bed-and-breakfast on the seafront in Oban, staring blankly at the tartan wallpaper. He caught the morning ferry for Barra.

'I thought that if I didn't see you for a while I might feel better. But I didn't,' she said. Flora and Jonah were standing in front of the window in the kitchen of the house on Barra. They were both holding mugs of tea. Flora was looking at him, chewing her lip, searching his face for some clue to his response. 'It's an inside job, I guess.'

How was he supposed to respond? Tell her that he should never have got married, and that she shouldn't have either? That he should never have taken up with Miranda? That with each step that he took away from Barnhill, it became clearer to him the mistake that he had made?

'How is it with her?' Flora asked.

'Miranda? She's grieving. She lost her son. She wasted ten years looking for him.'

'That doesn't answer my question.'

'I thought I loved her. No . . .' he corrected himself. 'I did love her. I really did. With all my heart. For a while I didn't have to think about you or Sarah, any of that bad stuff from my past. I thought it would be enough. But it wasn't.'

'And now?'

'We live in a kind of limbo,' Jonah told her. 'We're both waiting for something to happen.'

'And now you're back in the game.'

'Am I?'

'You know you are. I'll leave it to Beech to explain.'

'How is it with him?'

'He's a good man and a principled man.'

'And that doesn't answer my question . . .'

They heard a car pull into the yard and its door slam.

'That's him. He'll want to take you out on the hill.' She rolled her eyes. 'Does he really think that I don't know what this is all about?'

'What is it about?'

She was suddenly angry. 'It's about you and Nor, and my crazy father, and the hothead Americans and our supine government and the ridiculous idea that you can meddle overseas and not have to face the consequences.'

Jonah and Andy stood side by side on the cliffs on the north side of the island, looking down on the crescent of beach that served as a landing strip stretching away to the north-east, and beyond it the island of South Uist. They had hiked across the hills in silence. They knew how to be quiet together. Jonah attributed it to shared marches across the knife-edge ridges of Afghanistan in the heyday of the Guides.

'Flora's happy to see you,' Beech told him.

'You have a beautiful son and a beautiful wife. You're very lucky.'

'And I don't intend to lose them.'

Jonah sighed. 'What is it, Beech?'

'I had a call from Alex.'

'I'm done with Alex,' Jonah said. He wanted to say – *I'm free of his blackmail*. But he was squeamish about saying such things aloud. And it wasn't true.

'It's about Nor. Something you need to know.'

'I haven't seen Nor since 2003,' Jonah told him. Not since Nor had disappeared into northern Iraq with the diamonds and Jonah was dispatched to Kuwait in disgrace. 'I'm no longer in contact with him.'

'Listen to me,' Beech said. 'You can't hide from this one, it's serious. Nor has confessed to everything. He's posted a video on the Internet. He made a full confession of his crimes, including the death of Kiernan and the Department's part in covering it up.'

Jonah rubbed his face. 'Shit.'

'Worse than shit. The Americans are incandescent with rage. They want scapegoats. Monteith has been suspended. Fisher-King from MI6 has taken control of the investigation. He's put an inquisitor from MI5 in charge of the Department. They're going through all the files.'

'What would Five want with the Department?'

'That's not all that's in the video. Nor has sworn revenge, starting with a spectacular infrastructure attack on London.'

'Shit.'

'Alex told me to warn you. You're not safe any more. None of us are. Christ, I don't need this, Jonah. I don't want to lose my family.'

'You'll be OK,' Jonah said, in an attempt to reassure him.

'Don't be so bloody stupid,' Beech snapped. 'You know what happened. You killed a CIA agent. You think anybody is going to give a damn that I had an attack of conscience and walked away. We're tainted goods. Given the chance, they'll tear us limb from limb.'

'Monteith will protect us.'

'Do you really believe that?'

Jonah breathed out heavily. 'I don't know.'

'Why would Nor come out of hiding now?' Beech demanded. 'Nothing for a few years and now suddenly he blows the whole thing wide open. Why?'

'I don't know,' Jonah said.

'You know that they suspect you of being in league with him.'

'Do they?'

'You were so close for so long. Nor was your joe.'

'That doesn't make me complicit,' Jonah said. 'Did Alex say anything else?'

'He wants you to go and see him,' Beech replied. 'He says that he needs to talk to you urgently.'

'Do you think I should?' Jonah asked.

'I don't know. I don't trust him any more than you do. I just want to live a peaceful life. I thought that you'd know what to do.'

But Jonah didn't know what to do. He thought that he'd revoked any responsibility for the safety of others. 'You want me to talk to him, don't you?'

'I want to be sure that my family is safe. I don't want to be caught up in this. Do you hear me? You need to sort this mess out.'

'I hear you,' Jonah replied.

'We shouldn't have gone back into Afghanistan,' Beech insisted.

'There's nothing we can do about it now.'

There was a pause.

'Alex told me that you had a chance to kill Nor in the Sahara in 2002; he said that you let him go.'

'I'm not an assassin. What would you have done?'

'You need to leave in the morning,' Beech told him.

The house was silent. Beech and Flora had gone to bed. Nor's hollowed-out face stared at him out of the tube and beside it the title:

A spy's confession
The Koran commands you to speak the truth, even if it be against your own selves (more)

Jonah clicked on the link and the clip played.

'I swear to God,' Nor said, speaking out of the tube, 'the greatest tide that ever was remembered in England . . .'

Afterwards he sat in Beech's chair, with his head tipped back, staring at the ceiling. He thought, *What are you playing at Nor?*

What caused you to make such a public declaration? Was the penitent's desire for confession or is it that someone paid you to do it? Or was it, as seemed most likely, the thirst for the public spectacle of revenge that compelled you? After all, he thought, revenge was nothing if it was not public. There was something else that bothered him. Why single out the British when there was an opportunity to ridicule the Americans too? Why not pour scorn on the neocon Winthrop, the hidden programme Eschatos and the millenarian Pastor Bob? Why not trumpet the ease with which you defrauded them of the diamonds? He wanted to ask the actor's question: what's your motivation? Most of all he wanted to ask: who's standing at your shoulder? Who lit your touchpaper?

The phone rang at 2 a.m. Beech was called to a domestic incident in Castlebay. Jonah was lying awake in the next room. He listened to the muffled sound of Beech getting dressed through the wall, the clomp of his policeman's boots on the landing and finally his Land Rover starting up, and driving off down the lane.

Flora came to him soon after, slipping soundlessly into his room and under the bed covers. She huddled naked against him, her head pressed against his shoulder, her whole body shaking with anger or remorse, he wasn't sure which. He lifted her face to his and she closed her eyes and inhaled, and he felt her eyelashes brush his cheek. Then she pressed her mouth hungrily to his – kissing her felt like dissolving . . .

She reached for his penis and he ran his hand up her side and cupped a breast, brushing the nipple between the fork of his fingers. Then he rolled over on to her and her legs parted and she steered him inside her; he plunged deep inside her, and his other hand moved down her back and between the groove of her buttocks, lifting her upwards. They slid back and forth on a film of sweat and it felt as if they were riding a wave, that there were no longer two bodies, but one single sensation building towards a climax. The savagery of his desire overwhelmed him: he came with his face in a violent grimace and she yelled: 'Fuck! Fuck! Fuck . . .!'

The vulnerable city riff again

August 2005

This time they met at Woolwich Reach, on the concrete apron at the entrance to the Thames Barrier visitors' centre. Alex was leaning against a picnic table outside the café, wearing a day-glo vest marked ENVIRONMENT AGENCY. The burnished-steel hoods of the barrier's concrete piers stretched across the muddy swirl of the Thames before them. A row of flags carrying the Environment Agency emblem rattled on flagpoles on the freshly seeded grass banks beside the control room. From where they were standing, looking west, you could see the Millennium Dome and beyond it the towers of Canary Wharf.

'Next to fire, water remains the greatest threat to the city.' Alex told him, jabbing an unlit cigarette at him. 'December 1663 – three years before the Great Fire – a storm surge in the North Sea carried a massive tidal wave down the Thames and flooded Whitehall. It swept away the government.'

He paused to light the cigarette, cupping his palms to shield his lighter flame.

'I've heard your vulnerable city riff before,' Jonah reminded him. He had little patience to hear it again.

Alex inhaled and waved the cigarette in his face. 'But have you been listening? London has always been vulnerable to flooding. Fourteen people died in the Thames flood of 1928, and three hundred and seven died in 1953. One hundred and sixty thousand acres of farmland were flooded. All it takes is a combination of two things: a storm surge and a spring tide. A storm surge generated by low pressure in the Atlantic Ocean tracks eastwards past the north of Scotland and is then driven into the shallow waters of the North Sea, where a giant wave is formed. From there it's funnelled into the Thames Estuary. You couple that with a spring tide on a moonless night and, all of a sudden, more than a million East Enders are rushing for the high ground. And that won't be pretty, mate.'

'We're British. We'll form a queue. Anyway, isn't that why we've got the Barrier?'

'It may not be up to the task,' Alex explained. 'In 1990, the number of barrier closures was one or two a year. In 2003 the Barrier was raised on fourteen consecutive tides.'

'Why?'

'Global warming and something called post-glacial rebound, which means that the south of England is tilting downwards like a badly made table.' Alex dropped his cigarette and ground the stub into the concrete. 'A Thames Barrier flood defence closure is triggered when a combination of high tides in the North Sea and high river flows at Teddington weir indicate that water levels will rise more than five metres in central London. Control usually has nine hours' warning; any less and we're waist deep in water – five hundred thousand houses, four hundred schools, sixteen hospitals and eight power stations, and all of it fucked. One and a half million people at risk. The estimated cost of a flood that overwhelms the Barrier is somewhere in the region of thirteen billion quid. They're making a film about it. Robert Carlyle – you know, Begbie from *Trainspotting* – but with a terrible cockney accent. He plays the engineer who has to raise the gates again after terrorists have stormed the control room. Terrible tosh, really. My people are working on it in an advisory capacity.'

'You think that it's a credible scenario?'

Alex gave him an incredulous look. 'Disabling the Barrier on a high tide? Are you stupid? Of course it's fucking credible. Nor's made a threat. He's a resourceful chap. People are taking him at his word. They're going to raise the threat level to critical. That means mobilisation of the emergency services and the armed forces, or at least what we can find at the back of the cupboard given that most of them are in Iraq or Afghanistan.' Alex sprang up from the table and strode to the edge of the grass bank leading to the water, as if expecting some sudden activity to follow on from his words. 'Ideally, that means the cavalry in tanks on the Barrier, SAS boys from Hereford camped out in the control room, marine commandos in ribs escorting shipping in the estuary, a cordon of navy divers on the immediate approaches, roadblocks, helicopters, underwater netting, maybe even a submarine. Come to think of it the submarine is probably the one thing you can count on. That's just to try and prevent it happening . . .'

Alex paused and gave him a significant look. Jonah dutifully fed him his cue. 'And if it happens?'

Alex ran a hand through his hair. 'Cobra is drafting a contingency plan for the flood relief effort and is discussing a full national disaster preparedness exercise. And nothing about it is easy. A flood on this scale will rip the heart out of the government. The emergency services won't fare much better. Scotland Yard is in the flood zone so their special operations room will have to decamp to Hendon. The Fire Brigade will have to abandon Lambeth, and besides, fire engines can't operate in water above exhaust level and they've only got two boats. The ambulance service is in worse nick. Their control centres are in Waterloo and Bow, both in the flood zone. Ambulances can't operate in water of any depth. Hospitals will lose power and sanitation. The police will retain overall command but they will require substantial support from the army in rescue and repair operations. Under normal circumstances that assistance would be forthcoming, but given the constraints currently on the army new thinking is required, and for this reason a significant role is envisioned for the private sector. We're talking about the establishment and maintenance of camps for the internally displaced, a guard force for first-aid points, morgues, et cetera, as well as the provision of close protection to workers re-establishing electricity and sewerage. On top of that a general capacity to secure neighbourhoods and confront criminals with lethal force.'

'You're talking about armed civilians on the streets of London?'

'Armed professionals,' Alex corrected him. 'The day-to-day burden of defending society is now too big for the state to handle alone.'

There was something about the idea of it that struck Jonah as deeply wrong. 'This isn't America,' he protested.

'It's Blair's Britain, mate, get used to it.'

'And I suppose that you've secured yourself the contract?'

'This is bigger than any British firm. We've had to take on American partners.'

'You're serious?'

'Let me put it this way, negotiations are at an advanced stage with a major US security contractor for the provision of manpower and services in the event of a catastrophic flood.'

Jonah looked out across the water. It didn't seem to matter how bad it got, Alex would find a way to profit from it.

'Beech said that Monteith has been suspended?'

'Monteith's a spent force,' Alex replied. 'Fisher-King has washed his hands of him. Five have stepped in with an audit team headed up by a wizened old spy-catcher called Holdfast. They're going through all the files. They're putting names to faces. It's only a matter of time before they pin the Kiernan assassination on you. You'd better start making plans. If I was you I'd be liquidating my assets, preparing to disappear somewhere without an extradition treaty. I've heard Venezuela is nice. Mongolia less so . . .'

'And you? What are you going to do?'

'What I always do. I'm cutting a deal.'

'With who?'

'Listen to me, none of us owes a damn thing to Monteith.'

'And the rest of us? Do you owe us?'

'I'm sorry, Jonah, but you had your chance. You could have put a stop to all of this but you did nothing. I'm not taking a fall for you. And as for the others, Beech should be fine, he walked away, after all. He can justifiably claim he knew nothing. And Lennard, he's in Burma, mate, he's revoked all things material. He's already in a cell.'

'Where is Monteith?'

'He's hiding out down near Bristol at his old alma mater, Clifton College. It's a little puppy kennel for would-be imperialists. They'll love you down there. Tell him to find somewhere better to hide.'

When he returned to the car park, Jonah discovered that his Land Rover had been stolen. He contemplated walking back to the visitors' centre to tell Alex but then thought better of it. He could do with a walk. He set off along the Thames path.

He spent that night in a hotel in Earl's Court frequented by backpackers. He lay on a single bed and stared up at the water-damaged ceiling. He could hardly bear to acknowledge the scale of his betrayal of both Beech and Miranda. Beech, who was an honest and loyal friend, and Miranda, who had given up everything to go with him to exist in virtual exile in Scotland, and who had waited patiently while he wrote his ridiculous memoir.

At the same time he could not clear from his mind the memory of Flora clinging to him, her mouth hungrily searching for his. He felt inflamed.

How much Flora was in love with him he did not know; she had once asked him whether it was a game of secrets. He wanted to tell her that it was not.

In the morning Jonah took a taxi to Paddington and a train to Bristol. He found Monteith sitting at a long oak refectory table in the Clifton College school library with a pile of manuscripts on the table in front of him. Term had ended and the school was deserted.

Monteith looked up with his reading glasses perched on the end of his nose and gave him a candid stare. 'Were you followed?'

Jonah shrugged. 'If there were enough of them and they were working in shifts. Do you know anyone that good?'

'Maybe,' Monteith replied.

'With respect, I don't think that they need to follow me to find you. They probably already know where you are. You should move somewhere more secure.'

Monteith grunted and returned to reading the manuscript on

the desk. '*The present age is generally thought to be more chaotic than those which went before it,* he said, reading from the manuscript. *Life has become more controversial; controversy is more violent; the unintelligent are perverting science into a new form of superstition.* For science read security and they could be talking about the present day. It is ironic really. The letter was signed by four Old Cliftonians: Field Marshal Haig, Birdwood, who commanded the ANZAC forces at Gallipoli, the poet Henry Newbolt, and Younghusband.'

Monteith was an avid student of Francis Younghusband, the repressed, headstrong Edwardian explorer who'd shadowed the Russians on the North-West Frontier, opened an overland route from China to India, and led a quixotic military invasion of Tibet. He was a student of anything that touched on the clandestine quest for information and power in the huge uncharted expanse of mountainous territory between the empires of Britain and Tsarist Russia that had been popularly known as the Great Game.

'Come on,' Monteith said, pressing his hands palms down on the table and rising, 'let's go for a stroll in the grounds.' He picked up a canvas Gladstone bag by its handles. They walked past empty classrooms and down a steep set of stone steps and across a quadrangle.

'It's difficult to see now from looking at the current crop but Clifton's founding ambition was to produce the sort of men who would run the British Empire. It was remarkably successful. Thousands of them set forth over the years: soldiers, sailors, political agents, civil servants. Men of moral and political integrity, imbued with the qualities of administration and leadership, and unsparing and unstinting of themselves in their country's service.'

They walked past the chapel and a memorial to those who had died in the South African War.

'Isn't that when we invented the concentration camp?' Jonah asked.

'Don't be flippant.'

In front of the playing fields there was a statue of Field Marshal Haig, the inventor of trench warfare.

'I'm trying to remember how many people died on the first day of the Somme,' Jonah said. 'Twenty thousand, was it?'

Monteith blithely ignored him. 'I often wonder what it was like for them, when the school had only just been founded. How they went out into the world, conscious that they were the first and that it was up to them to set the school's reputation. Sit down.'

They sat on a bench, looking out over the empty playing fields.

'For the rest of us it was merely a question of trying to live up to the standards that they set,' Monteith continued. 'I've tried my best. There have been some nasty jobs that have had to be done and I've not shirked from them. I've seen them through. I don't regret trying to assassinate Bin Laden in '99. If we had succeeded the world would be a very different place today.'

'We were played,' Jonah told him.

'My overriding concern has been to protect the safety and security of the British populace.'

Monteith was staring intently at the dark strip of woods in the distance.

'Is everything all right?' Jonah asked.

'Can you see someone?'

'Why?'

'I thought I saw someone.'

Monteith reached inside his canvas bag and produced a pair of binoculars and turned to focus them on the woods. After a pause he said gloomily, 'Ramblers.'

Jonah studiedly Monteith discreetly; he looked tired, but not unhinged.

'You sound as if you're disappointed.'

'I want them watching me,' Monteith explained, in a tone that suggested that he was having to explain himself to a small child. 'That way I'll know where they are when I decide to disappear.' He returned the binoculars to the bag. 'We've got a problem, a serious bloody problem.'

'Go on.'

'Fisher-King is suffering selective memory loss. He says he never sanctioned the parlay with the mullah. As if he wasn't there, sitting at the back of the room with his bloody sanctimonious smile. He denies all knowledge of an order to assassinate Bin Laden or a conversation with our American cousins. He knows nothing about the death of Kiernan or the Department's involvement in it. He knows nothing and his organisation knows nothing. Instead, Fisher-King has chosen to accuse the MoD of running a black-ops kill squad run by yours truly and staffed by a gaggle of mulatto flotsam of questionable loyalty.'

'Mulatto flotsam?'

'That's what he said.'

'I'll try not to be offended.'

'I'm offended on your behalf. But that's not the worst of it.'

'Go on . . .'

'They're going to let the plot run. They've no plans to intercept Nor before he gets here.'

'Why would they do that?'

'Because Fisher-King thinks that he can score a propaganda coup and smash an al-Qaeda cell in this country if they can lure Nor here and catch him red-handed. He probably thinks they'll give him a knighthood. How could he be so bloody foolhardy?'

'Where is Nor now?'

'The video confession was uploaded in an Internet café in Peshawar.'

'Pakistan,' Jonah mused. 'How is Pakistan these days?'

'Most of the money that doesn't go to service their international debt is spent by the military, which doesn't leave anything over for schools or hospitals. And the military, which I would say is the last bastion of credible power in the country, is increasingly infiltrated by Islamist factions allied with jihadist elements and assisted by our old friends in the ISI. Efforts to impose rule over Baluchistan and the Federally Administered Tribal Areas have largely been in vain. The Pakistan army was recently kicked out of South Waziristan by well-armed jihadis. Kashmir is a mess and there is, of course, the threat of loose nukes.'

'So it's my kind of place.'

'It is,' Monteith replied, without smiling. 'I suggest that you get yourself there straight away. Find Nor and finish the job once and for all. I mean kill him.'

'I know what you mean.'

'I can't afford for you to get cold feet again.'

'I'll do the job,' Jonah told him.

'Good.'

'But I'm not going to be able to take a step without the ISI knowing about it.'

'Of course.'

Jonah realised with a sinking feeling that he had no means of secure communication with Miranda. No means of telling her that he would not be coming straight back. A second betrayal.

'Let me explain something to you, Jonah.' Monteith was staring fixedly into the distance with his fists clenched on his knees. 'After the ambush and the death of Kiernan, I came under considerable pressure to take action against you. Fisher-King accused you of being in league with Nor. It didn't help that your personal life was a mess. The collapse of your marriage was judged to be a destabilising influence. I had to fight to keep you. At the same time, I had to fight to maintain my own standing. The Department was threatened. Certain compromises had to be made. I did not approve the kidnapping of your wife's lover six years ago. I did not initiate it. In fact I argued against it. But my arguments did not prevail. I regret now that I did not fight harder for you. You have never given me any reason to doubt your loyalty.'

In all the years that he'd known him, Jonah had never heard Monteith admit a mistake, let alone make an apology. He came from a generation of soldiers who viewed any admission of failure as a weakness. It was unnerving. 'I need to leave for the airport,' Jonah told him.

Monteith studied him for a while. 'Very well.' He opened his canvas bag again and delved about in it, retrieving a passport. He handed it to Jonah.

'They've put a stop on your personal passport. This one should still be good. I pocketed it before I left.'

The passport was Belgian. Jonah flicked through the well-worn pages, noting the mishmash of immigration stamps. He stopped at the photo page. 'Is that the best photo of me you could find?'

Monteith grimaced. 'You look almost human.'

'My name is Ishmael?'

'Ishmael was Abraham's oldest son, born by his wife's servant Hagar. He was the world's first bastard.' He cleared his throat. '*He shall be a wild ass of a man, his hand against every man and every man's hand against him.* Genesis sixteen; verse eleven. Rather apt, I thought.'

Next Monteith passed him an envelope packed with cash.

'There's ten thousand dollars in there. In addition I have a line of credit with Yakoob Beg that you can utilise. I warn you, Jonah, they're preparing to make a scapegoat of you. You're not safe and nobody around you is either. I shredded everything I could before I left but it won't make any difference. They'll build a conspiracy out of your schooldays with Nor. They'll use the kidnapping as evidence of sociopathy. With her history, they'll have a field day with Miranda. She'll be cast as an accomplice. They'll plant evidence tying you to the plot. And it's certain they'll use it as the pretext to bring down your mother and end the reforms to the intelligence community that she has championed. The only chance you have to prevent all that is to find Nor and put a stop to him before he gets anywhere near this country.'

The North-West Frontier

In Peshawar there was a layer of brown smog that trapped the acrid smoke from the refuse fires of Afghan refugees. Each morning Jonah sat in the courtyard at Green's Hotel and listened to the songbirds in cages on the roof. For four days he had been waiting on permission to travel up into the tribal areas in the mountainous border regions where Afghanistan blurred into Pakistan.

It was a week since he had travelled as Ishmael to Lahore via Dubai. In Lahore, he stayed in a cheap hotel above a row of gold shops and ate curried chicken and dhal on Annarkali Street. The following morning he flew to Peshawar, the bustling city at the foot of the Khyber Pass, the gateway to Afghanistan.

It was more than six years since he had last stayed at Green's Hotel. That was in the immediate aftermath of the shooting of the CIA agent Kiernan, in the final days before Monteith, who was terrified of discovery, dispersed the Afghan Guides to the four winds. Jonah was sent to the Kosovo/Albanian border and a few weeks later his wife ended their marriage. Six years in which the landscape had irrevocably changed: Iraq and Afghanistan were under occupation and there was a blockade of fuel and food supplies to the tribal areas, where thousands of Pakistani troops backed by tanks, helicopter gunships and artillery were rolling northwards into the Pashtun villages, searching for jihadis.

And two men in a beat-up Toyota Hilux followed him every time he stepped out of the hotel.

★

Ms Nasir of the Narcotics Section of the Home Department of the Federally Administered Tribal Areas had all the trappings of a Pakistani bureaucrat – a dingy private office, a locked filing cabinet, a huge red telephone and a stapler, a desk fan for when the electricity worked and a view out of the window of a jumble of bricks. Her purpose was to stamp and initial permits for the tribal areas. It was a job that gave her absolute bureaucratic power and she knew it. On his first visit Jonah filled in the forms and told her that he was looking for his brother; on the second he brought her a packet of duty-free dates from Dubai; and on this third visit a bottle of perfume.

'The tribal areas contain a very sensitive frontier,' she told him. 'We must protect our borders.'

'I'm very worried about my brother,' Jonah explained. He was squeezed into a chair that was far too small for him, leaning forward and trying to appear eager without toppling forward on to the desk.

'Does your brother also have a Belgian passport?'

'No. He has a Jordanian passport.'

Ms Nasir eyed him sceptically. 'Excuse me, but what is he doing in the tribal areas?'

There was a sticker on the desk that read SAUDI RELIEF COMMITTEE FOR AFGHANISTAN. 'He's working for an Islamic relief organisation helping refugees,' Jonah explained.

Ms Nasir pursed her lips in a disapproving manner. 'We have a lot of problems with foreigners in the tribal areas.'

'I want to bring him home,' Jonah said. 'His father is sick. It is possible that he may not survive much longer.'

A smartly dressed man in a white shirt and black tie knocked, entered and whispered in Ms Nasir's ear. She listened intently. The man finished and left. Ms Nasir contemplated Jonah with renewed scepticism.

'Come back at four p.m. tomorrow.'

The corridor outside Ms Nasir's office was no longer empty. Someone had produced a light bulb and a white plastic chair.

Sitting in the chair, in a pair of pressed slacks and a tweed sports coat, with a bamboo cane across his crossed knees and a group of well-dressed, eager young men around him, was the man whose dog-eared likeness was stapled at the centre of the Afghan collage, the man who more than any other was responsible for the rise of the Taliban, Monteith's arch-nemesis, 'The Hidden Hand', Brigadier Javid Aslam Khan, retired former head of the Afghan Bureau of the Directorate of Inter-Service Intelligence, the ISI.

'You are looking for Mr Nor ed-Din, I believe?' the Brigadier said.

'I am,' Jonah told him.

'You know, you do not look much like Nor's brother. You are much darker. Not so slight. I think maybe you had different mothers. Is that right?'

'Something like that,' Jonah agreed.

'But there's no mistaking the father. I can see it in your face. The Scotsman Monteith fathered you both. He sent you here to bedevil me. Do you know who I am?'

There wasn't any point denying it. 'I do, Brigadier.'

'Am I still on his wall?'

Jonah nodded. 'You are.'

'Am I still at the centre?'

'You are.'

The brigadier laughed. The well-dressed young men laughed alongside him. 'I do not deserve it but I count it a great honour to be so revered. Come on, young man. I know these tribal people. I understand how their minds work. I'm going to help you find your brother.'

They ate freshly caught fish in a makeshift hut on the banks of the Kabul river. The brigadier peered over the top of his bifocals into a plastic cold box and used the tip of his bamboo cane to indicate his choice of fish. The cook, a Pashtun with a hennaed beard, weighed and gutted the fish, then rolled it in seasoned flour and chilli flakes and slid it gently into mustard seed oil. While it cooked they walked across a stone causeway and past a fairground, the darkened shapes of carousels looming out of the wood smoke around them. The brigadier's assistants followed, maintaining a discreet distance.

'As the snow melts in Afghanistan the water level rises and these people are forced to leave,' said the brigadier, pointing to the collection of shanty-town restaurants with their chugging generators and vertical strip lights. 'They've only got a few days left here . . .'

He looked thoughtful. Khan had taken it upon himself to educate Jonah.

'You know, it is not true that we created the Taliban. They were an indigenous movement. Of course, we started supporting them when they became powerful. Pakistan just wanted a stable and peaceful neighbour to the west. That's all we have ever wanted. What you in the West fail to understand is that the Taliban bought stability to Afghanistan. Before that it was anarchy. Warlords and gangsters flourished in the vacuum left by the Soviets. Afghanistan is a tribal country where you need strong tribal leaders and strict tribal laws. The Taliban provided that.'

'I'm sure that you had the best intentions, Brigadier.'

The brigadier snorted. 'You are in too much of a hurry. How much do you really know about the history of the Taliban? Not much, I can see by your expression.'

'Brigadier, please. There's no time.'

'Nonsense,' the brigadier said. 'I will tell you. The movement originated in a village madrasa near Kandahar. A band of students led by their teacher, Mohammed Omar, freed two women who had been raped by local commanders. They hanged the commanders from the barrel of a tank. A few months later, two commanders fought a battle on the streets of Kandahar over a boy that they both wished to rape. Omar arrived with his students, freed the boy and executed the commanders. This was exactly what the people needed.

'Straight away we saw an opportunity. Afghanistan is a perfect corridor for goods from Central Asia. These countries needed an outlet for their oil and gas. At the time the route to Central Asia through the north was blocked by the fighting in Kabul, so we decided to try the southern route. We put together an aid convoy, thirty trucks or so, that was to drive from Quetta and travel via Kandahar and Herat to Askhabad in Turkmenistan. The convoy was a sweetener, to encourage meaningful negotiations on energy supplies. In October 1994 the trucks left Quetta with several young military officers and a number of irregulars. Your colleague Nor was among them.' He glanced across at Jonah. 'I remember him. He was a quiet and courteous young man.'

And by that stage recruited into the ISI, Jonah thought. One of your prized assets, your eyes and ears inside the Taliban, though ours first. He sighed. 'Go on, Brigadier.'

'Near Kandahar some of the city's militia leaders blocked the convoy's route, demanding money, and Nor was among those who were taken hostage. For three days we waited. After a suitable pause, we turned to the Taliban for help and Mullah Omar agreed to free the convoy by force. The students carried out an assault on the village where the convoy was parked and chased out the commanders and their men. That same evening they attacked Kandahar, and after two days of fighting captured it. It was the beginning of a campaign that brought Afghanistan under control in just two years. Early in 1995 they took Herat, and a year later they were in Kabul.'

'You must have been pleased.'

'Of course we were pleased,' said the brigadier with a shrug of his shoulders, 'and let me tell you we were not the only ones. The Americans were ecstatic. They had a new route for a pipeline. American oil companies opened offices in Kandahar. But of course it didn't last. The Taliban became too ambitious. They weren't content to bring peace. They wanted to create the purest Islamic society in the world. There were excesses. We did not approve of the restrictions that they placed on women, but they no longer consulted us. There was nothing to be done.'

'And Nor?' Jonah prompted him, gently.

'He went with them all the way to Kabul and that's the last I heard of him. Obviously he turned bad.'

'Brigadier, please don't treat me like an idiot.'

'What do you mean? I'm trying to help you to understand.'

'Brigadier. I've been here for almost a week now.'

'I know what you are going to say,' the brigadier said loftily, peering at Jonah through the drifting smoke. 'But you must understand that these things take time. It is a vast area. There are perhaps thirty or forty permanent training camps, and more than a hundred transient ones. Small groups and individuals are lodged with families. There are Arabs, Central Asians and South Asians, as well as Chechens, Bosnians and Uighurs from western China. We are looking for one man. One man! And even if we find him there is no guarantee that the tribal people will give him up. They do not give up guests easily. They have their own laws and their own customs. The rules of hospitality are inflexible. And the Taliban are resurgent. Frankly speaking, the army is struggling against them. There have been setbacks. Then there are the Americans, with their Predator drones and their Hellfire missiles. You must understand the difficulties that we face.'

Jonah repeated the question. 'Brigadier, when did you last hear from Nor?'

'A very long time ago. I would need to consult my records.'

'Brigadier, we both know that Nor was your asset.'

'He was never my asset,' the brigadier snapped, tapping his swagger stick against the tops of his boots in irritation. 'That's what I said to the FBI when they came to me. This Nor was a British asset, I said, nothing to do with us. They showed me the video of Nor's confession. Go and speak to Monteith, I said. He's the man who killed Kiernan.' He turned to Jonah and pointed the stick at him. 'Have I surprised you? I can see by your expression I have. Did you really think that I would hold up my hand and confess that Nor was ours? Your agency deliberately planted a spy in the Taliban and now that he has gone rogue you want us to sort out the bloody mess for you. Forgive me if we are not overjoyed about it.' He turned around and strode back along the causeway towards the shacks. 'Come on, the fish will be ready.'

'I need to speak to Nor, Brigadier,' Jonah insisted, hurrying after him.

The brigadier frowned, as if the idea was not agreeable. 'In good time.'

'Brigadier, Monteith is sitting on a filing cabinet full of evidence that links Nor to the ISI and in particular to you.'

The brigadier had stopped and was staring at Jonah. 'Are you blackmailing me?'

'Yes, sir.'

'You're an impudent pup.'

'No, Brigadier, I'm a fully grown dog.'

The brigadier sucked on his moustache for a moment. 'I can see you are.'

'Monteith knew that as soon as I mentioned Nor ed-Din's name in this town you would come looking for me. I've been ready and waiting. Now I need your help.'

The brigadier nodded. 'We'll talk after the food.'

He ducked under the awning of the nearest shack, and his assistants pulled up two string bedsteads.

'Sit,' he said. Jonah sat.

The cook delivered their fish on a large platter. They ate it with their fingers, lifting the flesh off the bone, and after the meal they tucked balls of snuff under their lips and passed around a flask of whisky.

'Well?' Jonah asked.

'We believe that Nor is being given shelter in one of the villages in Bajaur Agency,' the brigadier told him. 'Tomorrow we'll get you a permit. Then we can go and find him.'

The shadow army

It was after three when Brigadier Khan strode into Green's flanked by his assistants. Spotting Jonah, he crossed the courtyard towards him, weaving between the chairs and tables and acknowledging the greeting of several groups of businessmen with a smile and a wave of his cane. He came to an abrupt halt in front of Jonah and the smile vanished just as abruptly.

'Good afternoon, Brigadier,' Jonah said, looking up from the postcards that he was struggling to write. The brigadier tossed a folded sheet of A4 on to the coffee table. Jonah unfolded it. It was a standard Red Notice issued by Interpol's General Secretariat seeking the provisional arrest of a wanted person with a view to extradition based on an arrest warrant. There was a photo of Jonah and identity particulars (physical description, fingerprints, aliases, etc.) as well as details of the warrant.

'Shall I continue to call you Ishmael?' the brigadier demanded. 'Or would Jonah be more appropriate?'

Jonah wasn't surprised. Shortly after rising and showering that morning, he had walked a block to an Internet café, and sat at a terminal in a tiny curtained-off chipboard booth to check his emails. There had been two messages in his inbox. One from Monteith. One from Flora. He had opened the one from Monteith first:

US Attorney's office has issued warrant for your arrest.

Then he had opened the one from Flora:

I love you. There, I've said it. I wish it was not so. But I can't help it. I refuse to live in a world of lies. I've told Beech. Everything is in ruins.

'You can call me whatever you like, Brigadier,' Jonah replied.

'Nor spoke of you. I remember it. You were at boarding school together.'

'We were,' Jonah acknowledged.

Never underestimate Khan's snobbery or his attachment to all things British – he may be a jihadi but he's a pukka one, was Monteith's memorable line. Like Jonah and Nor, Javid Khan was the product of a minor boarding school in the English home counties. A generation separated them, but had been enough to suggest a form of kinship a decade before when the Department floated a freshly discharged and recently disgraced former British army officer named Nor ed-Din in front of Khan as bait.

'Why shouldn't I hand you over to the police?' the brigadier demanded.

'Because you'll be next . . .' Jonah was finding it difficult to reconcile the Anglophile with the jihadi. 'Why exactly did Kiernan have to die?'

The brigadier flicked his cane across his boot-tops in irritation. 'The Home Department has issued you a permit.'

'Good,' Jonah replied.

'We leave first thing in the morning.'

'Good.'

The brigadier turned on his heel and strode away.

Jonah finished his postcards and walked over to the post office opposite the hotel to buy stamps. He snarled at one of the watchers when he got too close. The man slunk away.

'Al-Qaeda has re-established the predominantly Arab and Asian paramilitary formation that was formerly known as Brigade 055 as part of a larger, more effective fighting unit known as the Lashkar al-Zil, or Shadow Army,' the brigadier explained, staring out of the window of his Nissan Patrol at the passing landscape, the ragged peaks veined with marble and the fortress-like compounds. They were driving up through Mohmand to Bajaur in a four-vehicle convoy with a squad of tribal police as escort. The brigadier's mood had much improved.

'The Shadow Army has units analogous to battalion, brigade and division formations. They have good weaponry and better communications systems than our own army. Even the sniper rifles they use are better than ours. Their tactics are sophisticated and they have defences including trench and tunnel networks as well as bunkers and pillboxes that are taking us days or weeks to dismantle. It's mind-boggling. This is not a ragtag militia. They are fighting like an organised force and they have been instrumental in the Taliban's consolidation of power in the tribal areas.'

They passed a pile of Soviet aircraft bombs outside a scrapyard in Muhmadkut and clusters of collapsing mud hovels that had once housed Afghan refugees who had since returned. Jonah wondered how long it would be before the bombs followed them over the border and were used to manufacture improvised explosive devices.

'We believe that Nor has put together a specialist unit of the Shadow Army, trained to undertake acts of sabotage overseas,' the brigadier told him.

'How do you know this?' Jonah asked.

'The army has captured one of them.'

They passed a column of Pakistan army trucks towing artillery pieces. It began to rain, a light drizzle. The tribal police squatting in the back of the pick-up ahead drew their *pattus* around their shoulders and clutched the barrels of their assault rifles more tightly.

'The prisoner is in the custody of the Government Agent in Khar. That's where we are going.'

A Cobra attack helicopter flew directly overhead, its undercarriage so close that the driver ducked his head and swore, and the police were buffeted by the rotor-wash.

The Government Agent's office was housed in a wooden building with dripping eaves which resembled a large and long-neglected cricket pavilion. On the walls of his office were several wooden panels engraved with the names of his predecessors; a succession of government agents dating back to the early nineteenth century, when the first ones were young subalterns of the British Raj.

The current incumbent was a bearded Pashtun, a member of the Wazir clan of South Waziristan, who, according to the brigadier, had been disowned by his family since accepting the post and lived with a considerable bounty on his head. He greeted them in his office and then led them through a side door and down a dark and mouldy corridor to a storeroom that smelt of wet canvas.

The prisoner was hanging by his dislocated arms from a length of chain attached to a roof beam. He was naked and his body was covered in livid bruises. There was an expression of utter dejection on his swollen face. There were two large Pakistani soldiers standing on either side of him. Each of them was holding a four-foot metal bar.

The brigadier spoke to them in Urdu and they replied at some length. The brigadier looked back at Jonah, who was standing in the doorway, trying not to remember being similarly strung up in a basement beneath the stables in Baghdad.

'This chap attempted to sell a diamond in the market, a very large diamond.'

'Who is he?'

'He's a deserter.'

'What unit was he serving with?'

'He was a Black Stork, a combat diver of the Naval Special Services Group based in Karachi. He is one of five. They are trained combat divers. Until three months ago they were working at the new deep-water port in Gwadar. Then there were some difficulties. Since then, they have been hiding out in a family compound towards Loyesam, near the Afghan border.'

'And?'

'Three months ago they were approached by an individual who meets Nor's description. He offered them highly paid employment.'

'What kind of employment?'

'An underwater demolition job.'

'Where?'

'He wasn't told.'

'Ask him again.'

The brigadier spoke to one of the guards, who stepped up to the prisoner and struck him across the ribs with the metal bar. The prisoner screamed.

'Not like that!'

The brigadier appeared surprised. 'You don't approve of our methods?'

'Just ask him the question,' Jonah replied, through gritted teeth.

The brigadier lifted the man's chin with the tip of his cane and spoke to him softly. He had to hold his ear close to the man's lips to hear him reply.

'He says that they were told that they would be given further details as well as passports with the correct visas and airline tickets on the night before they travelled. They were told that they would be met at the destination and taken to a safe house where they would be provided with the materials necessary to manufacture plastic explosives. Further briefings including the location of the target would be provided in due course.'

The helicopter touched down on the edge of the escarpment and Jonah, suddenly jolted out of sleep, hit the quick release on his safety belt and leapt for the ground like a shipwrecked man scrambling for the shore. Ahead of him, the brigadier strolled to the cliff-edge beside the mortar line and engaged in conversation with the battery commander, who pointed at something in the distance. The mortars sprang out of the tubes with a pop like champagne corks.

The houses in the valley below resembled fortresses, with square turrets and mud-walled compounds the same khaki colour as the surrounding rocks. Several had been destroyed. The explosions caused by impacting mortars looked like tiny blossoms of dust on the distant hillside. A tower took a hit and crumbled.

There was sporadic answering fire: flint-sparks in window-slits and bunkers.

A machine gun opened up and a line of tracer snaked across the space. The brigadier summoned him over. Jonah approached the precipice.

'The infantry are advancing up the valley,' the brigadier said, and pointed with his cane at the line of troops strung across the valley floor. As the soldiers approached the first of the houses the mortar line fell silent. Farther up the valley it was possible to see a line of women on a mountain path, tiny blue dots in burqas fleeing in the direction of Afghanistan.

'Why haven't they closed off their escape route?' Jonah asked.

'Don't presume to tell them their business,' the brigadier scolded him. 'Anyway, it's not their fault. They lost the element of surprise. Just before dawn the Americans fired two missiles from one of their drones at a house in the village.'

Several hours later, standing in the ruin of one of the houses, the brigadier turned over a transistor radio with his cane. A soldier held up a charred exercise book. The only body they had found was that of an elderly Pashtun, curled round a Kalashnikov in a stairwell.

'The miscreants were here, of course,' the brigadier said. 'But it appears that they received prior warning of the attack. The women and the elderly stayed behind to delay our advance and give the fighters long enough to escape.'

'Who warned them?'

The brigadier shrugged. 'I don't know. Do you?'

Bitter with frustration, Jonah continued to pick through the wreckage.

'We had better leave soon. The helicopter has gone. We'll have to drive back.'

'Hold on,' Jonah called. He knelt down beside the open door of a wood-burning stove and reached in to remove the charred mass of papers stuffed inside. He prised them apart. Nothing was legible. There was nothing of value in the house. He wanted to punch a wall.

'Come on, we need to get back before dark,' the brigadier said.

'I'm not coming with you, Brigadier.'

The brigadier frowned. 'What are you going to do?'

'I'm going to follow them.' He pointed towards the mountains of the Hindu Kush. 'I'm going to Afghanistan.'

He knelt down to prise the Kalashnikov out of the elderly man's dead hands.

'I admit that I knew that Kiernan was travelling in that convoy,' the brigadier told him. 'It was my business to know. But I'm not the one that tipped off Nor. He walked away from us at the same time as you walked away from him, whoever he offered his allegiance to . . . the Taliban, al-Qaeda, whoever . . . they are the ones that wanted Kiernan dead, not us. Our fingers have been as badly burned as yours. Remember that when the Americans finally catch up with you. I am not the guilty party.'

'I'll remember,' Jonah replied. Cradling the Kalashnikov in his arms, he set off in the direction of the setting sun.

The new Great Game

The suburban enclave of Wazir Akbar Khan, on the north side of Kabul, once home to the senior ranks of the Taliban and their Arab supporters, had been overtaken by NGO workers, diplomats and journalists. One of its long-time residents remained, though. Yakoob Beg's compound had grown to include several adjacent houses and now occupied an entire city block. There was a checkpoint on the main approach and in front of it a loose knot of petitioners, beggars and hangers-on.

'Coming through,' Jonah called out in Dari, heading for the main gate with its twelve-foot steel doors. People made way for him, staring at him in sullen silence. Jonah greeted one of the guards in Dari and gave his name. Within ten minutes he was being shown into the *hujra*, the guest room. There were about a dozen bearded, turbaned men sitting on silk cushions arranged against the walls, and there was a strong aroma of hashish in the air. Yakoob Beg was reclining beneath a gold-stitched tapestry with a sitar player on his right. He looked larger and sleeker than Jonah remembered, like an overfed cat. He motioned for Jonah to come and sit beside him on his left side.

'Greetings,' he said.

'I hope that you are well,' Jonah told him.

'Business is good, *inshallah*.'

A small boy brought Jonah a beaten metal pot, poured warm water on his hands and then dried them with a towel. He was passed a glass of vodka. Solemnly the men raised their glasses and drained them.

Jonah reflected that there was a certain irony that in their final months controlling the country the Taliban had outlawed opium cultivation and come close to eradicating the crop and as a consequence ending Yakoob Beg's considerable influence and power. But with the triumph of the Northern Alliance and their American backers the opium trade had rebounded and was now flourishing. Yakoob Beg was more powerful than ever.

'How is my friend Colonel Monteith?'

'He is in hiding,' Jonah replied. 'The Department has been disbanded.'

'It is an unfortunate business.'

A dancer entered the room. Dressed in a long blue skirt and a crimson blouse with silver bells attached to hands and feet, face disguised by a red veil, the dancer stepped across the room. The men reached out to touch the skirt as it brushed past.

'I'm here looking for Nor,' Jonah told him.

Yakoob Beg nodded slowly, watching the dancer twisting and turning. 'I understand.'

'Has he been here?'

'He was here in Kabul for a matter of hours,' Yakoob Beg acknowledged with a wave of the hand. The dancer was moving faster and faster, arms held high above a lean, muscular body. The sense of excitement in the room was palpable. 'But he has gone . . .'

'And the men with him . . .?' Jonah asked.

'They were also here and they have also gone.'

'I'd like to know more about them.'

'There is someone that I can ask.'

Finally the veil dropped, revealing a young man's face with the beginnings of a moustache. He was a *bacha* dancer, literally a *boy for play*. One of the men grabbed the veil from the floor and pressed it to his face, inhaling its aroma.

'I appreciate your assistance,' Jonah said.

Another round of vodka followed and then more sitar music and another dancer. The dancer was even younger than the first and wearing lipstick. Yakoob Beg's eyes were almost closed, and

Jonah wondered whether he was asleep, but then he reached into the folds of his robe and retrieved a business card.

'There is an American that wants to speak with you,' he said, passing Jonah the business card. A name was printed on it. Mark Mikulski. And a New York telephone number. He turned over the card. On the back, written in pen, was a telephone number beginning with 070 followed by six figures: an Afghan mobile number. Beneath it, the same pen had written: *Let's talk.*

'He's here in Kabul?'

Yakook Beg nodded.

'He knows that I'm here?'

'An educated guess; he knows that you were in Pakistan and that you crossed the border into Afghanistan.' He made a fluttering gesture with his hand. 'Everybody knows it.'

'What is he doing here?'

'He is leading a team of FBI investigators that are out at Bagram airbase. They have one of the Uzbeks involved in the shooting in custody. He was a child at the time but he is an adult now. He is singing. Since they have been questioning him, they have recovered the wreck of two vehicles from the Khyber Pass and it is said some charred bones.'

'Are you exposed?'

'Perhaps,' Yakoob Beg replied. 'But I have also been careful. The leader of the Uzbeks was dealt with several years ago. The remaining witnesses were very young at the time of the incident. It was a chaotic time and nobody has a clear recollection. Of course, like you I am concerned about further revelations from Nor. It would be unfortunate if he found himself in American custody again. But I also have safeguards in place that will offer me a measure of protection if that occurs.'

'For your own safety, I should leave,' Jonah told him.

'Nonsense, you may stay here for as long as it is safe. But I also think that you should talk to Mr Mark Mikulski.' From his robes he retrieved a mobile phone and passed it to Jonah. 'Take this.'

'Why do you want me to call Mikulski?'

'Kiernan's widow and his eldest daughter are here.'

'If I could take back what happened I would,' Jonah told him. 'Monteith is the same. Any of us would.'

'They have offered a substantial reward for information,' Yakoob Beg explained. 'People are coming forward. The Uzbek was the first, others will inevitably follow. Kiernan's family are being told what they want to hear. Monteith is being painted as a gullible fool and you are being demonised. They accuse you of being al-Qaeda. If you have a chance now to present your side of the story, perhaps you should take it. Who knows when the opportunity might come again?'

'I have to find Nor,' Jonah said, pocketing the phone.

'First you should sleep. In the morning I will make enquiries.'

As he got up to leave, one of the *bacha* dancers took Jonah's place beside Yakoob Beg. He rested his head in the opium trader's lap.

Jonah woke to shafts of sunshine falling through the windows of his room. There were segments of blue sky and racing scuds of cloud. After washing in a bucket, he crossed the courtyard to the *hujra*.

Yakoob Beg was sitting on a cushion watching BBC World coverage of Hurricane Katrina. On the screen Ray Nagin, the mayor of New Orleans, was speaking: 'Every person is hereby ordered to evacuate the city . . .'

Watching it, Jonah found himself reminded of Nor's confession on YouTube, his barely veiled threat: *I swear to God, the greatest tide that ever was remembered in England . . .*

'Will they all leave?' Beg asked.

'Most will,' Jonah replied, 'but some will stay. Others may not be able to leave.'

'What will happen to them?'

'I guess they'll wait for the government to give them assistance.'

'And will the American government ride to the rescue?'

'They should.'

'I have arranged for you to meet someone who can help you,' Beg told him. 'My driver will escort you there.'

A couple of hundred metres beyond the martyr's shrine on Char-i-Shahid, and through a set of large arched wooden doors, there was a small, concealed graveyard with about a hundred and fifty graves. Jonah recognised the wizened old man who was sweeping leaves among the graves, but if the cemetery guardian recognised him in return he gave no indication of it. The old man had tended the graves at Kabul's Christian cemetery for more than fifteen years, paid and unpaid, throughout the civil war, when Jonah had used it as a clandestine meeting place, and subsequently during the Taliban regime, when continuing to care for Christian graves was an invitation to a beating or worse.

There had been some changes since Jonah's last visit. The most recent additions were memorial plaques to fallen soldiers from the International Security Assistance Force (ISAF) Afghanistan. On the right as he entered he saw that there was a newly placed plaque to British soldiers and opposite it, at the other end, there was one to German soldiers. Others were embedded in the perimeter walls.

There was a man standing by the grave of the Hungarian-born explorer Mark Aurel Stein of the Indian Archaeological Survey. He was clutching a brown leather satchel and he looked up as Jonah approached.

'You're a long way from the sea, Commander.'

Naval Commander Raja Mohan of the Indian navy smiled indulgently. 'Not really, Mr Said. In fact, for natural gas from Central Asia this is the shortest route to the sea.'

'You're going to build a pipeline?'

'My country will soon have a population that is the largest of any country in the world,' Commander Mohan explained. 'We have a mighty appetite for energy. So yes, I would say one day natural gas may flow through Afghanistan to Indian cities and ports.'

'It's been tried before.'

'By the Americans perhaps, but not by us,' Commander Mohan replied. 'And this is our time for greatness.'

'What can you do for me, Commander?' Jonah asked.

'Like many other people, including you perhaps, I owe Mr Yakoob Beg a debt of information. He has offered to free me from that debt if in turn I provide you with certain information.'

'I'm listening,' Jonah said.

'Let me put this in context. India is expanding her interests to the west, the east and the north. In the navy we like to think of the Indian Ocean as a single expanse, from the Arabian Sea to the Bay of Bengal. We refer to it as our patch. It is our duty to ensure that goods travel freely within it. Therefore it is also our duty to monitor any potential local threats. For instance, hundreds of millions of Muslims live along the Indian Ocean's edges, most of them law-abiding citizens of viable states, some of them not. The western reaches include countries such as Somalia, Yemen and Pakistan, which constitute a network of trade but also a network of global terrorism. At the same time, we see China attempting to establish a major presence in the Indian Ocean. This is a matter of great concern to us.'

'Commander, I don't have a lot of time.'

'Why is that, Mr Said? Are you concerned that the Americans may come and snatch you here?'

'Do you have something for me or not?'

There was a pause.

'Very well, Mr Said,' Commander Mohan agreed. 'The Chinese are building a naval base and listening post in Gwadar in southern Pakistan, on the approaches to the Gulf of Oman. It is a massive construction effort with a considerable security presence. For political reasons the Pakistanis are not willing to allow the Chinese military to provide protection to the staff and the site. Instead Pakistani security forces are assigned to the role. Our under-standing is that the security forces assigned to protect the base were infiltrated by Islamic extremists sympathetic to the cause of Muslim Uighurs in western China. Several members of an elite squad of the Special Services Group, trained combat divers, killed their commanding officer and went on a rampage on the construction site, destroying machinery and killing five Chinese engineers before escaping. We believe that they then sought refuge in the tribal areas, where they made contact with al-Qaeda. Our intelligence apparatus maintains files on all identified members of Pakistan's Special Forces.' He removed a buff envelope from his satchel and passed it to Jonah. 'Inside you will find photographs and identity particulars for the people that you are looking for.'

'Thank you.'

'Don't thank me. Thank Yakoob Beg. It is lucky for you that you are under the protection of one of the most powerful men in Afghanistan and that his influence reaches beyond the borders of this country, even to Delhi. If it was up to me I would have told the Americans that you were meeting with me and they would be surrounding us as I speak.'

'I'm glad that you didn't,' Jonah said.

'I have my orders. I am told to cooperate. But looking at you I am sure that it is a mistake.'

The Indian turned around and walked out of the cemetery.

Jonah stood for a while, listening to the swish of the old man's broom among the gravestones, and then he dialled the local mobile phone number handwritten on Mikulski's business card.

He answered on the second ring. 'This is Mikulski.'

'It's Jonah.'

There was a pause.

'You were going to tell me, weren't you? In 2001, in the department store, that's why you came to see me in New York. You were going to confess?'

Mikulski was right. He had been about to confess. 'It was bad timing.'

'Events intervened,' Mikulski acknowledged. 'There's no way to avoid it now, though. There's a warrant out for your arrest for the murder of James Patrick Kiernan and his bodyguard.'

'We killed the wrong people,' Jonah told him. 'We thought that we'd got Bin Laden.'

'Who gave the order to execute the ambush?' Mikulski asked. 'Was it Monteith acting on his own? Did he hate Kiernan that much?'

'I don't buy that,' Jonah said. 'Monteith was far too professional to let his personal feelings get the better of him. He didn't like Kiernan but he didn't hate him. And we never, ever acted on our own. We were arm's length, deniable, that's true, but there were clear lines of communication from us to Fisher-King at MI6. We didn't take a step without authorisation.'

'Fisher-King ordered the hit?'

'Monteith spoke to Fisher-King before the ambush. My understanding is that Fisher-King approved the hit with the tacit approval and possibly the encouragement of somebody on your side: Langley or the Pentagon, perhaps even the National Security Council. I'm not sure who. The message he received was: *Go ahead and do it but we don't want American fingerprints on it.* That's the way it worked, that's the way it has always worked, dating back to the war against the Soviets. We did your dirty work. The Afghan Guides were formed specifically as a means of cutting through the red tape in Washington. Somebody on your side okayed the hit to Fisher-King, who passed the message to Monteith, and Monteith went ahead and organised it. He was as shocked as the rest of us when we discovered we'd killed Kiernan.'

'Who knew that Kiernan and not Bin Laden was travelling in the convoy?' Mikulski asked.

'Nor says he got the information about Kiernan's movements from the ISI, from Javid Khan's mouth. Khan denies it. Khan and Kiernan were long-time allies from the fight against the Soviets. Sure, Kiernan was exasperated by ongoing ISI support for the Taliban, but things weren't that bad.'

'So what are you saying?'

'I'm saying that we didn't deliberately kill Kiernan and I'm not convinced that the ISI did either.'

'You believe Nor when he claims he thought it up himself?'

Jonah paused. 'Nor's mercurial,' he said. 'He was absolutely furious at us for abandoning him in '96. What better way to really fuck us over?'

'You don't sound entirely convinced.'

Jonah sighed. 'I can't see him acting completely on his own. Nor always wanted to belong to something. Sure, he didn't last very long with any particular institution or organisation but he never stopped trying.'

'Surely by that stage he belonged to al-Qaeda?'

'I don't believe that he ever belonged to al-Qaeda. If he took an oath he had his fingers crossed and it was only because he was reporting to someone else . . . a third party.'

'Who?'

'I don't know. I'm trying to find that out. There's another thing. Nor's confession is partial. It's not the whole story. Why stop at the death of Kiernan? What about Eschatos and stealing the diamonds? Why just pick on us Brits?'

'Surely because he holds you responsible for what happened to him?'

'Maybe, but I think he missed a chance to create an even bigger drama and it's not like him to have passed over the opportunity.'

'Are you willing to give a statement about what you've just said?'

'When the time is right,' Jonah agreed. 'But right now my priority is trying to stop Nor. I take his threat very seriously.'

'So you're not going to hand yourself in?'

'I can't yet.'

'It's better if you come in. We can talk about a deal. There are people here that are less reasonable than me, influential people. They want to hunt you down. You want to die by Hellfire missile?'

'No.'

'Yakoob Beg isn't going to be able to protect you much longer. I don't care if he's bankrolling the entire Karzai family, as soon as there's enough evidence linking him to the crime he's going down. Nobody gets to act with impunity.'

'I need more time,' Jonah said. 'I have to stop Nor.'

He cut the connection, popped open the back of the phone,

removed the SIM card and crushed it in the dust beneath his heel.

That afternoon Yakoob Beg secured him a seat on the UN Humanitarian Air Services flight out of Kabul. In Dubai he caught a plane to Amman, Jordan.

Inside al-Qaeda

The late afternoon traffic trundled along the road from Amman, leaving trails of dust and exhaust smoke. Jonah sat in the back of a battered yellow cab and stared out of the window as they drove through weathered limestone hills past quarries, factories, military camps and scrapyards. It was four hours since his plane had landed in Jordan.

Zarqa was a dilapidated town of filthy, garbage-filled streets, exhaust fumes, donkey carts and low breeze-block buildings. Young men in jeans stood on street corners and women in hijabs scurried to and fro carrying heavy loads. Jonah caught the occasional glimpse of bearded Salafists, veterans of the Afghan jihad, flitting between doorways. The town was infamous as the birthplace of Abu Musab al-Zarqawi, the recently killed leader of al-Qaeda in Iraq, who was held responsible for a deluge of atrocities, including the bombing of the UN's headquarters in Iraq which resulted in the death of the special envoy Sergio de Mello and the destruction of the Imam Ali Mosque in Najaf. It was less than three months since Zarqawi's death in an American ambush. Jonah tried to imagine Nor's early childhood in this place of wary hostility, but it was difficult.

Nor's father, Nazir, lived in a walled compound in a dusty side street festooned with overhead electrical cables. Jonah asked the taxi driver to wait. He was a couple of minutes early, and so he walked the length of the street.

When he returned a serious-looking boy was sitting on the doorstep of the house. Jonah smiled at him. 'Are you a policeman?' the boy asked.

'No,' Jonah told him. 'I'm a journalist.'

The boy shrank back into the shadows at his feet as Jonah stepped up to the door. He knocked twice.

Walid, Nor's younger brother, opened the door. He had been five the last time Jonah had seen him, a small, round-faced boy. Twenty years later he was burly and fierce, with a long bushy beard and a prayer cap. He was wearing a shalwar kameez with short trouser legs in the Wahhabi style, in accordance with the saying of the Prophet which states that clothes that touch the ground are a sign of pride and vanity. Jonah had also heard it described as 'al-Qaeda height'. If Walid recognised Jonah he did not show it, but he stepped back to allow him to enter. Jonah glanced down briefly, not wishing to step on the boy, but he had gone.

Nor's father Nazir was standing in the hallway. Jonah remembered him as a quietly spoken man with owlish sunglasses and his thumbs tucked into the pockets of a neat grey waistcoat. He looked older, his hair was grey and his face lined, and he used a stick, but it was unmistakably him, even down to the waistcoat, which was threadbare now. They shook hands formally.

'I remember you,' Nazir said. He may have been frail, but he had lost none of his powers of observation. 'You were always covered in sticking plasters as a boy. I didn't approve of you, as I recall. I thought that you were a bad influence. Your name is not Ishmael and I don't believe that you are a journalist.'

'No,' Jonah conceded.

'Please, you had better come this way.' He turned on his heel and walked slowly back down the darkened hallway, using the stick for support. About halfway down he stopped and peered over his shoulder. 'How is your father?'

'He is dead,' Jonah replied.

They stared at each other in silence for a few moments and then Nazir said, 'I'm sorry to hear about that.'

He resumed his slow walk. At the end of the hallway, he opened a door that led into a sun-drenched courtyard with a blue ceramic-tiled fountain and carefully tended plants in terracotta pots. He pointed with his stick to a table and chairs. 'Sit down.'

Walid served tea, and before the conversation started he produced a tape recorder and set it down on the table. 'It's not that we don't trust you,' Nazir explained apologetically, 'but we can't take a chance.' He glanced at Walid, who nodded to confirm that the tape was running. 'All my children were bright but Nor was very bright. Maybe too bright. He was a sensitive sort of person. He cared about the plight of others.'

Walid stared at the tabletop without comment.

'I'm looking for him,' Jonah told them.

'The FBI are also looking for him,' Nazir replied, 'and because they cannot find him they have decided they need a scapegoat. My family has been selected. They send their lackeys in our Jordanian intelligence services, our Mukhabarat, to persecute us. I am not welcome any more at the faculty in Amman. My wife has been suspended from the hospital. My younger son cannot get a job.' His face cracked into a mirthless smile and his eyes shone brightly. 'When it rains in Washington, we have to put up umbrellas.'

'I don't mean you any harm.'

'Your word?'

'My word.'

'It's rather late for that, I think. You were my son's friend but you turned him into a spy, didn't you?'

'Yes,' Jonah acknowledged.

'We have a saying: a young boy's company determines his destiny. It was unfortunate for Nor that you ever met him. Why are you looking for him?'

'Because, like you, I am accused of being his accomplice. Because I was his controller they have decided that we must be conspiring together.'

'Is that why you are Ishmael?'

'Yes,' Jonah acknowledged.

Nazir paused, his teacup shaking ever so slightly in his hand. 'Then perhaps you are the only one that can understand our tragedy.'

'Where is he?'

'He has vanished. Maybe he is in Iraq, maybe in London. He may have been yours once but he is al-Qaeda now and he means to right his previous wrongs, starting with your country.'

He reached forward and switched off the tape recorder. 'Find my son for me, Jonah,' he pleaded. 'Tell him to stop. And tell him to do it before they put his family in jail.'

'There's a problem with that.'

'Life is full of problems. Everything is a problem.'

'How am I supposed to find him?'

'He was your agent.'

'Not any more,' Jonah replied.

'Go to them, Jonah. Go to al-Qaeda. Tell them you are his friend. He will confirm it. Tell them to take you to him. They may. They may not. They may kill you. What other choice do you have?'

Standing to leave, Jonah looked down at Nazir. He had his eyes closed and his cheeks were wet with tears. Walid walked him to the door.

'Go to your hotel,' he said.

Jonah climbed back into the waiting taxi.

The telephone in his hotel room rang just after three in the morning. Jonah was lying awake watching the television. Desperate New Orleans residents were screaming at helicopters from balconies and rooftops, waving towels and blankets. There was something both horrifying and compelling about the footage.

He picked up the receiver. 'Yes?'

'You are Ishmael?' asked a softly spoken man.

'Who is this?' Jonah asked.

'This is Tariq. What do you want from us, please, Ishmael?'

'I'm a friend of Nor.'

'What is your business in Jordan?'

'I have to speak to Nor.'

The line went dead. Jonah stared at the ceiling. Fifteen minutes later the phone rang again.

'What is your real name, Ishmael?'

'Jonah.'

Tariq put the phone down. Twenty minutes later he called again.

'Jonah?'

'Yes.'

'It is Tariq.'

'Yes, Tariq.'

'A car is waiting for you outside the hotel. It is a black Mercedes. The driver is Zein. Please come now.'

'Where will it take me?'

The response was an order, strident in tone. 'Come now. Right now.'

Jonah threw on his clothes and ran down the corridor to the stairs. He stepped through the concrete blast barriers and out into the street. A battered and elderly black Mercedes was parked on the opposite side of the road. A small man with sparkling eyes and a big smile was holding the passenger door open. Jonah crossed the street to him. There was a second man in the shadows of the back seat, his face disguised by a red-and-white chequered scarf.

'Jonah,' said the small man. Jonah nodded. They shook hands vigorously. 'My name is Zein.'

Jonah got into the passenger seat and Zein closed the door on him. He rushed around and slipped into the driver's seat. He turned the ignition and the engine backfired. They all flinched and across the street the security men took cover. Zein cursed. They set off, weaving between the potholes in the road, with Zein watching his rear-view mirror all the time.

'You are Jonah?' asked the man in the back of the car.

'Yes,' Jonah said, recognising the voice from the telephone. 'You are Tariq.'

'That is correct. What do you know about this man, Nor?'

'He used to work for the British intelligence services.'

They turned off the tarmac road on to a bumpy, unpaved alleyway hemmed in by warehouses. Zein peered over the steering wheel, navigating between piles of drifting rubbish.

'What is your status in your country?' Tariq asked.

'I am a fugitive.'

'When did you last see Nor?'

'In Nevada in 2002. He was on his way to Iraq.'

'Why do you want to speak to him?'

'He is planning a terrorist attack in my country. I want to stop him. It's a trap.'

'Why do you care about him?'

'He is my friend.'

The car shot out of the narrow alleyway and bounced on to a busy tarmac road.

'We are taking you back to your hotel.'

'I'm telling you the truth,' Jonah protested.

'Tomorrow you must take a bus to Damascus. Tell them at the border that you want a transit visa and that you are travelling overland to Turkey. We will be waiting for you at the central station in Damascus.'

The car rattled to a halt opposite the hotel.

'We will be waiting for you,' Tariq repeated, in an encouraging tone.

Sure enough they were there in the crowd at Damascus bus station the following day. Zein darted forward through the heaving mass of people and their suitcases and cardboard boxes and wicker baskets full of chickens. He took Jonah's backpack from him and led him by the hand back through the crowd to the Mercedes, where Tariq was waiting.

'Is Nor here in Syria?' Jonah asked.

'You must be patient,' Tariq told him.

It was the first time that Jonah had got a clear view of Tariq. He was younger than Jonah had expected, and slight, with slender fingers that he used to punctuate his speech, and large brown eyes. A familiar type, Jonah thought.

'Are you Nor's friend?' Jonah asked.

Tariq looked at him. 'Yes, I am his friend.'

'Then you must help me.'

Zein propelled the Mercedes forward through the bus-station crowd with one hand on the horn and the other gesticulating out of the window.

'Where are we going?' Jonah asked.

'You will see,' Tariq replied, staring back over his shoulder to see whether they were being followed.

The car entered a warren of narrow streets festooned with electrical cables and laundry. They careened around corners and accelerated across intersections. Several times people were forced to jump out of the way.

Abruptly, the car slammed to a halt beside a small metal door set in a high wall. Zein leapt out and banged on the door with his fist. Tariq reached forward and placed his hand on Jonah's shoulder. 'Be calm,' he said.

A few moments later a man with a Salafist's beard and a Kalashnikov stepped out of the doorway and cast a wary eye up and down the alleyway. He ordered them to get out of the car and watched while Tariq patted Jonah down. Satisfied, Tariq took Jonah by the elbow and guided him through the door, along a corridor that was damp with mould and down a steep flight of rough concrete steps to another metal door. Tariq knocked on it and waited. The door opened and a cloud of cigarette smoke engulfed them. Jonah heard a man screaming. Two men in bala-clavas loomed out of the smoke with Kalashnikovs in their hands. Behind them there was another man in a balaclava holding a video camera. The door behind Jonah closed. Tariq and Zein had gone. The two men marched Jonah down a corridor to a window-less room with a wall that was hung with green jihadi flags and lit by floodlights. In front of the flags there was a blindfolded man in an orange jumpsuit. He was handcuffed to a chair on a large plastic sheet. He was slumped forward, and quietly groaning. Opposite him there was a large man with a full beard with two white tufts that stretched from his ears to his chest. He was sitting on a bench with a scimitar that he was sharpening on a whet-stone resting on his knee.

'Are you Jonah known as Ishmael?' the man asked.

'Yes.'

'Where is your passport?'

'In my pocket.'

'Give it to me.'

Jonah handed it to him.

'Lock him up.'

The two men in balaclavas led Jonah through another door and down a corridor and bundled him into a cell.

When he woke he could hear footsteps and whispering voices outside the door. He was lying on a cracked concrete floor, handcuffed to a radiator in an otherwise empty room. There was no window, only a ventilation grille that was far out of reach. Other prisoners had been held in the room before him; their names were scratched on the wall behind him, none of them more than a couple of feet above the floor. He wondered whether any of them had survived.

Twice the men in balaclavas came into the cell and beat him with sticks. They beat him about the thighs, the shoulders and the back. Jonah was no stranger to being strung up and beaten. He knew that you go into a kind of glide. One blow becomes much like another – he could sustain a certain amount of it. It was important to let it wash over him. He also knew how to behave. He knew from his training that interaction with his captors should be kept to a minimum. He must not make eye contact. He should not be uncooperative or short-tempered. But on this occasion he felt outrage. He had come of his own free will.

The second time, one of the Salafists got too close and Jonah tripped him up and was on in him in a second and, using his head as a battering ram, broke the man's nose and dislodged several teeth.

He felt exultant. They beat him unconscious.

They had rigged a blackboard on the wall behind the camera so that he could sit on a chair with his cuffed hands wedged between his knees and read the text while staring into the camera's lens.

'The British state will taste a tiny portion of what innocent Muslims taste every day at the hands of the Crusader and Jewish coalition to the east and to the west,' Jonah said. Blood spooled out of his mouth as he spoke. 'The duties of Islam are magnificent and difficult. Some of them are abominable. The hour of death can be neither hastened nor postponed. Death will find you, even in the looming tower . . .'

He looked around him. It was satisfying to engage the fear in their eyes. He was convinced that they had been instructed to keep him alive.

'Come on, then . . .' he said, in a low voice.

They advanced on him with sticks.

'Jonah!' He woke with a shudder. Tariq was squatting on the floor well out of reach.

'Nor says that you are beautiful but you think that you are ugly,' Tariq told him. 'I believe he must be right. He understands people. He is not frightened to say what he thinks. Is it true that he was your student?'

'He was my friend,' Jonah replied.

'He says that you taught him everything he knows, that you are the one who made him into an instrument of God.'

'Not me,' Jonah says.

'Why are you here?'

'To warn him . . .'

'He is warned. He knows that he is in danger. He is content. He is in danger but your country is in greater danger. Do you understand? You should be proud of him.'

'Where is he?'

Tariq's chest swelled with pride. 'He's in Iraq, fighting the Crusaders.'

'Can you take me to him?'

'He is leaving soon. He is going to take the fight to the Crusaders on their home soil. He says that he is going to sweep away an entire Kuffar city. He says that you will be amazed. I believe him.'

Systems sabotage

They came for him at dawn, in the midst of a sandstorm.

'We must leave at once,' said Tariq. His phone rang and he listened and nodded before someone cut the connection. One of the Salafists knelt beside Jonah and unlocked his handcuffs while another held the barrel of a Kalashnikov against his temple. It was satisfying to feel the man's fear as he fumbled with the lock. 'Get up,' said Tariq. 'Follow me.'

Jonah climbed shakily to his feet and staggered after him into the corridor.

'Quickly,' hissed one of the Salafists, and prodded him in the back with his gun. Jonah spun around and yanked the gun out of his hands. The Salafists fell over themselves to get out of his way. He threw the gun after them.

He climbed the stairs and went through the metal door and down the corridor and out into the alleyway where the car was waiting with Tariq at the wheel.

They turned on to a main road and lorries roared past. Tariq slapped his palm on the horn and kept it there until he found a gap in the traffic.

'Where are we going?' Jonah asked.

'Iraq,' Tariq replied irritably. He switched on the windscreen wipers to try to clear the dust.

They left the outskirts of the city and passed empty fields and rows of pylon lines. After an hour or so Tariq stopped the car and told Jonah to get in the boot.

'Be very quiet,' he told him, before slamming the lid closed on him.

The car started again and they drove for twenty minutes or so before slowing to a halt. For a while they proceeded in fits and starts as if lined up in a queue. The boot steadily filled with a fine cloud of dust. Jonah pulled his T-shirt up over his mouth and nose. He heard voices and imagined papers being inspected and perhaps money changing hands. There was no attempt to search the vehicle. They set off again. Jonah groaned and stretched limbs that were numb from remaining still for so long. Suddenly, the car veered off the road and rattled along the verge for a while before stopping. The doors slammed. Seconds later, Tariq opened the boot and helped Jonah out. 'Welcome to Iraq.'

'My favourite bloody place,' Jonah replied through gritted teeth, rubbing the backs of his legs to rid them of cramp.

'Come on, get in the car,' Tariq said.

They drove for several hours on a narrow strip of blacktop across a bleak and unremitting landscape filled with clouds of ochre-coloured dust and the wreckage of abandoned vehicles. On the outskirts of a town they turned off the road and pulled up alongside a beaten-up Land Cruiser parked next to a petrol pump. Tariq jumped out of the car and Jonah followed. Tariq gripped Jonah by the upper arm and steered him towards the Land Cruiser. There were several men inside: the driver and another in the passenger seat beside him; two more Iraqis were squatting on a pile of wooden crates in the back. They were covered in dust. All had their features obscured by scarves.

'Get in,' Tariq said, and slid in along the bench seat beside him. The driver turned the key in the ignition and the engine started with a throaty growl. They drove off, abandoning Tariq's car.

The man in the passenger seat unwrapped the scarf that disguised his features and turned to look at Jonah. By the light filtering through the dust-encrusted windows, Jonah recognised the harrowed beauty and numinous stare of his oldest friend.

'Hello, Jonah,' he said.

'Hello, Nor.'

Iraq was a place of barren desert and swirling dust, and endless potholed roads, desiccated orchards and drab, empty settlements. The only sign of the occupation was the Apache helicopters, sleek as hunting wasps, which skimmed along the distant horizon.

They were racing south. Jonah was wedged in the bench seat between Tariq and another Iraqi with a Kalashnikov between his knees.

'Why would you willingly walk into a trap?'

Nor glanced back at him. 'What makes you think that I haven't worked that into my calculations?'

'They'll stop you long before you present a real danger,' Jonah said. 'You won't get within a mile of the Thames Barrier.'

'Maybe I don't need to,' Nor said, his cold eyes roaming the desert outside. 'The other side may be strong but they are not strong in all things and our side may be weak but we are not weak in all things. This is what I tell my people: we are small and agile and we have surprise on our side. We create our own super-iority. I say it is up to us to identify and exploit our enemy's key vulnerabilities. I say, when you are trying to create the edge, the first thing you need is an imbalance, an asymmetry.'

A mobile phone on the dashboard began to vibrate. Nor snatched it up and listened briefly before cutting the connection. He sat up, took a water bottle from between the seats, poured water over his hand and slapped it on his face. He was energised again.

'We're going to see a man about a map.'

The convoy was pulled over by the side of the highway. Three armoured black Humvees, two of them with .50-calibre machine guns on top. The top cover gunners were wearing black body armour over their fire-retardant Nomex jackets and helmets that made them seem bulbous headed and insect-like. Greysteel was written in white lettering on the side of each vehicle.

The Land Cruiser pulled alongside the middle Humvee, close enough for Nor to speak to its passenger, an American with a buzz cut, sunglasses and a T-shirt with a logo just above the left breast of a wolf's head in a rifle's cross hairs. Jonah had seen the logo before but he couldn't remember when. The American passed over two packages. One was bulky and the other was flat.

'You'll receive the balance on completion of the task,' the American told him.

'Jolly good,' Nor told him with a mocking smile, and winked at Jonah. He nodded to the driver and they drove off. He tossed the larger package to Tariq in the back and ripped open the flat one. Inside was a map. Nor unfolded the map on the dashboard and Jonah saw that it was an Iraqi pipeline schematic printed by the American company Halliburton.

Beside him on the seat, Tariq opened the larger package and removed several bundles of hundred-dollar bills held together with rubber bands. He grinned broadly and held them up for all to see.

'From the Christians, Emir. Gifts . . .'

'An attack on systems can magnify the effect of a small attack into a major event,' Nor explained, his fingers tracing lines across the map. 'Provided that we can identify a key enemy weakness, a small cell like ours, with minimal costs, can accomplish an attack that generates a rate of return that is out of all proportion to the initial investment. Take the next left.'

The driver glanced across at him, his teeth bright white in the sunlight. 'Yes, Emir!'

Nor took a GPS from the pocket of his jacket and switched it on. 'The optimal size of an autonomous cell is between five and eight. Nine is the limit that I am prepared to work with, any more and we'd show up on the radar.' He turned around and leant over the back of the seat, so that he was face to face with Jonah. 'Our small size is compensated for by the overall size of the market. The market behaves like a bazaar: people trade, haggle and share. For specific skills we outsource to freelancers in the bazaar. For instance, for a vehicle-borne IED we buy in a hollowed-out car from a chop shop and a stack of artillery shells from a local insurgent group. We aim for simple attacks that have immediate and far-reaching effects. Our actions are designed to provoke copycat attacks, as other networks in the bazaar innovate from our original plans and swarm on identified weaknesses. At the same time they create protective system noise that masks our identity.'

'What were you doing in Pakistan?' Jonah asked.

'Sourcing expertise,' Nor explained.

'Explosives-trained combat divers for whatever you are planning in the Thames Estuary?'

Nor grinned and turned back in his seat. 'You don't give up, do you?'

'You know I don't. I never have.'

'That way,' Nor said, pointing. They veered off the road and raced across the desert.

'Stop!' Nor jumped out of the car and took several steps with the GPS in his hand. He stopped and scuffed the sand with his heel.

'Here,' he shouted cheerily. 'X marks the spot.'

They all got out of the car. Tariq removed a spade from the trunk and Nor took it from him. Nor and Jonah stood opposite each other on the sand.

'About six foot down,' Nor told him, before handing him the spade. He put on a pair of shades with small round lenses. They reminded Jonah of coins placed on the eyes of a corpse. 'Dig.'

Jonah began to dig. It must have been forty degrees. Within seconds, he was sodden with sweat. Tariq took the video camera from the car and started to film him.

'Brother Ishmael,' Nor said, 'tell me this: what gets larger the more you take away?'

Jonah continued digging.

'A hole!'

'Am I digging my own grave?' Jonah asked.

'Don't be melodramatic,' Nor said. 'You're digging for oil.'

Jonah threw the spade down. 'What the fuck are you up to?' he demanded.

'I'm getting even,' Nor told him, 'for every insult, for every slight. I'm getting my own back.'

'This is about revenge?'

Nor produced a pistol from the back of his waistband and pointed it at Jonah.

'Dig!'

Jonah resumed digging.

Nor shook his head wistfully and tucked the gun back in his waistband. 'Look at the mess you are in.'

'What is that supposed to mean?' Jonah demanded.

'It means that your ridiculous sense of loyalty is going to be everyone's undoing. You should have killed me when you had the chance. Think of all the lives you would have saved.'

'There's still time to stop you,' Jonah said as he dumped another spadeful over his shoulder.

'No there isn't. Not for you.' Nor looked away at the horizon and for a moment he seemed profoundly sad. Then he forced a smile. 'It's ironic really, the unforeseen consequences of what was set in motion on 9/11. The Sheikh's intention was to provoke the United States into an invasion and occupation that would bleed the United States financially, cut it off from its allies, and cause the Islamic world to rise up against it. His error was to think that the place where this would happen was Afghanistan and not Iraq. Bush and Blair gave us more than we could have hoped for. When I first started working with these people, just after the invasion, all it would have taken to put down their weapons was for the occupiers to leave. But now, if you ask them what they would do if the occupiers leave, they say that they must follow them wherever they go.'

Jonah paused with his foot on the spade. 'They know you're coming.'

'Of course they do. I told them. I announced it to the world on YouTube. How else can I make the world sit up and listen? Keep digging.'

After a few more minutes of digging, Jonah's spade struck metal.

'Hey presto,' said Nor, standing on the lip of the hole.

'What is it?' Jonah asked.

'It's a forty-eight-inch high-pressure pipeline. Out you come.'

Jonah climbed out of the hole and slumped on the sand with the sweat pouring off his forehead. One of the Iraqis carried a wooden crate from the Land Cruiser and set it down next to the hole. A second put an olive-drab ammunition box beside it.

'You're going to blow it?'

'Of course I am,' Nor replied. 'Identify and attack key enemy vulnerabilities. That's what I've been talking about. That's what I do. I blow things up. I fuck with the system. I spend a lot of time thinking up new ways to do it.'

He knelt beside the wooden crate and opened it. It was filled with rectangular packets of C4 explosive wrapped in plastic. He removed one, unpeeled the wrapping and kneaded the explosive into a ball in his hands.

'We buy the C4 from the Iraqi army. It is generously provided to them by the Americans. That's how asymmetric warfare works. We use their tools against them.'

He set the ball of explosive on the crate's lid. Next he removed a loop of white detonating cord and unravelled it, measuring it out from hand to elbow. Satisfied, he cut it with a knife from his belt, making a diagonal slice across the cord. He bent one end of the cord back on itself and tied it in a knot. He then folded the ball around the knot so that it was deeply embedded in the explosive.

'Tell me this, how come a private security contactor is paying you to blow up a pipeline?'

'Think about it for a moment,' Jonah replied. 'Who benefits? This pipeline moves nearly four hundred thousand barrels of oil a day. Who gains the most from its destruction? Certainly not the Iraqis and definitely not the American taxpayer. I'll tell you who benefits. Generally speaking, anybody who profits from a hike in the price of crude – obviously the contractor who rebuilds the pipe but specifically the private security company that secures the site. The daily rates for securing a rebuild like this are astronomical. In Iraq the post-war business boom is not oil. It is security.'

'Winthrop works for Greysteel,' Jonah said.

'Of course he does.'

'You knew that?' Jonah asked, genuinely taken aback.

'Sure.'

'Will you work for anybody?'

'Yes, if our interests coincide. Don't look at me like that, like you're outraged. Don't be so fucking naive. We're bleeding America dry and I'm enjoying the irony of getting paid by rich Americans to do it.'

He jumped into the hole with the detonating cord trailing behind him. Tariq advanced on the hole and filmed Nor as he placed the charge.

'I spoke to your father,' Jonah told him.

A flicker of irritation. 'There's nothing I can do for him.'

'You could stop.'

'It's too late for that,' Nor said, looking up at him from the hole. 'I've told you already.'

'You've identified the Thames Barrier as a key vulnerability. Well done. But so have we. And you've given away your game plan. You've lost the element of surprise. It doesn't matter how well trained your combat divers are, you're not going to get anywhere near the Barrier.'

Nor smiled as he got down on his hands and knees to earth himself; dissipating any static build-up before handling the detonators.

'You have no idea,' he said. He unlatched the lid on the ammo box. From it he carefully removed a small box of detonators and a length of safety fuse. He cut away a length of fuse the width of his outstretched hand and discarded it. Then he cut another length of a similar size and lit it with a box of matches from his pocket. The fuse hissed as it burned – a wisp of smoke travelling from one end to the other – while Nor consulted his watch to time the burn rate. Satisfied, he measured out two minutes' worth of fuse.

'People are expecting great things of me.'

'Which people?' Jonah asked.

'Have you heard of Those Who Seek The End?'

'Those Who Seek The End? The end of what?'

'Forget it,' Nor said. 'It's a joke.'

'It's very funny,' Jonah said. 'You're not going to attack the Barrier, are you?'

Nor looked at him with sympathy and sadness. 'Do you really think that I'm going to come clean with you? Do I look like I'm afflicted with a cinema villain's brag reflex?'

'The only way to negate the Barrier without taking control of it or sabotaging it is to overwhelm it. To do that you need a tidal wave that comes out of nowhere. How are you going to manufacture a tidal wave?'

'Start the car,' Nor said, and one of the Iraqis headed for the Land Cruiser and seconds later the engine rumbled into life.

Nor removed a small aluminium-cased detonator from its box and, holding it carefully between his thumb and forefinger, inserted one end of the safety fuse into the aperture.

'You are going to blow something up in the Thames Estuary.'

Nor crimped the fuse in place using a set of pliers from the ammunition box. 'You're not making this any easier for yourself,' he said.

'You're going to blow up a ship,' Jonah said.

Nor grinned. In fact, he never could resist showing off. 'Not just any ship. The biggest IED in history.'

'You think they're going to let you sail a ship full of explosives into the Thames Estuary?'

'Maybe it's already there,' Nor told him, briskly. He used insulating tape from his pocket to attach the detonator to the cord.

'Where?'

'There. Just sitting there. Ready to blow. Has been for sixty years. Sort of like the Statue of Liberty guarding the mouth of the Hudson. Do you want to light this?'

'No thanks.'

Nor shrugged and cupped the end of the fuse in his hand.

'You're going to have to kill me if you don't want me to stop you,' Jonah told him.

'Sure.' Nor set a match against the exposed tip of the fuse and scraped the striker across it with a flick of the wrist. The fuse hissed and commenced its slow burn.

'You think you could?' Jonah asked.

'Sure.'

'You didn't in Sierra Leone.'

'I didn't need to,' Nor replied. 'I caused you much more harm by letting you live. Let's go.'

They sprinted for the Land Cruiser. As soon as they had slammed the doors it accelerated away.

Then the explosion, filmed from the rear window of the Land Cruiser: the flash, the shock wave rattling the car windows, then the leisurely unfolding of a mushroom cloud; and coming up through it, a high-pressure jet of oil from the ruptured pipeline and a spreading pool.

The atmosphere in the car had changed. They were racing northwards alongside the Euphrates, using the main highway this time. Several times they had passed massive US military convoys. Nor was pale and jittery, scanning the road ahead. Jonah wanted to ask, *What is it? What's the matter?* But he thought he knew the answer. Nor was preparing to kill him.

'I remember now where I saw the logo of the wolf in crosshairs before,' Jonah told him. 'The guy from Greysteel who gave you the map had it on his T-shirt. And it was on the baseball cap that Kiernan's bodyguard was wearing in 1999. Kiernan's bodyguard was employed by Greysteel, wasn't he?'

'He was,' Nor acknowledged, staring out of the window.

'They knew the route that Kiernan was taking that day.'

'Of course they did,' Nor acknowledged.

'Is that where you got the information about Kiernan's route and timings? Did Greysteel deliberately leak the information to you?'

'I knew you'd figure it out one day.'

'I don't understand. Why would Greysteel be prepared to sacrifice one of their own bodyguards? Why would they want Kiernan dead?'

'Kiernan wasn't the only Greysteel client in Kandahar in those days,' Nor explained.

'Who else, then?'

'Think about it.'

They were entering the outskirts of Fallujah, their headlights lighting up the shredded palms and shelled mud-brick buildings that lined the street. Everything was in ruins. Soon the old metal bridge over the Euphrates appeared ahead.

Jonah was remembering his conversation with Fisher-King in the MI6 headquarters when Fisher-King had told him that the Taliban could play a central role in restoring centralised government in Afghanistan: *Lodestone are going to run a thousand miles of pipeline straight through the middle of it and pump a million barrels of oil a day. They've opened an office in Kandahar.*

'Lodestone . . .'

They drove on to the bridge, the shadows thrown by the girders causing them to plunge through stripes of darkness and light.

'What did Lodestone have against Kiernan?'

'Stop!'

The driver hit the brakes. They slewed to a halt at the centre of the bridge.

'Kiernan was threatening to go to the Securities and Exchange Commission,' Nor explained. 'He claimed he had evidence of Lodestone executives paying bribes to Taliban officials going back to the mid-nineties and in direct contravention of the Foreign Corrupt Practices Act. There was no way Lodestone could let that happen.'

'And so you killed him?'

'No. You killed him.' Nor turned on him angrily. 'I don't think you understand what it was like for me in Afghanistan after you abandoned me. I don't think you have a fucking clue how much danger I was in. The ISI wanted me dead. The CIA wouldn't touch me. Lodestone were the only people who were prepared to give me the time of day. They had big plans for Afghanistan. They were going to make everybody rich. And they needed someone like me. I walked into their offices in Kandahar and you know who I met? I'll tell you. Richard Winthrop. Yes, that's right! He was on contract from Greysteel, doing a risk evalua-tion for Lodestone. I can tell you, it was the best move I ever made. Right away, he saw my potential. Go ahead, look at me like that. I've been working for Winthrop for the best part of ten years. I was his joe, not yours. And because of your ridiculous sense of superiority you never saw it. You were so keen to dismiss Winthrop as a naive fool that you failed to notice that we were playing you from the very beginning. Now get out of the car! Everybody out!'

One of the Iraqis dragged Jonah out on to the bridge. His head was reeling. It was difficult to comprehend. He'd been duped. Not just the assassination of Kiernan. In the cages in Kandahar, in the Sahara and Nevada, in Kurdistan – it was obvious now that he'd been window-dressing, a cut-out, a means for Winthrop to disguise his relationship with Nor.

'What about the diamonds?' Jonah asked softly.

Nor shrugged. 'Eleven of the twenty couriers made it out of Afghanistan and to the rendezvous point in Kurdistan. Pakravan and I were waiting for them.'

Jonah was remembering a press cutting – the discovery of eleven disembowelled bodies in a mass grave. 'You killed them, gutted them for the diamonds and dumped the bodies in a hole.'

'Sure. We stole millions of dollars' worth of diamonds from al-Qaeda. You could say we did the world a favour. We got rich. Winthrop bought a McMansion on the Chesapeake. So what?' Nor retorted, moving around to the front of the vehicle. All eyes were on him. 'Wait here.'

'What is it, Emir?' Tariq asked.

It was the bridge where the corpses of American contractors working for the security company Blackwater had been strung up the year before. Standing on the structure, looking up at the metal girders, Jonah saw that someone, presumably a Marine, had written on one of them: *This is for the Americans of Black-water that were murdered here in 2004, Semper Fidelis. PS Fuck you.*

'Wait.'

Ahead of them, several armed men materialised out of the shadows. They were wearing black uniforms and balaclavas and carrying M4 carbines with night vision scopes.

'Emir?' There was a hint of desperation in Tariq's voice. 'What's happening here?'

'Wait there,' Nor repeated, advancing towards the soldiers.

'Aren't you going to say goodbye?' Jonah asked. Beside him, one of Nor's team made his weapon ready.

'What are you talking about?' Tariq demanded.

'He's abandoning you. He's switching sides again.'

'What?'

Nor stopped by the nearest Iraqi soldier, who pulled off his balaclava and embraced him; Jonah recognised Mohammed, the Iraqi general's son who had lived with Nor in his caravan in the Nevada desert.

'You're going to die,' Jonah said.

'I don't understand,' Tariq protested.

Nor looked back at them. 'I'm sorry,' he said, meeting Jonah's gaze. 'I'm truly sorry.'

Jonah thought of Flora and Miranda and his daughter Esme. All the mistakes that he had made. There was so much to do to put things right.

The soldiers opened fire.

Jonah started running. Not away from the soldiers but towards them. A bullet picked him up and spun him around. He fell forward over the bridge's handrail and dropped towards the water.

MIRANDA
Takfir: Apostasy

The practice of declaring that an individual or a group previously considered believers are in fact Kuffar (non-believers in God).

The Red Road Flats

Alex Ross was standing on the jetty at Oban waiting for her when the ferry docked. He was looking sleek and expensive, wearing a black cashmere overcoat and sunglasses on the crown of his head. As Miranda hurried down the gangway, trying to get off the boat as quickly as she could, he took his hands from his pockets and spread his arms out wide. 'I couldn't live without you,' he called. He was smiling, but his eyes were as hard and shiny as stones.

'I know who you are,' she said.

'Of course you do. I'm Jonah's closest friend. Here, let me take that.' He held out his hand for her rucksack.

'I'm taking the bus.'

'Like fuck you are,' he said cheerfully, and then in a low and threatening voice, 'You're going to get in my car and I'm going to drive as fast as I can as far away from here as I can, because very soon now the police are going to be searching the fucking length and breadth for you.'

She bit her lower lip.

'This way.' He strode across to his car and opened the passenger door. The car was almost unrecognisable, it was so covered in mud. The dog knew it, though – he streaked ahead of her and leapt in the back. *Traitor*, she thought.

'Where are you planning to take me?' she demanded.

He pulled his sunglasses down on to his nose and she saw herself reflected in them. It was not a reassuring sight.

'I'm taking you to a safe house,' he said.

'Why?' she asked.

'Duh! To keep you safe.'

There was something disturbing about Alex, a mixture of immaturity and cunning that suggested that he was capable of almost anything. 'Safe from whom?' she demanded, and as she did so she glanced back up the gangway, but there was no sign of the ginger-haired man.

'Get in. I'll explain on the way.'

She wasn't someone who liked to find herself in someone else's power, particularly not someone like Alex, but she didn't seem to have any choice. She slung her rucksack in the back of the car with the dog and got in. He closed the door after her and strode round to the driver's side. She stared at her hands in her lap, her nails chewed to the quick. She tried to imagine herself in warrior pose, fearless, crouching with her arms outstretched. Alex slid into the driver's seat beside her and switched the engine on. They drove up the hill out of the town and on to the A85 heading east.

'I heard that Jonah had found himself a woman,' Alex said, 'but Christ, no one said how beautiful.'

'Fuck you,' she said.

Alex was impervious. 'Jonah Said . . .' He pronounced the name with respect. 'A very talented operator. One of the best. You know, I saw him just before he left for Pakistan. He arranged to meet me at the Thames Barrier. I thought that it was an odd choice at the time.'

'What are you talking about?'

He smiled indulgently. 'You know, I've been wondering about his motivation. What has driven him to this? Is it money? Could it be revenge? Was he pushed too far? Is he being blackmailed? Is it about making history or the very biggest bang?'

'Where's Jonah?' she demanded.

Alex glanced at her. 'Don't you know?'

She stared at the dashboard.

He laughed. 'We thought we'd lost you after you did a runner from Barnhill. We didn't know about the boat. It was stupid, really. Of course Jonah would have a back door. It's in his nature. We should have anticipated it, but once we'd worked out you were on your way to the mainland, it was just a question of laying a string of checkpoints out and waiting for you to cross the tarmac. Sure enough you did, and I happened to be close at hand. And I understand you giving me the slip in Spean Bridge. I was less than subtle, I admit that. But we knew you were heading for Barra. Where else were you going to go?'

Miranda repeated the question. 'Safe from whom?'

Alex shrugged. 'Take your pick, any of a cupboard full of spooks and sheriffs: CIA, FBI, MI5, MI6, ISI, Interpol. Since Nor pulled his publicity stunt we're all out of friends.'

They sped south through the zigzag bends of Loch Lomond-side, weaving between lumbering caravans. Rain slashed the windscreen. She was in an impossible situation: she didn't know whether to trust Alex or not, she could not tell whether he was friend or foe. All she could focus on was Jonah's reply to a question that she once asked him – *What did they teach you at spy school?* His reply when it came was succinct and serious – *Always suspect. It's the only rule. Never trust anyone.*

'Jonah went looking for Nor,' she told him.

'And now he's accused of being Nor's accomplice.'

'That's ludicrous.'

'Is it?' Alex said. 'How well do you really know him?'

'Well enough.'

'You can explain that to Monteith.'

'You're taking me to Monteith?'

'He's coming to us. First, he has to come out of hiding.'

'He's in hiding?'

Alex laughed. 'Right now, I'd say Monteith's not far behind Bin Laden on the CIA's most wanted list.'

'And what about you? You were one of the Afghan Guides.'

'You think that this is government work? You think that any of this is official? I'm still Monteith's boy. I'm as deep in the shit as you are.'

His phone rang. 'Yes? Right. OK. We're approaching now. Are the cameras down?' He paused, listening. 'Good. What about the perimeter?' He glanced across at Miranda. 'OK. That's grand.'

He cut the connection.

Staring up at the nearest tower with its garish cladding of mustard and fire-engine red, taking the full force of the rain on her upturned face, Miranda was filled with a profound sense of unease. Nothing about the Red Road Flats looked safe. On the approach to the estate, the only shops that weren't boarded up were a heavily fortified betting shop, a solicitors' office and a fish and chip shop. There was a primary school ringed by a barbed-metal stockade at the base of the cluster of towers but no children in sight. Waste ground stretched for as far as the eye could see. They were somewhere on the outskirts of Glasgow, but it reminded her of the Balkans in the nineties, when she'd been looking for her husband. Alex had already told her that many of the inhabitants of the towers were refugees from the Balkans, Kosovars and Bosnians. She remembered trudging up and down countless staircases, and sitting with soldiers on the bare boards of unheated apartments on the front lines. She had offered packages of tea, coffee, butter, slivovitz – whatever she could get her hands on – in return for news of the Arab fighter named Bakr. She had not found him, although she had collected reports of his deeds. Most of it was garbage, lies told in exchange for what she was offering, but she developed a talent for spotting the truth among the falsehoods, enough to keep her going, even though he was always a few steps ahead of her. Her life seemed to be repeating itself.

They had parked beside a shipping container, in a small car park at the foot of one of the towers. Water was running off a grass bank, washing a tide of litter across the tarmac. There was only one other car in sight, the carcass of Jonah's Land Rover. The windows and wheels had been removed and it was sitting on four breeze blocks.

'Jonah was here?' she asked.

'Before he took off,' Alex acknowledged. 'Excuse me.' He spoke briefly into his mobile phone. 'We're on our way up.'

She watched a woman in a headscarf pushing a pram between the large granite boulders at the approach to the tower. The boulders had presumably been put there to keep joyriders off the small playground with its rusty swings and slide.

'It's on the fifteenth floor,' Alex said, snapping on a pair of latex gloves. He went round to the boot of the car, popped the lid and removed a pair of green wellington boots. He swapped them for his shoes. 'The lifts don't work.'

He set off across the tarmac. She stood for a moment, with a protest half formed in her head, but he was already halfway to the tower's entrance, and the only alternative appeared to be to stay and get soaked in the car park. Reluctantly she followed, with the dog at her heels.

At the entrance, there were three sets of fire doors, one after the other, like airlocks, and she had to set her shoulder to each successive door to force it open. The wind howled between her legs and she heard snatches of what sounded like distant shouting. In the foyer, the elevator's doors gaped. A cardboard sign announced it was out of order. She made for the stairs. Alex was ahead of her, and as she climbed after him, up steps that were scattered with broken glass, it was if she were ascending through a subterranean passage. Somewhere above she heard a woman shouting abuse and a door slam. At each level there was a fire door with a wire-core glass window like an embrasure which looked into a passageway. She was forced to pause several times and catch her breath. There was a sense of people shrinking back into the shadows before her. She felt her discomfort intensify, as if experiencing an ear-popping change in altitude.

On the fifteenth floor, Alex was waiting for her by the elevator shaft, with his hands on his knees and his head down, sweat pouring off his brow.

'I should quit smoking,' he groaned.

'It'll kill you,' she said, quietly. She was reminded suddenly of the whiff of stale smoke carried into the house at Barnhill on someone's clothes. She felt a sudden wave of fear.

Alex straightened up and pushed through the fire door. There was a stocky man in jeans and a hoodie standing in the passageway beyond. His face was almost entirely in shadow.

'This way,' the man said, as if he had been expecting them.

Halfway down the passage, the man stopped in front of a grey, steel-plated door with a plastic number and a spyhole. He produced a key from his pocket and let himself in. Alex and then Miranda and the dog followed. There was a short hallway with several pairs of running shoes neatly arranged against the skirting board and a door that led through to a living room.

Beneath the living-room window there was a cheap synthetic sofa and opposite it two matching armchairs. Alex collapsed into the nearest armchair. Miranda looked around. There was a glass coffee table with a packet of cornflakes, a bottle of Irn-Bru, a pile of loose papers, an overflowing ashtray and a couple of Xbox consoles on it. In the corner of the room there was a television set. On one wall there was a framed quotation from the Koran and an Islamic calendar. The place stank of cigarettes and unwashed bodies.

'You can withdraw to the perimeter, Taff,' Alex told the man in the hoodie, and waved him away. 'Wait for further instruc- tions.'

'OK, boss,' the man identified as Taff said.

'Have a seat,' Alex told her.

'What's going on?' Miranda asked.

'Sit.'

She sat on the sofa and the dog ranged up and down the skirting boards.

'Monteith is coming,' Alex told her. 'He wants to talk to you.'

'How long will he be?' she asked.

'I don't know. Not long, I hope. He has to be sure that he's safe.'

'Doesn't he trust you?'

'Of course he trusts me,' Alex said, irritably.

This is fucked, she thought. She was suddenly desperate for a pee.

'I need to go to the toilet.'

He didn't seem to be listening. He was scratching the dog's neck. 'Good boy,' he said.

She stood up. 'I need to go to the toilet.'

He glanced up at her. 'First door on the right,' he said.

She got up and went through the door into the narrow corridor that led to the rest of the flat. She closed the door behind her. There was another door immediately to her left and one to her right. She opened the door to her left. It was a bedroom. There were two single beds with bare mattresses. On one of the beds was a large cardboard box marked HEXAMINE BLOCKS FOR CAMP STOVES. There was a rolled-up prayer mat and propped against the far wall a samurai sword. She closed the door softly. The door to the right led to the bathroom. There was a toilet, a sink and a bath with a shower attachment and a shower curtain that was stained with mildew pulled across it. She dropped her trousers and peed in the bowl. When she was done she turned on the seat, searching for paper. There was none visible. She looked around. With a feeling of trepidation she pushed aside the shower curtain. The bath was filled with several industrial-sized bottles of drain cleaner and some discarded fertiliser bags. She stared at the empty bottles and torn-open bags. It took a second or two for the significance of them to sink in, and then she felt the panic welling up and threatening to overwhelm her. She pulled her trousers up, flushed the toilet and then stared at the handle, her fingerprints clearly visible on the chrome surface.

Shit shit shit

She opened the door and almost jumped out of her skin. Alex was standing right in front of her.

'Why don't you make some tea?' he said in an amused tone. He inclined his head. 'The kitchen's that way.'

He made no effort to make room for her and she had to brush past him to get down the narrow corridor. She felt his breath on her neck – his extreme alertness, arousal even. She took two more steps and opened the remaining door.

She stepped into the kitchen. It was here that they had manu-factured the explosives. There was a gas mask and beside it a row of cloudy retort bottles and several glass beakers on the linoleum-topped table. The kitchen counter was stacked with coffee filters, ice-cube trays and several large bags of salt.

'They seemed to know what they were doing, don't you think?' Alex asked her from the doorway. 'Real professionals. You'd know, right? Isn't this what they taught you in the Lion's Den?'

'Why did you bring me here?' she asked.

'Mine's white with one sugar.'

She took a deep breath and went over to the counter, picked up the kettle and carried it to the sink to fill it. There was a kitchen knife with a six-inch blade lying on a chopping board beside the sink. Miranda stared at it, listening to the water running into the kettle. She tried to decide whether she was in a suffi-ciently life-threatening situation that she might need it. When she looked up she saw that Alex was watching her. He looked amused.

'Give me the knife,' he said, holding out his hand to her.

She paused.

'Give me the knife,' he repeated, menacingly.

She picked it up and held it out to him, handle outwards.

'That's a good girl,' he said, taking it from her. He tapped it against his thigh. 'The tea bags are in the cupboard.'

She carried the kettle back to the wall socket and plugged it in. Next she opened the wall units. The first cupboard that she opened was stacked with jars of Vaseline. She stood for a moment, holding the door handles. *Petroleum jelly: they'd used the Vaseline as a plasticiser.* And her fingerprints were all over everything. She was conscious that he was watching her. She closed the doors calmly and opened the adjacent unit. Inside there was a packet of tea bags, a bag of sugar, a sliced white loaf, some honey and jam.

She dropped tea bags into two mugs.

'We think that they were here for two to three days,' Alex told

her. 'They ate eggs, toast and honey. They prayed. They manufactured explosives. Then they walked out the door. How much
by weight do you think they made?'

The kettle boiled and she poured water on the tea bags. Her
gaze was drawn inexorably to the fridge. She was in desperate
trouble – she knew that – she shouldn't touch anything else, but
she wanted to know. She opened the door and the interior light
clicked on. On the shelves were rows of glass beakers, twenty or
so, some with a residue of yellowish liquid. It was as she'd guessed:
they had made red fuming nitric acid using a mixture of sulphuric
acid and potassium nitrate, obtained from drain cleaner and
fertiliser. They had heated the mixture in retort bottles, and then
collected the acid in glass beakers cooled by iced water. They
had then mixed the acid with powdered hexamine from the fuel
blocks to create the explosive slurry RDX. Adding a plasticiser
and plastic binder had given them a malleable explosive.

To get at the milk she had to remove a beaker. She set it gently
on the counter and reached in for the milk. She sniffed at the
carton. The milk was fresh. They had made their explosives and
left. Not long ago. She closed the fridge door without returning
the beaker.

She poured milk in his tea and added a spoonful of sugar. She
handed him the mug. He took it in his left hand. He was holding
the knife in his right. She held her own mug of tea in both hands
and sipped at it, watching him over the rim.

'I've been reading your file,' Alex told her. 'It turned out that
the Americans had much more on you than we did. A hard-copy
file: longhand, cross-referenced entries, Post-it notes, the lot. I
assume that they bought it in a job lot from the Pakistanis. It's
now circulating. We know that you were at the Lion's Den. We
know about the sleepovers with your husband's business partners in Baghdad. There's a school of thought that says that you're
a dangerous terrorist.'

The doorbell rang. Alex smiled menacingly. 'He's here.'

Why isn't she wearing gloves?

When Monteith stepped into the kitchen, she was standing with her back to the sink, as far from Alex as she could get.

Monteith was wearing a Barbour jacket over a shabby tweed suit, the same suit that he'd been wearing when she last saw him in August 2003, after Iraq, when he had spoken to her in his basement offices in Whitehall. Away from his desk he looked shorter than she remembered. His brogues were muddy and his thinning hair was plastered to his skull. He seemed tired, like a man who had been thinking too many gloomy thoughts. He didn't look at her at first. He stood and studied the room, the chemical apparatus, bottles and beakers, and crusts of explosive residue. He held out his hand briefly for the dog to sniff.

'Well?' he asked.

'They came in on last Friday's Dubai–Glasgow flight,' Alex told him. 'Four Pakistan nationals with temporary work visas. The names on the airline tags in the rubbish match those we obtained from the Home Office. The photos on their visa applications match those passed to us by Yakoob Beg.'

Monteith grunted and made no comment.

'They were employed by an Aberdeen-based commercial diving company called Filkins-Storr that provides offshore divers to the North Sea oil industry,' Alex explained.

'And?'

'Filkins-Storr obtained visas for four divers who answered an advert calling for experience of welding and drilling work, surveying and working with explosives.'

'And?'

'They didn't turn up for work in Aberdeen on Monday.'

'What pictures do we have?'

'Just the photos with their visa applications.'

'Cameras?'

'Here?' Alex shrugged. 'They've been down for the last week. You could ask Border Agency at the airport.'

'Any sign of the Security Service?'

'None.'

'I don't like this,' Monteith said. He looked across at Miranda and frowned. 'Why isn't she wearing gloves?'

'You don't need to give me a lecture on forensics,' Alex told him.

She looked from Alex to Monteith. Alex stepped up to Monteith and stuck the knife in his back.

Monteith didn't seem particularly surprised. He tried to reach around to grasp the knife but the attempt defeated him and he toppled face forward, crashing into the table, smashing several bottles, showering the room with broken glass. The handle of the knife stood proud from his back. He looked up at her and then rolled off the table, landing on his back, the force of the fall pushing the point of the blade up through his ribcage. The dog cowered.

'This one they will pin on you,' Alex told her in a matter-of-fact way, 'as well as the deaths of tens of thousands of Londoners. When the flood waters subside you're the one they're going to be pointing their fingers at. You're going to be the stuff of screaming headlines.'

There was something incredibly smug about him. He seemed to assume that because of his physical strength he was invulnerable. He was mistaken. She was of the Isaaq Clan. It was her father who had taught her that the results of most fights depend on speed in the first few moments. When she had moved to England from Somalia and was put in a girl's boarding school she encountered for the first time the persecution of those who are different. In her new class she was the only one with dark skin and black hair. There was one girl in particular, in a class several years above hers, who taunted her. The girl was brutal, feared across the school, even by the teachers. She didn't stand a chance. Miranda followed her into the showers one night. She didn't bother working herself into a fury and she didn't give the girl the chance either. She just went straight up to her and head-butted her, breaking her nose. She kicked her legs out from under her, and slammed her head up and down off the tile floor a couple of times. Nobody bothered her after that.

This time she didn't pause either. She grabbed the beaker from the counter-top and flung its residue of nitric acid in Alex's face. He screamed and staggered backwards, folding over on himself. She jumped over Monteith, and dashed out of the room and into the corridor.

'Come on!'

She glanced back. Alex was holding the dog by his collar and in his other hand there was a gun. He reached over the dog to point it at her. He was screaming.

She didn't have any choice.

She ran across the living room and out into the passageway. Pressing her face to one of the windows, she saw a van disgorging men into the car park. Already doors were being slammed the length of the passage. She ran to the stairwell, leant over the railing and saw two men in hoodies, several floors below, advancing up the stairs. She took a deep breath and headed down towards them. On the next level down, she pushed through the fire door and ran down the passage. Halfway down she passed a small black girl with dandelion hair and the sharp, Semitic features she associated with the Horn of Africa, standing in the doorway of a flat. She stopped.

'Help me,' she said in Somali.

The girl stepped aside and gestured for her to come in. She found herself in a living room with a television playing Islam Channel. A woman in a black abaya but with her face uncovered looked up as she entered.

'Help me,' she said again.

The woman looked at the child and they reached some unspoken agreement. The girl took Miranda by the hand and led her down a corridor that was the mirror of the one in the apartment above. The girl opened the door to her room. There was a bed with a colourful bedspread covered in toys. The girl led her to a built-in cupboard and opened the door. At the bottom of the cupboard was a cubbyhole, created from cushions and pieces of embroidered cloth.

Miranda squeezed herself in, thankful for the years of yoga that had made her supple enough to fit into small spaces. The girl also squeezed in and pulled the door closed behind her. They sat in the darkness, with only their breath to give them away. The girl rested her head against Miranda's shoulder.

Beech was dead. Monteith was dead. She was being framed for the death of Monteith and, who knows, maybe also for the death of Beech. She had lost Esme's dog. Now it might not be enough to just run.

She walked as carefully, as full of composure, as she could manage, out of the tower block and past the swings. There was a man still standing by the van. He was smoking a cigarette and paid her no attention. She was wearing a full niqab, her face and body covered in shapeless black cloth; a shape only, invisible in plain sight.

She crossed the car park and turned the corner. Then she was running, bent almost double, through rain and darkness, away from the flats. She stripped off the robe, leapt down a slope and waded across a thundering brook, while blackened cloud-stacks raced across the sky and rain dashed against her in gusts. She stumbled onwards. Reaching the road, she flagged down a truck driver who gave her a lift into Glasgow.

The streets of Londonistan

9 September 2005

Within minutes of leaving Glasgow, most of the passengers were sleeping with their heads resting against the gently vibrating windows. The only sounds were the hum of the engine and the soft hiss of the air conditioning. Miranda's fellow passengers were entirely foreign: migrant workers, students and budget tourists. She slipped easily into their midst.

She was heading for London, but she carefully avoided a direct route. For the first leg she sat next to a Nigerian business student who tried to chat her up, and for the stretch from Newcastle to Birmingham next to a Slovak beautician who tutted over the stubs of her nails.

In the toilets at Digbeth coach station in Birmingham, she took a penknife to her hair, hacking at her thick curls and discarding them in the bowl. She had not worn her hair this short for twenty years, not since her days in the Lion's Den. Afterwards she sat for an hour, waiting for her connection in the vast hangar-like garage. She ate a stale cheese savoury sandwich from the station kiosk and glanced intermittently at the phone box. She bit her lip, steeling herself.

She had to. She walked over to the phone booth, fed change into the slot and dialled the number. It was answered on the third ring.

'It's Miranda.'

'Where are you?' Flora demanded. 'Why did you just disappear?'

'What did the police say to you?'

'That there had been a sighting of Beech near Dover.'

'They're lying or they're being lied to, Flora.'

A bad pause.

'What do you mean?'

'Is there somebody you can go to? A neighbour. A friend. Somewhere safe.'

'What are you trying to tell me, for fuck's sake?'

She told her. 'Beech is dead. He's in the rocks up on the hill. I'm sorry.'

She had no idea whether Flora was hearing her. She thought she heard a door slam and the sound of something crashing. 'Flora?'

A further pause.

'Flora?'

After a while she ended the call.

She called BBC Television Centre from a phone booth on the concourse of Victoria station as soon as she arrived in London, gave a name and was immediately put through to *Newsnight*.

'Saira speaking.'

'Hello. It's me, Miranda.'

Silence. Saira was mystified. 'Miranda?'

'From Sarajevo . . .'

'Ah, that Miranda.' There was a pause. 'The cold-hearted Miranda.'

'I'm in London.'

'The prodigal returns . . .'

'Are you all right?' Miranda asked.

'I'm just tired,' Saira told her. 'I've been working flat out since the 7/7 bombings. How much trouble are you in?'

'Plenty.'

'So nothing's changed, then.'

'Nothing's changed,' Miranda acknowledged.

They arranged to meet in a couple of hours at the Frontline Club in Paddington. Miranda hung up and stepped out on to the pavement. She paused for a moment, feeling oddly confused and guilty all of a sudden. Guilty because she had walked out on Saira several years before without so much as leaving a note and confused because hearing her voice down a phone line had revived a very specific physical memory of lying naked, more or less sated, in a hotel room in Sarajevo.

She walked slowly north towards Hyde Park. She kept looking down, but there was no dog at her heels.

Saira poured her a large glass of wine and then filled her own glass to the brim. They were sitting on the red leather sofas in the club room at the Frontline.

Saira was sitting with her legs curled under her on the sofa, wearing jeans, dark suede shoes and an open-necked white silk shirt that was so crumpled it seemed likely that she had been wearing it for days. She was tall, and her cheekbones were high and handsome. It was easy for Miranda to remember why she had found her so attractive.

They had met in Sarajevo, during the siege, when mortars and shells could fall anywhere and at any time. It was a period when you ran into people. You drank together in mobs. You drank so much and then by accident ended up in bed with someone; with men, and very occasionally with women. It just happened that way. Saira was working as a producer for BBC World Service and Miranda was following a rumour of her husband Bakr. It was Saira who had taught her the *Sarajevo walk*: relaxed when protected by the cover of buildings or barricades, brisk and alert when crossing streets, and breaking into a sudden sprint when crossing open ground, cobbled squares or crossroads exposed to sniper's rifles. They had met in the warren of lanes around the old Turkish Bascarsija market. You couldn't miss Saira, she was as tall as Miranda, head and shoulders taller than most other woman, with skin the colour of a cinnamon stick. They were the same waist and shoe size. The similarities didn't end there. Saira's father, like Miranda's, had been an opponent of the Siad Barre regime and had had to flee Somalia. Both their families had been forced into the peripatetic existence of political exiles – constantly on the move as the regime concluded deals with countries to prevent its opponents from settling. Saira's family had lived in Saudi Arabia, Ethiopia and Kenya before finally settling in Cardiff, Wales.

For a while Saira and Miranda were lovers and had shared a room at the Holiday Inn. There had been a couple of chance encounters since then, in Peshawar and Grozny.

'So what brings you here?' Saira asked.

'I'm looking for someone,' Miranda replied.

'You're not still . . .?'

'No. Someone else.'

Saira studied her warily. 'Did you find Omar?'

Miranda bit her lip. She really didn't want to burst into tears. 'Omar died in 1991. He was dead all the time that I was looking for him.'

'I'm so sorry,' Saira said.

Miranda took a deep breath. 'I found out just over two years ago.'

'I don't know what to say.'

'What can you say?'

'What have you been doing?' Saira asked.

Walking, she thought, walking on the moor, and drinking vodka and fucking Jonah. I got up every morning and saluted the sun, even when it was overcast, in the hope that one day it might scorch me off the face of the earth. 'I've been living on an island in Scotland,' she said. 'I met someone.'

'You always had someone,' Saira observed with a sigh.

It was true. She had never left a man without abandoning him for someone else.

'He's gone missing,' Miranda said.

'Missing as in disappeared?' Saira asked, sceptically.

Miranda nodded.

'That's what happens to your men.'

'He was in Peshawar and then Amman,' Miranda told her. 'After that, nothing.'

'Who is he?' Saira asked.

'He's a spook. Military intelligence. A retired agent.' She paused and stared at her wine glass. 'At least, I thought he was retired.' She leant forward. 'I need you to arrange a meeting for me with someone at the House of Lords.'

'I can get a peer's number in no time. You can give them a call and make an appointment. It's not difficult. Who do you want to speak to?'

'Norma Said.'

Saira sat up slightly and her eyes narrowed. 'Baroness Said sits on the Intelligence and Security Committee.'

Miranda gripped her knee. 'I need you to go to Parliament and speak to her. Tell her that I am a friend of her son.'

Miranda had raised her interest now. 'Norma Said's son is a spook?'

'Yes. And he's in trouble.'

'Why can't *you* go to Parliament?'

'I can't.'

Saira frowned. 'Why not?'

'There are people looking for me.'

Saira rolled her eyes and leant closer. 'Don't tell me the police are looking for you?'

'I need your help.'

Saira gave her a resigned look. 'Come on, let's get out of here.'

They walked down Praed Street towards the Edgware Road. Saira's two-bedroom flat was on a corner opposite the tube station.

'I was here on the seventh of July, on the day of the bomb- ings. It was supposed to have been a day off. I got up late. I stood outside the tube station all day and all night with a cameraman,' Saira said, walking briskly down the street, 'the same station that I've been using for years. Some people were asking why Muslims would bomb a tube station in the heart of the largest Arab Muslim community in London. But it was bloody obvious, it was because the Edgware Road is *takfir*, it's a symbol of everything the bombers despised. They targeted it because it proves that Islam as a religion and Muslims as a community can thrive here in the West. Come on.'

They climbed several steep flights of steps to Saira's flat. She paused with the key in the lock. 'I share with a journalist from *World Affairs*. Luckily for you, he's overseas at the moment, so you can have his room.'

'Thank you.'

She sat on the sofa and unlaced her boots while Saira made her tea.

'Parliament is in recess so Baroness Said is unlikely to be at Westminster,' Saira called to her from the kitchen. 'I think she lives in Sussex. I'll ask some questions at work tomorrow. I'll speak to her office. I'll see if I can find out what her schedule is. Perhaps we can get her alone for a few minutes.'

Saira returned and handed her the cup. 'You look exhausted,' she said.

'I'm OK,' Miranda told her.

'I really need an explanation.'

Miranda told her everything in detail. About Jonah's departure. About the policemen Mulvey and Coyle. About Mark Mikulski and Richard Winthrop IV. About the Department. About Nor's confession. About Alex Ross. About Beech's murder. About the ginger-haired man. About the bomb factory. About the death of Monteith. About her fingerprints on the murder weapon. She spread the items from her pocket across the carpet: a postcard from Peshawar, a print-out of the Sheerness tidal gauge, the diagram of an unnamed ship with a set of coordinates, and Inspector Coyle and Mark Mikulski's business cards.

As soon as she started, Saira lit a cigarette. It took five cigarettes for Miranda to finish. Once she had finished they sat in silence for a while.

'You really do have a capacity for getting yourself in trouble,' Saira said, eventually.

'I need your help.'

'I'll make some enquiries in the morning. Check elements of the story. But I warn you, if I get anywhere with this I'm going to have to go to my editor. He'll want you to give an interview.

I don't need to tell him that you're here or how I know you, but I'll have to give him something.'

'I understand.'

'You knew that when you called me.'

Miranda nodded. 'I did.'

'Is that what you want, to go public?'

'I'm being set up. I'm going to try to speak to Norma Said but I don't know whether she can help me. I don't trust the police. You're the only friend I have. What else can I do?'

'You did the right thing,' Saira assured her. 'Come on, I'll show you your room.'

There was a freshly made double bed and beside it a pile of dog-eared reference books, a pair of Levi's slung over a chair and a guitar propped against a wall.

Miranda sat on the bed.

'It's good to see you,' Saira said, pausing in the doorway with her fingers resting on the frame. 'It's been too long.'

In the news

Miranda woke suddenly. Momentarily she was panic-stricken. Something was terribly wrong. And then she realised that for the first time in ages she had not been woken by the dog's paws prodding her through the blanket.

She swung her legs on to the floor, ran her hands through what remained of her hair. She looked up and stared out of the window at the imposing tower that was Paddington Green Police Station, and beyond it the directionless grey sky. She knew that there were underground cells at Paddington Green used for the questioning of terrorist suspects and it reminded her of the complications of her situation. The forces against her seemed too great for her to succeed. She decided to get up and go out, giving it as little thought as possible.

Walking into the lounge, she found that Saira had left her a spare set of keys and a note with her mobile phone number, telling her to make herself at home and help herself to anything.

There was a time, in Afghanistan, when she had found oblivion in the five daily prayers, in the succession of physical movements and recitation called the *rak'a*. But she'd never been able to stick at Islam. She'd never been much of a joiner. Now she found a kind of mindlessness in the sun salutation, its succession of coordinated postures and breaths.

She was in Hyde Park with her bare feet on the warm grass and her palms pressed together. She was wearing a T-shirt and jogging pants from Saira's wardrobe, and her ankle wallet was

balled up in a pair of Saira's trainers. Ten times she raised her
arms to the sun, ten times she held herself rigid in the plank
position until her arms shook with the strain, before jumping
forward. With the obligations of the salutation done, she ran
through a succession of her more challenging postures. Sweat
ran down her back and pooled at the base of her spine. For a
time, she felt free of care.

Then she ran around the Serpentine, and north on the path
parallel with Park Lane, gathering speed as she ran, breaking into
a sprint for the final stretch to Speaker's Corner. From Marble
Arch she walked north up the Edgware Road, past the Lebanese
cafés that were filled with crowds of Arabs sharing narghile pipes
in the warm summer air. It was just after noon.

As she was walking, she noticed a bank of televisions in the
window of an electronics store showing tanks and soldiers
surrounding the Thames Barrier. Only when it cut away to armed
police standing outside the Red Road Flats did she stop and
stare.

No sound came from the televisions. There was footage from
a bystander's mobile phone of army bomb disposal experts in
bulky green bomb suits emerging from a van and entering the
building. Beneath it ran a breaking-news strap:

POLICE RAID GLASGOW BOMB FACTORY

Then the photograph of Nor from the Interpol Red Notice,
his mocking smile filling the screen. Beneath it the strap:

TERROR MASTERMIND THREATENS LONDON

And then, to her dismay, there was grainy security-camera
footage of a dark-haired woman with a backpack walking across
a petrol station forecourt with a dog at her heels. It was her. The
petrol station outside Spean Bridge on Tuesday morning – in
contrast to the dark surroundings, a digital effect had been used
to highlight Miranda's face.

ARAB WOMAN SOUGHT BY POLICE

She called Saira from a payphone. Buses roared past and she was forced to raise her voice.

'Are you watching it?' Saira asked.

'I'm standing in the street staring at it.'

'You're in a phone box?'

'Yes.'

'Are you all right?'

'I guess so. I'm a bit shocked.'

'The police haven't named you yet. And if that's the only footage they've got you're not likely to get recognised in the street. We're OK for now.'

'There were two policemen in my kitchen on Monday. They know who I am.'

'And if you're right this whole thing will be over in a couple of days. We can keep you hidden until next Tuesday,' Saira told her, in a reassuring tone. 'Don't worry.'

Miranda forced a smile. 'What's there to worry about?'

'That's the spirit.'

'So what have you found out?'

'The police have slapped a cordon around the flats and they're not letting anyone in or out. However, I have a friend who writes for the *Glasgow Herald*. His contact within the Strathclyde Police has confirmed that as well as scene-of-crime officers and the Bomb Squad, officers from Strathclyde CID's Counter-Terrorism Intelligence Section and MI5 are in attendance. And they pulled a body out, a white male in his late fifties.'

'Monteith.'

'Looks that way. Your story holds up. I spoke with Brian Judd, our Security Correspondent. He already knew about Nor's confession. He told me that he uses a freelancer who monitors extremist websites and tips him off if anything interesting comes to light. He forwarded the link to Brian soon after the video was uploaded. Brian made some enquiries at the MoD and at MI6 after it was posted. At first they told him that it was a prank and then, after he dug around a bit, they slapped a DA notice on him. A DA notice means that he is prevented from public disclosure of information that might compromise UK military and intelligence operations. That was a week ago. The notice is voluntary so he can break it, but he's been holding back until now. He's pretty sure that this Department of yours really exists. Or at least it did. He believes that it refers to an offshoot of the Defence Intelligence Staff called the Afghan Crisis Cell. Strictly speaking it's part of the Ministry of Defence, although it doesn't appear anywhere in the armed forces budget. It's supposed to be a group of analysts, both military and civilians with a technical expertise, who provide assessments for the Chief of the Defence Staff and the Permanent Secretary of the MoD. Actually, he thinks that's just cover. He believes that it is in fact an arm's-length black-ops unit run by MI6. Or at least it was. It was closed down about a month ago, just like you said. I have some information on this guy Monteith from the Army List, but it's not very revealing. It's the same with your friend Jonah and his friend Andy Beech. According to the army they both retired years ago. I'm going to keep digging around.'

'What about Alex Ross? He's the one that murdered Monteith.'

'According to Companies House, up until a month ago he was listed as the director of a security company called Threshold. Then they got bought out by a much larger American company called Greysteel. That's the company that your Richard Winthrop is now vice-chairman of. They call it the fifth branch of the US military: army, navy, air force, Marines . . . Greysteel. Alex Ross is now listed as a non-executive director of Greysteel UK. They have offices in Kensington. I called them up. They told me that he wasn't available. They seemed pretty interested in me, though.'

'What did you tell them?'

She laughed. 'I told them that I was from the *Today* programme.'

'You should be careful,' Miranda told her.

'Hey, careful is my middle name.'

'I'm serious.'

'I know you are. If you're still interested, I know what Norma Said's doing tonight.'

'I'm interested.'

'She's going to the theatre. The Almeida in Islington. It's the European premiere of a new David Mamet play. You could buy a ticket or just turn up for the interval. According to the blurb it's a courtroom drama, and it has all the ingredients: the Israeli–Palestinian conflict, sexual fidelity, world peace, et cetera, et cetera . . . You know where it is?'

'I know.'

Her parents had lived close by, in Highgate, and she had gone to school there in what seemed like a different life.

'I'll meet you at the flat later?'

'Yes. Can I borrow something to wear?'

'Sure, and get yourself a mobile phone. Call in regularly.'

Farther up the Edgware Road, Miranda stopped at an Arab-owned electronics store and bought five pay-as-you-go mobile phones. Back in the flat she switched the TV on. It was on Sky News. There was further footage of the Red Road Flats. She pressed the mute button. She set about unpacking the phones, plugging them in to charge at sockets in various rooms. She chose a dress, a simple black dress, from Saira's wardrobe. It had been a long time since she'd worn a dress. She justified it on the grounds that she was going to the theatre. She hung it up on the back of the kitchen door, then took a shower. She realised that she would need shoes. She chose a pair of plain black pumps. And a handbag for her money and the phones – there was one on the back of Saira's door.

She made herself toast and Marmite. She dozed off on the sofa.

Miranda woke to a split screen, a Sky News anchorman on one side of the tube and on the other Richard Winthrop IV with a caption identifying him as a former White House National Security Advisor. She grabbed the remote and turned up the volume. The anchorman was speaking. 'Do you honestly believe that we have come to a place where the most senior people in the highest office in the land won't do the right thing in the end? They won't see the error of their ways?'

'No, sir, they will not,' Winthrop replied, and suddenly he had the whole screen to himself. 'The only chance that we have right now is for Osama Bin Laden to deploy and detonate a major weapon in Europe. It's going to take grassroots bottom-up pressure, because these politicians prize their office and prize the praise of the liberal media above the safety of their citizens. It's an absurd situation. Only Osama Bin Laden can execute an attack which will force Europeans to demand that their government protect them effectively, consistently and with as much force as is necessary.'

Infuriated, she changed the channel.

On CNN, a car was burning on an overpass in New Orleans. Beneath it was the caption:

SHOOT-OUT IN THE NINTH WARD

A Greysteel security contractor was explaining that his convoy had come under fire from black gangbangers on an overpass in the Ninth Ward neighbourhood. 'I was talking to my wife,' he said. 'Then suddenly we're in an ambush. I dropped the phone and returned fire with my AR-15. After that there was just yelling and screaming. And bodies everywhere. I'm telling you, it's like Baghdad on the bayou.'

'This is a trend,' said a spokesman for Greysteel. 'You're going to see a lot more of guys like us in these situations. Our rapid response unit has global reach and can make a positive difference in the lives of those who are affected by natural disasters and terrorist attacks.'

Miranda changed channels. BBC News 24. The next image was of the Home Secretary at a speech that afternoon to the Association of Chief Police Officers, being asked by a reporter whether there was any truth in the allegation that the intelligence services had been infiltrated by terrorists. 'I have full confidence in the intelligence services,' the Home Secretary said, looking rattled and unprepared.

She changed channels again. In Iraq, a suicide bomber had detonated his charge next to a petrol tanker south of Baghdad; sixty died in the ensuing fireball and hundreds were injured.

She changed again. A weatherman was tracking the progress of a depression from its origins on the Grand Banks off the coast of Canada, across the Atlantic towards the North Sea.

She changed once more. Sky News again. The anchor announced, 'We're going live to our correspondent Scarlett Taylor who is outside the US embassy in Grosvenor Square. What can you tell us about the American reaction, Scarlett?'

'So far there has been no official comment from the American government on the allegation that British military intelligence officers colluded to cover up the assassination of a CIA agent in Afghanistan in the late 1990s. However, we do know that the US Attorney's office in New York has today unsealed warrants for the arrest of a list of six individuals who are believed to have belonged to a secret British military unit. At least two of those individuals are believed to have died under mysterious circumstances in recent days. One of them on the remote Scottish island of Barra and the other in what the Strathclyde Police has just confirmed was a bomb-making factory in the Red Road Flats in Glasgow.'

She switched off the television and immediately dialled Saira's mobile phone.

'Who is this?' Saira asked.

'It's me, Miranda.'

'Thank God you called. Are you in the flat?'

'Yes.'

'Get out of there right now. Whoever is following me is probably also watching you. Go somewhere public, a train station, department store. See if you can lose them. Call me again in an hour. I'll have fixed up somewhere safer for you to stay.'

Saira cut the connection. Miranda got dressed. She put the mobile phone she'd used in the rubbish bin and scooped up the other four. She put them together with the money and the papers from Jonah's collage in the handbag.

For a short time she stood on the pavement, studying the Edgware Road with as much indifference as she could muster. It was busy and there were people everywhere – walking on the pavement, getting on and off buses, emerging from the underground. Even some of the parked cars along the kerb had people in them. It was impossible. She walked to the kerb and hailed a cab. She told the driver to take her to Selfridges.

As soon as they were under way Miranda noticed a car opposite the entrance to Saira's block of flats pull out into the traffic. It was an ordinary-looking blue car and Miranda could not tell what make it was. It stayed several cars behind them as they headed down the Edgware Road and along Oxford Street.

At the front entrance to Selfridges, she thrust a ten-pound note into the driver's hand and hurried in under the clock tower without looking behind her. She walked through the crowded perfume counters with such haste that shop assistants turned to look after her.

Ascending on the escalator, Miranda watched the door she had come in. To her horror the ginger-haired man, who she had last seen standing on the deck of the ferry from Barra, hurried in and looked angrily around the crowd. Miranda had almost reached the next floor when the man looked up towards her and their eyes met. He scowled. The first floor was as crowded as the ground floor. She rushed around the central well to climb to another floor. Stepping from the escalator, she ran past racks of women's designer wear and shoes to the stairs at the back.

She sprinted down the stairs, following the signs for the car park, and ducked out on to Edwards Mews. She hurried across Portman Square towards the glass-canopied entrance of the Radisson Hotel. She crossed the lobby to the mezzanine, where there was a bar with a view of the doors. The bar was furnished with red leather chairs, and there was a woman playing a piano in the corner. Miranda ordered a vodka and tonic and sat and watched the doors. There was no ginger-haired man.

She drank deeply. Her choice of Selfridges had not been entirely an instant improvisation. She had been chased through Selfridges before. It had been Christmas and the store was crowded and decorated. Her pursuer at the time was an overweight store detective who had caught her shoplifting in the Virgin record store. She had managed to evade the detective's grasp but then he had pursued her along Oxford Street through the lunchtime crowds. At last she had darted into Selfridges and escaped by a very similar route to the one she had just used.

There was something strange about it, when she reflected on it. It must have been about a year after her parents' death and just before she set off for Pakistan. The record that she'd stolen had been for Digger, her companion on the trip. Perhaps if the store detective had been a bit quicker she might not have ended up in Afghanistan; she might not have got pregnant; she might not have been sucked into Jonah's world; she would not be sitting here now, hiding from the ginger-haired man.

She ordered another drink. If she had not been so headstrong as a child, so heedless of the consequences of her actions, she might have achieved some semblance of contentment. It was too late now. She didn't think that she was going to live very much longer and she didn't much care. Her death would be as point-less as everything else in her life.

She paid for the drinks and went down to the lobby. She stood beside a column for a while and then stepped out on to the pave-ment. No ginger-haired man. When she had crossed Baker Street she turned in her tracks and looked around, but she could see no sign of pursuit. She was reasonably satisfied that she was no longer being followed, and for some reason that made her feel confident and bold.

She walked into Top Shop and bought a red halter-neck dress, a bra and underwear and then on impulse a dark blonde wig. The label said the colour was cappuccino. She paid for them and then changed in the fitting rooms, folding the black dress into her handbag. Once again she had lustrous, long hair. She strode down Oxford Street to the tube station with the same boldness that had carried her down al-Arasat in Baghdad more than a decade before.

★

It had turned into a warm evening and as she turned into Almeida Street from Upper Street she saw that the theatre crowd had spilled out on to the pavement for the interval.

There was an elegant-looking black woman, of indeterminate age, with large eyes, strong cheekbones and closely cropped black hair, standing with the white walls of the bar behind her. She was wearing bold jewellery and a cashmere shawl wrapped around her shoulders. She was talking to a tall man in a vivid tie who Miranda recognised as the anchor for a rival television news programme to the one that she had been watching earlier. The man was animated. The woman was, by contrast, calm and self-possessed – there was something about her manner that reminded Miranda of Jonah's surprising capacity for stillness and observation when he chose to exert it. She waited for a break in their conversation and then approached, easing her way through the chattering crowd.

'Baroness Said?' she asked.

Norma Said contemplated her without expression. 'Yes?'

'My name is Miranda. I'm Jonah's friend.'

Calmly, Norma Said turned to her companion and said, 'Will you excuse us for a moment.'

The news anchor ducked his head and withdrew out of earshot.

'Thank you,' Miranda told her.

Norma Said took her time looking her over and then said, 'Well?'

'I think Jonah is being set up to take the blame for a terrorist attack here in London.'

Norma Said's equanimity did not waver even for a moment. She was clearly a woman who responded with the greatest calm to events that might be expected to cause anyone else extreme anxiety. 'Can you prove it?'

Miranda hesitated.

'Well?'

'I have seen certain clues that suggest the date and the target of the attack. I can identify one of the people behind it. A man named Alex Ross. He used to own a security company called

Threshold, which has been taken over by the US company Greysteel.'

Norma Said was silent for a time.

'I need your help,' Miranda told her.

'Come to Ripe in Sussex tomorrow,' Norma said. 'I'll be in the graveyard at eleven a.m. We can speak then.'

She turned her back on Miranda and walked over to the news anchor. She was smiling by the time she reached him.

Whistle and duck

Saira looked thoughtful and serious as she dumped an overnight bag on the bed. They were in adjacent rooms in the vast hangar-like Hilton across from Terminal 4 at Heathrow Airport. There was a camera on a tripod pointing at an armchair arranged in a corner of the room. Miranda was sitting collapsed in it. The wig was discarded on the floor.

'I see you made a start on the minibar,' Saira said.

'We need more vodka,' Miranda said, 'if you want me to tell all.'

'There's a bottle in the bag. And some clothes.'

'You think of everything.'

'I try to be thorough.' Miranda was aware of Saira watching her as she got up out of the chair. 'You look good in a dress,' Saira told her.

'Why, thank you,' Miranda replied, retrieving the bottle. 'You should see me in my wig.'

'Do you know who's been following us?'

Miranda poured two shots. 'I have some idea.'

'Did you lose them?'

'Yes. In Selfridges.' She handed a glass to Saira. 'What about you?'

'In the crowds at King's Cross,' Saira replied. 'What I don't understand is why they were so obvious.'

'Maybe they are trying to frighten us.'

'They succeeded.' They both downed their shots. 'Who are they?'

'I think they work for Alex Ross.'

'Greysteel?' Saira said.

'Yes.'

'You said that Alex Ross was a member of the Afghan Guides?'

'That's right.'

'Are you sure about that?'

'Of course. I told you he was in the photo that was stolen from the wall at Beech's house. Flora confirmed it.'

'Then he's getting some pretty heavyweight protection, probably courtesy of his employers at Greysteel.'

'What do you mean?'

'His name is not on the list of warrants issued by the US Attorney's office.'

'They're covering up his involvement,' Miranda said.

Saira nodded. 'It looks that way. It explains why he stole the photo of the Guides that you described, and from what you're saying it appears that he's busy murdering or implicating in a fabricated terrorist attack anybody that had any connection to the Guides. Presumably without a live witness he's in the clear.'

'You think the terrorist attack is a fabrication?' Miranda asked.

Saira frowned and shook her head. 'It's a fairy tale. It's got to be.'

'What do you mean?'

'Nor's not coming here, he'd be crazy to. He's caused all the damage he wanted to on YouTube. Intelligence and security are at each other's throats. We've got senior sources in MI6 briefing journalists against the MoD, accusing them of running a death squad. The MoD are claiming that they were infiltrated by private contractors paid by MI6. The police want to haul everybody in. The Americans are furious. Both the Defence Secretary and the Home Secretary are looking vulnerable.'

'I'm not so sure. Nor's threat seemed pretty real to me. Flora thinks he has reason to want revenge. And in the Red Road Flats, when Alex spoke to me after killing Monteith, he made it sound like it was really going to happen.'

'There's nothing you can do about it now.'

'I can try and stop them.'

'The best way for you to do that is to tell your side of the story. You want to do this now?'

Miranda sighed. 'All right.'

'Then take a seat in front of the camera,' Saira told her.

Miranda sat. Saira knelt before her for a moment and smoothed her eyebrows. As she got up she paused briefly to press her lips to Miranda's forehead.

'Good luck.'

She stepped up to the camera and pressed Record.

'Tell me everything.'

They lay outstretched on the bed with the empty foil trays of their takeaway dinner and an empty wine bottle spread out on the floor beside them. Saira was smoking a cigarette, with the back of her head resting on the headboard.

'Do you remember the whistle and duck?'

The whistle and duck. It sounded like the name of an English pub. The phrase had probably been coined by an Englishman. It was the sight and sound of Sarajevo. The two things happened simultaneously and, curiously, in slow motion. A loud whistling overhead and, because it was a sound that everyone recognised, they would all duck, in perfect unison. Then the shell would thud into the ground or the side of a block of flats, explode and let out a belch of black smoke.

'I remember it all,' Miranda said.

'Are you going to elude me again?' Saira asked.

'I can't,' Miranda replied.

'You've never known a boundary in your life. You used to say that we could do whatever we wanted.'

'I'm sorry,' she said. But she remembered a time when she felt drunk with kissing, when they spent hours merely kissing. There was a part of her that wished that she could lose herself so completely again. Miranda shifted on the bed, dropping her feet on to the carpet. 'I'm going to take a shower,' she said, going through the interconnecting door to her own room. 'I'll see you in the morning.'

She was standing under the shower head with her eyes closed and a bar of soap in her hands and the shampoo flowing out of her hair when she felt a sudden rush of cold air as the glass door opened behind her, and another body stepped into the shower with her.

'Saira,' she protested.

'Sshhh . . .'

Saira took the soap from her, lathered her hands and rubbed Miranda's back before reaching around and stroking the inside of her thighs. Miranda sighed as Saira's hands travelled up her belly, her left hand caressing Miranda's navel while her right hand lathered her breast.

She remembered how boldly she had walked down Oxford Street that evening. Saira was right. She'd never given a damn for the consequences of her actions. *Why not?* she thought. *Why not just give in to the moment?* That was all she had ever done. She let her head fall back against Saira's shoulder. But when she closed her eyes, it was not Saira that she imagined stroking her ribs and touching her nipples. It wasn't even Jonah. It was Nor.

'Stop,' she said.

Saira let go of her and stepped back.

'I'm sorry,' Miranda told her, 'but I can't.'

She turned in the shower stall to face Saira and saw disappointment turn to anger.

'What is it with you?' Saira demanded.

'I'm sorry.'

Without another word, Saira stepped out of the shower stall and wrapped herself in a towel. She went through into the next-door room and closed the door behind her.

Miranda dreamt of Nor again, his face and his naked body in the darkness. He reached out to touch her with fingers that were as soft as silk.

She woke in a curious state of arousal, with no single point of pleasure. Instead the entire surface of her skin glowed. She kicked off the sheet and lay back, struggling to control her breathing. Pleasurable images of the dream filled her head but were followed close on their heels, as so often before, by the urge to flee. She did not want to be there when Saira awoke.

Miranda got out of the bed and washed her face. She put on a new bra and pants from Top Shop and tiptoed through into the adjacent room. Saira was lying on her back and gently snoring. From Saira's bag she chose a pair of jeans and a silk shirt. She put them on. From beside the camera she recovered Saira's sneakers and from the back of the door she took Saira's tailored black coat with pink satin lining. Saira had left the keys to a hire car on the bedside table. She picked them up and pocketed them. The last thing she did was remove the tape from the camera. She put it in her bag with the other evidence. She would be the one who determined when it was released.

Minutes later she was walking across the car park, pointing the fob at each car in turn until finally one clicked and flashed and came to life.

'The British state will taste a tiny portion of what innocent Muslims taste every day at the hands of the Crusader and Jewish coalition to the east and to the west.' It was Jonah talking, his voice strangely flat and toneless on the radio. 'Death will find you . . .'

She pulled over on to the hard shoulder, and sat for a moment with her hands on the steering wheel, her whole body shaking, while traffic roared past.

'This new footage released on extremist websites overnight shows another former member of the British Army's secretive Afghan Crisis Cell confessing his involvement in the death of a senior CIA agent in the 1990s,' the announcer said. 'He is also shown engaged in a recent act of sabotage against an Iraqi pipeline and has repeated the threat of an imminent terrorist attack on British soil. We asked both the Ministry of Defence and the Home Office to speak to us but they refused to put anyone up for interview. With me here in the studio I have our Security Correspondent, Brian Judd. Brian, what can you tell us about this latest video?'

'Well, John, according to a banner headline on the video it was produced by the media section of the Islamic Army of Iraq. I should say that this is not a group that we are familiar with. The video begins with a man of Middle Eastern appearance reading from a statement in which he claims that he is a former British Army officer and a double agent; a jihadist who infiltrated the highest echelons of British military intelligence. He calls himself Ishmael. As I said, he is reading from a written statement and he appears to have been beaten. It is not clear at this stage whether he is a hostage or a willing participant.'

'And what can you tell us about the attack in Iraq?'

'I can tell you that it happened. Three days ago terrorists blew up the main pipeline that carries nearly half a million barrels of oil a day out of southern Iraq. Repair crews rushed to the scene but they are operating in an extremely insecure environment, in dangerous circumstances. According to my sources this attack may cost Iraq hundreds of millions of dollars in lost oil exports before the damage is fixed. The terrorists knew exactly which pipe to destroy and where to find it. That suggests a level of sophistication the like of which we have not seen before. It seems entirely possible that this is indeed the work of an international gang made up of trained former intelligence agents.'

'And they have repeated their threat against us?'

'That's right, John. In his statement the man calling himself Ishmael says: *Economic jihad is one of the most powerful ways in which we can take revenge on the infidels at the present stage. The right target may generate a rate of return many times greater than the size of the initial investment.* The signs are that this gang intends to pull off a spectacular attack on our infrastructure, possibly on the city of London. The security forces here appear to be concentrating their efforts on securing the Thames Barrier in advance of the coming storm.'

'That's because in the earlier video, released several weeks ago now, there was reference to a tidal wave.'

'That's right, John. The Barrier seems to be the target. And the warning issued today by the Met Office Storm Tide Forecasting Service of a low-pressure area approaching across the Atlantic, together with a projected higher-than-normal tide, suggests that we may be facing a scenario that tests the Barrier to its limit. If the terrorists chose this moment to attack, London could suffer cataclysmic damage . . .'

The sudden whoop of a police siren and a wash of coloured lights in the rear-view mirror startled her. There was a police car behind her on the hard shoulder, flashing its lights at her. Terrified, for a moment she thought of running. On her right lorries thundered by and on her left was an exposed bank of grass. A policeman was approaching. There was nowhere to go. She jabbed at the off switch on the radio. The policeman tapped on the window.

'Are you all right, madam?' he asked once she'd opened the window.

'Yes,' she said. 'I felt dizzy, that's all.'

'How do you feel now?'

'Better. I'm OK now.'

'I'll tell you what,' the policeman said, 'there is a service station just up ahead. We'll escort you there. You can take a rest.'

'Thank you,' she said.

She drove seven miles in the slow lane to the service station and the police car followed her into the car park, before tooting its horn and leaving. She sat for a while with her head in her hands.

In the cemetery

Miranda stood for a moment by the stile at the back of the grave-yard with the Sussex Downs behind her and the spire of the early Gothic church before her. The air was full of petals from the wisteria on the cemetery wall. She had no idea what to expect.

Norma Said was standing by a graveside among the yew trees, wearing a long dark-blue cashmere overcoat and court shoes. She looked up as Miranda approached and her eyes were shining. Miranda realised that her cheeks were wet with tears.

'I'm sorry,' she said. 'I miss him. He was a difficult man ...' She tailed off, contemplating her husband's grave, which was decorated with a fresh bouquet of lilies. 'The right hemisphere of his brain, which is what you use for sorting and recognising faces, was damaged. Towards the end he developed something called Capgras syndrome. He took it into his head that Jonah was being impersonated. In his eyes Jonah was no longer Jonah. He used to become very agitated on those rare occasions when Jonah visited. He would shout at him. It must have been very hard for Jonah to see his father in that condition.' She shook her head sadly. 'It was typical of my husband that even his delusions were prescient.'

They stood for a moment.

'Thank you for coming,' she said. 'I thought that it was best to meet discreetly.'

'The police are looking for me,' Miranda told her.

'As far as the Secret Service is concerned my son is a terrorist traitor and you are one of his accomplices.'

'I don't believe that Jonah is a traitor,' Miranda said.

'When I joined the Intelligence and Security Committee I fully expected to learn things, often unpleasant things. I did not expect them to be so close to home. I admit I underestimated my son. I knew that he was determined. He was a very determined child. When he was small he had a plastic horse on springs that he called Go. Sometimes when he rode it he would pass into a kind of trance and bounce for hours, back and forth, back and forth, with a blankness in his eyes. I found it worrying. I used to have to hold his shoulders down to stop him. What is worrying in a child rapidly becomes disturbing in an adult. I suppose I was taken in by his impersonation of a directionless and unsettled young man. He was my son but I did not like him very much. When I first read his name in a file I admit I was deeply surprised. I was forced to reappraise him.'

'There's somebody coming,' Miranda observed.

A serious-looking man in a grey suit approached from the direction of the highly polished black car parked at the cemetery's main entrance. He stopped just within earshot.

'Are you OK, ma'am?' he asked Norma, cautiously.

'Yes, thank you,' she said, pleasantly. 'I'm fine.'

'Very well,' he said, and retreated to the car.

'I was unused to protection,' she said, 'but then I learned secrets and lies and I grew to believe that the prime minister was right when he said that I must have it. You'd better not stay long. The people who protect me may also be watching me now. I have submitted a letter of resignation. I do not believe that it will be long before the prime minister accepts it.'

'I think that Jonah is trying to stop a terrorist attack.'

Norma glanced at Miranda, an impatient glance that said: *You don't get it, do you?* 'It's a conjuror's trick. A plot plucked from the air: an article of faith.'

'I don't understand,' protested Miranda.

'There are forces at work,' Norma Said explained, 'forces at the heart of this administration that sincerely believe that the overriding purpose of intelligence is to shape the public mood.

They believe that any deception is justified as long as it serves that purpose and then it is not deception at all. In believing this they expose us to the gravest risk. I'm afraid that during the course of the last decade, under our current leadership, lying has become integral to the functioning of intelligence.'

'You are suggesting that there is no plot?'

'No, I'm not saying that. There may be a plot. There is certainly a threat. There are files full of worst-case scenarios. The vulnerability and interdependency of modern society means that any disruption to the infrastructure has the potential to cause mass civilian casualties. There are genuine terrorists, of both the home-grown and overseas varieties, who mean this country harm. There are individuals like myself and my son, who, for whatever reason, have become embarrassing or surplus to requirements. The ingredients are all at hand. What I am saying to you is that it suits certain individuals who seek preferment within the intelligence services to nurture and encourage an apocalyptic plot, a threat to the very fabric of this nation, so that in foiling it at the very last moment they provoke a strong national reaction – the righteous indignation of the tabloid press – and in so doing hand to their political masters the means to advance draconian legislation at home and project massive force overseas. You have to understand that the belief persists within certain sections of the administration and the Secret Service, even now, after all that has happened, that countering terrorism involves defeating a global insurgency. Afghanistan, Iraq – these are simply moves in a long war, a multi-generational conflict in which pre-emptive attack and regime change must be used to defeat terrorism and spread liberal democracy throughout the world.'

Miranda opened her mouth and abruptly closed it again.

'It has been my intention since I joined the committee to control the Secret Service,' Norma Said declared, 'to shift its powers to separate, smaller agencies and to make each of them separately accountable, and in doing so to dilute their powers.' She shook her head wistfully. 'I had not counted on the resourcefulness or ruthlessness of my adversaries. I have been blocked at every turn.

And now, by manufacturing a plot and implicating my son in it, they have managed to discredit me.'

'What should I do?' Miranda asked.

'A senior intelligence official within MI6 is behind this. His name is Topcliffe, though he goes by the code name Fisher-King. I do not know the exact details of the conspiracy that he has manufactured but I do know that he will stop at nothing to ensure his own preferment.'

Miranda was suddenly aware of movement behind her and, turning, saw the American FBI agent Mikulski with his hands in the pockets of his battered leather jacket. He seemed to have materialised from the nearest yew tree – not moving, just standing there, half hidden, expectantly waiting.

'This is Mr Mikulski. I believe that you have met him before. He tells me that he is not a member of any conspiracy. He says that he is simply interested in the truth. In my experience, America gives us the worst of itself and the best of itself. I sincerely hope that Mr Mikulski is a product of the latter.'

'It's good to see you again,' Mikulski said.

She stared at him, unsure of what to say. There was a pause. 'I didn't kill Monteith,' she said, 'or Andy Beech or anyone else for that matter.'

'That's not really what I'm here about.'

'Then what are you here about?'

'Can you tell me where Jonah is, Miranda?'

'I'm looking for him myself.'

'What about Nor ed-Din?'

She paused. 'If he comes, then perhaps . . .'

Mikulski nodded. 'I'll walk you to your car,' he said.

'We must not let terrifying threats cause us to degrade what is valuable in our society,' Norma Said told them. 'God go with you.'

Mikulski walked in the direction of the stile and after a moment's hesitation Miranda followed. When she caught up with him he said, 'I don't know whether by luck or skill, but you've done well to evade capture. What have you got for me?'

'Items that were planted in Jonah's study . . .'

'Show me.'

They sat side by side in the rental car and he quickly leafed through what she had to offer. The postcard, the tide tables, the ship's diagram, the coordinates. It didn't seem like much.

'The time of tomorrow's high tide is highlighted,' Miranda told him. 'Whatever they are planning it's for tomorrow night.'

'I see that.'

When he came to the diagram of the ship Mikulski frowned.

'It's a Liberty ship,' he said.

'A what?'

'A Liberty ship. It's a distinctive profile, like a child's imagining of a ship. They were hastily constructed freighters used to move supplies across the Atlantic during the Second World War. Tin cans really. They've got one in Baltimore harbour. It's a floating museum. My grandfather worked in the port. He used to take me on it as a child. What about the coordinates?'

'They mark a point about a mile and a half off the coast of Sheerness in the Thames Estuary.'

He handed the things back to her. He seemed mildly disappointed. 'What else can you tell me?'

She told him about the death of Monteith at the hands of Alex Ross in the bomb-making factory and finding Beech's body on Barra. She told him what she had learned about Threshold and Greysteel.

When she mentioned Greysteel he became briefly animated and asked, 'Have you heard the term Those Who Seek The End?'

'No.'

'They're a loose-knit group of powerful people linked to the security industry,' he said, 'CEOs, policy-makers, politicians and the like. They are extreme in their views. Let me give you an example. They argue that military and economic functions should be reunited, as in the time of the British Empire when firms like the East India Company were the main instruments of foreign policy, cutting deals and making war. They believe that the commercial security companies that are increasingly responsible for our defence in America and overseas should have a much greater say in the running of the state. Some call them a millenarian cult. Personally, I regard their activities as treasonous. I believe that Richard Winthrop answers to them.'

She explained that all reference to Winthrop had been removed from Jonah's collage.

'They're covering their tracks,' Mikulski told her. 'These people are ruthless and utterly unscrupulous. They murder people and call it collateral damage. They thought nothing of executing a CIA agent in Afghanistan because he was threatening their financial interests. They clearly think nothing of fabricating a terrorist attack on British soil. They will not spare you.'

'So what should I do?' she demanded.

'The best thing you can do is to stay out of their reach.'

'You expect me to do nothing?'

'Tomorrow they will play their hand. When they do it will be easier for the authorities here to take action.'

'You can't protect me, can you?'

'I can't,' he admitted. 'I told you, these are powerful people. They are very well connected.'

'I'm going to Sheerness,' she said.

'That's the last place you should go. Didn't you listen to what Norma Said was telling you? Don't give them any further excuse to pin this on you.'

'Nevertheless, that's where I'm going.'

'You've obviously made up your mind.'

'I have,' she said, grimly.

He got out of the car and paused before leaning in the open window. 'Call me. You've got my card, right?'

'I have. Wait.'

She reached into her bag and withdrew the tape of her interview with Saira.

'Take this,' she said, handing it to him. 'It's my side of the story.'

The Montgomery

11 September 2005

Miranda crossed into Kent on the motorway, driving through chalk cuttings and past red-brick housing estates with red-tiled roofs and pylons with their legs in flooded grass fields. She came off the motorway and on to the A249 northbound, following the signs for the Isle of Sheppey.

She stared through the windscreen at the passing landscape, the barren mudbanks and grasslands of the marshes, and across the Medway the steel stacks and tubes and winking lights of a power station on the Isle of Grain. She crossed the Swale on the elegant arc of the high bridge at Sheppey Crossing, and once on the island, drove through marshes dotted with occasional sheep. The first sign of the port was a chain-link fence and a series of access roads blocked with boulders. The road curved around to the right and she drove alongside a dense leylandii hedge and then past the entrance to a steelworks. On the other side of the road there was a yard filled with rows of concrete Buddhas and a banner advertising CONCRETE GARDEN ORNA-MENTS MANUFACTURERS. Beyond it was a sign for Blue Town and a glimpse of the twenty-foot-high brick wall that ringed the oldest section of the port.

The first of two roundabouts signposted the port and the second, on the far side of a brackish stretch of canal, signposted the town centre and a supermarket; circling back, she followed the sign for the port and performed an abrupt U-turn as soon as the checkpoint with its uniformed guard came into view. She fed back into the traffic and crossed the canal again, heading for the town centre this time, passing the railway station and after it a police station, then turning left on to the High Street.

She drove slowly down a narrow one-way street that was festooned with multicoloured bunting, past a Victorian clock tower and rows of shops selling knick-knacks and seaside souvenirs, and emerged confusingly, at the end of it, back at the second roundabout and the green-tinged canal. This time she headed for the broad expanse of the supermarket car park. Cautiously, she drove the length of it.

At one end, hidden behind the supermarket, there was a run-down mall, with an amusement arcade, a boarded-up nightclub and a sunken playground in a stretch of grass. Young women, who looked as if they were barely out of school, were standing beside pushchairs on the grass. At the other end of the car park there was a recycling point and an old man in shorts throwing bottles from a cardboard box, one after another, into a green skip, the glass smashing in staccato accompaniment to the raucous cry of gulls. Beyond the row of skips there was a steep incline covered in brambles and the concrete sea wall. She parked along-side the stairway leading up to the wall. It was plastered with warning signs. She hadn't been this close to the sea since leaving Barra on the ferry, and the contrast couldn't have been greater. She glanced at the print-out of the tidal gauge and the ship's diagram. This was it, all she had, a print-out of the Sheerness tidal gauge and a set of coordinates for a point just offshore. If there was nothing here then she was out of possible leads.

She got out of the car, locked it and climbed the cement steps. On the top of the wall, she stood for a moment staring out to sea. From where she was standing, she could see the mouth of the Thames, a large town on the far side of the estuary and the North Sea. The water was gunmetal grey and still for as far as the eye could see. There were several large ships in the shipping channel. She closed her eyes for a moment and listened to the lapping of the waves on the shingle beach and the gulls. She opened them again. A row of dark wooden groynes stretched along the beach in both directions. To the right there were exposed mussel beds and to the left a jumble of concrete pillboxes that might have dated back to the Second or even the First World War, and, dividing the beach from the port, a moat filled with dark green algae.

She jumped down off the wall and trudged along the shingle beach towards the jetty where the tidal gauge was located. There were several men sitting in folding chairs at intervals along the shoreline, with their fishing rods on cradles beside them. Lying next to a large bald-headed man in an Arsenal shirt was a brown-and-white Staffordshire bull terrier on a leash, which raised its snout as she passed.

The beach ended abruptly with a jumble of rocks, barbed-wire fencing and signs saying KEEP OUT. If she wanted to reach the jetty she was going to have to hire a boat or swim. She turned around and trudged back along the beach. As she did so a small tugboat passed the end of the jetty and she watched it strike out perpendicular to the beach. It took a moment or two to under-stand what she was looking at. She felt her mouth go dry. It was there staring her in the face. A mile and a half offshore with warning buoys at four corners: the tops of the three masts poking out of the water, a glimpse of the deck.

The Liberty ship.

The three-masted freighter pinned to Jonah's collage by persons unseen.

It was a wreck. There in plain view, in the shipping lane.

She sat down on the beach and watched as the tugboat weighed anchor beside the forward mast. It was too far off to see what it was up to. She looked around, searching for inspiration. The man with the Staffie wasn't that far away. She took a couple of fifties out of her handbag and palmed them. She undid one of the buttons of her shirt and scooped her breasts together in her Top Shop bra. Ready. She reflected that there was a time when she wouldn't have bothered with the money.

The Staffie climbed to its feet warily as she approached. It was stocky and muscular, with a broad, wedge-shaped head and large round eyes. She squatted and held out her hand for it to sniff. The bald-headed man in the soccer shirt blinked and squinted suspiciously at her before his gaze was drawn, as intended, to her cleavage.

She withdrew the first fifty-pound note from the sleeve of her coat with a magician's flourish. She held it up in plain view tucked between two fingers. The man licked his lips and looked from the note to Miranda's cleavage and back again. Miranda leaned forward, ruffling the dog's neck, and smiled encouragingly.

'The boat out there. What can you tell me about it?'

'That's the *Goney*,' the man said, 'she's the port tug.'

'And the wreck?'

'The *Montgomery*,' he answered.

'What are they doing out there?'

After a moment's pause, the man smiled slyly. She held out the fifty and before she could pull it away he had grabbed her hand and was stroking her fingers.

'They're diving on the wreck,' he told her. 'They do it every year or so.'

He let go of her and swiftly pocketed the fifty.

'Why?' she asked.

'Check the hull.'

'And if I want to speak to the crew?'

The man's eyes became smaller and shinier. 'What have you got for me?' he asked.

She produced the other fifty-pound note from her sleeve and held it up for him to see. 'Just money.'

He looked disappointed.

'They drink at the Albion in Blue Town,' he told her.

'Thank you,' she said.

'You look familiar,' he said. 'Are you on the television?'

'I'm a TV reporter,' she told him. 'I'm doing a story.'

'I don't watch the news,' he said.

She laughed. 'Of course you don't.'

'If you want to know about the *Montgomery* you should speak to the Swampie,' he told her.

She looked in the direction that he was pointing with his plump finger. The shape of a man in a large overcoat was huddled against the nearest groyne. There was a brief flash of light on glass. A pair of binoculars.

'He's been watching her for years. When he's not wandering the marsh he's here. They reckon his father was on her for salvage when she broke up.'

'Thank you.' She stood up. The dog sat and stared up at her, cocking its triangular head to one side. 'Hope you find a fish.'

She started trudging across the shingle towards the groyne, intent on getting a look through the binoculars.

'Hello,' she called out. The man lowered the binoculars and stared fearfully at her. His face was filthy and his hair formed a wispy halo around his head.

When she stepped closer to him and was about to talk to him, she found that he stank terribly of piss, enough to make her eyes smart. Up close it was as if his face was peppered with shot. There were shiny black marks in the pores of his skin. Miranda felt queasy. Across the beach the man with the Staffie was laughing.

'She come out of Hog Island with her holds full, bound for Cherbourg,' the Swampie muttered, his eyes darting this way and that, 'beached on a reach of shoal they come off her like rats scrambling scrambling over themselves to get ashore the sound of her back breaking on the middle sand like gunshot the bombs will blow they said she'll blow, she'll BLOW . . .'

'When did this happen?' Miranda asked, after a pause.

He wouldn't meet her eye. 'Sunday morning,' he mumbled, 'twentieth of August 1944.'

'Can I look?' Miranda asked.

The Swampie clutched the binoculars tighter.

'I heard 'em,' he said, and a sly expression came over him, 'talking like spittin' I was listening at the window of a cottage by Bedlam's Bottom or Ladies Hole can't remember which minding my business.' He looked scared suddenly. 'He's not nice he's a Paki dark dark face in the darkness took my hand twisted it crying crying I said I ain't seen nothing I ain't heard nothing.' He looked sly again. 'But I did she's already rigged to blow forward and aft.'

The Swampie turned his back on her and raised the binoculars to his eyes and continued muttering unintelligibly to himself.

She sat at a keyboard in an Internet café on the High Street and
stared at the Google home page with its letterbox slot. She tapped
Montgomery + Sheerness in. One million eight hundred and ten
thousand results. Fifth down the list was a link to Wikipedia. She
clicked on it:

> The **SS Richard Montgomery** *was an American Liberty ship
> built during World War II, one of the 2,710 used to carry cargo
> during the war. The Montgomery was wrecked off the Thames
> Estuary in 1944 with around 6,000 tons of ammunition on board,
> which continue to be a hazard to the area . . .*

She swore softly under her breath and looked around suddenly
in case anyone was watching. There were only a couple of other
people in the café and neither of them seemed interested in her.
She turned back to the monitor and continued reading.

> *. . . The ship was built in 1943 by the St Johns River Shipbuilding
> Company . . . given the official ship number 243756, and named
> after General Richard Montgomery, an Irish-American soldier who
> was killed during the American Revolutionary War.*
>
> *In August 1944, on what was to be its final voyage, the ship left
> Hog Island, Philadelphia, where it had been loaded with 6,127 tons
> of munitions.*
>
> *It travelled from the Delaware river to the Thames Estuary, then
> anchored while awaiting the formation of a convoy to travel to
> Cherbourg, France, which had already fallen to the Allies . . .*
>
> *. . . When it arrived off Southend, it came under the authority
> of the Thames naval control at HMS Leigh . . . The harbourmaster,
> responsible for all shipping movements in the estuary, ordered the
> Montgomery to a berth off the north edge of Sheerness Middle
> Sands. On 20 August 1944 it dragged anchor and ran aground on
> a sandbank around 250m from the Medway Approach Channel,
> in a depth of 24 ft (7.3m) of water. The ship broke its back on sand-*

banks near the Isle of Sheppey, about 1.5 miles (2.5km) from Sheerness . . .

. . . Due to the presence of the large quantity of unexploded ordnance, the ship is monitored by the Maritime and Coastguard Agency. In 1973 it became the first wreck designated as dangerous under Section 2 of the Protection of Wrecks Act 1973 and there is an exclusion zone around it monitored visually and by radar . . .

. . . According to a BBC news report in 1970 it was determined that if the wreck of the SS Richard Montgomery exploded, it would throw a 1,000-foot (300m) wide column of water and debris nearly 10,000 feet (3,000m) in the air . . .

It was a bomb.

A bomb that it turned out had been sitting, right under people's noses, at the mouth of the Thames Estuary for sixty years. A ship packed with aircraft bombs intended for Allied forces in Europe – an open invitation to mass destruction. It beggared belief.

It was obvious what the divers were up to out at the wreck. It was no different to using any piece of ordnance – artillery shells or mortars, for instance – to build an improvised explosive device. No different to doing it on land. You just had to pack enough plastic explosives in enough bomb fuse-wells to initiate the main charge, link it all up to a ring main with detonating cord, attach detonators and then blow it – the sympathetic detonation wave would be enough to set the whole lot off simultaneously; do it on a high tide during a storm surge and the result would be a tsunami, a wave big enough to overwhelm the Barrier and flood London. It wouldn't matter what defences were put in place.

The high tide was tomorrow night, 12 September, just when the storm was expected to strike. They were going to blow up the ship tomorrow night, Monday night – four years and one day after 9/11.

She paid for her time online and left the shop. As she stepped out on to the street, she saw that the Swampie was sitting in a doorway opposite. He pointed an accusatory finger at her.

'Cunt!' he shouted.

She turned away from him and strode through the small seaside town. She should not panic. She had to stay cool and calm, rational, for only that way could she negotiate her way out of this nightmare.

She should call Mikulski. She had his card. It was in her bag.

He answered on the second ring.

'Where are you?' he asked.

'Sheerness. I found the ship. The Liberty ship. It's called the *Montgomery*. It's a wreck full of unexploded bombs. It's just sitting there in the Thames Estuary, in full view in the shipping lane. They're going to blow it up!'

There was silence at the other end of the line.

'Listen to me,' she said. 'There's a team of divers working on it right now, preparing it for detonation. They must be nearly finished. There are no police here. There's nothing to stop them. Do you understand me? Mikulski? Are you there?'

There was a pause.

'You should walk away,' Mikulski told her. 'You've done what you can, so leave the rest to us.'

'Us? Who's that?'

'I can't tell you that.'

She cut the connection. She continued walking. She threw the phone in a bin in disgust. The American didn't care about whether or not terrorists were trying to flood London, whether or not they were trying to frame her for it, she saw that now. When she had told him that she was not responsible for Monteith's death he had simply said *that's not really what I'm here about.* Clearly, all Mikulski cared about was tracking down Jonah and charging him with the murder of some long-dead CIA agent.

No one was going to stop this if she didn't, she saw that now.

She must go to the police.

She had to. She had to warn them. If she went into a local police station, where there were witnesses, where there was no armed response unit or Counter-Terrorism Command, there was some chance they might listen to her. She might be given the chance to warn them. They might investigate. She headed towards the blue lamp of the police station on Millennium Way.

She walked through the police station's public entrance. There was a small waiting room full of people that, apart from a few chairs, was devoid of furnishing. A large red-faced man was sitting holding his head in his hands beneath a poster about dangerous dog breeds, and in one corner a teenage girl was sobbing. Behind the counter a female receptionist and a uniformed policeman were dealing with people in the queue, trying to sort the confusion into some kind of order.

She stood in the line, three from the front, practising what she was going to say – *My name is Miranda Abd al'Aswr, I wish to make a statement* – when a waft of piss filled her nostrils and she became aware of a familiar voice muttering in the room behind her. It was the Swampie and he was agitated. 'She'll blow,' he said, 'on the black moon.'

A policeman came through a door and was walking towards the Swampie when he started shouting, 'It's a bomb! A bomb!'

All around her people recoiled. She was pushed against a wall.

'Thousands of 'em and ammunition and incendiaries and fragmentation bombs and general purpose,' the Swampie yelled at the top of his voice.

And then there were more policemen, spilling into the room wielding telescopic batons.

There didn't seem like any good reason to stay. Nobody was going to believe her now. Keeping close to the wall, she eased herself towards the door and out on to the steps. She continued walking.

She sat on a bench in a car park. She picked up a newspaper that was lying on the seat next to her. She gasped. On its front page was a picture of Jonah sufficient to scare a nation. He'd been beaten. His shaved head was lumpy and distorted and his empty eye socket gaped. The headline screamed: DEATH WILL FIND YOU.

Beneath it, in slightly smaller font, it said: TERRORIST THREATENS TO DESTROY LONDON.

On the inside page there was a photo of her in a hijab. It appeared that it had been taken in Kuwait. Beneath the photo it said: TERRORIST ACCOMPLICE TRAINED IN BIN LADEN'S AFGHAN CAVE.

She was furious. She stared around her wildly.

She remembered after she was freed from Abu Ghraib, when she thought that she might never see her son Omar again, and she was filled with rage at the world. There were times when she believed that humans were a cruel and undeserving species. They did not deserve to survive. It was not for her to take responsibility for the savagery of others, for the savagery of men.

Now she faced a choice – either she ran or she stayed. Running was the obvious answer. Mikulski was urging her to do it. She did not think that, even if tens of thousands of people died in the tidal wave, she would know even one of them by name. But if she turned her back and ran there was no guarantee that she would survive. If the Barrier was breached and London was flooded, the public's fury would be boundless. The police would hunt her down with guns and helicopters and they would undoubtedly kill her.

If she stayed her future was equally uncertain. She didn't know a bloody thing about anything. She had no resources at her disposal to direct against a conspiracy on this scale. The police were hunting for her.

She could only keep going.

This is England

11–12 September 2005

The Albion bar was on the south side of a narrow cobbled street opposite the twenty-foot-high Victorian brick wall that ringed the port. She walked past it slowly, staying close to the wall. An emaciated man wearing a barman's white shirt and black tie stood in the doorway smoking a cigarette, and he nodded to her as she passed. She doubled back. The barman studied her impassively.

'Are the crew of the tugboat in?' she asked.

He sighed. 'They've been in here all week, from when the doors open to when they close.'

She wondered whether she had heard him correctly. 'They haven't been out?'

He shook his head. 'Not since the Ministry commandeered the boat.'

'The Ministry?'

'The Ministry of Defence.' He dropped his stub on the pavement and crushed it with the heel of a scuffed patent-leather shoe. 'Are you going in?'

'Yes, I am.'

He held the door open and followed her in and went around behind the long polished bar. 'What would you like to drink?'

'Vodka and tonic. A large one, please.'

She looked around. There were two men sitting huddled at the bar and one more near the back of the pub, a large man in a check shirt sitting alone at a table. The barman nodded towards the back of the pub. 'That's Charlie, he's the captain.'

'What does he drink?'

'Lager. Rum and Coke. Either or both.'

'Give me a rum and Coke. Make it a double.'

She picked up the drinks and went over to him. He gazed up from the table as she approached. His eyes were red and struggled to focus on her.

'Are you with the *Goney*?' she asked.

He grunted in a non-committal way.

'May I sit down?' She sat down, gave him the rum and handed over one of Saira's business cards. 'I'm from the BBC and I'm doing a piece on the *Montgomery*.'

He glanced at the card and drank the rum. When he spoke his voice was slurred. 'There's nothing to tell.'

'The MoD commandeered your boat and that's not a story?'

He looked briefly angry. 'Tell me this, how is it less of a national security risk to pull my crew off the boat and use foreign contractors?'

'What are they doing out there?'

'Checking the hull.' He paused and sniffed. 'Ultrasonic hull thickness analysis.'

'How do you know?'

'They do it every year as regular as clockwork, at the end of summer.'

'They don't usually take your boat?'

He shook his head slowly from side to side. 'No. We always crew it for them. It used to be navy divers we'd take out there but it's contract divers now, it has been for years.'

'But not foreign divers?'

He stared at her. 'They come in from all over. It's not the first time we've had foreign divers – we've had Poles from the port of Gdansk, for instance. These guys are Pakistanis from the port of Karachi. So what? As long as the company they're working for is legitimate and approved by Medway Ports. I didn't give it any thought and then I got a call from the owners, telling me to hand over the boat, and on Monday the MoD man turned up with the paperwork and the harbourmaster confirmed it.'

'The MoD man?'

'The MoD has someone on the boat at all times.'

'Describe him.'

'Smith.'

'That's what he's called?'

'Yes. He's the MoD man responsible for wrecks and downed planes.'

'Where would I find him?' she asked.

'The Abbey Hotel over in Minster. You'll find him there. And the divers.'

'Thank you,' she said. She stood up to go, but paused for a moment. 'Your man Smith is not from the Ministry.'

Charlie stared at her.

The Abbey Hotel was a modern red-brick single-storey sprawl with a fake clock tower and an expansive car park that was dotted with cars, the sort of place that was frequented by travelling salesmen and couples conducting clandestine affairs. She parked on scrubland adjacent to the Minster marshes with a view of the entrance to the hotel and settled in for a night of fitful sleep.

She dreamt of a massive wave, a wall of water advancing towards her, and just as the wave crested and threatened to plunge down upon her, she woke up, sitting bolt upright in the car seat. It was several hours before dawn.

She switched on the radio. There were reports of a fishing boat lost off the west coast of Scotland. The storm was approaching, veering into the confined space of the North Sea. With north-westerly winds blowing on its flank, it was being compressed between the converging coastlines of England and continental Europe, and funnelled towards the Thames Estuary.

The divers emerged just after 7 a.m., bulky in their drysuits and buoyancy vests, and advanced across the hotel car park towards a waiting black people carrier. Walking beside them was a man in a bright red Gore-Tex jacket, holding an aluminium flight case. She guessed that he was the official called Smith who claimed to represent the Ministry of Defence, in all likelihood one of

Alex's red team members. She sat up in her seat and switched on the car's engine. The people carrier pulled out of the car park and joined the sparse traffic bound for Sheerness. She followed.

It was incredible to think that for a week now the divers had been prepping the wreck under the noses of the port authorities in one of the country's busiest shipping lanes. But then she remembered what Jonah had once told her – if you're confident enough and you have the right paperwork you can get away with anything once – *you just stride in and take over.*

The people carrier followed the coast road alongside the sea wall. Leaves skittered along the pavement below the wall. A high-sided white van overtook her and obscured her view of the people carrier. Another car cut in front of her. The traffic was suddenly busy and she was falling farther behind. A helicopter raced over-head.

It started spitting with rain. She turned on the windscreen wipers, craning to see the people carrier.

Suddenly, a police car with its lights flashing and its siren blaring came rushing up behind her on the wrong side of the road. Then sirens were converging from all directions. She braked hard and hunched her shoulders in a self-protective cringe. Ahead, the white van swung out into the oncoming traffic and jack-knifed, smashing into the people carrier, throwing it up against the sea wall, shattering the side windows and crumpling the driver's door. The police car screeched to a halt right behind the people carrier and a black Range Rover reversed at high speed, taking up a position directly in front of it. The white van was positioned sideways to it with its white doors open and policemen with guns were spilling out. They surrounded the people carrier, dragged the divers out and threw them in the van.

Then, to her amazement, Alex Ross climbed out of the Range Rover and walked over to the people carrier at a leisurely pace. He helped the man in the Gore-Tex jacket climb out through the shattered windshield, half-carried, half-dragged him to the Range Rover and bundled him inside. Alex jumped in after him and slammed the door. The Range Rover accelerated away, leaving police officers with incident tape to start cordoning the area. Another police officer was advancing towards the rapidly forming queue of cars, one arm windmilling.

After seconds of just sitting and staring, Miranda recovered her wits. The car in front of her was indicating that it was turning left into a side street lined with shabby red-brick houses. She indicated similarly and followed. She turned right and left again, lost in the warren of streets, and then, spotting a parking space, pulled into it, allowing the cars behind to pass. She switched off the engine. She let her head sink back against the headrest and waited for her heart to stop racing.

It was done. It was over.

She got out of the car and stood, peering down the now empty street in the direction from which she had come. The wind was rapidly gaining in strength, and she could hear the waves striking the sea wall. She felt a need to see it, to feel the spray on her face. Her wig had slipped slightly. She righted it and started walking down the street. She cut left and right, heading diago- nally to avoid the incident area. She crossed the Minster Road. The cordon had enlarged to include several blocks and many more police cars. Men in white suits were walking back and forth behind the incident tape.

She climbed the cement stairs to the sea wall. Along the beach, huge grey swells were rolling in from the North Sea and large patches of foam were blowing in dense white streaks in the direc- tion of the wind. Farther along the wall she watched the Swampie struggling against the wind. It was beginning to rain hard.

The first sight of him was like being shaken. She glanced up and Nor was there beside her, standing by the bench, as if he'd stepped out of her dream, smiling at her from beneath the peaked cap of his baseball hat.

'Ahoy, as they say,' he shouted, above the roar of the waves.

'What are you doing here?' she demanded.

'Come on!'

He took her firmly by the hand and led her back down the

stairs and across the Minster Road, past the cordon, and through the densely packed streets to her car. He got in beside her, unzipped his jacket, swept off his cap and ran his hands across his face and his scalp. She glanced at him while he was looking up and down the street. He was as she imagined: lean and brown with long slender limbs. Long-lashed eyes the colour of polished walnut, a feral stare. So beautiful that at first she didn't realise why she couldn't breathe.

'My father brought Jonah and me here once,' he told her. 'Not long after we first met. I remember we had red plastic spades with long handles but there was no sand to make sandcastles. Instead, we fenced with them. I was quicker than he was. But he was dogged. You couldn't stop him. He just kept coming.'

Nor glanced at her and down the empty street again. There were tears on his cheeks. She resisted the sudden urge to reach up and touch them, to press the salt to her lips.

'I used to think he was indestructible,' he said, sadly. 'I can't bear to think of him gone.'

She closed her eyes and opened them again. 'He's dead?'

'I'm sorry.'

Several times she had wondered what she might say to Jonah if they were ever reunited but she had not found a formulation of words to describe the impossibility of their situation. For the briefest time, in Kuwait and then in Baghdad in the opening days of the war, there had been a passionate intensity that they had both mistaken for love. She had convinced herself to believe in love at first sight. That you just knew. But it was all wrong. There was no love, not of the lasting kind. They had sleepwalked through two years on Jura. And now she found that she had stopped being angry with him. In a way, his death relieved her of a burden. She was no longer under any obligation to explain or to listen to his explanation. She could live entirely in the moment. It was hers to seize.

'We have to get out of here,' he said. 'We are still being hunted.'

It was not lost on her, his use of the pronoun 'we'. As if they were co-conspirators.

'What are you doing here?' she asked.

He ignored the question. 'Let's have a drink. That's what Jonah would have wanted. Come home with me'

'Cobra's job is to ensure that everything that can be done is being done,' a government minister was saying on the radio. News of the terrorist attack averted that morning had been swiftly replaced by that of the coming storm. The minister informed the listeners that Police and Environment Agency staff were patrolling in Norfolk, Suffolk, Essex and Kent, offering advice. 'If you are advised to evacuate please follow those instructions, there are rest centres that are being set up for you. And it's really important to keep away from the sea because, as well as the storm surge, there will also be very large waves, and this is dangerous – people need to keep away from it.'

'A long way away,' Nor commented.

She turned her back to the sink and watched him as he paced back and forth. The kitchen seemed too small to contain him. From the freezer compartment he withdrew a bottle of Absolut.

'We are doing all that we can but we are just going to have to wait and see what happens as the surge makes its way down,' the minister said.

There was a gun on the table between them, a compact black pistol. He caught her looking at it and smiled.

'Have a drink,' he said.

'OK.'

He rinsed two glasses and poured vodka in them.

'Nothing to mix it with here,' he said.

She downed the shot. Her head reeled.

'And if there was it doesn't look like you'd need it . . .'

'Why did you go for this?' she asked.

'Why did I go for what?' he asked.

'Blowing up the *Montgomery*?'

'You understand,' Nor told her, 'that it's not personal. It's just what I do. It's a vocation.'

'Was it your idea?'

He found the notion amusing. 'No. It was Fisher-King's idea for a propaganda coup. MI6 and the police swoop in on conspirators manufacturing the biggest ever IED in the Thames Estuary. All they wanted me to do was recruit the dive team and manufacture the plastic explosives and detonating cord. They'd handle access to the wreck as part of a routine MoD survey and provide the detonators, duds of course. They then sweep in at the eleventh hour. Simple really.' He brought the bottle over to the table and poured them both another shot. They were side by side, leaning against the table. 'It was the Americans, Those Who Seek The End, who had the idea of really doing it.'

Those Who Seek The End – it was Mikulski, the FBI agent, who she had heard first use that name. She'd been wrong when she had watched the divers being arrested and she had thought that it was all over. She'd suspected that since she had looked up from the bench on the sea wall and seen him standing there. Now it was confirmed.

'Yesterday morning they connected the ring mains that link the ammunition stacked in the forward holds and that in the aft holds,' he explained, 'and after lunch, while you were watching them from the beach, they attached real detonators and activated the ignition assembly, which is fixed to one of the warning buoys. It's simple really – a regular phone connected to an electrical circuit in a waterproof box. It's set to blow on receipt of a phone message. All we have to do is wait for the tide.'

'You'll do it?'

He shrugged. 'You can't have a war on terror without spectacular acts of terror.' He put on an American accent and rolled his *r*'s: 'We have to terrify them to make them agree to what is necessary for the protection of their freedoms.' He poured them both another shot. 'Why did you come here?' he asked.

'To tell the truth,' she said, shocked to hear herself saying it. 'I was looking for you.'

'That's the craziest thing I've heard all week,' he said, laughing a little. He stared into her eyes. She thought that his eyes were the eyes of someone who would never be tamed. 'You should run.'

It was ridiculous. She laughed and at the same moment so did he. An instant when they were as one. Bound one to the other. She caught her breath.

'You're shaking,' he said.

'No,' she said, with a laugh. She could hear the rising hysteria in her voice.

He held the back of his hand to the side of her jaw and she closed her eyes and exhaled softly, the tumult rising like a tide within her. He gently squeezed her shoulder and she felt as if she were sinking towards him, as if his outstretched arm was all that was preventing her from falling. She felt his lips brush hers and she let her mouth open. And then she was hungrily kissing him, devouring him.

He pulled his T-shirt over his head and she unbuttoned her shirt and shrugged it off. She undid her bra and let it fall to the floor. She reached for his smooth, hairless chest and ran her nails down his sternum, across the plain of his stomach. She unbuckled his belt, unbuttoned his jeans and reached in to hold his engorged penis, feeling it thickening in her palm. She pushed him back on to the table and bent to his penis in an act of deliberate surrender. She plunged her mouth on to him, again and again, feeling him tense from his knees to his shoulders. Her nose was filled with the smell of him, and above her he was groaning, and his hands were making fists. He did not offer any warning before he came. He suddenly shuddered and groaned and she tasted the briny wash of his discharge in her mouth.

He lay back on the tabletop with his mouth open and his eyeballs rolled back into his skull. She felt a shudder of elation. For the first time since she had left the island of Jura she felt truly fearless and bold.

She took him by the hand and led him up the stairs to the bedroom. They removed their remaining clothes and she pressed herself against him. He held her away for a moment to look at her and she felt triumph as she recognised the need rising in him again. He turned her around, bent her over the bed and lifted her hair from the nape of her neck, wrapping it around his fist and pulling her up so that she was pressed against him, his breath on her neck, his other hand cupping a breast, the arm rising across her collarbone and encircling her neck. She was trapped with his penis pressing against her. He went in, pushing into her, and she felt as if she were falling. She felt so full. He made a roaring sound, and spent himself again.

They lay together in the bed, with the sheets and blankets tangled between their legs, sleepy and hot, with his sperm trickling out of her, and it felt as if some part of her was melting.

She felt at peace. She remembered Saira once describing Stockholm syndrome to her, the fondness and loyalty one could come to feel for a captor.

'What happens at high tide?' she asked.

'I press speed dial.' He put his mobile phone against a nipple and moved it downward across her belly until it pressed against her labia. He whispered in her ear, 'And everybody's dead.'

JONAH
Covert Transit

'... of three days' journey'
The Bible, Jonah 3

From Fallujah to Dover

Jonah fell. It was no more than fifty feet from the bridge to the surface of the Euphrates, no more than a second of weightlessness before he plunged into the water. But in that second after he was shot, and while he was falling through the air, he stared wide-eyed into the approaching depths and saw death there waiting. Its howling maw. *You have betrayed everyone that ever loved you.* Then he struck. He was dragged down. Panicking, he tried to scramble for the surface but he was tricked by the current, and instead funnelled down into the murky depths, among dark and menacing shapes. Voices whispered to him: *Traitor! Adulterer! Thief!* Close to passing out, he gave up the last of his breath, watching the air bubbles rising around his face, urgently seeking the surface. Then a moment's clarity, a life-saving spark – sheer bloody-mindedness – caused him to strike out with one arm and chase the path of his ascending breath. His head broke the surface, his mouth open and gasping, filling his lungs with the humid night air. Above him were cars and buildings, a moving field of light. And he was spinning, powerful currents swirling and eddying around him, sweeping him towards the centre of the river. There was no strength in him to fight it and so he let himself be carried forward.

He had been shot in the front of his upper body, he was sure of that, in his neck, shoulder or chest. There was no pain as such, just a dull throbbing. His left arm was paralysed but his right arm was working, and soon he discovered that by using the blade of his good hand as a rudder, he could edge across the face of the current. He must get ashore and soon if he was to survive. He steered towards the bank.

Soon, his fingers slid through soft mud and he grabbed a fistful of reeds, and, using the current's momentum, allowed himself to be washed on to the rubbish-strewn bank. He could not afford to rest. He knew that he must keep going if he were not to be sucked back into the water. He crawled forward one-armed through the ooze, grabbing debris and other organic matter, anything he could get a purchase on to haul himself forward.

Creatures scuttled across him. A nauseating stench filled his nostrils. He could no longer see and he had no idea how far he had to go. His left arm felt massive, like an anchor dragging alongside him. His legs were useless. He was cold and getting colder. He must keep going. Death would not have him yet.

It felt like crab claws tickling his sides, then a wet sponge on his face and a snuffling sound. A dog licking his face. Jonah smiled. It was Esme's nameless dog to the rescue. Then two hands, rough and calloused, travelled up and down his body, exploring his pockets and unbuckling his belt.

'I can give you money,' he said.

A man grunted in surprise. Jonah wondered what language he had spoken and tried again, careful to use Arabic. The man shooed the dog away from Jonah's face and leant down to look at him. He was a large man in a grubby djellaba. His breath was if anything worse than the dog's.

'You're alive,' the man said. He grinned toothlessly and shook his head in wonderment.

'I'm glad,' Jonah told him, 'because this would make a shitty paradise.'

'You're a gift,' the man said.

'Get me to a phone,' Jonah said.

The man took hold of him by the ankles and started to drag him through the debris and waste.

*

He heard the first note of the dawn call to prayer. He opened his eyes. Two donkeys were staring down at him. They were attached to a wooden cart that was stacked high with rubbish.

He looked to one side. He was lying outstretched on a concrete apron beside the river. At the back of the cart he could hear the dog yelping at what it thought was a game and the man muttering as he shifted bundles of trash to make a bed.

Rag-pickers, charcoal burners ... Jonah wondered what it would take to get found by actual Search and Rescue. A different line of work perhaps? He shut his eyes against the throbbing in his head and waited for the sun to come.

'You are lucky the bullet did not break up in your body. Your clavicle is fractured but not splintered,' a voice said. He opened his eyes. An elderly man in a white coat was holding the bullet up to the light with forceps. He had a hooked nose and prominent chin and resembled a geriatric Mr Punch. Behind him on the wall there was a poster with all the different breeds of dogs on it. Somewhere close by, several dogs were barking. 'Frankly, I am more concerned about your swim in the Euphrates. You are very lucky that old Hassan found you. I am giving you intravenous antibiotics. When did you last have a tetanus shot?'

He realised that the man was speaking to him in English. 'I need a telephone. I need to speak to Yakoob Beg,' he said, struggling to hold a thought.

'Yes, yes, it is being taken care of,' said the man in the white coat. He held a needle up to the light and with one eye closed threaded suture material through it. 'We have heard all of your speeches. We have spoken to Mr Yakoob Beg in Kabul. A very nice man. Now hold still. I'm going to stitch you up, first the deeper layers and then the surface skin.'

Jonah wondered whether he'd heard right. 'You've spoken to Yakoob Beg?'

'Yes. As soon as I have finished here you are leaving. You are going home.'

Home?

Out of the corner of his eye, Jonah watched as several times the man pulled the thread tight, tied a knot and snipped the ends of the thread with scissors.

'I'm not feeling any pain,' Jonah told him.

'That's because you are receiving five-star service, no expense spared, orders of Mr Yakoob Beg and courtesy of the swiftest international cash delivery I have ever encountered. I gave you enough ketamine to knock out a bear. I worked at Baghdad zoo for a while, before the current difficulties. You are like a bear, I think?'

'I'm hallucinating,' Jonah said.

'No doubt. You know I must tell you, I'm not used to patients who can speak.'

'Where am I going?' Jonah asked.

'I don't know,' the man said. 'I don't want to know. And frankly it's better for me and for old Hassan if you don't remember us. If we are asked we will say that we were coerced.'

There was the sound of vehicles growling to a halt and several cars doors slamming. Then shouting. Someone banging on a nearby door.

'You will need to have the sutures taken out in about seven days.' The man smiled. 'If you are still alive, of course.' He paused. 'I hope they don't break down the door.'

They broke down the door. There were four of them and more outside, and drifts of blue smoke followed them in as they came barrelling down the corridor. They were carrying M4 carbines with under-slung grenade launchers and wearing body armour and helmets. The man in the white coat backed against the wall with his hands in the air.

'I'm Sergeant Stone,' the nearest one yelled in Jonah's face. 'Third Squad, First Platoon, Charlie Company. I'm your escort out of here. This way please, sir.'

He grabbed Jonah by his good arm and together they ran out into the smokescreen, towards four Humvees that were rolling back and forth so that snipers couldn't get a fix on a door. Jonah was bundled into the back of the nearest one. He wedged himself against a storage rack, with his sling braced against his chest, and the top gunner's legs in front of him. The vehicle's sound system was cranking out the Eminem and Obie Trice track 'Go to Sleep':

'Die, motherfucker, die! Ugh, time's up, bitch, close ya eyes . . .'

Opposite him a soldier who could not have been more than eighteen scowled ferociously at him. 'Are you mean-mugging me?'

'Sir, you're in a four-vehicle convoy,' Sergeant Stone called out from the front seat. 'Tango's One through Four. This is Tango Two. We're heading east on Route Fran.'

'Why are you still alive?' the turret gunner sang.

'Where am I going?' Jonah shouted.

'Wayne County Jail.' The sergeant grinned manically. There were several rifle shots nearby and then a burst of automatic fire. Jonah tried to curl up on himself. Then he realised that there was something wrong with the noise; it was coming out of the speakers. It was part of the track. The eighteen-year-old opposite him was laughing uproariously.

'Rot, motherfuckers, rot! Decay, in the dirt, bitch, in the mother-fucking dirt! Die nameless, bitch.'

'I'm just fuckin' with ya!' Stone said. 'We're going to Camp Baharia.'

'Every day in this fuckin' place,' Command Sergeant Major Frydl said, 'we see the strange and the downright weird.'

They were sitting in a refrigerated Portakabin surrounded by breeze-block walls in Camp Baharia. The walls were grey, but now and then patches glistened purple – he was pretty high on the ketamine and prone to hallucinations. There were no windows.

'If it was my call,' Frydl continued, 'I'd really tighten things up around here. We've got people here who are spooks, mercenaries, assassins, God knows what. I got Delta boys coming in from all over Anbar and depending on me for their next meal.'

'What am I doing here?' Jonah asked. He knew people who claimed to have gone into combat on ketamine but he had never believed them.

'I don't know what you are doing here,' Frydl said. 'With respect, sir, I'm not your commanding officer or your goddam shrink. I'm waiting for a phone call.'

'Can I use your phone?'

There were people that he needed to speak to . . . Monteith, Yakoob Beg. He wished that there was a phone line to Barnhill – he felt a strong need to explain himself to Miranda, to apologise.

'Let me guess, sir, you want me to step outside my bomb-proof office into the world of shit outside so that you can whisper secrets down my phone line? I'm not fuckin' stupid. Get a phone card like everyone else.'

The phone rang. Frydl picked it up. He nodded and put the phone down.

'You're out of here on the next convoy,' he said. 'And by the way, sir, you look like shit.'

The convoy was four kilometres long with forty vehicles: armoured trucks, MRAPs and Humvees. Jonah sat in a litter of canned coffee drinks and sodas between Ensler, the blurry-eyed nineteen-year-old driver of Truck 21, and Blickstein, the vehicle commander. Ensler had already been driving for fourteen hours. Jonah recognised several of the tracks on the iPod playlist, including 'Hell's Bells' and 'Welcome to the Jungle'. There were several others that he thought were by Metallica and Slayer. The playlist belted out of the speakers on a continuous loop. Apart from the occasional flash at the edges of his vision he wasn't that high. It was manageable.

'Three southbound cars in the northbound lane,' reported the first truck, and each vehicle commander repeated it like a mantra as the cars approached. *Three southbound cars in the northbound lane . . . Three southbound cars in the northbound lane . . .* Twenty times before they caught sight of the cars and then it was their turn and Blickstein said, 'Three southbound cars in the northbound lane.'

The cars drove past, the Iraqi occupants inside staring sullenly out at them. Blickstein made his finger and thumb into a gun and fired an imaginary shot.

'How often do you get shot at?' Jonah asked.

'Every fuckin' day,' Blickstein said.

The mantra continued, nineteen more times: *Three southbound cars in the northbound lane.*

Jonah was sitting shovelling mashed potato into his mouth with a spoon when he was approached by a security contractor with Redbriar Security written on his black baseball cap. He was in a massive logistics base in the middle of the desert. The chow hall was as large as an aircraft hangar and had a sign that said WE NEVER STOP SERVING.

'You're Ishmael?'

'That's correct.'

'I'm delivering you to Mosul.'

'I have difficult news.' There was something in the tone of Yakoob Beg's voice that made Jonah pause before he confirmed that he was indeed listening. 'Prepare yourself . . .'

'Tell me.'

Jonah was in the front seat of an armoured Redbriar Range Rover, racing north on the highway with a satellite phone held to his ear.

'Monteith is dead.'

Jonah closed his eyes and opened them again. 'How?'

'He was murdered. And Beech too. Somebody is killing the Guides.'

He struggled to articulate words. 'What about Flora? What about Beech's wife and their son? What about Miranda?'

'I don't know. I'm sorry.'

There was a pause.

'It's not safe for you to return to the UK,' Yakoob Beg said.

'Nevertheless, that's where I have to go. Can you contact Mikulski for me?'

'I can.'

'I want you to tell him that Nor is Winthrop's joe and has been since '96. Tell him that Winthrop conspired with Nor to have Kiernan killed to prevent him from exposing bribes paid by Lodestone to senior figures in the Taliban.'

'Is that it?'

'Can you get me into the UK?'

'Wait.' Beg moved away from the phone and then returned. 'Your travel arrangements were designed to be deliberately flexible.' For a few seconds Jonah listened to Beg flicking through the pages of his Moleskine and then he was talking to someone in heavily accented Russian on another phone. After a couple of minutes he came back on the line. 'Covert Transit has agreed to your request.'

He had punched the numbers into the phone. It was simply a question of pressing the call button. But to do so would be to alert them that he was alive and that he was coming. It was foolish to think that Flora's line would not be monitored. Besides, what would he say?

I'm sorry. It's my fault that Andy is dead. I should have finished the job and killed Nor when I had the chance . . .

He set the phone down on the seat beside him. He had destroyed everything that was precious to him. There was nothing that he could say that would change that.

'They got rich here,' Yanov said, 'at this very spot, three thousand years ago, at the world's first truck stop, on a highway that ran all the way from the Indian Ocean to the Mediterranean.'

They were standing beneath the vaulted arch at the mud-brick Mashki gate in the ancient ruins of Nineveh. To the west lay the suburban sprawl of Mosul. The Redbriar security detail had dropped Jonah in the car park and directed him towards the ancient gate where the Bulgarian Yanov was waiting for him.

'Until God made an utter end to the place.' Yanov flicked his cigarette butt away. He looked like a gangster complete with five o'clock shadow and a bespoke Turnbull and Asser shirt worn open-necked with massive gold cufflinks. 'Of course, the route is still viable, if your money is good.'

Jonah met the black glitter of his stare.

'You are Ishmael?' Yanov asked.

'I am.'

'I'm sorry that I couldn't meet you in person in Fallujah but I find for extractions from Iraq on insecure routes it is best to subcontract the work.'

'It's an impressive level of influence that you have.'

'It's nothing really. A sentence inserted here or there by an amenable logistics coordinator in a set of routine orders. We do it all the time. This way, please . . .'

They walked back through the gate to the car park where Yanov's silver Mercedes E500 sedan was standing, with its engine running. 'Any friend of Yakoob Beg is a friend of mine. Get in.'

Jonah walked around to the passenger side, opened the door and climbed in. The air inside was freezing and stank of cigarettes. It made his eye smart.

'Do you need a doctor?' Yanov asked, beating an impatient rhythm on the dash with his left hand, while his bodyguards climbed into their escort vehicles.

'I'm fine for now,' Jonah replied.

Yanov pumped the horn a few times with his fist and after a few seconds the vehicles set off.

It was no surprise to Jonah that the Bulgarians were running people out of Iraq. In 1994, soon after he had joined the Department, Jonah had spent several months as a British Army liaison officer ostensibly monitoring the front lines in Gorni Vakouf in Bosnia but in fact gathering information on the movement of weapons through Croat lines and into Sarajevo by a gang calling itself the Covert Transit Directorate, led by a consortium of former Bulgarian secret service agents. The original Covert Transit Directorate had been established by the Bulgarian State Security Service in the 1970s, ostensibly as a means of smuggling weapons to Soviet-allied insurgent groups in Africa, but had soon expanded to include people-trafficking and drug-smuggling. Like most

Soviet-era intelligence operators, Yanov and his colleagues had embraced the opportunities offered by the open market that followed the collapse of communism, initially in the Balkans and then farther afield.

'Cigarette?'

Why not? Jonah thought. *Almost everybody you know is dead. Dead as a result of your own actions or lack of them.* He accepted a cigarette, his first for a couple of years. The sudden rush of nicotine made his head reel.

'It's in my blood,' Yanov told him, sprawling beside him on the back seat of the sedan. They had picked up a driver in Diyabakir, the first of several relay drivers tasked with transporting them across Turkey. 'I'm Bulgarian. I'm a smuggler. Some of my colleagues prefer to call themselves commodity traders or whole-salers but not me. I'm a smuggler. You want a drink? There's a bottle of fine Scotch in the glove compartment.'

Sure enough, there was a half-finished thirty-year-old Lagavulin. 'I don't think that they made many bottles of this,' Jonah said, holding the bottle up and reading the label.

'Just over two thousand.' Yanov winked. 'I did an old friend a favour. Pass it over.' He pulled out the cork with his teeth, took a slug and passed it to Jonah, who wiped the neck and took his own slug. They continued in that way for some time, passing the bottle back and forth, as the car raced west towards Istanbul.

'Smuggling is my country's cultural heritage,' Yanov told him. 'It's how we cope. My country has always been squeezed between ideologies, between Orthodoxy and Roman Catholicism, between Islam and Christianity, between capitalism and communism, between empires suspicious of each other. If you want to make progress in the Balkans you have to learn how to make the boundaries disappear. We can cross the roughest sea and traverse the highest mountain. We know every secret pass and, failing that, the price of every border guard.'

★

The only time that they stopped was to refuel or collect a new driver. Jonah slept fitfully and his dreams were filled with images of cataclysm, of a city swept away by an immense wave.

They entered Bulgaria at the Kapeten-Andreevo border crossing. From Bulgaria they drove through Serbia to Montenegro. The car was waved through each successive border crossing after payment of what Yanov referred to as 'transit tax' by means of bulky brown envelope.

Jonah first caught sight of the crystal-blue water of the Adriatic just north of Lake Shkoder, the cliffs falling hundreds of feet to the sea. In the port of Bar there were hundreds of sleek, expensive-looking speedboats bobbing in the packed marina, the fruits of a thriving trade in contraband.

'This is as far as I take you,' Yanov told him. 'From here the Italians have you. They will deliver you to your final destination . . .'

'Thank you.'

They shook hands.

Jonah made the 130-mile sprint across the Otranto Strait to Italy with a cargo of cigarettes, landing on a beach in Puglia after midnight. Another Mercedes was waiting. They drove him to a truck stop outside Milan. From Milan to London Jonah travelled in a specially adapted ten-foot-by-ten-foot compartment hidden inside a standard truck-mounted shipping container. He shared the compartment with four Moldovan girls. He spoke to the Moldovans in pidgin Russian and they replied in pidgin English. They were expecting to work as shop assistants. It didn't seem very likely.

Once in the European Union, Jonah did not have to cross a single police control point before Dover.

Death will find you

'Wherever you are, death will find you,
Even in the looming tower.'
Koran, Sura 4

The rain fell

Monday, 12 September 2005

A flood of commuters emerged from the buses and underground entrances and from the train station, looking dusty in the morning sunlight. The sky was a fierce blue but there were thunderheads advancing from the east and there was an ozone taste in the air as if lightning might strike.

Jonah was standing in the midst of a loose gathering of people arriving, removing their helmets and locking their bikes to the collection of steel hitching posts located opposite the entrance of 89 Albert Embankment, an office block with a café on the ground floor. Motorcycle couriers came and went. Close by, a cluster of early smokers were standing or sitting in a covered shelter that faced the side wall of the MI6 building with its loading entrance and green cathedral-like windows.

It was Monday morning. Dead on 9.50, Fisher-King strode past, briefcase in hand. Jonah followed from the opposite side of the road as Fisher-King walked along the pavement past the police building and Alembic House, towards the roundabout by Lambeth Palace. He crossed Lambeth Bridge. Instead of entering Thames House as expected, Fisher-King strode purposefully across Horseferry Road and down Dean Ryle Street, past the baroque church, St John's Smith Square, with its leaning towers, and into the rows of Georgian houses beyond. Racing clouds made the streets narrow and elongate. Fisher-King did not look back once. He walked down Great College Street, past the crumbling wall of the medieval abbey precinct and through the gateway into Dean's Yard. Jonah followed at a discreet distance.

Fisher-King crossed Victoria Street and cut down Dean Farrar Street and along Dacre Street, entering Scotland Yard at 10.05.

Two hours later, Fisher-King re-emerged with his briefcase in hand and strode down Broadway and along Queen Anne's Gate into St James's Park. There were people everywhere, jostling crowds of tourists on the paths and sitting on the grass, and there was a fervent quality to their chatter, as if they must cram as much enjoyment as possible into the remaining time before the approaching storm.

Jonah spotted Ginger, one of Alex's bodyguards, standing by a tree and surveying a field of deckchairs, and then Taff by an ornamental flower bed, similarly observant. Fisher-King strode straight past them both and towards the bridge at the centre of the park. And waiting for him there, head and shoulders above the crowd of Japanese tourists around him, the creases in his suit trousers and in his hair parting as sharp as ever, was the former deputy proconsul and arch neocon, the father of the Eschatos programme, chairman of Greysteel, Richard Winthrop IV.

Jonah was careful to keep himself out of the line of sight of both Ginger and Taff as he circled around behind Winthrop and Fisher-King as they crossed the bridge, their heads together in intimate conversation. The crowds helped and hindered him. They masked him from the watchers protecting Winthrop and Fisher-King but several times he lost sight of them. He was forced to push his way forward, craning his neck this way and that.

For a moment he thought that he saw Pakravan cutting across the crowd, brushing Fisher-King's shoulder and then disappearing again. He lost them. He pushed sideways. He was aware of someone swearing behind him.

He caught sight of them sitting beside each other on a bench, but then Winthrop stood up and strode purposefully north, holding Fisher-King's briefcase. Jonah looked from Fisher-King to Winthrop and back again. Fisher-King was leaning to one side on the bench. Something was wrong. He was toppling into the lap of a woman who had sat down on the bench in the inter-vening seconds. The woman pushed him off and sprang up with an expression of disgust.

Jonah darted forward. He pressed his fingers to Fisher-King's neck, feeling for a pulse, but there was none. His chest wasn't moving. He lifted one of his eyelids. No pupil reaction. He was already dead.

Jonah walked swiftly away, scanning the crowds for signs of Winthrop. He caught a glimpse of him standing by a litter bin. Winthrop removed a brown envelope from the briefcase and then dumped the case in the bin. Somewhere behind Jonah there was a commotion. A woman was yelling. Winthrop spoke briefly on a mobile phone, before continuing north towards Buckingham Palace. Taff and Ginger fell in behind him. Jonah followed. A black Range Rover pulled alongside them as they reached the Mall and they got in. It made an abrupt U-turn, heading in the direction of Trafalgar Square. Crossing the road, Jonah hailed a passing black cab.

'Follow that car,' he said, pointing.

'Just get in,' said the cab driver, rolling his eyes. He was an overweight man visibly perspiring in an England football shirt. On the back seat there was a discarded newspaper with Jonah's scowling face on the front page. Jonah crumpled it in his fist.

From Trafalgar Square they followed the Range Rover down Northumberland Avenue to the Embankment.

On the cab's radio a presenter announced that the police had carried out a major anti-terror operation in Sheerness, Kent, and broken up a plot for an attack on London. The presenter added that they were going direct to a press conference being given by the Commissioner of the Metropolitan Police at Scotland Yard.

The Commissioner said, 'The arrests are as a result of a month-long joint investigation which commenced after intelligence and law enforcement agencies identified a potential threat to the UK's national security. This investigation has been a massive physical and electronic surveillance effort. The alleged members of the group are Pakistan nationals from the Baluchistan region bordering Afghanistan.'

The Commissioner paused and there was an immediate barrage of shouted questions. The taxi was following the Range Rover east on Victoria Embankment, driving alongside the Thames. Cleopatra's Needle flashed past. Fat drops of rain began to strike the windscreen. There was a rumble of distant thunder.

'We continue to take the threats made on the Internet very seriously,' the Commissioner assured the journalists. 'We believe that with these arrests the immediate threat has been averted. However, I am in constant contact with my counterparts in other police forces nationally as well as with the UK Border Agency. I am confident that if the individuals identified as Nor ed-Din and Jonah Said attempt to enter this country they will be apprehended.'

As they emerged from under Blackfriars Bridge, a wall of rain advanced down Upper Thames Street and buffeted them as it struck. The Range Rover was still visible by its brake lights just ahead of them. At London Bridge, Upper Thames Street became Lower Thames Street.

'Our correspondent Brian Judd is in Sheerness,' the presenter said. 'What can you tell us, Brian?'

'What we do know is that this is one of the UK's biggest ever security operations, involving hundreds of police officers from forces in England and Scotland, which came to a head this morning in a pre-dawn raid in Sheerness.'

'Do you have any information on what the target might have been?'

'The police haven't given any specific details or told us what charges these men are likely to face. But we understand that the conspirators were planning to detonate a huge quantity of explosives in the Thames Estuary. And I can tell you the police have cordoned off the centre of Sheerness town. Local people here are pointing to the presence in the estuary of the wreck of a Second World War cargo ship, the SS *Richard Montgomery*, which is believed to contain up to two thousand tons of unexploded shells.'

They passed the Tower of London and turned left, heading up Mansell Street towards Aldgate.

There was then a statement from the Home Secretary, saying

that he had full confidence in the intelligence services and the authorities' response to date in arresting the conspirators and continuing the search for the alleged mastermind. He said that it was, however, necessary that everyone remain vigilant.

At Aldgate they turned on to the Whitechapel Road.

'Vigilant!' scoffed the taxi driver. 'How's that gonna help? What a load of old bollocks.' For the first time he glanced in the rear-view mirror and then his glance became a stare. ''Ere, you look familiar. You're on television, right? You're famous. I can't place it – is it *Big Brother*?'

'Not me,' Jonah said.

'I've seen your face.'

'You're mistaken.'

'Jesus Christ! You're the terrorist!'

'Stop the cab!'

The driver slammed on the brakes. There was a slow screech, then the sound of metal crumpling and glass smashing. A Renault had ploughed into the back of them and a white van into the back of the Renault. Jonah was thrown to the floor. He landed on his shoulder and groaned as the edges of his broken clavicle ground against each other. An alarm was wailing and somewhere someone was shouting. He pushed himself back on to the seat with his good arm and grabbed at the nearest door but it was still locked.

'Let me out,' Jonah said.

The driver was shaking his head in a daze. 'What?'

'Let me out!'

'You're the terrorist.'

'So let me out or I'll blow myself up. I'll fucking do it!' Jonah yelled.

The locks clicked open. Jonah tumbled out of the cab into the rainstorm. Another sudden jolt of pain. He picked himself up and started running up the street. He could hear police sirens behind him. The Range Rover was maybe fifty feet away, stuck at an intersection with a bendy bus blocking its way. He ran up on its passenger side.

The door opened. Ginger rolled out and into a crouch with his arms outstretched and a gun in his hands. Jonah ducked between two cars. He heard the crack of the shot and a windscreen shattering behind him. He scuttled forward between rows of cars. There were several more shots. People were screaming. On one knee by the front wheel of a Volvo, Jonah risked raising his head for a look. They had abandoned the Range Rover. He caught a glimpse of Winthrop being rushed up a side street, past Whitechapel Bell Foundry, with Ginger, Pakravan and Taff in a protective huddle around him.

Without thinking, he rolled across the bonnet of the car and sprinted after them. He ran down Fieldgate Street behind the East London mosque, dodging between women in niqabs and men with Wahhabists' short trousers. They turned down a street of shabby Georgian houses. At the end of the street they sprinted across the road, passing a video store with its shop window filled with Bollywood posters.

Jonah turned a corner at speed and Pakravan hit him with a plank of wood from a skip. Jonah staggered backwards, hit a brick wall and thumped down into a sitting position. Pakravan hit him again, bringing the plank down in a great arc. A door slammed in Jonah's head.

He came to on his back, looking up at the mannequins in a sari shop. He was stretched out on the pavement with his hands in steel handcuffs. There were sirens converging from all directions.

'Nor said you were tenacious,' Winthrop mused. 'Unstoppable was the precise word he used. When he explained to me that you had shown up in Iraq, I told him to tie rocks to you and throw you in a river.'

'They forgot the rocks,' Jonah groaned.

'I see that.' Winthrop glanced over his shoulder and raised his voice angrily. 'We need to get out of here.'

Ginger was consulting his BlackBerry. 'There's a helicopter pad on top of the Eastern General Hospital. The chopper can land there. We'll be with them in minutes.'

'I will never forget the expression on your face the first time that I met you when I told you that we were holding Nor in the cages in Kandahar,' Winthrop said.

'You played me all along.'

'You were very useful. You provided a level of separation between Nor and me and with it plausible denial. You did us all a favour.'

'What should we do with him?' Taff asked, appearing at Winthrop's shoulder, pointing a gun at Jonah.

'I think we should take him with us,' Winthrop said. 'Provided that he behaves . . .'

Winthrop reached forward and placed the heel of his palm against Jonah's shoulder. He pressed down on the bandage. Jonah gasped and passed out from the pain. When he came to again, he was lying in the gutter, in a pool of his own vomit.

Taff pulled him to his feet and pushed him along the street.

'Run.'

He staggered after Winthrop with Taff pushing him from behind. They crossed Mile End Road by Whitechapel station, running through the market stalls to the road and into the crowds of people spilling out of their cars. Somewhere to their left a police car was inching its way forward through the traffic, its siren pulsing. The hospital was beside them. They ran across the access ramp to Accident and Emergency and into an alleyway where there was a steel staircase bolted on to the side of the red-brick Victorian building. They ran up the stairs and emerged on to a broad helicopter pad on the roof of the building.

'There she is,' Pakravan said.

The helicopter came thumping out of the south-west. It was a Lynx with Greysteel Security written in large letters on the side. It touched down and they ran forward under the spinning rotors. Taff hauled Jonah in after him and the Lynx immediately lifted off again.

Jonah rolled over on to his stomach on the floor of the helicopter and looked out as they flew east along the Thames, skimming the surface of the river; around Canary Wharf, between Greenwich and the Isle of Dogs, over the top of the Millennium Dome and the Thames Barrier. He could see the corral of armoured personnel carriers around the control room on the south bank. The Barrier gates were rising out of their concrete sills on the river bed. He remembered Alex's words to him at the Thames Barrier what seemed like an age before: *Five hundred thousand houses, four hundred schools, sixteen hospitals and eight power stations and all of it fucked. One and a half million people at risk.*

Pakravan turned Jonah over and fitted a set of headphones over his ears. A burst of static was replaced by Ginger's voice: 'Storm tide warnings have been issued. The King George flood gate and the Barking Barrier are closed. The rising gates at the Thames Barrier will be closed within an hour, the falling radial gates soon after that.'

Then Winthrop spoke. 'It won't make any difference.' He was leaning forward in his seat, staring intently at the passing landscape. 'The tidal wave caused by the explosion will overwhelm the Barrier. The storm is an unexpected bonus . . .' He glanced back at Jonah. 'Only the British would keep thirteen thousand unexploded aircraft bombs on board an unstable wreck smack bang in one of the country's busiest shipping lanes at the entry point to your administrative and financial heartland. What did you think it was . . . a museum? Yet one more memorial to a war that ended more than half a century ago? Is everything in this damn city a museum or a mausoleum? As far as I can see, up to now the only thing that has stood between London and total annihilation is a failure of imagination on the part of the terrorists.'

Ginger cut in again: 'We have less than five hours to highest tide.'

'We've reserved the best seats in the house,' Winthrop said, 'ringside seats. You are going to witness what few others have, Jonah . . . the death of a once great city.'

And the wind blew

The helicopter flew east along the Thames in the driving rain, over the bridge at the Dartford Crossing and the town of Gravesend, heading out towards the sea. Out of the left side of the aircraft Jonah could see vast fields of storage tanks, refinery stacks and pipework on Canvey Island and beside it, in the shipping lane, a supertanker waiting to deliver its cargo of crude.

'Oil refineries, storage facilities, liquid gas installations,' Winthrop said, 'all of it in the path of the wave . . .'

The helicopter veered to the east and they passed over the cooling towers and sodium lights of the power station on the Isle of Grain, then the dark mass of the Medway Channel and beyond it the Isle of Sheppey.

They touched down on a grassy hill just south of Sheerness town.

'Welcome to Furze Hill,' said Ginger. He kicked Jonah out through the side door and jumped out after him. Winthrop and the others followed.

Ginger grabbed Jonah by the collar and pulled him out from under the rotor-wash and towards the treeline. The helicopter lifted off and banked steeply, thudding back along the Thames towards London.

'I almost lost my faith.' Winthrop was forced to raise his voice. The wind was moving heavily in the treetops, blowing clouds of dead leaves across the exposed summit of the hill. 'Not in God, but in our endeavour.'

Jonah was kneeling with the barrel of Pakravan's gun pressed to the back of his neck and water from it running down his spine. Winthrop was beside him, on the summit of the hill, with the hood of his raincoat swept back and his face exposed to the rain. Ginger and Taff were standing a few feet away, speaking into their mobile phones. They were on the highest point of the island. There was churning water on all sides, the vast estuary before them and the Medway and the Swale at their backs.

'We made mistakes. We trumpeted our achievement before it was fully accomplished. We didn't have enough troops to secure neighbourhoods or prevent looting. Bremer should never have disbanded the Iraqi army. But our intentions were noble. We delivered the Iraqi people out from under the yoke of tyranny and gave them the gift of freedom and democracy. The ingratitude! That was what I could not bear, the ingratitude, the sullen hostility, the fratricidal childishness of the Iraqi people. When I flew out of Baghdad last summer, I can tell you that I was sick to my back teeth of the whole project. I allowed doubt to enter my heart.' He paused. He seemed oblivious to the rain and the wind. 'You know what I did? I took a sabbatical. I went on a pilgrimage to the Holy Land. And you know what? I had an epiphany! I renewed my faith in our endeavour. I recovered my ambition. I'll tell you about it . . .

'One morning I climbed a path to the ancient fortress city of Megiddo and I stood upon its ramparts and what I saw there amazed and horrified me. I looked down upon the fertile Jezreel Valley and its vineyards and orchards – the breadbasket of the Holy Land. Twenty different civilisations have risen and fallen there within the last ten thousand years. Alexander, Saladin, Napoleon, all the great warriors of antiquity fought there. But that wasn't it. That's not what amazed and horrified me. For its real test is yet to come. For the hill of Megiddo will be the site of the final battle between Christ and the Antichrist. When Christ will come with blazing eyes, in a robe that is dipped in blood, and out of his mouth will come a sword and he will reap and reap and reap. And all the souls that have matured but rejected

God will be cast into the wine press of the wrath of God and there they will be crushed and blood will flow out of the wine press: *even unto the horses' bridles, by the space of a thousand and six hundred furlongs.* I stood there astride that hill and I tried to imagine, with all the power of my intellect and my imagination, the entire valley filled with blood to the height of a horse's bridle, that's a two-hundred-mile river of blood, four and a half feet deep. I've done the math! That's the blood of two and a half billion people . . .'

Ginger glanced across with his mobile phone clamped to his ear. He said, 'The Thames Barrier is closed. Four hours to highest tide.'

'Two and a half billion people dead in an instant, the horror of that,' Winthrop said, through gritted teeth. 'But the scale of it! The grandeur! You know what? The destruction of an old, tired city is nothing compared to that. This is just a wake-up call. A fright! Something to make everyone sit up straight and take notice again. To stop taking their liberties and comforts for granted and complete the job that began the day after 9/11, the job of remaking the world as it should be, in preparation for the return of Jesus Christ, our saviour.'

Two black Range Rovers appeared over the brow of the hill, churning the wet grass and spraying water. They skidded to a halt. Alex got out of the lead vehicle and the dog leapt out after him. Smudge, another of Alex's employees, got out of the second vehicle.

Alex strode straight up to Winthrop. He looked jittery and exhausted. There was a livid burn mark across his face and one of his eyes was partially closed.

Winthrop handed him the brown envelope. 'Fresh route out for Nor. Take it down to Chetney Marshes. He's waiting for you. Tell him his big moment is here. Tell him we're all counting on him.'

Recognising him, the dog yelped and licked Jonah's face.

'Well, well,' said Alex. 'I thought you were dead.'

'You know me better than that,' Jonah replied.

Alex sneered. 'I do. You're a tenacious fucker. You're renowned for it. You know the last thing that Beech said to me before I cut his throat? I mean, setting aside the pleading. I'll tell you. He said you can stop me but you'll never stop Jonah. I was like, I feel your pain, mate. After all, you couldn't stop Jonah fucking your wife, could you? He was upset about me saying that.'

'You bastard,' Jonah growled. Pakravan screwed the barrel of his gun farther into the back of Jonah's neck.

'Yeah, yeah. I know the drill,' Alex said. '*It's not wise to upset a wookie . . .*'

'Why are you doing this?' Jonah asked him.

'Clear and simple, mate. We're going to get rich beyond our wildest dreams. Greysteel's got planes on standby in Iraq and Afghanistan ready to fly seasoned professionals here at just a few hours' notice. I told you when I last saw you. The government doesn't have enough resources of their own to cope. They're going to need our help. We're going to guard the camps and the first-aid points. We're going to clear up the bodies. We're going to provide the protection necessary to get the infrastructure of society up and running again: power, communication, transportation. They'll throw open the doors of the Treasury to us. We'll be heroes.'

'You'll be mass murderers.'

'I think that particular epithet will be reserved for you and your fellow conspirator Nor, and, of course, your terrorist girl-friend.'

'What have you done with Miranda?'

'She's alive, I think. She's quite something. I underestimated her. I mean, killing Beech and Monteith and fitting her up for it was easy in comparison with trying to keep her tied down for more than five minutes. She's a slippery little bitch.' He paused. 'She's the one that burned my face. Make no mistake, when I catch up with her, I'm going to kill her.'

'I'll kill you first,' Jonah told him.

'Oh no you won't! Oh yes you will! Oh no you won't!' Alex mocked him. He stepped up to Jonah and slapped him across the face. 'This isn't a fucking pantomime . . .'

'Take one car,' Winthrop told him. 'Leave us the other.'

'All right, boss.' Alex turned on his heels and strode to the nearest Range Rover with the dog and Smudge following on behind. They drove away down the hill in the direction of the Sheppey Crossing.

Taff and Ginger retreated inside the remaining Range Rover to shelter from the rain.

'We didn't think we needed your actual body to lay the blame for this at your door,' Winthrop told Jonah, in a conversational tone. 'After all, there will be so many bodies in the water, most of them unrecognisable. But now you're here we can use you. Greysteel can make sure the police find your corpse. We'll deliver it. You and your girlfriend will be an international sensation – the traitors who sank a city.'

Miranda was dimly aware of the sound of tyres on gravel above the drumming of the rain, then a car door slamming and a few seconds later someone banging on the door. Nor slipped out of the bed beside her and prowled at the window. She thought she heard him say, 'It's the prick with the passport.'

He came back to the bed and pulled on his jeans. He bent over her briefly, with his lips against the rim of her ear, and whispered, 'Go back to sleep.'

He padded barefoot down the stairs. She rolled in the tangle of sheets, sliding easily back into sleep.

The next time she woke it was raining even harder, the raindrops hammering on the cottage roof, and she was being prodded by a familiar wet nose. Instinctively she reached out a hand to scratch under his chin. 'Dog . . .' she whispered.

She sat bolt upright. The dog was yelping and scratching at the covers.

'Come here,' a familiar voice yelled from the hallway, closely followed by the thump of his feet bounding up the stairs. She drew the sheet around herself. The dog leapt on to the bed.

'Come here . . .' Alex burst into the room. He stopped and stood still for a moment, staring at her. There were red burn marks running diagonally across his face. The dog was looking from one to the other, barking excitedly.

She nuzzled him. 'Shhhh . . .'

'What the fuck is she doing here?' Alex demanded, furiously.

'She's with me,' Nor said, slipping into the room behind him.

Alex rounded on him. 'Are you insane?'

'Somewhat so,' Nor acknowledged, with the hint of a smile. 'Miranda's going to push the button. Aren't you, honey? You're going to send the signal that blows the boat.'

She felt a sudden shiver run down her spine. 'Sure.'

'We'll need another passport,' Nor said.

'You'd never get her out on a plane,' Alex sneered. 'Her face is on the front cover of every tabloid. Besides which, you'll be lucky if I don't cut her up here and now. In fact, maybe I will.'

'You talk too much,' Nor told him, calmly. 'I've always thought that.'

'Have you seen what she did to me?' Alex demanded. 'Look at my face.'

'If you touch her I'll kill you.'

Alex's eyes widened in astonishment. He stared at Nor as if unsure whether he was joking.

'We'll take the boat,' Nor said.

'Take the fucking boat, then,' Alex retorted, and it seemed that at the heart of his astonishment there was some admiration. 'If you think you can surf the wave. Personally, I think you'd have to be crazy to go to sea at this time. I'll tell you what I'm doing – I'm heading back to the high ground.' He turned to leave. 'Come on, dog.'

She gripped the dog's collar more tightly. 'The dog stays,' she said.

Alex turned on her. 'No fucking way.'

'You're annoying me,' Nor told him.

'Hey, fuck you!' Alex snarled, and lunged at Miranda.

Nor sprang forward and she saw the flash of a blade and an arc of crimson and then he was bending over Alex, who was curled up on the floor, and his elbow was working like a piston, thrusting the knife in again and again. 'Let's hear you talk now, motherfucker . . .!'

When Alex had stopped struggling, Nor stood up again and flung the knife into the corner of the room. There was blood on his forearms and on the sleeves of his shirt.

Miranda stepped around him and knelt over Alex. His mouth hung open like a broken door. She put two fingers to his throat but there was no pulse. 'He's dead.'

'I never liked him,' Nor said, striding back and forth. 'I really, really didn't like him.'

'What do we do now?' she asked.

'There's another one in the car outside.' Nor knelt beside her and turned Alex over. He withdrew the pistol from a holster on his belt. He checked the magazine and made ready. 'Wait here.'

She listened to the sound of his bare feet on the stairs and then he was charging out through the front door into the pounding rain and firing the pistol. Fifteen shots in rapid succession and then the sound of falling rain again and the crack of approaching thunder.

In the interval between thunderclaps she heard the distinctive buzzing of a phone. She reached into Alex's pocket and retrieved it. She looked at the flashing screen. *Winthrop calling . . .*

'Alex?'

'No,' she replied.

'Where's Alex?' Winthrop demanded.

'He's dead.'

'Who is this? Who am I speaking with?'

'Miranda.'

'Where's Nor?'

'I'm not going to let you get away with this,' she said. She cut the connection. She reached into her bag and took out Mikulski's card. She wrote him a text.

Ship is rigged to blow by phone signal at highest tide. Miranda

She pressed Send.

When Nor reappeared at the top of the stairs he was holding an assault rifle.

'Get dressed,' he said. 'It's not safe here. We're going out to the boat. We'll ride out the storm there.'

She glanced at the dog and he returned her gaze. If she hadn't known better she could have sworn there was reproach in his eyes.

And the floods came

Standing beside the duty controller at the windows of the Thames Barrier control tower, Mikulski watched huge swells march upriver from the horizon in even bands, their white crests streaming sideways in the wind. They exploded against the Barrier gates with a force that seemed to shake the whole structure. Air trapped inside their grey barrels was blown upwards in geysers higher than the steel rigging of the Millennium Dome.

According to the controller, predictions from the Met Office computers were systematically exceeding all atmospheric models, and the storm had developed such a steep pressure gradient that an eye had begun to form. The print-outs showed clouds swirling into its centre like water down a drain.

Mikulski was furious. He had been since that morning. The decision not to attempt to send a team of specialist police divers from Thames Division to the wreck had been justified to him on the grounds that the detonators had been recovered by the police before the terrorists had the opportunity to attach them to the charges and, besides, any attempt to dismantle the charges before the storm had passed was unsafe and probably impossible. What made him angry was that immediately after the raid the man who was masquerading as the MoD official on the boat had been spirited away from the scene in the back of an unmarked Range Rover by persons unknown, presumably from the intelligence services. The police were given no opportunity to question the man and now Fisher-King, who was the sole police point of contact with the intelligence services, had gone missing. The divers were in the cells at Paddington Green but so far had remained silent. Nobody

seemed to know whether Nor or Jonah was at large. He hadn't
heard from Miranda in nearly twenty-four hours. Norma Said
had been right: the whole thing stank of entrapment and cover-
up. It was sloppy and feckless. As irresponsible as leaving a wreck
full of explosives in a busy shipping lane for sixty years.

His phone beeped. A text from an unfamiliar number.

Ship is rigged to blow by phone signal at highest tide. Miranda

'Shit!'

Inspector Coyle glanced at him from a nearby bank of monitors.

'Where's Fisher-King?' Mikulski demanded.

Coyle looked uncomfortable. 'I don't know.'

Mikulski showed him the text message.

'You better get on to Cobra and find out where the hell he is.'

Coyle reached for the nearest landline.

Mikulski turned to the controller. 'When will the water be at
its highest?'

'Peak surge is projected for about ninety minutes before highest
tide,' the controller replied. 'Eight thirty p.m.'

Mikulski glanced at his watch. Two hours. 'Fuck!'

Coyle looked across at them, and held his hand over the phone's
receiver. 'Fisher-King's body was found in St James's Park earlier
today,' he said.

'What?'

'He was murdered.'

'When were they going to tell us this?' Mikulski demanded.

Coyle looked stricken.

'Well?'

'Gold Commander says that it's too late to initiate a London-
wide evacuation.'

'Can you kill the phone networks?' Mikulski demanded.

A brutal wind lashed the marshlands. Miranda followed Nor with
the dog at her heel. Each step was a struggle and icy needles of
water struck her face and stung her eyes. On the horizon there
were occasional flashes of lightning. They crossed under a pylon

line, the wires moaning in the wind, and on to an ancient dyke that ran alongside an overflowing ditch. Water coursed across their boots. Warning lights blinked on marker buoys riding the swell in the channel at the approach to the crossing, and sodium lights boiled on the raised walkways of a sewage works.

They struggled along an overgrown footpath that was choked with swaying nettles, veering to the left, heading north-west along a sea wall with the wind buffeting them from behind. Foamy water was already lapping at the top of the wall.

The dinghy was directly in front of them, and it had been lifted from its mooring and deposited on the footpath. The well of the boat was awash with water and they had to tip it over before they could launch it into the channel.

They leapt aboard and the dog leapt in after them. They were immediately swept south towards the crossing, spinning in the rising tide, while Nor repeatedly yanked on the ignition cord.

'Come on!' he shouted.

The engine roared into life. Nor steered the boat around and into the tide and opened the throttle. They slammed into each successive wave, following the channel north through the marshes towards where it emptied into the Medway.

They went around a narrow spit of land, into the sudden shelter of a meander, a bend in the river that offered shelter from the storm. There was a concrete pier nestled against the land and a forty-foot steel-hulled tugboat moored against it. They came alongside and Nor heaved himself over the port gunwale. He reached down and scooped up the dog, swinging him aboard. Miranda followed.

The dinghy was swept away.

Jonah was kneeling in ankle-deep water that was rushing across the grass and cascading down the hillside. Pakravan still had his gun pressed against the back of Jonah's neck. Beside them, Winthrop was trying to get through to Nor. He had been ever since he had spoken to Miranda on Alex's phone. 'Answer the phone, damn it!' he snarled.

Taff got out of the Range Rover and walked towards them. 'What's the problem?'

Jonah thought he understood the problem. 'Why don't you just go ahead and dial the number and blow up the ship?' he asked.

'Be quiet,' Pakravan told him.

'Because you don't have the number, do you? Only Nor has the number. I mean, he's not stupid. And now you can't get hold of him. And what about Alex? Who was that you were talking to on his phone? Has Alex been arrested or is he dead?'

'What is he talking about?' Taff demanded, looking from Winthrop to Jonah.

'Shut the fuck up!' Winthrop yelled.

'There are cop cars on the motorway,' Ginger shouted from the open car door.

Abruptly, the blinking lights went out on the twin masts on the nearby hill.

Ginger looked at his phone. 'I've got no bars.'

'Me neither,' said Taff. Nobody had a signal.

'They shut down the networks,' Jonah told them. 'They know all about you. They're coming for you.'

'Damn it!' yelled Winthrop. He flung his phone into the water.

Then they saw the flashing lights of police cars approaching from Sittingbourne, heading for the Sheppey Crossing.

'If they control the crossing we're cut off,' Ginger said.

'Where's the helicopter?' Winthrop demanded. 'Bring it back here.'

'We've got no comms,' Ginger told him.

Jonah laughed out loud. 'You're so fucked.'

Attention all shipping, especially in sea areas Humber and Thames. The Meteorological Office issued the following gale warnings to shipping at 1900 GMT today. Humber, Thames, south-west gale 8 to storm 10, veering west, severe gale 9 to violent storm 11 imminent.

Nor and Miranda were standing together in the wheelhouse, listening to the radio while the boat slapped against her moorings and the wind howled in the wire stays and outrigger cables.

Rain battered the windows. Nor had cut the running lights and they could see only by the greenish light of the instrument panel and the occasional flash of lightning.

Nor looked down at his phone and frowned. 'I'm not getting a signal.' He switched it on and off again. 'Nothing.'

'What does that mean?'

'Either that the storm knocked out the masts or someone's switched off the networks.'

So Mikulski had come good. 'What do we do now?' she asked.

He reached for the radio that was now issuing a soft, sibilant hiss. He switched several channels. The same hiss. Either the air was too highly charged or the police were jamming the frequencies. It didn't matter which. 'I have to take the boat out to the wreck.'

'You're going to take the boat out in this?'

'I don't have any choice,' he said with a sort of weary resignation. 'I have to reach the buoy and blow the charges manually.'

'It's not worth it,' she said. 'We could just run. We could go away somewhere together.'

'They'll kill us anyway,' he said, and turned the key. The diesel engine roared into life and the planking in the wheelhouse throbbed with the power of it. 'You can get off here.'

'I'm coming with you,' she said, without hesitation. He stared at her. Another shared moment, another shiver down her spine. She had committed herself to this, to stopping him, whatever it took. 'You can't do it on your own.'

He went out on to deck and cast off the ropes securing the boat to the pier. Then he was back in and edging them away from the pier, with the engine in reverse. He opened the throttle and black smoke spewed out. They sailed out into the Medway approach channel. They could see, through the wheelhouse window, the size of the oncoming waves. Her face flushed, her eyes grew wide.

'Oh my God,' she said. 'Oh my God, look at it.'

In the eye of the storm

Mikulski and a police sniper ran across the tarmac towards the waiting Search and Rescue helicopter, a bright yellow RAF Sea King. They climbed in the jump door and knelt down beside the auxiliary fuel tank at the rear of the aircraft, while the pilot completed his pre-flight checks. They were wearing immersion suits, wetsuits and inflatable life vests. The sniper was carrying a .50-calibre Barrett rifle, a weapon strong enough to punch a hole through metal plate.

The rotors began to thud into life, losing the sag of their weight, and the helicopter shifted on its tyres and was suddenly airborne. They flew east along the Thames into the eye of the storm.

Gravesend Port Control Centre was reporting that on the radar a boat had left the Medway and was sailing towards the *Montgomery*. It had to be Nor.

The Range Rover was slipping and sliding as it came down off Furze Hill. Ginger was at the wheel with Taff beside him, a map on his lap, shouting directions. Pakravan and Winthrop had Jonah hemmed in the back with his cuffed wrists jammed between his knees. There were spinning blue lights on the crossing a couple of miles to the south and more police cars racing north towards the port.

They bounced on to a farm track and slid across a farmyard, accelerated over a roundabout and slammed into the side of a police car, sending it careering across the road and into the marsh. They turned north away from the crossing and over another roundabout with police cars pursuing them.

'Left,' Taff shouted.

They drove past low red-brick bungalows, over a railway track and across a small stone bridge. There were sheds on either side – it was some kind of factory – and then a narrow road of crumbling asphalt with the River Swale on one side and marshland on the other, curving to the right and around the bend a narrow spit of land and at the end of it the pier. The Range Rovers screeched to halt.

'Cover us,' Pakravan shouted. Winthrop pulled Jonah out of the car and on to the tarmac. They ran out along the pier. Behind them Taff and Ginger scrambled to opposite sides of the road. They crouched behind their weapons with their legs out behind them, and when the first police car came out of the bend they opened fire.

'Where's the fucking boat?' Winthrop yelled.

'He's gone,' Pakravan shouted back at him, 'Nor's gone!'

Which was the point at which Jonah decided to act: he threw his cuffed hands over Pakravan's head and yanked backwards, tightening the chain across his neck. Pakravan gasped and Jonah pulled him backwards and on to his knees on the pier. His left shoulder was screaming. He pushed down on his right side until all his weight was in his right shoulder and his hip. Pakravan's neck snapped.

The boat groaned as if she was being crushed and the engines raced as the bow went down in a trough and the propeller blades were lifted out of the water, and then another wave slammed the deck and Miranda was swept off her feet, carried aft with the gaffe in her hands.

Things unravelled in slow motion. Looking back across the moving deck at the wheelhouse, Miranda saw Nor's face, an unearthly green by the light from the instrument panel, and beyond him the wall of water. It was terrifying. A massive swell. There was no horizon, just surging green water and the rising and falling deck.

The wind was making a sound she'd never heard before, a deep tonal vibration that made her think of the end of the world.

And suddenly she glimpsed a flashing red light – the buoy with the ignition assembly that carried the detonators.

She heaved herself upright against the transom and swung the gaffe around so that the hook on the end of the pole was hanging over the water. She lunged for the buoy.

And a spear of white light came out of the sky towards her.

Mikulski couldn't believe what he was seeing, massive foam-laden swells rising and falling in the cone of light, some barely missing the belly of the helicopter.

The searchlight swept across the boat. She was plunging into the crest of each wave and launching out the far side, with spray streaming off the wheelhouse and green water sheeting out of her scuppers. Mikulski could see Nor standing in the wheelhouse and Miranda, barely keeping her feet, at the stern of the boat, with the gaffe in her hands. He looked back at the sniper crouching in the fuselage. He was throwing up.

The pilot could barely control the aircraft. They were getting batted around the sky.

By the time Jonah had got the keys out of Pakravan's pocket and uncuffed himself, Winthrop was halfway across the River Swale, his arms flailing as he rose and fell with the waves. Jonah glanced back in the direction of the firefight. Armed police were trading shots with Ginger and Taff, who were falling back, taking it in turns to provide covering fire while the other sprinted backwards. Bullets ricocheted on the tarmac around him, and peppered the hedgerows, chewing up leaves and branches. If he stayed where he was he was going to get caught in the crossfire.

He looked back along the pier towards the marshland on the far side of the Swale and in the distance, beyond the Medway, the burning lights of the power station on the Isle of Grain. The Swale was only a few hundred yards across. Winthrop was practically on the other side.

Fuck it.

He sprinted to the end of the pier, took a running jump and

plunged into the churning water. He swam with one arm, side-stroke, shovelling his hand into the water.

Nor rushed down the ladder from the wheelhouse and out on to the deck with the assault rifle in his hands. As the boat pitched and the helicopter came at them, he raised it and bellowed. Then he was firing, the scalding cases cascading on to Miranda's exposed skin as she cowered on the deck behind him. There was a rush of wind and noise, the rattle of the helicopter's engine and the blur of its rotor blades as it passed overhead, and the staccato crack of the rifle. The boat pitched forward again. There was no one at the wheel. Another wave struck. She was knocked off her feet again. She'd lost the gaffe. The dog was washed past her and overboard.

She slammed against the transom. The helicopter came around again. It tipped down, with the howling storm behind it, its search-light rushing towards them. Beside her, Nor's rifle had jammed and he was struggling with the rifle's bolt to unblock the stop-page. It was then that she saw it, rising behind the helicopter. The whole horizon was blotted out by a huge grey wall. It had no crest, just a thin white line along the whole length, and its face was unlike the normal sloping face of a wave. It was a wall of water with a completely vertical face.

There was no time to think or to act, only to marvel at the sheer size of it.

The wave engulfed the bow, the foredeck and the wheelhouse, blew out all the windows and flipped the boat end over end.

The last thing she saw was white water coming at her like a massive fist, then darkness and a moment later dazzling blue sparks, like lightning, arcing down into the water as the ship's electrics shorted out. The boat was upside down and she was under it. The water was freezing cold and blurry with silt. She surfaced briefly in a small air pocket, took a breath and struck out to get clear of the boat, but within moments a powerful force had her in its grip and was dragging her farther downwards. She was being sucked down by the vacuum created by the sinking boat.

Down down down . . .

It felt as if she was in a vice. Her ears were agony. She equalised, pinching her nose and blowing. She felt suddenly light headed, which was followed by a sensation of darkness closing in from all sides, like travelling down a long tunnel. So this is drowning, she thought, this is how my life ends.

A shape materialised out of the shifting silt, a looming cave. She was swept inside. Her first thought was that they were monstrous cocoons, dark grey tubes of muscle and matter stacked in rows, waiting to erupt. And then she realised that she must be inside one of the holds in the broken back of the *Montgomery*. She reached out, and as she passed her hands brushed the casing of the nearest bomb, dislodging clouds of rust. Then the current had her again and she was being carried along the top of the stack, through lines of fluorescent white detonating cord converging out of the darkness. She was buffeted from all sides, sucked down and then just as suddenly propelled upwards. Above her the detonating cord formed a single braided cable as thick as her wrist, rising from the stack towards the cargo hatch. She shot through the hatch and was swept along the top of the deck.

There were more cables twisting out of the darkness, forming a knot of explosives tethered against one of the masts, linking all five of the ship's holds in a single explosive circuit, a ring main. And as she rose alongside the mast, she saw that at the centre of the knot, hanging suspended in the water with his arms outstretched, was Nor's lifeless body.

She surfaced beside the buoy and grabbed at it. She held on for a few seconds, gasping for air between each crashing wave. Then she looked up and saw it, just within reach, the ignition assembly: a clear plastic box containing a bundle of explosives, detonators and blinking circuitry, and feeding into it the twin ends of the cable. With the last of her strength she pulled, tearing the cable away from the box, unravelling the charge . . .

It was done. She was swept away.

Death will find you

Miranda dreamt that she was on land with her back to the sea and something was slithering across the mud from the water's edge. She couldn't look back. She couldn't turn around. Something had risen from the depths and was coming for her, slowly and deliberately. She couldn't move. She couldn't run. She was filled with ancient dread. The thing was right behind her. It had been searching for her for ten long years and she knew that it would be the most dangerous thing that she ever had to face. Saliva spooled from its open jaws. There was a foul smell and a child's voice at her ear saying, *Mother, I'm here. I'm here.*

She woke up.

She was lying face down in the mud, in corpse pose. Rain was pounding the earth beside her and water was lapping at her ankles. All around her, she could hear the storm raging, but where she was, on a worthless spit of land, there was an eerie calm. She scrambled to her feet and sloshed through the mud and the reeds away from the crashing waves, away from the water's edge, away from her son's voice.

Walk.

The first part of the walk was the most difficult. There was the rain and the mud. Several times she sank to her thighs in the mud. Each time she had to pull herself out by grabbing fistfuls of reeds, and each time she felt herself growing weaker. She was forced to wade across a narrow creek. On the far side she pulled herself on to the remains of an ancient earthwork and lay there breathlessly. She was tempted to close her eyes again but it didn't seem like a very smart idea.

Are you tough, little bird?

'I'm tough,' she said, as she always did when her father asked. 'I'm Isaaq.'

Then hit my fist.

She looked up and for a moment it was if the curtains of rain parted and a couple of hundred yards away, across a stretch of marsh, she could see a pylon line. Pylons lead to plugs, she thought, transmission lines lead to houses. She was genuinely glad to see the ungainly metal structures.

Are you tough?

'I'm tough.'

She took a few deep breaths and set off again through the mud, pulling herself forward with fistfuls of reeds. She was cold but she hardly noticed the rain now.

She heard the sound of a helicopter from somewhere behind her and, turning, saw the long white beam of light sweeping the marshes, searching the barren ground.

'I'm here,' she shouted, but no one heard.

Beyond the pylon line there was a raised hard-core track full of ruts and potholes. It made her think of Jura, of the long walk to Barnhill from the end of the country road. Walking, that was what she did. There was a rhythm to it. It was what she'd done every day since she discovered that Omar was dead. It was what she was: a forked animal, following a track one step at a time.

'I'm tough,' she said, but it sounded hollow in her ears. The helicopter had wrecked her concentration. 'Damn it, get a grip of yourself.'

Walk.

She came to a cattle grid, with a locked wooden gate beside it. Who would lock a gate here, where there were no fences? Rather than cross the steel bars of the grid or risk her footing in the surrounding marsh, she climbed over the gate, falling across it and tumbling on to the wet earth beyond.

She stood up again. The rain was falling in horizontal sheets.

She was blinded. She took several steps and sank to her thighs in the mud. She had lost the track.

Omar was there walking beside her. Sixteen years old. He was almost as tall as his father. She was no longer afraid of him.

'I don't think I'm going to make it,' she said.

I know.

He smiled sympathetically.

'Am I going to make it?' she asked.

Follow me.

'I love you,' she said. 'I love you so very much.'

I love you too, Mom.

Ahead there was a metal structure, a dilapidated lambing shed with sheets of roofing metal flapping in the wind. He had led her through the marsh to the only nearby shelter. He was a determined and resourceful boy.

I'm going now.

'Come back soon,' she said. She was so glad to have seen him, so glad that he had turned out so well. She struggled towards the barn. Soon she would be out of the rain and somewhere that she could lie down and rest until Omar woke her.

As she approached a man that she did not recognise at first stepped out of the shadows at the entrance to the barn and lifted something towards her.

He was pointing at her.

It was Richard Winthrop IV. She knew immediately that he was accusing her of something. She had done so many wrong things.

There was a loud bang and a blinding flash of light and she felt a tremendous shock. There was no pain, only a violent shock, as if she had been electrocuted, and immediately after it a sense of utter weakness, a feeling of being stricken and shrivelled up to nothing. The barn in front of her receded to a great distance. The next moment her knees crumpled and she was falling. Her head hit the ground with a thud which, to her relief, did not hurt. She had a numb, dazed feeling, an understanding that she must be very badly hurt, but no pain in the ordinary sense.

She tried to get back up again, but discovered that her legs would not work, they slid uselessly in the mud, and as she tried to lift herself up on her elbows a lot of blood poured out of her mouth. She sank back into the ooze.

There was no point trying to move. It was only then that it occurred to her to wonder where she was hit. She couldn't feel anything, but she was conscious that the bullet had struck her somewhere in the front of her body. When she tried to speak she found that she had no voice.

Jonah saw the muzzle flash in the distance and started running, sloshing through the mud. He fell several times and each time got up again and forced himself forward.

The shape of a building emerged out of the rain. A long metal shed. There was a man running north along a raised dyke away from the shed.

Winthrop.

Jonah ran after him.

Several times Winthrop stopped and looked back, aware that he was being followed. Several times he fired his gun wildly at shadows.

Jonah kept on running.

For a mile or so the track and the pylon line ran parallel to each other and then began to converge as the land narrowed towards the end of the spit. There was water on two sides and water ahead. Winthrop was running out of options. He was at the end of the line.

There was nothing but rushing water, and unreachable beyond the Medway the blazing lights of the power station. He turned back and kept firing his pistol until he was out of ammunition.

'What do you want?' he screamed.

Jonah came roaring out of the darkness.

You did it. Omar was kneeling beside her. *You saved a million lives.*

Miranda laughed at the irony. 'I really did.'

There had been several minutes during which she had assumed

she was dead. It was interesting to note what her thoughts had been at such a time. It made her unaccountably glad that her son was so proud. It made her think that her father would have been similarly proud. Perhaps she had not wasted her life after all. Happy as she was, she began to cry because her father had not lived to see it.

She took a deep breath between sobs and as she exhaled the blood bubbled out of her mouth. She tried not to breathe deeply again. Short, shallow breaths, she told herself. Everything was very blurry.

Are you ready?

It was Omar again.

'Ready for what?'

You know.

'I'm frightened.'

And he was gone. This time somehow she knew it was for good. She had been searching for him all her adult life. In the end that was all there was, that was all there had been . . . the searching.

The helicopter passed directly overhead. It was close enough that she could see its oblong yellow undercarriage, lit up by red running lights, and for a moment her hopes were raised, but the searchlight swooped far off across the reed beds, away from her.

The searchlight abruptly went off.

There was no one there in the darkness. Not her father. Not Omar. Not even Jonah.

She heard the helicopter coming back.

It hovered about fifty yards away and the light snapped on again, reaching out through the prop-wash, to find her.

She shielded her eyes and through her fingers watched it land. A figure jumped down from its side and ran towards her through the searchlight's beam, throwing a vast and hulking shadow across the marshes.

She heard the rotors slowing down.

The man walked up to her out of the glare. It was the American, Mikulski. He knelt by her side and cradled her in his arms.

She died.

A bright day after

It was about an hour after sunrise on the thirteenth and the morning sky was untroubled by aircraft. It reminded Mikulski of the days after 9/11 when the skies over New York had been completely empty. He looked around at the blasted landscape. There was water everywhere, bubbling in the rivers and creeks, and sparkling on the reeds and pylon lines and on the lambing-shed roof and the helicopter's plexiglas windshield and rotor blades.

He watched a large man come slouching out of the marsh, dragging something behind him. After a while he saw that it was Jonah and he was pulling Winthrop by his ankle. Mikulski looked down and with his hand he smoothed the hair away from Miranda's face. He had seen the tape. He had watched her as she recalled the events of her life, including the raw emotion on her face as she described the loss of her son. She looked peaceful in death. As beautiful as when he had first seen her, standing in the kitchen at Barnhill, just ten days before, but no longer harried. Jonah dragged Winthrop on to the track beside the lambing shed and dumped him there.

'Is he alive?' Mikulski asked.

Jonah nodded. 'Just about.'

He walked over, looked down at Miranda, and then sank to his knees beside them. His face was battered and bruised and one of his arms hung uselessly at his side. He tipped back his head and let his mouth hang open. Mikulski looked away; he couldn't bear to see the anguish on Jonah's face. About a mile away a police Range Rover was bumping along the track towards them from Chetney Cottages. The police sniper had climbed out of the helicopter and was standing beside it, with his rifle in his hands, unsure of what to do. Mikulski waved him away.

It was a mess. Kiernan's family were demanding justice. Various agency heads would have to draw strongly on their reputation for preserving public safety if they hoped to keep their jobs. There were people all over that would have to be arrested. Others, in Iraq, Afghanistan and elsewhere, would disappear. Rendition protocols would be enacted.

Winthrop made a sound in his throat. A groan.

From what Mikulski had learned about Those Who Seek The End it seemed unlikely that Winthrop would ever make it to trial. He did not envy those who would find themselves charged with protecting him in custody.

'You should go now,' Mikulski said.

Jonah held his head up and gritted his teeth, and there was in the line of his jaw, visible for anyone to see, the determination, the refusal to fold under any circumstances, that had driven him this far.

'Go on,' Mikulski urged.

Jonah looked at him.

'There's no reason to stay,' Mikulski told him.

Reluctantly, Jonah climbed to his feet and, after spending a few moments staring down at Miranda's pale, lifeless face, he sucked in a deep breath, turned towards the marsh and staggered back into it, a solitary figure wading through dark vegetation.

Sources

Greg Campbell *Blood Diamonds*, Steve Coll *Ghost Wars*, Dexter Filkins *The Forever War*, Misha Glenny *McMafia*, John Gray *Al Qaeda and What It Means To Be Modern*, Michael Griffin *Reaping the Whirlwind*, Rohan Gunaratna *Inside al Qaeda*, Michael Isikoff and David Corn *Hubris*, Ed Husain *The Islamist*, Lutz Kleveman *The New Great Game*, Chris Mackey and Greg Miller *The Interrogator's War*, Pankaj Mishra *Jihadis*, John Robb *Brave New War*, Iain Sinclair *Lights Out for The Territory*, Bruno Tertrais *War Without End*, Mark Urban *War in Afghanistan*, Paul Virilio *City of Panic*, Ed Vulliamy *Seasons in Hell*, Edward O. Wilson *The Diversity of Life*, Lawrence Wright *The Looming Tower*.